THE NIGHT VISITOR

Something splashed in the river. A fish?

Jerr leaned over the rail of the ship. But with only one moon risen, night was still pitch-black. She could barely see the water.

There was another splash, and she felt a bump. Something had struck the *Handmaiden*'s hull.

Jerr heard the scraping of claws on wood. A crocodile?

Before she could step back, she found herself staring into the face of a bregil. His tail curled up and wrapped around the rail. He was dripping, and he was naked. He was not a crocodile but something far worse—

Jerr let out a strangled cry.

"Sssshhhh!" hissed the bregil. "Take me to Threok!"

THE CHRONICLES OF AELWYN
by Robert N. Charrette

Timespell
Eye of the Serpent
Wizard of Bones

Published by HarperPrism

HEREIN

WIZARD
OF
BONES

THIRD CHRONICLE OF AELWYN

A Tale of a Journey Made amid Conflicts
Both Old and New and of the Tangled
Mysteries of the Great Art
wherein a Man Comes to Understanding

Robert N. Charrette

HarperPrism
An Imprint of HarperPaperbacks

HarperPaperbacks
A Division of HarperCollins*Publishers*
10 East 53rd Street, New York, N.Y. 10022-5299

ISBN 0-06-105603-0

HarperPrism is an imprint of HarperPaperbacks.

HarperCollins®, ❦ ®, HarperPaperbacks™, and
HarperPrism® are trademarks of HarperCollins*Publishers* Inc.

Cover illustration by Jean Francois Podevin

First printing: April 1997

Printed in the United States of America

Visit HarperPaperbacks on the World Wide Web at
http://www.harpercollins.com/paperbacks

❖ 10 9 8 7 6 5 4 3 2 1

For Peter.
Now go out and feather me a rast, or two.

PROLOGUE

THE WALLS OF THE CITADEL known as the Rock were built for defense: thick, solid, and pierced only by narrow windows. Even high above the pounding surf at the crag's base, high above the range of any shipborne cannon, the windows were no wider, simply taller. Through them could be seen only blue sky, white cloud, and the occasional wheeling rapenar. The sharp cries of the hunting birds penetrated to the long corridor, their insubstantial voices reaching where no cannonball ever could.

A man sat in the third embrasure, and, though his face was turned outward, he seemed to pay no heed to the birds, nor to the sky, nor to the sound of the surf below at the base of the Rock.

Iaf Smyth knew the seated man, by name and profession at least. "Handrar" was all the name this man used. He claimed neither clan nor family connections, letting the appellation *ser* be his distinction. That title was usually reserved for the wisest of men and the greatest of scholars, an accolade earned over a lifetime; but magicians, even newly certified ones, often adopted it as well. Handrar was not just a magician but a master of the Art—in short, a wizard—and who would deny a wizard whatever title he chose?

Ser Handrar was newly come to Sharhumrin and the

court, having arrived for the Solstice festivities only a fortnight gone. He seemed young, only a year or two older than Iaf—and was whispered by some to be too young to have reached his stature through honest achievement. But who was Iaf to be a judge of that? Hadn't he himself been proclaimed a general officer of the empire, by order of His Majesty Dacel IV, at the very festivities at which *Ser* Handrar had been presented to the emperor? There were those, even among Iaf's friends, who said that Iaf was too young for the honor. Achievement and distinction sometimes came early in life, despite the jealous gossip of rivals.

How strange to have something in common with a wizard!

But strange seemed to be the order of the day. The summons to Iaf's puzzling and just-concluded audience with Sorigir Renumas had been an unusual way to begin the day. Now here sat *Ser* Handrar to add another curious twist to the still-young day. The wizard had been leaving the sorigir's presence chamber as Iaf was being ushered in; yet here he remained, in the empty corridor that served as an antechamber. No one else was visible in the bars of light that the tall, narrow windows threw across the polished stone floor. No one lurked in the few pale shadows that the bright morning sunlight allowed to exist in the long hall. Why had the wizard remained?

Ser Handrar turned his head at the sound of Iaf's boots on the hard stone floor. A flash of avid interest, so quick that Iaf wasn't entirely sure that he had seen it, was replaced with a congenial smile as the wizard rose from his window seat. It was a courtier's smile, and Iaf expected the wizard to pass him without a word on his way back into the sorigir's presence, but *Ser* Handrar did not turn toward the great doors at Iaf's back. He moved toward Iaf. Iaf himself, it seemed, was the reason that the wizard had lingered. This was a day of unusual interest in

Iaf. Or, perhaps more accurately, in what Iaf knew. First Sorigir Renumas, now *Ser* Handrar.

Sorigir Vornor Renumas, besides being feudal ruler of the largest island in the empire, was chancellor to his cousin Dacel IV, ruler of the Coronal Empire. The chancellor had the wardship of the realm, so his interest in a general of the empire was unsurprising—although the relevance of today's interview to the realm's security was obscure.

But this wizard's interest in Iaf—*any* wizard's interest in him—was surprising, and a little unsettling. Iaf had met magicians before, but he'd had little to do with their kind; wizards were not known for their interest in military men. In Iaf's experience, the sort of magician who used the appellation *ser* never dabbled in Iaf's trade or associated voluntarily with its practitioners. The interest that *Ser* Handrar was showing in Iaf marked the wizard as an unusual sort—though one could hardly call any wizard a *usual* sort of person.

Not that *Ser* Handrar looked unusual, save perhaps for the dark complexion which made him stand out among the inner islanders who thronged Sharhumrin. And, of course, the silvery *claviarm*, the badge and tool of a magician, that he wore on his breast. *Ser* Handrar bore no fanciful staff of power, nor was he festooned about in charms and amulets, nor did he dress in flowing, multilayered robes such as wizards always wore in plays. He did wear a long-flapped scholar's cap rather than the common broad-brimmed hat of a gentleman, but otherwise he looked the part of a well-to-do member of the gentry. The wizard's coat was a sober, deep blue, and his boots were well-polished, but ordinary, tandra hide. The lace-fringed edges of his shirt's stark white collar and cuffs showed at neck and wrist: finer linen than Iaf wore, richer, as were the gilt buttons warding his coat's turnbacks and marching down his coat front and along the satin ribbons that striped the flanks of his pants. Yes, this *Ser* Handrar looked nothing more than an up-and-coming merchant or a gentleman scholar with taste for flashy medallions, but Iaf knew better.

So far, proper deference to superiors—as well as deference to those who were only *possibly* superiors—had eased Iaf's life in the capital. Since his hat was still in his hand after his departure from the sorigir's presence, he could not whisk it off as was fitting for a properly respectful bow. He swept his arms wide and gave reverence as best he could.

The wizard gave an acknowledging nod. "Your audience with Sorigir Renumas went well, General Smyth, did it not?"

Knowing the wizard's face and name was easy; newcomers to the court were easily marked, and often discussed—of times without any facts to support the gossip. Iaf had learned nothing reliable of *Ser* Handrar's politics or interests. He did know that *Ser* Handrar had frequented the Imperial court often since his introduction, far more often than Iaf. Iaf had heard that the wizard had even had private conversation with the emperor. A new favorite? Caution was warranted. "Well enough, I suppose," he answered.

"Well enough compared to what, good sir? And well enough for whom?"

Well enough for Iaf, he supposed. Well enough that he hadn't been placed in an awkward position by Sorigir Renumas as he had feared he might be. Renumas was chancellor of the empire and Iaf a general of the empire, but their politics were not well matched. Fortunately for Iaf, the interview had had little to do with politics. "By your leave, *Ser* Handrar, his Grace did say that our conversation was to be held in confidence."

"A confidence which, as you can see by my presence here, I share."

Likely, but not certain. Still, how wise was it to anger a wizard by refusing to answer his questions? Gossip did not attribute tempestuous outbursts to *Ser* Handrar, nor was he rumored to turn those who annoyed him into prawns, but a man's reputation never encompassed all a man did. Iaf's hesitation prompted the wizard to speak again.

"Come now. His Grace showed you the object, did he not? I would not know of it were I not in the sorigir's confidence."

Clearly *Ser* Handrar knew something of what Iaf and Renumas had discussed. It seemed that *Ser* Handrar did share the sorigir's confidence. Perhaps Iaf could speak safely.

"He did show me an object," Iaf admitted. A hemisphere of carved bone, disturbing, but beautiful in its way. Iaf hadn't known what to make of it and had said as much to Renumas. The sorigir had moved on to other subjects. "His Grace seemed more interested in asking me about someone I know."

"Ah, the wizard Tanafres."

Ser Handrar certainly was demonstrating that he knew what was going on. Iaf relaxed a little. But only a little: all this sudden attention focused on his old acquaintance pricked his suspicions. He would be more comfortable talking of other things. "As you say. The object, though. It seems very strange. Do you know where it came from or what its purpose is?"

"Its history before coming to the attention of my patron is, to speak mildly, obscure—at least as obscure as its purpose—and it is its nature that is of more concern than its purpose at the moment. Concerning that nature there are varying opinions, all troubling in one way or another. What is your opinion of it?"

"I am a simple soldier, *Ser* Handrar. I doubt that I could tell you anything about it that you do not already know."

The wizard let Iaf's flattering dodge slide past him. "You claim that, even after your campaign against the drakkenree, it is totally unfamiliar to you?"

How could he? "I did recognize the carven shapes as drakkenree."

Iaf had risen to command in an Imperial expeditionary force aiding continental allies against a rogue host of the saurians that had invaded Kolvin. His deeds in that campaign had earned him his current rank. And his current nightmares. If the matter worrying Renumas and *Ser* Handrar had to do with the drakkenree, there was a storm on the horizon. "It is a mystery to me."

"Do you think that Tanafres will unravel that mystery?"

Iaf thought that Master Tanafres could do just about anything to which he set his mind. Most everyone in the empire credited the winning of the Battle of Rastionne to Iaf and the patronage of the war god Vehr, but Iaf knew otherwise. The victory was as much, if not more, due to Master Tanafres and his magic. Master Tanafres was the smartest man and the greatest wizard Iaf had ever met. But that was almost certainly not the sort of response to give this wizard, so he said, "I think so."

Ser Handrar smiled like a soldier who had won a bet. "Because of his knowledge of our ancient enemy? Or has he other resources to draw upon?"

Iaf bristled at what the wizard was suggesting. It was the same suggestion that the priest at Sorigir Renumas's side had made. Iaf hadn't liked it from the priest; he liked it less from the wizard. "Master Tanafres knows more about the drakkenree than I do. Of that there is no doubt. And his knowledge is hard earned. You do know that he spent time as a captive of the lizards, don't you? You are wrong to imply any other source of his knowledge. The Master Tanafres I know would have nothing to do with the forbidden side of his Art."

"And it has been some years since you last saw the wizard Tanafres, has it not?" Iaf didn't see what the passage of time had to do with the matter, and said so. The wizard shrugged off his remark, asking, "And even with your defense of Tanafres, his Eminence approves of you?"

His Eminence? Was the wizard referring to the priest who had stood at Sorigir Renumas's side during Iaf's interview? Renumas had not introduced the Churchman, and Iaf hadn't recognized him. Though relatively new to the intrigues of the capital, Iaf had recognized the ploy and had known better than to ask for the priest's name. Still, he had wondered at the Churchman's presence; Renumas had a reputation as a dutiful but not overly devout Triadic. The Churchman—a high-ranking priest, to judge by *Ser* Handrar's according him the honorific Eminence—had been a scowling, dour sort. Iaf hadn't liked him.

"He said nothing against me."

"You should be relieved by that," *Ser* Handrar said in a tone that hinted at ominous consequences had matters gone otherwise.

The wizard's hint troubled Iaf. Recalling the priest's questions, Iaf said, "His Eminence seemed deeply concerned with matters of spiritual purity."

"Indeed." *Ser* Handrar leaned closer in a gesture of confidentiality. "I found him so myself. One might almost say obsessed."

Iaf had been raised in Scothandir, where the memories of the dark times were stronger than they were here in the islands. Just thinking about those terrible times made him uncomfortable. The thought that the followers of the old heresies might be rising again was disturbing, disquieting, and—he had no qualm about admitting it—frightening. "Has he concerns to justify his attitude?"

Striking right to the heart of Iaf's thoughts, *Ser* Handrar said, "You have, no doubt, heard rumors about a resurgence in the faith of the ancient heretics." Iaf nodded. "Though there is no hard evidence, some of our spiritual fathers seem to be taking these rumors very seriously. One might almost say that fuel is being set aside to feed the purifying fires. It is, perhaps, a time for men to be circumspect, especially if they practice arts which the Church already finds uncomfortable."

Such arts as magic? The Churchman's oblique questions about Master Tanafres's habits and practices came into a new light. "Are you warning me?"

"You? I think no warning is necessary for *you*." *Ser* Handrar shrugged. "However, I cannot speak to the peril in which others stand. You would apprehend that better than I."

Does Master Tanafres need to be warned? "But you think that someone needs to be warned? That there is trouble?"

"There is no doubt that trouble wings through the air. Where it shall alight—well, I expect we shall learn that when we reach our destination."

"Destination?"

Ser Handrar's brow creased. "You are not to be part of the expedition?"

The orders the chancellor had given Iaf were for him and him alone. "Nothing was said of an expedition."

"I see." *Ser* Handrar took a step away from Iaf, straightening his coat as he did. "Perhaps we should not be speaking." The wizard turned away. His last words, spoken over his shoulder, were: "Perhaps it would be wisest to say that we never spoke."

"Perhaps so," Iaf agreed, offering a bond of confidentiality. The wizard nodded.

Iaf stood, perplexed. What was afoot? An expedition—apparently—but to where, and why? Questions concerning heresy. Questions concerning Master Tanafres. The drakkenree bone carving. Iaf feared that he saw how they were linked. Suspicion of colluding with the drakkenree had fallen on Master Tanafres before, and terrible accusations had been made. *And* disproved, to everyone's satisfaction—or so Iaf had thought. Had he been wrong?

Iaf wished that his connections in the capital were better. He had questions to ask, but no time to ask them. The chancellor's orders required him to leave on the evening tide. Was it by coincidence or design that the chancellor was sending Iaf out into the western islands, farther away from the continent, farther away from Master Tanafres? Iaf suspected that *Ser* Handrar's expedition wouldn't be heading away from Master Tanafres.

If the wizard had betrayed a confidence, it would certainly be best for him if no one learned that he had spoken to Iaf. But Iaf was grateful for *Ser* Handrar's misconception that Iaf's presence today made him a member of the mysterious expedition. If he hadn't made that mistake, they would not have spoken, and Iaf would not have received the wizard's veiled warning. A warning that the chancellor's orders prevented Iaf from taking to Master Tanafres.

Ser Handrar had barely returned to his window seat when the inner door opened. Hand on the latch, the Churchman scowled at Iaf, but said nothing. He summoned *Ser* Handrar within. The wizard passed Iaf without a word, not even a nod of good-bye. The door closed, leaving Iaf alone in the antechamber, dismissed. But Iaf's worries were not dismissed.

Whatever was afoot involved Master Tanafres, and Iaf had been cut out of it. Or had he?

"Teletha S." was the name written on the letter. Teletha recognized Iaf Smyth's hand. She also recognized the seal, and that aroused her misgivings. She knew Iaf had done well for himself in Imperial service, but since when had he been entitled to the use of an Imperial dispatch seal? Her stomach knotted tight. It could be nothing but trouble. She read it at once.

> *I pray that this letter finds you in good health and that the gods have been kind. May They remain so.*
> *I, whom you heard called* mardiarouna *in my home*

village, will soon find myself at risk. Thus this letter, which I know you are not expecting. There are those who would condemn me for what I do, but to run away from this peril would damn me in their eyes and perhaps even in the eyes of the gods. Ever do we stand under Their watchful eyes.

Know that there are those who wish me ill. They will tell you that I am not what I should be. I pray you, watch for these vipers. They do not hold your best interests in their hearts.

My feelings you know. At least I pray that you do. I commend them to your attention, before others do the same. I also pray that my sensibilities are wholesome, in your eyes if no other.

I am a different man now, but you remain in my thoughts. I know that these are not the words you wish to hear, but do not dismiss this letter as you have all those others. I had hoped to find some other way to tell you what I know you must know, but could think of no other. Matters between us cannot be as I once hoped they might be. I know this. Horesh alone knows what the future holds.

I beg that you read the words I have set down here with understanding. I fear that my words are not clear because so much is not clear to me. Yet I felt compelled to attempt this letter. I hope that it finds you in the gods' good grace. I begin to ramble.

It is said that winter leaves the Waters of Travel early this year, and that is perhaps why I must be gone. I am told that there are great matters of state that must be attended to, but I fear that I travel as much at the personal interest of some Great Lord or another as at the Emperor's will. I know not the Truth behind what I have been told, but I am sent, and I must go. Ever must the servants of the empire move at the expressed will of his Majesty. Already ships sail from Sharhumrin, bound to Glaebur and Tradestad, to Brandespar and beyond.

Worry not for my safety. I shall be well. If you are

inclined, a word of your health and well-being would be a kindness.

I wish I had time to tell you more, but the tide turns, and I must leave soon. The gods willing, this letter will go where I cannot at this time go. Perhaps I abuse slightly the trust so recently placed in me in order to send this note on its way, but no person with a heart will fault my motives. I pray that the gods will not delay this letter, and I trust that They will not, for They know, Lord Einthof especially, that Truth must be served.

Written by my hand, at the Inn of the Red Anchor in the Old Harbor district of Sharhumrin, I am, as always, your obedient servant,

Iaf Smyth

By his Majesty's wish, general officer of the empire.

Teletha hadn't really known what to expect when she opened the letter, but she hadn't expected to be quite so puzzled once she finished reading it. It read like a love letter from a confused young boy. It was true that when Iaf was younger, he'd had a crush on her, but they had settled that issue long ago. *So what is this all about?*

Clearly—or rather, unclearly—Iaf was trying to tell her something without giving his message away to a casual reader.

She examined the seal. The damage she had done in opening the letter was obvious. Careful examination revealed that the seal might have been tampered with before she received it. She couldn't be sure. Iaf's caution was, perhaps, justified. Unfortunately, beyond communicating a sense of impending danger, Iaf's letter told her little. If he wanted to write in riddles, the least he could have done was to give her a clue.

As she was reading the letter a second time, Peyto Lennuick found her. "Ah," he said. "That must be the Imperial dispatch."

There were damned few secrets in a village the size of

Lizard's Cave. Sometimes it seemed that the clerk knew all of them.

"It's a personal letter," she told him. He raised a doubting eyebrow, daring her to explain. She didn't bother, asking instead, "What's a *mardiarouna*? It sounds Scothic."

"It *is* Scothic," he confirmed, but said no more.

She really didn't want to barter information. After all the years they had adventured together, she knew that Peyto could be accommodating, but sometimes it seemed the clerk had the heart of a merchant, and a stingy one at that. "So what does it mean?"

Peyto shrugged. "I don't exactly know."

"Not *exactly*, eh?" She was annoyed with him, and put her annoyance into her voice. "But you've heard it used? You recognized it!"

Her outburst had the desired effect. Peyto dropped his dumb act. "I have heard it before, but in only one context. It was connected to some sort of provincial superstition, I think," he said, finally succumbing to the need to prove he knew more than she did. "The folk of that abysmal Scothic village that consumed a year of my life used it. It's what they called Tanafres after they pulled the two of us out of the sea. I was a *chaelddur*. Another superstitious term. One thing was clear about a *chaelddur*: a *chaelddur* was in some way subsidiary, or perhaps subservient, to a *mardiarouna*."

She didn't care about *chaelddur*. "And you never heard anyone else called a *mardiarouna*?"

"Not as long as we were there. What about your letter brings on this interest in things Scothic?"

He took her "Later" with ill grace and departed huffily. He'd be as much joy as an aching butt for a while. Just now, she didn't care. She had thinking to do.

Mardiarouna. Yan. Suddenly the letter looked completely different.

1

THE RAIN WAS HEAVY, soaking the ground and running in rivulets across the clearing, past the assorted structures belonging to the village, and down to the stream. The black Kolvin earth, softened from winter's iron grip by previous rainfalls, was a thick, viscous mud. Already the stream's rushing flow was dark, hardly more liquid than the banks at which it ate.

Yan Tanafres stared out at the rain. The overhang protecting the cave's mouth shielded him from all but those drops driven by the hardest gusts. It was a cold, unpleasant rain, and it would continue to rain for hours, or so his weather sense said. Yan wasn't always right about the weather, but he felt sure that this time he was.

He should have paid attention earlier, when he'd felt the first stirrings of the storm. But he had been too intent on puzzling out the implications of an obscure passage in Armiacodi's *Transluekkia*. Now, unless he wanted to get drenched to the skin, swathed in muck to the shin, and spattered all over with mud, he was stuck in the cave. Being somewhere else just wasn't a good enough reason to leave the dry, relatively warm cave. Fra Bern would have said that the gods were telling Yan to be about his business where he was, to stop putting things off. While Yan could understand how the gods might be interested

in his results, he didn't like being pushed into things—
even by the gods. He didn't like getting soaked and
sloppy either, which was what would happen to him if he
tried to walk to his house now.

No point in torturing himself. He dropped the curtain
of coarse, heavy Megeed wool. The noise of the rain was
softer now, muffled. He walked back along the entrance
corridor to the workroom, consoling himself with the
thought that he hadn't seen any smoke emerging from
the chimney pot of his house. With no fire, the house
would be cold, offering no ease for anyone coming in out
of the rain. At least here, he was dry. As he went deeper
into the hillside, the steady drumming of the rain grew
softer still, and the air grew warmer.

Not that it was truly warm—he needed the long wool
gown he wore for comfort—but the cave was warmer
than a house in winter and cooler than a stream in summer; the air always felt like a summer night on his home
island of Merom. The warmth of the air in the cavern
was unchanging, separate from the turn of the seasons
outside. The locals thought the effect magical, some even
attributing it to Yan. Yan knew that there *was* magic
here, but the steadiness of the cave's warmth was no part
of it. That was a totally natural phenomenon, part of the
nature of the place. The magic was more subtle, had
been brought here by the ancient drakkenree, and it
remained—even to him—obscure and tauntingly elusive.
Yan's struggle to understand it was ongoing.

He *knew* so little. After years of exploring the far
reaches of the tunnels, excavating the collapsed sections,
and studying the things he found there all he could say
was that he had a better understanding of what the caverns had meant to the drakkenree. Better but far, far from
complete. All his conclusions were speculative; all his
answers only tentative. There was no way to be certain.
Each new discovery seemed to unearth more questions
than answers. Sometimes he felt his efforts were futile.

He recalled his old master's admonition that great mages learned, but were not taught. He was certainly not being taught, but was he learning? Did he really know more now than when he'd decided to settle here and study the cave, or was he fooling himself by mistaking imaginative guesses for honest scholarship? Had his dedication to the mystery of the cavern and its former inhabitants gained him anything?

Yan called his magelight into being to illuminate the chamber. Though the meager glow from the fist-sized ball of cold light would not be enough for one unawakened to the Art, it was sufficient for him. There were some advantages to his chosen profession.

The work chamber looked little different from the days when he had served here as the drakkenree mage's slave-cum-assistant. The shelves carved into the walls still held jars and glassware. There were fewer jars than before, but the pottery held powders and pastes and oils of Yan's making rather than Yellow Eye's; the stuff the saurian mage had left behind was gone, expended in Yan's experimentation. Behind a locked panel whose hinges were set into the stone itself lay Laird Gornal's books and Yellow Eye's grimoire, along with Yan's own collection of arcane works—a small library, but bigger than it had been before he had arrived in Kolvin. Less rare tomes sat openly on the shelves. The big cabinet in the corner still held dried foodstuffs, a heavy crock of water, and assorted implements of the craft. Bunches of herbs and roots dangled from the rod set in brackets over the worktable in the opposite corner. Yan had added some chairs, of course—he was not suited to lie with his belly on the floor as the saurian had been—but mostly the chamber was furnished as it had been by Yellow Eye; the drakkenree wizard's arrangements had been practical and well thought out.

Yan told anyone who asked that he had left the place alone simply for practical reasons, which wasn't quite true. There were other reasons as well, reasons that he could not quite identify. Sentimentality wasn't the right word for what he felt; the saurian mage had been more of a slave's master to him than an apprentice's. Sometimes, upon entering the chamber, it seemed to Yan that perhaps Yellow Eye was not dead, that perhaps the drakkenree might return to work new magics in the chamber.

A pointless fancy, held to ease his guilt. Yan knew what he had done to Yellow Eye, and no amount of imagination could change the facts. He had done what he had done. Killing the saurian mage had been a kindness. It had certainly seemed so at the time.

Yellow Eye was gone, and the room wasn't his anymore. It was Yan's place now; Yan's by right of—what?—conquest? Inheritance? Possession, anyway. Hadn't he entered the cave before Yellow Eye set up his workshop here? Yan had found it first. Did it matter that he had been no more than a cowering fugitive at the time?

Yellow Eye was dead and gone.

It was Yan's workplace now. The protective circles chalked on the floor in the open center of the chamber were Yan's, too. They were nearly complete; just the last touches remained to be made. By all that Yan understood, they would be as efficacious as those drawn by Yellow Eye. It had taken Yan nearly a year to reconstruct the structure and content of those circles. He was confident that they matched, as near as Yan could make them, the circles Yellow Eye had made. Naturally, the arrangement could not be exactly the same; Yan had an approach to the magics involved that differed from Yellow Eye's. Additionally, Yan had not drawn the circles with the expectation that he would be working with an assistant, as Yellow Eye had done.

Were the circles as potent? The circles had lain almost finished all winter. Was it fear that his circles would be inferior that kept Yan from completing them and beginning the ritual? Or was he just afraid that this latest attempt to reactivate the Eye of the Serpent would be as useless as all the rest?

When he had used the Eye, that long-ago day on the battlefield at Rastionne, he had felt like a great mage. He'd seen everything around him from a godlike perspective. He'd felt the mana all around him, and in him, and known its power and beauty and sorrow. He'd understood how all he'd felt was connected, linked inextricably in a pattern of intricacy outdoing the most complex spell construct or ritual of which he had ever heard. He'd been a part of that pattern, standing at its heart and able to impose his will upon it. For a shining moment, his will had indeed constrained the world. He *was* the magic!

Yan wanted to feel again the way he'd felt that day, and he was afraid that he never would.

Of course that wasn't the only reason to delve into the secrets of the Serpent's Eye. The Eye's very nature was strange and, by Einthof, it wanted understanding. The Eye was a puzzle to attract and fascinate anyone with the slightest understanding of the Great Art. Its essential qualities needed to be known, its essence plumbed, its potencies recorded, its energies mastered. Tasks at which he had been less than successful. His every attempt to reawaken the Eye of the Serpent had failed. Its secrets still eluded him. He knew that the Eye was drakkenree magic, made in a way no merin magician understood, but a merin magician could use it. *That* he knew. *He* had used it! He just didn't understand how to call forth its magic.

Although the Eye's secret eluded him, some of the mysteries of the drakkenree and their magic were his now. The glosses in drakkenree script that Yellow Eye had made in Yan's copy of Costigern's *Of Light and Air* had been helpful beyond description in understanding the language. Yan had translated much of Gornal's collection now, more than the Scothic laird had. Yellow Eye's personal grimoire had helped, too, as had Yan's contact with live drakkenree. The combination of sources made the work easier, but Yan suspected that his greatest insights had come from his single use of the Eye, a source now closed to him. And there was so much still unknown! And so much of Yan's work was just speculation; so much remained locked away and hidden in his sources.

Locked in the Eye.

Yan and the drakkenree mage had first discovered the Eye of the Serpent on a spirit journey into the lower levels of the cavern. A spirit journey was no longer necessary to reach the chamber that had been the Eye's resting place. The toil of King Shain's laborers had changed that condition, opening the passages between the upper and lower caverns. Would that secrets could be excavated so directly! Often Yan stood in the chamber and looked up at the monstrous draconic statue and the dark indentation where the Eye had been set between the beast's glittering eyes of gemstone. Hours spent contemplating the carven idol had brought no enlightenment. Magical examination of the beastly idol and its chamber offered no insights. The only track he had not trodden was the one he and Yellow Eye had used when they discovered the Eye. The spirit path. Was that the key?

He walked around the outside of the triple circle chalked on the floor, studying the symbols he'd written there. All seemed correct. To his inner eye, the circles looked no different than they had when he and Yellow Eye had made their trip into the depths of the cavern complex below and gained the Serpent's Eye. These circles' symbols were different, attuned to Yan rather than Yellow Eye, but the circles had the same resonance.

Could a retracing of that astral journey uncover the secret of activating the Eye? It had to. Yan had tried all the other avenues that he knew. If this approach failed, he would be sure that he lacked the magical competency necessary to control the Eye.

Had not his old master often told him that the journey was more significant than the destination?

He looked again at the circles. Once closed, all that remained was actually to begin the ritual.

A great magician wouldn't hesitate.

A great magician wouldn't need to do this; he would be able to use the Eye.

But *if* a great magician needed to do such a ritual, he wouldn't hesitate as Yan was doing.

As he would do no more! Yan strode to the locked cabinet. Behind the lock, behind his spells, behind the door, and behind treasures of his library lay a greater treasure: the small casket in which the Eye rested. He turned the key in the lock, speaking the word that released the wards. The door opened with only the slightest of creaks. Reaching in, he plucked the casket from its hiding place. The pebbled leather and silver of the box felt hard and unyielding in his hand; the protective spells made his skin tingle even though they were attuned to him. He was the only one who could safely open the casket—a precaution somewhat less than necessary, given the inaccessibility of the Eye's power.

Entering the circles through the unfinished section, he laid the casket on the floor in the center and placed his magelight ball beside it. The cold light cast the casket's shadow ominously across the entry point. Yan stepped away, working in that shadow to seal the circles.

With the protective spells emplaced, he returned to the center and opened the casket. The Eye lay within, a dull ocher sphere resting in a hollow carved in the mahogany woodblock that filled most of the interior. Drakkenree symbols—a ward—were carved around the edge of the hollow that held the Eye, ringing the sphere with their physical presence as their power enwrapped the eye arcanely. A second circle of symbols enringed the first—Yan's own ward. The dull lifelessness of the Eye seemed a mockery of the protective charms.

The Serpent's Eye had not always been so passive, and if Yan succeeded, it would no longer be inert. Teletha and Peyto had argued against the wisdom of his quest, as had Fra Bern. Normally Yan would have listened to their advice, but they didn't understand—couldn't understand—how the mystery of the Eye demanded unraveling. The mystery of the Eye was what really drew him, the need to understand. It wasn't just the power he'd felt that day. *Power is fleeting*, his old master would have said. *Understanding is forever.*

Today he would see how well he understood.

He spoke the words that activated the fullest protections of the circles. His *claviarm*, made of gold, set with gems, and hanging from a chain of gold, lay heavy on his shoulders and chest. The materials had been the gift of the grateful King Shain, a reward for services rendered to the throne and a retainer for future services. Yan had accepted the gold and gems without too much hesitance; their extravagance was great, but finer materials made for better conductivity of magical energy, and he had needed to replace the *claviarm* that Yellow Eye had destroyed. Yan's hand tingled where the scarred imprint of that destroyed talisman marked his skin, as he slipped into *prœha*, the state of magical awareness.

His spirit form drifted free from his physical shell. Leaving the confines of the circles, he headed down the path by the great abyss and into the lower depths of the cavern. He did not wander as he and Yellow Eye had that day, but went straight to the now-cleared passage where he had once feared to follow Yellow Eye through the blocking stone. He passed into the guardian's chamber, floating up to the opening that led beyond, rather than climbing the ladder as his physical body would have had to do. Entering the place that Fra Bern, with priestly certitude, had identified as a worship hall, Yan drifted over the edge of the balcony and across to the great draconic idol. The statue's serpentine form, with its six legs, horned head, and barbeled snout, looked no different than it had that day; but knowing it to be an idol, Yan did not start at its lifelike nature as he had then. Yet he was nearly as nervous. There was still a faint echo of power here, although the magical barriers Yellow Eye had breached were gone.

Yellow Eye had called the thing "Baansuus"—or something like that—when they had confronted it that day. "Baansuus" was as close as Yan could get to a name that meant little more to Yan now than it had then. He knew now that the Baansuus was a deity to the drakkenree, but he remained ignorant of the being's spheres of influence, nor had he any idea of what correspondences it held with the Great Beings of the Celestial Court.

In the air before the idol's nose, Yan's spirit hand sketched the symbol he had come to associate with the Baansuus. He began with the broad curved and recurved central line. The uncompleted symbol reminded him, as it always did, of a snake. With a zigzag pass of his hand, he crossed the serpentine line with three other, more slender lines. The symbol hung glowing in the air until, having been crossed with all three of the subsidiary lines and completed, it flared and vanished.

The empty hollow between the Baansuus's eyes stared at Yan, a pit of profound darkness that seemed as if it might reach all the way to the lowest levels of the Under Court. Yan put aside the suggestive religious imagery. He knew the nature of the Eye of the Serpent; it was thaumaturgic, not theurgic. Despite its resting place in the brow of an idol, it was born of magic, not gods. Still one did not casually flout the Great Beings of the universe. Yan hesitantly reached toward that darkness.

In the workroom, within the circles, his physical hand reached forward to caress the orb of the Eye.

He touched the Eye—he touched the darkness—and he touched the past. Pain exploded in the side of his head and he felt his lost ear burn away again as it had when

Yellow Eye had sought to enforce his control over Yan. Banishing the phantom agony, Yan concentrated on the Serpent's Eye, recalling its glow and sorcerous feel to his mind. He was jarred as the images before his physical and spirit eyes overlaid each other. He blinked, trying to force clarity into his vision.

Erratic images assaulted him, flashes of viewpoints not his own. The steading outside the cave. Riders on the road. Distant storm clouds gathering on the flanks of strange mountains. Jerr Kansti stumbling through a heavy downpour—no—through a dense tangle of undergrowth, pursued by something. A circle of six dreaming wizards. An ancient wall, immaterial but impervious. The images came in shorter, fuzzier flashes. Yan didn't know whether they were true visions or shards of memory or pieces of dreams. He couldn't be sure. There was none of the godlike certainty he'd experienced at the climax of the Battle of Rastionne.

He felt confused, lost. The images melded into a chaotic stream of flickering color and light. He felt dizzy; he was still having trouble separating the arcane from the physical. The world spun around him as he stood still, frozen in time. The magic he'd built into the circles was around him, cloaking him. The air seemed to thicken, the magic hardening it as winter hardened water to ice. His stomach clenched from fear as memories of the labyrinth beneath Laird Gornal's keep rose up. He saw Teletha descending the stairs, slow, slower, slowing to immobility—frozen in time. They'd been trapped there in a timespell, trapped while the world went on without them.

No! I won't be trapped that way again!

He fought the magic hemming him in, rejecting it, tossing it aside in his bid to be free. The *præha* awareness shattered, and he found himself face down in the dirt floor of the workroom. His scarred right hand ached, and his left hand stung as though he'd struck it against something hard. The leather and silver casket lay on its side just beyond his hand, the orb of the Eye rolling away across scuffs in the protective circles.

A soggy Jerr Kansti scrambled toward the rolling sphere. She was ignorant and unprotected. She should not touch such a thing as the Eye.

"Leave it be!" he shouted.

Jerr froze in mid-reach.

"Get away from it."

Jerr backed away, stumbling over a chair. She looked frightened. Let her be scared. Magic was scary stuff. Anyone in their right mind should be scared of getting involved with the Art. The Great Art was a prime path to frustration, a good way to prove you didn't know half what you thought you did.

"Go on," Yan snapped. "Get out of here! This is no business for you. You shouldn't be here. I don't want anyone here! Go on, get going and don't come back till I call."

She looked hurt, and Yan knew he should care, but just now he didn't. Jerr mumbled apologies and backed out of the chamber. Yan could hear her sobbing as she fled down the entranceway.

Jerr was a gangly, shy girl, clumsy and awkward with youth, and she fancied herself his apprentice even though they hadn't exchanged formal vows. Yan had recognized some little talent in her and had not sent her packing as he had all the others who thought that he could give them power. Jerr had proven herself diligent and useful, if not a quick student in the Great Art. Before she had attached herself to Yan, she hadn't even been able to read, but she could fumble her way through a little Nitallan now, though she spoke it better than she read it, and even that accomplishment was more due to Fra Bern's attentions than anything Yan had done. Yes, Jerr was an eager student, but she wanted magic, not letters, and did not yet comprehend that magic was based in knowledge; she, like so many others, thought the Great Art was all waving hands and intoning spells and having things happen the way you wanted them to happen. The magic Yan had taught her was next to nothing, which was the only way it could be until she understood reality better. Until then, there was little he could do for her. She was, he supposed, a suitable apprentice for a fumbling, hedge wizard like himself.

Great magicians learn, the ghost of his old master's voice said.

Learn, indeed! Just what was one supposed to learn in this old cave? Was one to learn about incompetence? Was one to learn how little one knew about real magic. Perhaps how stupid one was, and how poor one's education was?

Oh, Yan had learned all right. He had learned that his stubborn insistence that he *would* learn on his own was getting him nowhere. He'd learned that his ambition to be a great mage was too high a mark for a shoemaker's son from Merom. His friends told him he had magic, but they were hardly qualified judges. To be sure, he did touch the magic, but his was clearly a minor art. His experience with the Serpent's Eye was a fluke, a mockery. He could see now that without Yellow Eye to activate it, the talisman was useless to him, beyond his ability to touch in any meaningful way. The magic, the real magic, was beyond him.

He could hear the rain outside; Jerr must not have pulled the curtain closed behind her. He let it be. In a way, the sound was comforting. Rain was a part of the world, an aspect of the natural order. He was a small part of the world, too, a minor aspect of the natural order. He should let himself play the role he was meant to play, let things come in their natural way. Wasn't that the way he had always been the most successful? Hadn't his will *constrained* the world best when his will accorded with the way of the world? Perhaps it was his ambition that was at fault, more than his self or his abilities. The rain became a rivulet, then a stream, then a river. What ambition did a drop of rain have?

None that he could perceive. It was simply what it was. And what was he?

Not what he thought he was. That was for sure. Perhaps it was time to just be what he was. Whatever that was.

Tired.

Tired was what he was. The soothing sound of the rain sent him drifting toward sleep. Should he get up and drag out the blankets from the cabinet? No. Too much effort; it was easier to lie amid the remains of his failed effort to touch the Eye, easier to welcome the sleep beckoning him.

Tomorrow, when the rain is gone, clean the place up. Make a new start.

2

JERR KANSTI HUDDLED just outside the mouth of the cave, too frightened of Master Tanafres's anger to go back inside. She was afraid that the mage might turn her into a worm—not that she'd ever seen him do that to anyone, but he had sounded so angry. She had to work to gather enough courage to creep back within the entrance and get out of the wind and rain.

But not very far in. Not far at all. Just far enough to get out of the weather. She crept past the curtain, not daring to pull it closed because he'd know. She went just far enough to find a place to huddle against the wall. Hunching up against the wall in the lee of the curtain, she hugged her legs to her. She was just far enough inside so she could shiver some warmth back into her stiff fingers and toes. Not too far at all.

Still, she feared that Master Tanafres would know that she was disobeying his command to go. She prayed to Mannar, hoping that the merciful Lady would protect her from the mage's wrath. Jerr was halfway through her third appeal to the Lady when she remembered that magic wasn't a part of the Green Lady's responsibility; magic belonged to V'Zurna, the Lady of Mysteries, or so the old grannies said. Jerr hadn't had much to do with the secrets of the Elder of the Three; she was barely initiated into the rites of the Maiden. But now, she was the magician's student, which meant that some of her life was under the light of V'Zurna's sphere. Though she was far too young to be a regular devotee of the Elder, she offered a prayer to her, asking that She find better things for Master Tanafres to do with his magic than to catch his apprentice in her disobedience.

Though Master Tanafres still refused to take her on formally as his apprentice, Jerr thought of herself that way. Others, she knew, did not. Perhaps the Lady of Mysteries might hold such a view and find Jerr's prayer presumptuous. Knowing that the gods always answered the prayers of presumptuous mortals in unexpected and usually unpleasant ways, she raised her eyes to the sky, made the sign of the Triad, and tried to explain herself to the Elder. Before long she realized that she was talking much and saying little to put her in a good light. She felt foolish.

"I don't mean to put myself above my station, Great Lady," she ended sincerely. "Please think no ill of me, and shine in kindness upon me."

The Elder did not speak. Jerr was not surprised; the gods did not speak to silly girls. Not in words, anyway. She would get her answer in time. She hoped she could live with it.

She looked down the corridor toward the workroom. Master Tanafres's magelight shed the faintest of glows on the wall at the bend in the tunnel. The light grew no stronger, or fainter. He was staying in the workroom.

Master Tanafres had ordered her to get out. She had gone at his word, but not far. It wasn't as if she had somewhere to go; the cave—on Master Tanafres's sufferance—was where she lived. Her blankets and tick—her warm and dry bed; her unreachable bed—were stuffed into the crevice behind the cabinet in the workroom. That room was the closest place to a home she had. It wasn't a bad place to live. By Horesh's light, she liked it better than the drafty, smelly hut her family lived in; Master Tanafres had no animals to bring in for the night. Master Tanafres had told her to get out, but shivering against the stone wall made her long for her dry, warm bed.

She wished that she dared go in. It would be warmer in the workroom; she could dry herself off. Being dry and warm sounded so very nice. But to go back would risk increasing the magician's anger; when he shouted at her, he'd sounded more angry than she'd ever heard him. If he got angry enough, he might tell her to go away forever. Or turn her into a worm. Or worse. She didn't know what could be worse, but she was sure that he would know something that was; he knew so much about everything that she was sure he could make her life horribly, utterly miserable.

Not that she was happy right now, she thought, stifling a sniffle. But it could be worse. A lot worse. Before Jerr had come to Master Tanafres, she had been an ignorant farm girl, looking forward to an ignorant farm life, marrying an ignorant farm boy, and raising ignorant farm children. The very thought of such a life made her want to cry. Mannar and the Maiden both knew that she had cried often enough over such thoughts.

A wet, cold night of shivering was little enough price to pay for a chance at a better life. And a better life was what being Master Tanafres's student offered her. Before she'd come to him, she hadn't known anything beyond the stupid, everyday things that farmers and farmwives knew. She hadn't even been able to read. By Horesh's light, she had barely understood that words could be written down! Words, always saying the same thing, were as reliable as the memory of a tale teller. No, more reliable! It was magic without being magic! A mystery that she had conquered!

Sort of. She really wasn't that good at reading. She knew a few words of Kolvinic, her native tongue, and could recognize names once she'd seen them and had them pronounced for her. She was better at the Church language, Nitallan, though she spoke it more easily than she read it. That was an accomplishment; two years ago she had thought the language something one had to be a priest to learn. Now she knew that Nitallan was used by people in many lands so that they could all talk to each other and understand what was said.

She'd been so ignorant!

She was *still* ignorant. Only now she knew that there was so much more than she had ever thought she *could* be ignorant about. It was scary sometimes. But now she also knew—knew in her head as she had always felt in her heart—that there was more in the world for her than farm life. She knew that if she hadn't run away from her family, her heart would have shriveled and died inside her.

She'd come to Master Tanafres with a lot of foolish ideas in her head. She'd wanted him to teach her magic so she could change her life, so that she'd never, ever have to be an ignorant farmwife. She was going to wear fine clothes of silk and necklaces of gold, ivory, and jasper that she pulled from the air; to make crops grow in winter with the flick of a finger, and reap them with the wave of a hand; to speak to horses in their secret language; and to go wherever she wanted to, whenever she wanted to. Knights and ladies would bow to her. Maybe even the king would speak to her. Master Tanafres had laughed at her dreams, told her such things belonged to the magic of goblin tales and daydreams. "The Great Art," he'd said, "is something else altogether."

His laughter hadn't been meant to be cruel, but it had cut her deep. Although she had wanted to, she hadn't run away from him; she'd stood, feeling her face burn with shame. But she hadn't cried. No, she hadn't cried.

So why was she bawling now?

Master Tanafres had relented. He *had* taught her about

the Art. Not much, true, but enough for her to know that she did have a chance to learn how to touch the mana, the energy of magic, on her own. He'd help her make the talisman she now clutched in her shivering fingers. The charm wasn't a *claviarm* such as he had; it was just a student's tool. Yet under his guidance she'd seen the strange, wonderful, and unforgettable beauty of the world as seen through a magician's eyes.

She knew why was she crying. It was because she feared that her new world was dissolving away beneath her feet like mud on a rain-soaked riverbank. She wasn't sure what she had done to earn Master Tanafres's anger, but she'd done whatever it was. She was such a bungler! This time she had bungled one thing too many and made the mage regret that he had ever taken her in. What if this rejection was complete? Would he take away the talisman? What if he wouldn't teach her anymore? What would she do? What *could* she do? She knew of no other magicians. If Master Tanafres was truly casting her out, where could she go? She couldn't go back to her parents now, even if they would have her back. She didn't belong there anymore. She pictured herself wandering a perpetually rainy countryside, homeless and hopeless.

And if he hadn't completely rejected her, why was she tempting such rejection by disobeying his order to leave the cave? The steady hiss of the rain told her: she could not face the cold, wet night. She had nowhere to be but here. If only the rain would stop. Or if it were a little warmer; summer rain she could have faced. Or if it wasn't so dark. Or maybe if . . .

If only Master Tanafres wouldn't catch her. That was her only real chance; she just didn't have the courage to leave as he had ordered. She prayed again to Mannar and to V'Zurna, too. Her entreaties became a litany that she chanted over and over until the drumming rain seemed to fade away and she slept.

The sky was lightening when Jerr awoke, stiff and

cold and soggy, but still a girl and not a worm. At least one of the goddesses had taken pity on her; Master Tanafres had not discovered her. And, for a mercy, the rain had stopped. Seizing the chance to keep her disobedience hidden, she tottered outside on creaky legs. It was still cold, and her breath steamed past chattering teeth. She wanted to be warm so badly that she would have sold herself just to spend the time near a fire. No, she really wouldn't have sold herself, not just because of one cold night anyway, but she *did* want to be warm. Looking down at the village in the predawn grayness, she envied the folk their dry, warm beds. Like her, those folk were here because of Master Tanafres. Unlike an unsworn apprentice, they had a real place here; Master Tanafres was glad of their presence. *They* slept warm and dry.

The small enclave in the wilderness was not a real village and had no name that everyone agreed upon. Some called it the Wizard's Stead, others Lizard Cave, while still others, mostly the warriors, called it Kopell's Hall, after their master, Sir Kopell Mastillan. Jerr called it the village when she called it anything at all.

The place was nicer than when she'd first arrived. There'd been no houses then, just tents and makeshift hovels. Now there were three houses for the finer folk and a handful of huts for the common folk. There were sheds and stalls, too, and a proper corral for the horses. Since there were no farmers here—something she was glad of—every few days a wagon of provisions arrived from Baron Yentillan's steading, bringing foodstuffs, ale, and whatever supplies Master Tanafres had requested.

Baron Yentillan provided for them because he was a good king's man and the mage stood high in the king's favor—a fact that was not the least of the things that made Master Tanafres such an attractive master. If he still was her master, that was. If he wasn't, she wouldn't be here much longer. She hugged herself, feeling the

cold, and her gaze traveled out across the wild forest surrounding the village.

Distant movement on the far side of the Tersrom
River caught her eye. People on horses, they were.
Though her eyes were sharp, she could make out no
details. The riders were moving slowly along a ridge on
the far bank of the river. As they disappeared behind
trees from time to time, she could not even be sure of
their numbers. They were not on the road from Baron
Yentillan's steading, although they appeared to be heading for the ford where the road crossed the river on its
way to the village. A group of horsemen this far from
steadings could only be coming to the village, and if they
were traveling already at this hour, they were on no ordinary business.

She ought to tell someone. Master Tanafres was the
obvious choice, but she wasn't ready to face him yet. She
especially didn't want to enter the cave unbidden. Sir
Kopell Mastillan was the baron's knight and held the village for him; Sir Kopell needed to know, but he was a
knight. Jerr dared not go directly to him. Her eyes fell on
the house which Master Tanafres shared with his clerk,
where he usually spent his nights. A wisp of smoke
curled from the chimney pot, telling her that someone in
the house—it had to be Master Lennuick—had woken
the fire from its embers. Jerr didn't like the old man's
ornery manner, but she knew that he could speak freely
with both Master Tanafres and Sir Kopell. She would tell
him of the riders.

Jerr made her way down the path, less careful of the
slick earth than she should have been. She fell twice, skin-
ning her hands and ripping her skirts, before she reached
the level ground of the clearing. Once on more level, if
not firmer, ground, she hiked up her skirts and ran.

As she passed Sir Kopell's house, she wondered if she
should be so worried about not disturbing the knight; he
seemed more easygoing than Master Lennuick. She might

not even have to talk to him directly; she could just tell her news to his servant. Then she heard someone shifting wood in the crib behind the biggest of the village's houses, the long hall where Sir Kopell's warriors resided. A rattling crash of falling wood made that someone curse, and Jerr recognized the voice. It was Mistress Teletha Schonnegon, the islander warrior.

Jerr changed her plans at once and cut toward the wood crib. Mistress Schonnegon was a warrior and Master Tanafres's friend; her connections were as good as the old clerk's and her manner far more friendly. If Jerr could catch the islander before she went back into the long hall, Jerr wouldn't have to deal with the other warriors, whose manner made even Master Lennuick's look attractive.

Jerr rounded the corner of the hall just as Mistress Schonnegon emerged from the wood crib. The islander was having trouble juggling her armload of mismatched faggots and keeping her cloak snugged tight around her. She almost dropped the wood when she caught sight of Jerr.

Jerr tried to address her politely, but she was out of breath and shivering. Her words came out making no sense at all, chopped to pieces by her chattering teeth.

"Jerr?" Mistress Schonnegon furrowed her brow. "That *is* you under all that mud, isn't it, girl?"

Still unable to speak, Jerr nodded awkwardly.

Mistress Schonnegon dropped her load and swung her cloak from her shoulders, settling it around Jerr's. The hem sagged into the mud, but Mistress Schonnegon didn't seem to care. "Come on," she said. "Let's get you inside. You need to be dried off and warmed up before you take a fever."

Trust Mistress Schonnegon to have some sympathy for a cold, wet girl. Jerr let herself be turned around and led toward the back door of the long hall. The thought of being warm again emptied her of her natural fears about the place where the warriors lived. The warmth of the place was more important than anything else. Besides, with Mistress Schonnegon's protection, she ought to be safe enough.

As Jerr stepped through the doorway, she almost changed her mind, because the first thing she saw was the drakkenree stretched by the central fire pit. The big green monster didn't move, other than to curl its tail around itself when the breeze from the open door made the fire dance. The lizard lay there on its belly, its long legs folded up like those of a hen sitting a nest. The monster's long-muzzled snout was in profile to her, so when it opened its eyes, she could see only one emerald orb. The lizard glared at her balefully.

She hated lizards.

Master Tanafres had scolded her the first time she had called it a lizard. He never called the thing a lizard. He had told her to use the proper name for its kind, to call it a "saurian." The word sounded strange to her; she tried to use it, at least when speaking to the mage, but often she forgot. "Lizard" was what all good Kolviners called the monsters.

What else was it? It didn't wear any clothes and it didn't speak anything but its own tongue. Sometimes it seemed to understand what was said to it, but a smart dog did that—although a dog didn't look at you with cold emerald eyes and bare its teeth in a permanent, evil grin. When she was around it she often had the feeling that the lizard would suddenly start hunting her; and because of that, she always wanted to know just where it was.

Drakkenree were the ancient enemy, recently returned to haunt Kolvin as they had in the olden days. Having one in the village made nonsense of all the old tales her mother and granny had told her. Lizards were supposed to kill you or be killed by you—well, by the knights and their warriors actually, or by mages like

Master Tanafres. Lizards didn't live in a village with decent folk. Jerr didn't understand why Sir Kopell let this one live. Despite Master Tanafres's assurances that the drakkenree was cowed, Jerr didn't trust it. She didn't like the way it always lurked about at the edge of things, watching.

"Shut the door!" one of the warriors shouted from a muffling pile of bedclothes.

"This hain't no barn," added another, one of Sir Kopell's men-at-arms.

"Hey, Norlann, it's the farm girl. House is a barn where she comes from, eh?" said Senn. He was the newest of the three men-at-arms, just come down from the baron's steading a fortnight ago. Jerr liked him almost as little as she did the lizard.

"You oughta know, eh, Senn?" Mistress Schonnegon said. Taking Jerr by the arm, Mistress Schonnegon moved her out of the doorway and kicked the door shut. The latch rattled as it caught. "Come on, girl, you need to sit by the fire." Over her shoulder she said, "Senn, there's a load of wood just outside. Go get it before the damp takes it. We could all use a good fire this morning."

"I don't take no orders from you, Islander," Senn said haughtily.

"Do it, Senn," Myskell ordered. He was Sir Kopell's senior man-at-arms and indisputably of higher rank than Senn.

Senn started to complain. "Why me? Let one of the . . . "

"Do it! You hain't no knight; you can still get your hands dirty with honest work."

While Senn argued, Mistress Schonnegon led Jerr to the fire pit and sat her beside it. "Stay put," she ordered, before going over to a cask and drawing a mug of ale. Returning, Mistress Schonnegon dug at the end of the embers with fire tongs until she found a stone, which she snatched up and dropped into the mug with a plop and a hiss. From the other side of the fire, the drakkenree imitated the sound with eerie exactness; Jerr looked over at it and saw that the lizard was still watching her, but with both eyes now. She shivered and knew it wasn't from the chill she had taken. After receiving the mug from Mistress Schonnegon, Jerr turned so she wouldn't have to see the monster. Sipping carefully, she let the heat of the drink slide down her throat and into her belly. The steam from the mug smelled good, and the warmth spreading through the pottery eased the cramp in her fingers.

Myskell came over and spoke to Mistress Schonnegon. "What's afoot, Teletha?"

"The girl has something to tell, but she is so taken with chill that she cannot speak clearly."

Squatting before Jerr, Myskell looked at her sternly. "Something from the wizard?"

She shook her head. The heat and the ale were helping, but she didn't yet trust her tongue between her chattering teeth. It wasn't until the fire had been stoked up and she'd had her second mug of ale that her shivering abated enough for her to give an account of what she'd seen. Her threadbare tale was enough to make Myskell and Mistress Schonnegon look worried.

"No one without strong reason would have ridden through last night's rain," Myskell said when she finished.

"They'll be carrying bad news, then," Mistress Schonnegon suggested.

"Or bringing trouble," Norlann said.

Myskell looked as if neither possibility pleased him. "How many did you say, girl?"

"A half dozen, I think. Maybe more. I'm not sure, sir."

"And headed for the ford?"

Jerr nodded.

"River'll be high," Norlann observed. "Maybe too high to cross."

Jerr had been thinking that herself. Mistress Schonnegon

disagreed. "If they rode through the night, they'll not let the river stop them. We haven't seen all that much rain."

Myskell nodded. "Still take them more than the usual time to cross. Even if they ride hard once they're on our side of the river, I don't see them getting here before Horesh clears the trees. We have some time to prepare for the worst." Myskell sighed. "Norlann, ready the men. I'll go tell Sir Kopell."

3

WHEN TELETHA EMERGED from the long hall, clad in her buff coat and with the ties of her prawntail helmet snugged under her chin, Sir Kopell was already standing where the road entered the steading's clearing. He showed no agitation, only watchfulness, so she assumed he had yet to see any sign of the riders. Or, with Vehr's blessing, he had seen the riders and they had shown themselves to be no threat; it was too cold and damp for a fight.

A glance around decided her that Sir Kopell must not have seen them yet; he wasn't the sort to let the preparations for trouble go on unless he thought them, if not necessary, at least prudent. Sir Kopell took seriously his charge to protect the steading.

Bustling men pushed past her as they left the hall. Servants carried gear to the three men-at-arms who stood nearby, helping each other don their light harness. The foot soldiers looked to their own gear. The knight's four archers were loudly debating the wisdom of stringing their bows now or waiting until the riders were sighted. The steading's civilians watched nervously from the doors of the houses and from their huts.

Senn, the newest of Sir Kopell's men-at-arms, bawled for the knight's slave drakkenree to go and fetch their horses. The green-scaled saurian stared sullenly at the man and made no move to comply.

"You're wasting your breath. He won't do work for you," Myskell told Senn, before giving the same order to his own servant, who ran at once to do the senior's bidding. To the drakkenree he said, "Go get Sir Kopell's cote armor and his helm, then. They are in the common room of his house."

The drakkenree growled something that ended in a soft hiss.

"Armor! From Sir Kopell's house! Understand? Sir Kopell's armor," Myskell shouted at the saurian. As the drakkenree turned and headed for Sir Kopell's house, he added, "Light harness! His cote armor, no more!"

If the drakkenree heard or understood, the lizard gave no sign.

Teletha noticed that all the bustle among the men-at-arms and the talk of armor was upsetting Jerr. Wrapped in Teletha's cloak, the wide-eyed girl stood to one side of the long hall's door and watched all the activity. Teletha hoped for the girl's sake that there wouldn't be any real trouble; if the riders were going to be troublesome, and if there were more than half a dozen of them, this little force would have its hands full.

The drakkenree returned with Sir Kopell's armor and dumped its load near the knight. Backing away at once, it stalked to the edge of the clearing and settled to the ground. Its hide was patterned in darker stripes that made it almost disappear against the greenery, a disconcerting effect. Being what it was, the lizard always merited watching.

Sometimes Teletha found it hard to think of the drakkenree as a human being as Yan said she should. Though it was much smaller, its form was uncannily like that of the great beasts that Yellow Eye had sent against the Kolviners during his invasion: tooth-filled snout, cold eyes, sinewy limbs with taloned hands, heavily muscled birdlike legs with clawed feet, hunched posture, long tail, and scaly skin. The resemblance was even stronger now that the slave no longer wore harness or carried tools or weapons. And what Yan said was a language might be only the growls and hisses and posturing of an animal for all the sense she could make of it. But if its kind *were* only animals, they were clever, dangerous animals. Yan said they were more than animals, though, and he should know: he'd spent more time in their company than anyone, and he was too smart to be fooled by even a clever animal.

Sir Kopell called his men to him. Teletha, though not under contract to the knight, went as well. The masters of the Guild of the Sword understood that there were times when one used one's craft without payment; she'd done so before, and probably would again—but, with Vehr's grace, not today.

They heard the riders before they saw them. The strangers' lack of stealth suggested that the Kolviners' precautions were unneeded. She hoped so.

When they came into sight, she counted five riders. The foremost was a familiar local, a woodsrider: Dantil by name, called the Scout for his skill in the forests. He was a veteran of Yellow Eye's war and still served Baron Yentillan. The other four, by their dress, were not Kolviners. Their heads were covered in low-crowned, broad-brimmed hats of island style. All wore buff coats common to Imperial soldiers, a practical martial style that Teletha had seen too little of these last years. Their prawntail helmets were slung from their saddlebows, a sign of peaceful intent.

Teletha untied her helmet strap.

Sir Kopell raised a hand in greeting to Dantil, and the Scout waved back.

"It appears that our concern is misplaced. It is not danger we receive today, but visitors," Sir Kopell announced. The knight bade his men to relax their vigilance.

Peyto Lennuick was quick to note the change in attitude and join Teletha. The old clerk squinted down the road at the newcomers. "Hunh," he exclaimed mildly. Whispering to her, "Imperial visitors, by their clothes."

"Early in the season for ships to be on the water, isn't it?" she whispered back

"Upon the Waters of Travel, no. But to attempt a crossing to the mainland, I would have thought so. It is not too late for the Sea of Storms to send a tempest up the coast. I wonder what urgency drives them to such risk."

What indeed? "I expect we'll know soon."

Maybe she had been too quick to dismiss the possibility of trouble. Teletha looked the newcomers over, not that she expected to see familiar faces. Still, this wouldn't be the first Imperial expedition into Kolvin to bring pieces of her past along. However, none of the islanders looked familiar.

All but one of the strangers sat their horses awkwardly, as if unaccustomed to the Kolviner saddles. If they were newly come to the kingdom, that was likely; it had taken her some time to get used to the local rig. The one who rode comfortably had likely spent some time in the kingdom before now. She took a closer look at him.

Even without his more practiced horsemanship, he would have stood out among his fellows. The rain had taken a toll on his gear, but its quality was amply evident. He wore a buff coat of rich, pale leather—at least, it would have been pale had it not been soaked. Golden braid adorned the wings at the coat's shoulders and at the edges of its hanging sleeves, and the buttons in their braid frogs glistened brassily in the morning light. The bucket tops of his boots were of as fine a leather as his coat, though lighter weight, of course, and were rolled up to fully cover his legs. For all their extravagance in decoration, though, his clothes were practically cut for riding, and he had covered the hilts of his weapons with oiled bags, an old campaigner's trick. Though his hat brim was limp from the rain, he had somehow managed to contrive a fresh and dry spray of plumes. Both the feathers and the cockade that pinned back a portion of his hat's brim were black and white: the colors of a follower of the Imperial party. When a glint of silver on his chest caught her eye and she saw the half-concealed medallion that lay there, she understood much.

He was a *staliarm* man, an agent of the emperor!

His face was lean, his features finely formed enough to serve as a model for some sculptor. Handsome, even. He looked far more respectable than Raff Janden, the last *staliarm* man Teletha had known. She hoped this one would live up to his appearance. It would be a cruelty worthy of the Dark Lord of the Under Court Himself if such fair features hid a black heart like Janden's.

They said that a man's companions told much of him. Teletha looked for clues to the *staliarm* man's nature among the other islanders. She found them an odd lot.

The least impressive of the four islanders was a scrawny man in an ill-fitting, sleeveless buff coat. Beneath the armor, he wore plain and undistinguished clothes, and he was shod with shoes rather than more sensible riding boots. Despite the sword slung from a baldric across his chest, he was no soldier. The white sleeve of his shirt was stained with dark splotches where it showed beneath his jacket's cuff, by which Teletha took him to be a clerk. An unhappy clerk. His dejected frown and sodden clothing gave him a resemblance to a cat some prankster had dropped in a fountain.

Riding beside the clerk was a fellow who looked more a boy than a man, despite his soldierly coat and the sword and long dagger hung in bravo fashion, one beneath the other on a single baldric. The carefully groomed but sparse beard told the tale; this youth could not be more than a year or two older than Jerr, barely out of childhood. A bit young for campaigning. Was he a page to the *staliarm* man? The way his clothes mimicked those of the *staliarm* man, though of less rich materials, color, and decoration, suggested that if he wasn't attached to the man by duty, he found the man admirable and worthy of imitation.

The last islander rode a few paces back. His buff coat was unadorned and sleeveless, the sort a thrifty and practical soldier invested in. Beneath the coat he wore plain, much-worn clothes of dull, dark, muddy brown. The brim of his hat was barely wide enough to be fashionable and hung limply all around the crown. A single, bedraggled yellow feather sprouted from the band, held to it by an enameled cockade. The pattern on the disk—yellow circle with a blue surround—explained the drabness of his dress: he was a Solonite, a member of that dour sect which claimed that there was but one God, Horesh, and that all other Great Beings of the Celestial Court were reflections of the One. Solonites were uncommon in the empire and almost unknown outside its borders; few people held such a narrow view of godhead, and fewer still wanted a part in the Solonites' strict and rigid way of life. This fellow seemed a true example of the breed; the sour expression he wore as he looked about the steading radiated his disapproval.

"Sir Kopell, this here's Arun Schell, a captain in the Imperial Lancers," Dantil the Scout said, indicating the *staliarm* man. Dantil guided his horse off the road and out from between the knight and the oncoming islanders. Turning his head back to those who followed him, Dantil completed his unceremonious introduction. "Captain Schell, Sir Kopell's the man in charge here."

Schell nodded to the woodsrider. "You've been as good as your word, Dantil. Horesh give you just reward."

"As He wills," Dantil mumbled as turned his horse toward the cookshed.

He'd be seeking something warm, but he'd have to fend for himself; the cook and her scullions were among the crowd of steading folk come out to see the strangers.

Schell dismounted, and when he was afoot, his *stal-iarm* was no longer visible. He was making no show of his position. His eyes swept across Sir Kopell and the sol-diers. Teletha thought the man's gaze lingered briefly on Peyto, and she was sure that he gave her a second glance before looking over the craftsmen, their apprentices, and the servants. There need not have been any significance to his attention—Peyto had a single arm, a noteworthy lack, and Teletha, the only woman among the soldiers, was a somewhat unusual sight herself with her islander armor over Kolviner clothing—but Teletha would have bet silver that Schell had been matching their appear-ances to a description he had been given.

From a friend or an enemy?

She hoped he'd had their description from a friend, but his arrival in the company of Dantil didn't bode well. The woodsrider had been one of the blackguard Janden's henchmen.

Schell waited until the other islanders dismounted before speaking to Sir Kopell.

"Well met, Sir Knight. May I present Master Ab Nendern and Galon Martello." Each bowed as his name was pronounced. "The glum gentleman holding himself aloof is Caram Namsorn, a commissioned captain in the service of the most illustrious Emperor Dacel. We have a letter of passage from your king granting us safe con-duct." Schell held out a folded piece of paper. "It also bids all of King Shain's loyal subjects to lend us such aid as seems meet."

Teletha noted suspiciously that Schell made no mention of his position as a *staliarm* man. He *was* hiding his position.

Sir Kopell took the offered letter, unfolded it, and squinted at the writing. He nodded at the seal impressed in a blob of dark red wax near the bottom of the sheet. "Looks real enough."

"Would you like me to read it to you, Sir Kopell?" Peyto asked.

"Later," said Sir Kopell. He kept his eyes on the islanders. "Most travelers come by the road past Baron Yentillan's steading."

Schell smiled broadly. "Captain Namsorn, who knows this countryside somewhat, had suggested that very course of travel, but the gods put fortune in our way in the person of the baron's woodsrider. Dantil suggested a more direct route which, given the unkindness of the weather, has meant that we have spent less time enduring your Kolviner rain than we might have otherwise."

"The baron's roof would have kept you dry," Sir Kopell pointed out.

"It certainly would have," Schell agreed.

"So, Captain Schell, you've come a long way into the wilderness. And in a hurry, unless I miss my guess. Why?"

"That we will take up with the magician."

So they'd come to see Yan. No wonder Schell had recognized Peyto and Teletha. Once more she wondered if she'd been too quick to dismiss the possibility of trouble.

"Go fetch Master Tanafres," Peyto shouted to Jerr.

"He doesn't want to be disturbed," Jerr said timidly, her voice almost inaudible.

She sounded afraid. Now Jerr's cold and wet state made sense to Teletha. Somehow the girl had gotten herself in trouble with Yan. She normally spent her nights in Yan's workroom like a good apprentice, and the cave didn't leak. She must have spent the night outside. If Jerr had been willing to do that, she certainly wouldn't want to be the one to "disturb" Yan.

If Peyto noticed the girl's reluctance, he dismissed it. "I think he'll have a different opinion when he learns who's come. Go on. Tell him emissaries from the emperor are here. He'll want to hear that, no matter what he's wasting his time with."

Jerr took a step back. She looked ready to run—and it wasn't toward the cave that she was edging.

"Leave be, girl," Captain Schell said. "We are in no great haste to see the magician."

No haste?

Schell continued speaking. "The others are the ones who have business with him. Perhaps he'll be more open to disturbance by the time they arrive."

"Others?" Sir Kopell sounded as if he didn't like the idea. "Who are these others?"

"Scholars, mostly. One you may have heard of even here: a holy man of Horesh, one Löm Geroy Kerandiri," Schell said.

"The emissary of his Holiness, the primate," Namsorn added.

"I have heard of Löm Kerandiri," Sir Kopell said.

His response surprised Teletha; she hadn't heard of the priest. But then, though she believed in the gods, she had little faith in most of their priests; she'd paid little attention to Church hierarchy when she'd last been in the empire, and that had been some time ago. Whoever Kerandiri was, he was important if he was on a mission from the head of the Triadic Church.

A mission that involved Yan? *Vehr grant that the high-and-mighty Löm Kerandiri not be an inquisitor come to accuse Yan of some sort of trespass against the Church's strictures on magic.*

Sir Kopell was more concerned with practical considerations. "Captain Schell, could it be that you left the holy man to travel unescorted?"

"Not at all. The priest and his entourage are well protected," Schell assured him. "For Löm Kerandiri's comfort, they must perforce travel at a slower pace and take a less arduous route. They come by way of your Baron Yentillan's steading, in fact. I thought it best we come on ahead and ascertain that the magician here is indeed the man we seek. With all the rain, we feared the ford would be swollen beyond passage, and I saw no reason for Löm Kerandiri to waste his time waiting for the river to slacken if we'd come to the wrong place."

The answer seemed to satisfy the knight, for he abandoned his questioning and remembered to be hospitable. He invited the newcomers to the long hall and sent the cook scurrying to prepare food and drink for them. Teletha watched Sir Kopell bow the guests into the hall, but he didn't immediately join them. Instead he pulled Norlann aside and spoke briefly and earnestly. When they were done, the knight went into the hall, and the man-at-arms took to his horse and left the steading. The other soldiers went into the hall, and the steading's folk went about their business or gathered near the long hall to catch snatches of news and gossip from the conversation of the knight and the islanders.

She thought about Iaf's letter. Was this the danger he had tried to warn her about? Maybe she ought to go tell Yan about the newcomers, and about the letter. She wondered what he'd make of the whole thing, and wondered if he'd share his conclusions with her, something he'd been doing less frequently of late. Peyto had his own ideas and spoke freely of them.

"This is an interesting development," the clerk said. "An Imperial commission to find Yan."

"Namsorn suggests that it's a Church commission."

"Rare the Solonite who gives importance to earthly motivations. They harken only to orders from on high, though some, I've heard, prefer their consciences over even the primate's word. Mark me. Captain Namsorn, for all his Imperial commission, is less well informed about the motivations behind this commission than he believes."

"Why do you say that?"

"Practical experience," Peyto answered, but instead of explaining, he changed the subject. "This could be a call to Imperial service. Ha! But wouldn't that be a charm?

All these years of Yan fretting about how to make an impression when we reach Sharhumrin. It would seem he has already made his impression."

"Wouldn't Schell have been more open if that was the case?"

"You mean, wouldn't he have proclaimed himself a *staliarm* man?"

So Peyto had seen the talisman, too. For an old man, he was still sharp-eyed. "That, at least."

"I couldn't say. Perhaps his only charge is to ensure Löm Kerandiri's safety and success, or perhaps he thinks to save the revelation, to impress our good magician with the importance of the summons. We will know when the priest gets here."

"You sound eager."

"And why not? We'll be going back to the empire at last. Even Yan can't refuse a summons from the emperor."

What about one from the primate's inquisitors? And how would King Shain take all this? She guessed that the king thought of Yan as "his" wizard now. But Teletha didn't voice her fears, she just asked, "Have you had breakfast?"

Peyto hadn't; they went into the hall. Teletha would get to speaking with Yan later. Maybe by then she'd have more to tell him.

4

TELETHA BROUGHT YAN THE WORD about the visitors around midday. He didn't need her mysterious letter of warning from Iaf to tell him that he had problems. He spent the rest of the afternoon pondering the situation and doing what little he could to safeguard the workroom. His splendid and studious isolation was over. As he walked down the path from the cave, he decided that he should have listened to Peyto. He should have had the king's workmen install a door inside the cavern entrance, a door with a lock. He had thought it an unnecessary precaution at the time. Out here in the wilderness, whom would he have to keep out?

An Imperial delegation, it seemed.

The great Arkyn had blocked the pass at Gerhandascine with an impenetrable wall of force, but Yan was no Arkyn, and real life was no heroic ballad. He'd done what he could; a hedge wizard's solution for a hedge wizard's problem. His head was already starting to ache with the effort of maintaining the spell that he'd woven.

Trying to hold a spell on himself at the same time didn't help. More of real life putting the lie to the old tales. In the stories, wizards could move unseen whenever and wherever they willed. Real magicians knew that sorcerous concealment was best when the magician was stationary: movement was a concealing spell's bane, making the spell quite easy to penetrate. Nevertheless, he was trying to hold such a spell on himself as he returned to his house. He didn't want to meet with any of the Imperial visitors just yet.

He reached his house without incident. It was evening and the village seemed almost deserted. Was his sorcerous effort unnecessary? The only person he saw was Rosh the blacksmith, pounding away in his smithy, taking advantage of the last light. The smith was too engrossed in his work to pay heed to anything beyond his forge and anvil. Just as well.

As Yan closed the door behind him, he let the spell slip away. The pounding in his head dulled to a steady, slow throb. Peyto and Fra Bern interrupted their debate and turned to look at him. Peyto was scowling, his usual response at any interruption. Fra Bern looked surprised; the priest's hand strayed up to clasp the sun disk on his breast briefly before turning the gesture into a general resettling of his cowl. Teletha, lounging against the worktable where she could watch out the window, smiled and said, "You finished up there faster than I thought."

Upon seeing Yan, Jerr nearly dropped the pitcher she was wiping with a rag. She'd been jumpy since she'd gone up to the cave with Teletha and brought the news of the visitors. She hurried over at once to take Yan's satchel. Though he would have preferred retaining the bag to hand, he let her take it away and lay it beside his bed. She was being especially solicitous today.

"All went as I asked?" he asked.

Teletha's nod said that she had managed to get Fra Bern to the house without being seen. He wanted to talk to his friends before he spoke to the newcomers, and until he knew more, caution suggested that the conference was better kept confidential.

Peyto took in the exchange and nodded shrewdly. "So

you're the one who asked for this hooded-cloak tack. Has Teletha brought you to put faith in her fears, then?"

"She has expressed legitimate concern, I think." Yan sat on the bench by the door. "I have placed misdirection and concealment spells on the cave. The small cave to the east should appear to be the one to which the path leads. Please don't try to go up to the real cave without me."

"But everyone here knows that the eastern cave is empty," Jerr said as she brought a steaming mug of cider. "They all know where the real one is."

As he gratefully accepted the warm drink, Yan said, "With luck, no one will bother to ask."

"You're asking a lot from luck," Teletha said.

Yan shrugged. "Very few have been inside since the workmen left. If any of the people here try to point out the real opening, all that will be seen is rock. Perhaps our visitors will think I've confused everyone with my magic."

"You're confusing me with your feeble hopes," Peyto said.

"Oh, well." Yan shrugged. His head hurt beyond the remedy of the steam from his mug. "Maybe it's not important that the cave be hidden, anyway."

Fra Bern looked perplexed. "I'm afraid I don't understand. Mistress Schonnegon said that you wished to speak with me, but she said nothing to match your grim demeanor."

"You know about the visitors."

"Everyone in the steading knows. But I have heard nothing untoward about them, save that one of the captains is a misguided follower of Solon."

"Trust a priest to be worried about the fine points of doctrine," Peyto remarked.

"It is not just a matter of fine points," Fra Bern objected. "My bishop says that the Solonites are heretics."

"Your bishop is a narrow-minded country bumpkin who—"

"That's enough, you two," Yan told them. "I don't think they're here to deal with Captain Namsorn's theology. I fear they will be looking more closely at other people's beliefs."

Fra Bern blinked. "Why would Imperial soldiers concern themselves with anyone's faith?"

"Haven't you heard about the priests?" Peyto asked.

Leaning back, Fra Bern put on a sober expression. "There were no priests among the strangers."

"They're coming though," Peyto told him. "The delegation is headed by a löm. Kerandiri, I think the name was."

"The Church does not bestow the title of löm lightly," Fra Bern said with a trace of awe in his voice. "Fra Kerandiri must be a priest of exceptional holiness."

"Or exceptionally good connections among the princes of the Church," Peyto said.

"Priests from the empire?" Fra Bern was starting to sound worried.

"From the primate himself, if Captain Namsorn is to be believed," Peyto said.

Fra Bern went pale. "The Baansuus," he said in a strangled voice.

"Perhaps." Yan understood how the priest would leap to that conclusion. Along with Yan, Fra Bern had studied the drakkenree writings and the deep caverns. He had identified part of the complex as a temple dedicated to a drakkenree deity: the Baansuus. According to Fra Bern, the Baansuus was a deity that belonged to neither the Celestial Court nor the Under Court, something that orthodox Triadic doctrine held to be impossible. It was not just narrow-minded country bishops who could find a holder of such beliefs to be a heretic. Fra Bern was dedicated to Einthof, but even a priest of the Lord of Secrets was not given free rein to delve in all matters; if the purifying fires were to be lit over the matter of the Baansuus, Fra Bern would see them, and not as a disinterested observer. There was no evidence that the Imperial priests had the Baansuus on their minds, but Fra Bern was showing early signs of panic. Yan didn't want that; he needed clear minds among his friends. "By all accounts, these priests are coming to see me."

"You?" Relief flickered briefly on Fra Bern's face, almost instantly replaced by concern. "Why?"

"I wish I knew."

"You will soon," Teletha said.

"Perhaps this has something to do with what you did at the Battle of Rastionne," Peyto suggested.

"It might," Yan conceded. "But I would have thought that we would have heard before this, if the empire had an interest in what happened there. It's been years since Iaf went back and told his tale."

"Five winters," said Teletha.

That long? He'd have said three; he'd lost track of the time. "If it's Rastionne, why now?"

"And why priests?" Peyto asked. "That was magic. Why not send a wizard?"

"Maybe they have." Everyone turned to Teletha. She looked directly at Yan. "Since we spoke, I've heard that there *is* a wizard among the priests."

"What?" Yan wasn't sure he'd heard correctly. There were several minor orders devoted to the Great Art as well as to their sponsor deity, but those orders were small, and the practitioners within them little skilled; it seemed being a good priest conflicted with being a good magician. Yan had never heard of any order producing a magician powerful enough to be termed a wizard. "Are you sure? A *Church* wizard?"

"No, I'm not sure. I wasn't the one conversing with young Martello." Teletha turned her gaze on Jerr.

The girl shrank away as she became the center of attention.

Yan tried not to sound upset. "Jerr Kansti, why didn't you tell me of this?"

"I didn't think it important, Master Tanafres. I thought if it was important, you'd already know."

"Silly girl," Peyto chided.

"She knew no better," Fra Bern said in her defense.

"What's done is done," Yan said. "It's all right, Jerr. Tell me what Martello said about this wizard?"

"He didn't say much. We weren't talking about him."

"I won't ask what you were talking about," Yan said. "Tell me, did he say if the wizard was a priest?"

"No. I don't think so. But I don't think he is."

"And why is that?"

"We weren't talking about priests then."

"You're not being helpful, girl," Peyto said. "Did Martello name this wizard? Did he use any honorific for him?"

"I—I—" Jerr was gulping air, on the verge of crying.

Yan got up and went to her.

"Calm yourself, Jerr." He put a hand on her shoulder, extending his will upon her and calming. The work he had done with her, readying her to touch *præha*, made it easy for him to reinforce her attempts to steady herself. "No need to cry."

Jerr steadied. Her gasping stopped, subsiding into sniffling.

Beneath his hand Yan felt her calm. He reinforced it. "Remember, calm is the friend of memory."

Jerr nodded, eyes closed. She was almost in *præha*. Yan was pleased. Her memory would be clearer.

"Sit and be calm," he told her. At Yan's nod, Fra Bern vacated his seat. Yan guided Jerr to it. When she was seated, he said, "We need you to remember what was said. Can you do that for me?"

She nodded.

"Good. Now, put your mind back to when you were talking to young Master Martello."

A faint smile on Jerr's lips.

"He is a handsome lad, isn't he?"

Jerr nodded.

"So young Master Martello told you that there was a wizard coming here." Jerr nodded again. "To see me?"

"I don't know," Jerr said sleepily "I don't think Galon knows."

Behind Yan, Peyto whispered, "Who's Galon?" and Teletha whispered back, "Martello." Yan kept his attention on Jerr.

"But Galon knows the name of the wizard, doesn't he, Jerr?"

"Aye. He told me, but the name was strange to me. Hain't heard its like before."

"Think hard, Jerr. Can you recall it?"

Jerr's face scrunched up. Yan felt her mind churning. After a moment she relaxed her expression. Yan knew the answer before she said, "Nay, but I think Galon called him a sir."

"A sir? Are you sure that was what he said?" A knightly wizard was even more unlikely than a Church wizard. "Could he have said *ser*?"

Jerr thought about it and nodded. "Aye, that's the way he said it. I like the way he talks, but he's got a funny accent, and I'm not very good at Nitallan."

Nitallan, eh? That would account for Jerr's confusion. She would have heard what she most expected to hear and taken the Empiric honorific as one she knew. *Ser* was a term of neither martial nor priestly regard. This wizard was not a knight or a priest; he was a scholar, and an eminent one at that. *Ser* was a form of address reserved for the wisest of men.

"Jerr, did Galon tell you anything else about the wizard?"

"He said he was almost as important as the holy man."

"Did he say why the wizard was important?"

"Nay."

"Thank you, Jerr. Go in the back and get some sleep. You may use my bed. No one will disturb you."

Yan wouldn't be using his bed tonight, not with the Imperial delegation due to arrive tomorrow. He was thoughtful as he watched the girl take herself off to the bed. Why was this wizard coming to see Yan? And why was he coming in the company of Triadic emissaries? Questions without answers, the story of Yan's life.

"It seems," he said, "that matters are more complicated than ever."

5

JERR AWOKE WHEN SHE HEARD the door close. The sound
was soft, but enough to reach her and pull her from a
dream. She opened her eyes just in time to see a flickering light at the shutters. Whoever had left was passing by
the window, briefly blocking the early-morning light. She
shifted under the covers, feeling the drag of her skirts
against the blanket; she had gone to sleep fully dressed.
Odd, but no odder than the creak of the ropes beneath
the tick on which she lay.

Ropes? Ropes beneath her meant that she was on a
bed. Her sleepiness vanished like a snowflake in a fire.
Mannar's mercy! She *was* on a bed! Master Tanafres's
bed!

She was in trouble.

Dimly she remembered Master Tanafres telling her to
lie down on his bed and rest, but surely he had not meant
for her to sleep the night away. What had he done for a
place to sleep?

In a panic Jerr scrambled from the bed and peeked
around the curtain that screened the sleeping alcove from
the main room. The central table was littered with candle
stumps; someone had burned a lot of wax during the
night. Otherwise, nothing in the house looked out of
place, until she spotted an occupied bedroll over by the

worktable. A closer look told her that the form within was too short to be Master Tanafres. Who, then? She tip-toed around the central table until she could see a sword lying on the floor beside the sleeping figure. It was Mistress Schonnegon's sword; the anonymous sleeper must be Mistress Schonnegon.

Jerr heard a soft snoring coming from the other sleep-ing alcove and looked in that direction. The curtain there was not closed all the way, and through the opening she could see the white hair of Master Lennuick. Unlike Master Tanafres's bed, the clerk's bed was too narrow for more than one person at a time.

There was no loft, no second room, and Master Tanafres was nowhere in sight. Where was he? Feeling a dullard, she realized that it must have been he that she had heard leaving.

Looking at the candle stubs, she wondered if he had remained awake all night. Just so he wouldn't disturb her? A gallant gesture, but unlikely; she was barely rein-stated in his good graces. And only an apprentice at that.

Maybe he had spent the night studying his books. Yes, that had to be it. He'd been worried about why the islanders had come, and he'd been seeking answers in his books.

But if Master Tanafres had been seeking answers in his books, why would he have done it here? Most of his books were in the cavern. He hadn't brought any with him in his satchel last night; she knew, because she had carried the satchel to his bedside and she would have noticed any books.

She looked. The satchel was gone. It *must* have been Master Tanafres that she had heard leaving.

If he'd taken the satchel, he would be planning on doing some work; he would need assistance. A good apprentice was supposed to help, without being asked. She hesitated. If he'd been awake all night, his temper would be short. She had best follow him; it was what a good apprentice would do. But she'd have to be extra careful and do everything right. She'd imposed enough on his goodwill by stealing a night's sleep in his bed. If he were an ordinary craftmaster, he'd be within his rights to cast her out for such a liberty. After the incident the other night, he was close to dismissing her already. She suspected that she remained only through Mistress Schonnegon's intercession. She was grateful, but she also knew that her opportunity here would last only as long as Master Tanafres's goodwill; and that depended on her being a good apprentice.

A good apprentice wouldn't have kept her master from his bed. But he had ordered her there, after all. Still, it was wrong. She hoped he wouldn't hold it against her.

Standing around fretting wasn't helping. Master Tanafres had asked that no one go up to the cavern without him last night, and that was surely where he was heading; she'd have to hurry to catch up to him.

Should she even try? Wouldn't he have woken her if he'd wanted her? He was a little absentminded. She felt sure that he'd be in need of some help today, especially if he'd been awake all night. A good apprentice was always there when her master needed her.

She headed for the door. She would have to hurry. She didn't want to enter the cave without his permission; that was what had gotten her in trouble the last time. She closed the door behind her, slowly so as to not waken the sleepers inside, and heard the latch drop into place. Then she froze, suddenly apprehensive.

She felt with a certainty that someone was nearby, watching her. Someone who was somehow. . . menacing. It was a strange feeling, and a frightening one.

Slowly she turned around.

Barely a dozen yards away, Sir Kopell's drakkenree was hunkered down against the wall of the long hall. The lizard's head was pointing in her direction like an arrow set to a bow. It was staring at her with its cold eyes.

She wanted to run, but she was afraid to. The way the lizard watched her reminded her of the way a cat watched a mouse. She knew what a cat did when the mouse started to run. It was easy to see herself as a mouse to the drakkenree's cat. There was no doubt what her fate would be if the monster attacked; she had no defense against its claws and teeth. Not for the first time she wished that Sir Kopell had slain the lizard instead of taking it as a slave.

But for all the intensity of its stare, the lizard did nothing. She took a step to the side. It didn't even twitch. A second step. Nothing. With her third step, the drakkenree's head turned slightly, perhaps to keep her in sight better, but the lizard remained relaxed. It didn't rush forward, talons outstretched and jaws agape. It didn't even stand up.

She told herself she was being foolish. The drakkenree had lived among them for months and it hadn't done so much as snap at anyone. Even when the soldiers teased it or beat it, the lizard remained docile. What was there to be afraid of?

She *was* being foolish.

Deliberately, she turned her back on the lizard. There was no sudden rush of clawed feet on the dirt. Step by step she walked away. She wanted to hurry, but she made herself walk slowly, telling herself that she could run once she got around the building and out of the lizard's sight. The problem was, once she got around the building, she saw Captain Namsorn standing by the village's shrine. He saw her as well and beckoned her to him.

She had heard the man called a Solonite. She didn't know what that was, but she knew he was of the Imperial party and recalled the admonition of just about every adult in the village that she be polite around the islanders. "Treat them like guests," Sir Kopell had said. "More like the lord's men come to collect his due," the blacksmith had said later.

"Girl, come here," Captain Namsorn said. To her surprise, he spoke Kolvinic.

It wouldn't be polite to ignore him. Looking past the islander toward the rock face, she caught a glimpse of Master Tanafres. There was still time to catch up with him. If she was quick . . .

"Good morrow to you, sir," she said, putting on a smile she didn't feel.

The islander wasn't polite. "Is this the only shrine here?"

"Aye, sir."

Captain Namsorn scowled.

"Is there something wrong?"

"Nothing I should not have expected in this godforsaken land. As shadows grow longer when the Great Lord's light fades, so too does evil grow where He is not foremost in our minds and hearts."

Jerr didn't understand.

Captain Namsorn stared at the shrine as he spoke, so Jerr took a careful look at it. The shrine was a simple thing: a sheltered box on a post, just the sort one would expect in a small steading such as this one. The doors of the box were open, revealing the carved and painted devotional panel with Lord Einthof's symbols: the black-irised golden eye, the white feather, and the gray lumpy-looking thing that she didn't understand but knew was associated with the scholar god. The box and post had been made by Padam the carpenter, and the panel was the work of Fra Bern.

"Do you see nothing amiss here?" Captain Namsorn pointed at the panel.

Jerr looked. Lord Einthof was not a god she knew well, but His symbols appeared correctly rendered. Certainly the workmanship wasn't as fine as in the temple at Baron Yentillan's steading, but neither was it as crude as the devotional panels in her home village's shrines. The gold was only bronze powder in a tempera

suspension—Fra Bern had shown her how it was done—
and not real gold, but she didn't see anything wrong with
that; the gods understood that this was a poor village and
not the king's temple. Being from the empire, Captain
Namsorn surely expected even small villages to have
finer shrines.

"It is impious," Captain Namsorn pronounced.

Jerr decided that she didn't like being thought of as
impious because she worshiped at a poorly furnished
shrine. "I'm sorry if it is not to your taste, but this is all
you will see around here. Fra Bern did his best."

"Fra Bern, you say? The priest associated with the
magician Tanafres? This is *his* work?"

"Padam helped, but he did what Fra Bern told him to
do."

"And Fra Bern is the only priest here?"

"Aye. His sermons are a bit windy, but Fra Bern tends
well enough to our needs."

"Does he?" The islander reached out and shut the
doors of the shrine, saying, "The wrath of the Great Lord
is pitiless, and He shall show no mercy to those who
spurn His light."

Captain Namsorn's voice sent shivers down her spine
as he asked, "Do you stand in His light, girl?"

She stepped back from him, but his hand flashed out
and grabbed her arm. His grip hurt.

"Do you, girl? Answer me!"

Captain Namsorn's icy eyes frightened Jerr as much as
the drakkenree's stare. But she wasn't afraid to run away
from him. She tore herself from his grip and spun
around. She found herself facing the woods hard by the
carpenter's workshed. She ran toward the trees. She just
wanted to be away from the scary islander. He didn't
come after her, but she kept going past the shed and into
the woods.

It wasn't until later that she realized that she had forgotten about catching up to Master Tanafres, and by then

it was too late. She sat down with her back to a tree and cried.

She was not a very good apprentice.

With the long hall given over to the Imperial delegation, Teletha had spent the night in Yan's house. It wasn't the most comfortable arrangement; but since she wasn't sworn to Sir Kopell, she didn't get a place by his fire as his men-at-arms did, and she didn't care to join the common soldiers in the tent that had been hauled down from the long hall's loft and set up on the stream bank.

Yan, as usual, had other things than her on his mind. After she'd escorted Fra Bern back to the hovel he called his penitential hut, she'd come back to find Yan bent over a scroll. A single candle was enough for him, with his magesight, but it wasn't enough for her; she hadn't been able to make out what he was reading. She had planned on asking him about it in the morning, but when she woke, he was gone. A look into the sleeping alcoves told her that while Peyto still lay abed, Jerr was up and out, too.

Magician and 'prentice, both gone without disturbing her. Teletha wasn't used to sleeping so soundly. Had Yan used his magic to make her sleep through his departure? She hated to think he'd taken such a liberty; he knew how she felt about that sort of thing. She knew that she could ask him when she caught up with him, but she wasn't sure she wanted to hear the answer. If he said that he had done nothing, could she believe him? He was not above lying to keep peace between them. And if he said yes, she would have to consider killing him.

For at least a heartbeat.

Vehr, but she hated dealing with magicians.

Not that she would really try to kill him, but she hated the idea of one more magical thing coming between them. Why couldn't he let all that stuff go and take up an honest trade? Because he was who he was, of course. There seemed to be no more hope of changing Yan than of her coming to like sorcery.

His pulling out so early suggested that he had something on his mind. From the collection of candle stubs on the table, he'd been up all night. Had he been reconsidering the advice of his friends? Not that anyone had suggested much of use; they knew too little about what had brought Yan to Imperial attention. They had talked for hours after Jerr's revelation about the wizard, but despite all their talking, they'd only managed to conclude that the Imperial priests had to be met and talked to. If the priests were bringing trouble, running away wouldn't help; and if they weren't bringing trouble, running away would only make Yan look foolish, something to which he had an intense aversion.

Yan had agreed that the best course was to meet with the priests and their wizard, but all the while he had insisted that the problem was his. Over their protests, he had said that last night's discussion was to be the end of their involvement in this matter. Had Yan decided to make sure that they stayed out of the matter?

A glance around his worktable said he hadn't cleaned out his equipment, but then he would have had a hard time doing that without disturbing her, given where she had laid out her bedroll. Some of that stuff was difficult to come by; she couldn't see him abandoning any of it just to sneak out without telling her. He had to be intending to come back.

But until he did, what would he be doing? And why hadn't he confided in her?

For her safety, he would say. He might even be right; but she didn't like the way he presumed to know best, taking away her chance to make her own decision. This wasn't the first time he'd tried disappearing—and given the painful results of the last episode, one would have thought he had learned the folly of not trusting his friends to stand by him. Apparently, one would have been wrong.

This time, she wasn't going to go chasing after him. She could wait. He'd left his precious equipment behind; he'd be back.

And if not, she'd track him down.

Until then, she'd get on with her life in the steading. She pulled on her clothes, buckled on her sword, and snatched up her cloak. Mistress Grethann, Sir Kopell's cook, would be working up something special for the guesting Imperials' morning meal. Intending to cadge a share of it, Teletha headed for the kitchen shed.

It turned out that she wasn't the only one with that idea. Both Myskell and Senn were there before her. Likely Norlann would have been with them, save that he had yet to return from wherever Sir Kopell had sent him. The men-at-arms had already appropriated a cold haunch of mutton and bowls of something that steamed and smelled wonderful. Teletha took a bowl from the table and helped herself from the pot on the fire. She joined them in the sunny spot at the corner of the long hall.

"You up for a little exercise?" Myskell asked her. "Captain Schell has suggested we meet him for a few friendly bouts."

Senn harrumphed. "Like *we* need the practice. Schell's a show-off, if you ask me."

"Nobody's asking you," Myskell said. "I think it'll be good to try our hands against some new blood."

"I still think Schell will be the one to get any benefit from bouts with us. Those islanders always have a lot to learn about real fighting."

At least about the way men like Senn understood fighting, Teletha thought. The Kolviner man-at-arms was typical of his breed, caring little for any sort of fighting beyond that done by armored horsemen like himself. Fighting styles such as Kolviner men-at-arms used had their place, but heavy sidearms and the armor they were meant to pierce weren't very common in the empire anymore. The wars were no less deadly or skillfully fought, but what worked in one place might get you killed in another.

What did Schell want to see? Practice bouts would give him a good chance to get a gauge on the fighting skill of the locals. A man expecting trouble might want to know what sort of opposition he could expect. Was Schell expecting trouble?

"What about you, Teletha?" Myskell asked. "You're looking thoughtful. Thinking about a chance to cross swords with a countryman?"

"It *has* been a while," she said.

Myskell seemed to take her statement as agreement. "Thought as much. You've never really lost your preference for islander ways. I'll be interested to see what you can do with this Captain Schell. I hope he's got some skill."

"He'll have skill," Teletha said. He wouldn't be a *staliarm* man if he didn't.

They talked some more, mostly about differences in technique and weapons, but it was all old stuff. Teletha kept up her end of the conversation without thinking about it. She expected that the practice bouts would put the lie to some Kolviner opinions that she hadn't been able to change. Unless Schell held back, they'd see.

But Schell was holding back on some things, like his position as a *staliarm* man. She couldn't help but think that he was holding back other things as well.

As they were finishing up their morning meals, Galon Martello appeared and asked politely if they would be ready soon, saying, "Captain Schell is most anxious to try your mettle, gentlemen. And lady," he added, with a bow and a flourish of his hat.

"Tell him to ready himself for a lesson or two," Senn said as he heaved himself up. He and Myskell started for

Sir Kopell's house to gather their gear. As was their custom, the men-at-arms left their bowls and spoons for the
cook's helpers to gather, but Senn tossed the mutton
bone to the drakkenree as he would have done for a dog.
The saurian ignored the gift until Senn had passed, then
snatched it in to gnaw on the remaining meat.

"Milady?" Young Martello's voice took her attention
away from the lizard. "The Captain would be especially
pleased if you would attend."

"And why is that?"

"I wouldn't know, milady. The Captain didn't say."

"Hey, Schonnegon, come along," Myskell shouted.
"Senn says he's ready to teach a few lessons."

"I'm coming." Captain Schell's interest in her stoked
her own in him. The emperor expressed his will through
his *staliarm* men. Was Schell's interest in her part of the
peril of which Iaf had tried to warn them? He *was* part of
the Imperial army, as she had once been. Would he be
threatening her with a trial for desertion as Janden had?
It all seemed so long ago, and she didn't care to dwell on
the past. Here and now, she'd soon see Senn learn rather
than teach a lesson, and that would be a sight she'd
enjoy. For the moment, that pleasurable certainty out-
weighed the vague, and probably only imagined, danger
to her.

The practice session soon gathered a ring of watchers,
and not just the soldiers. After losing a dozen straight passages, Senn gave up trying to beat Captain Schell.
Myskell, having studied Schell's technique, said he'd try
a turn. About that time Jerr, without Yan, showed up at
the edge of the crowd. Teletha wanted to watch the
match, but she thought it better to find out what Jerr had
been about.

She didn't have to get too close to see that the girl had
been crying again; tear tracks cut through a smudge on
her cheek. Jerr refused to say why she'd been crying, and
"I haven't spoken to Master Tanafres since last night,"

was all she would say on the subject of Yan. The girl wasn't very far from crying again, and Teletha didn't want to deal with a weeping girl. Questions unanswered, Teletha went back to watching the sparring.

When Teletha's turn came, she found that Captain Schell's form was even finer than he had shown against the Kolviners. As she suspected he might, he appeared to be holding back a bit. Could he tell that she wasn't giving it her all, either? They split their passages almost evenly, he having the better of her by one exchange. Having felt his strength and experienced his speed, she decided that she would not care to have to truly test herself against him.

The practice session went on after Captain Schell declared himself winded. He set Martello to sparring with the soldiers, pitting the young man's rapier and dagger against a Kolviner's sword and buckler. Martello showed a fine form that echoed Schell's style.

"My student," Schell said.

Martello had clearly learned well. He had a youth's speed and suppleness, coupled with a skill advanced beyond his years. Teletha saw that the boy's moves incorporated some of Schell's more sophisticated techniques, and said so.

"You have a good eye," Schell said. "Though I think you watch him not half as closely as the young girl does."

Teletha looked where Schell indicated with his head. Jerr had found herself a place on the bench in front of the long hall, where she had a view of the sparring area. A bunched-up wad of cloth lay on her lap, a needle sparkled forgotten in her hand. Her eyes were on young Martello, though Teletha didn't think she was critiquing the young man's skill at arms. Had Jerr discovered something to interest her other than magic?

"He won't take advantage of her, will he?" Teletha asked.

"He will take what is offered. He is a lusty young man," Schell replied. "Is she under your protection?"

"She's Yan's student."

"The magician's?" Schell sounded thoughtful.

"Does that matter, Captain Schell?"

"My name is Arun," he said, ignoring the question. "Having tested our arms against each other, it seems to me that we need not be formal. May I call you Teletha?"

He brought the conversation back to Martello and Jerr, but somehow she got the impression that he was speaking of more than just the two youths. Arun's smile was warm, and his eyes dark and deep. Teletha tried not to let the way her name sounded on his tongue touch her, but she failed. As they talked, he said her name often, and each time he made it sound more intimate. She knew he was being deliberately charming, but she couldn't help herself; she found herself attracted to the man. In the midst of the steading's common, their talk was general, but there were hidden implications. He made comments, seemingly ordinary, but such that a careful listener, aware of the looks that passed between them and the way they stood, might take to have other meanings. Arun seemed sincerely attracted to her, chasing from her mind thoughts of priests and wizards, and even most of her dark thoughts about him.

It wasn't the way she thought things would go.

And their conversation was over sooner than she wished. Sir Kopell interrupted them to compliment Martello. Teletha used the opportunity to slip away and try to sort out what she was feeling. She didn't get the chance; Peyto found her almost as soon as she cleared the crowd.

"Have you heard anyone mention anything about Sharhumrin?" Peyto asked anxiously.

"No," she said, letting her annoyance at the disturbance color her tone. The Imperial capital hadn't even been mentioned in her hearing by anyone other than Peyto.

"I haven't either. Schell's clerk knows nothing, or I've

lost my skill at reading men." Peyto sounded frustrated.
Like Yan, once he got an idea in his head, he went after
it like a hungry, tired horse headed for the barn at night.
Peyto had his own hopes regarding the purpose of the
delegation's visit. "Captain Namsorn is impossible, but
you seem on good terms with Captain Schell. Perhaps
you could ask him about it."

She had wanted to turn her talk with Arun to the matter of the delegation's purpose, but had gotten distracted.
If she told Peyto that, he would only say she wasn't
skilled enough at extracting information. She *was* skilled
enough; it was just that . . . Well, she could say that Arun
Schell was only willing to talk about what he wanted to
talk about. Instead she said, "Why should I bother asking
him? If that was the plan, there would be no reason to
keep it a secret. Arun would have mentioned it."

Peyto raised an eyebrow at her use of the captain's
first name, but all he said was, "It might have slipped his
mind."

Not Arun Schell's mind. "I don't think so."

The pounding of hooves seized the attention of everyone on the steading common. The approaching rider was
Dantil the Scout. Sir Kopell had posted him at the ford
with orders to report the appearance of the Imperial delegation.

"The priests are coming," Dantil announced as he dismounted. "They're at the ford."

"And we still don't know why," Peyto said.

"Give it up, Peyto. Whyever they're here, they're
here. I doubt they're carrying an invitation for Yan to
come to the emperor's court." And even if they were,
Yan wasn't here to receive it. The Imperial delegation
couldn't be more than an hour away. "Have you seen
Yan?"

"I'm not his keeper," Peyto snapped, but despite his
aggrieved tone, the old clerk looked worried.

6

HAVING DONE WHAT HE COULD to conceal all that he didn't want seen, Yan gathered up those things that he could not do without for a few days and retired to the small cave that he hoped any strangers would think was the infamous Cave of the Lizard. He brought with him his best "mysterious magician" clothes as well. His old master Gan Tidoni had taught him the virtue of appearances.

The wool of the gown was so well fulled that its weave was near invisible, but the black dye was fading and it showed reddish brown highlights where light caught it. Over that he put on a surplice of fine black silk, belting it at the waist with a supple cincture of braided white leather. The effect was rather monastic, but he knew that the dark colors could also bring to mind unwanted thoughts of dark mages. Some other color might be more prudent, but he had no finer gown. A black cloth gave a rich look and a sober aspect; no one accused nobles or rich merchants of consorting with dark powers when they wore such garments. He could only hope that Löm Kerandiri was intelligent enough to place no superstitious value on the colors.

With a length of copper wrapped in fine silver wire and red silk ribbon, he bound his hair loosely at the nape of his neck, letting the hair sweep across the side of his head to cover his ravaged ear. He drew on long-cuffed gloves of tawny, supple kid to hide the scars on his left hand. The visible reminders of his struggle with Yellow Eye were not pretty and would undermine his appearance as a puissant magician.

Lastly he drew forth his *claviarm* from beneath his shirt and let it lie openly upon his breast. The gold gleamed brightly against the midnight silk. Normally he disliked displaying this ultimate symbol of his chosen calling, but today it seemed important that he wear it proudly.

He awaited the coming of the priests. For hours he waited, until he began to think he had misjudged the speed at which they would travel. He was thinking about taking off all his finery when the priestly delegation arrived at last.

Yan watched them ride into the steading from his vantage point within the shadow of his decoy cave mouth. He saw at once that his preparations were well advised. The priests were making a show of it, wearing robes instead of more practical everyday clothing. Yan counted seven clerics in ordinary Triadic robes of blue and yellow, and three more in partisan colors. One of the latter, the one wearing Horesh's pure yellow, would be Löm Kerandiri; he was by far the most richly dressed, to judge by the flashes of light from his clothing and from his horse's harness. The other two dedicated priests wore the habits of warrior orders: one in the green of Vehr and the other in the deep red of Baaliff. The presence of those two—and the dozen or so soldiers trailing behind the party—explained the small mystery of why an Imperial *staliarm* man felt safe in leaving his charges to find their own way here.

The resources of the steading would be strained beyond their strength if the delegation stayed long. But that wasn't why Yan hoped that they wouldn't be remaining long at all. This was *his* place, the place where he was supposed to be learning the secrets of the drakkenree. He couldn't do that with a bunch of nosy, self-important Imperial priests around—especially because they'd brought along their own wizard, a great scholar at that.

This wasn't the sort of company he'd had in mind when he'd wished for someone to share his studies.

From among the newcomers Yan picked out the man who had to be the scholar wizard. Not that it was difficult. There was only one among them wearing an academic's cap and a gown rich enough to be beyond the means of a clerk. The mage was a lean man with a complexion much darker than his islander companions. Was he from the coastal kingdoms? If so, there would be a tale in how he had come to be an Imperial scholar.

The priestly procession was met by a less formal grouping of folk in the steading's common area. Captain Schell, arrayed in his finery, took up a position between Sir Kopell and the newcomers. Yan didn't need to hear the captain's words to know that introductions were being made.

Time to arrange for his own appearance.

From where he stood, Yan could see a corner of the steading's corral. Black Stocking, the quarrelsome Senn's equally fractious mount, stood in that corner. Yan smiled. Black Stocking was a noisy, ill-tempered animal, well suited to what Yan had in mind.

He touched his *claviarm*, to improve the link; casting an illusion over distance, especially one good enough to fool the senses of an animal, wasn't easy. He dropped into *præha* and formed in his mind the image, sound, and scent of a diamond-banded rock snake. He imagined the snake coiling on the ground near Black Stocking's hooves.

Black Stocking hated snakes.

The horse reacted to Yan's illusion with a wild shriek. Black Stocking pranced away, but Yan moved the snake before the horse again and again until the animal was rearing and screaming. The other horses in the corral took up Black Stocking's panic, racing around and adding their own noise to the ruckus.

The people on the common turned toward the commotion. Yan waited until all eyes were turned away before he left the cave and walked toward the new arrivals. He was at the end of the common before anyone spotted him. That man, one of the newly arrived soldiers, looked startled; he elbowed one of his fellows. Before long Yan was the center of attention. He could hear the whispers among the crowd that he had appeared out of thin air.

"Appearances can be deceiving," Gan Tidoni had often told his student. "Use them for all they're worth." Encouraged by the success of his opening ploy, Yan addressed himself to the priest in Horesh's golden robes.

"I give you good day, Löm Geroy Kerandiri. May Horesh shine upon you." Yan gave what he hoped was a suitably elaborate bow. "I am Yan Tanafres, a magician. What service may I perform for you?"

"In Horesh's light we are well met, Master Tanafres." Kerandiri returned Yan's bow by inclining his head; a man of the gods acknowledged earthly courtesies but did not participate in their intricate structure of proprieties. Yan was not offended until Kerandiri said, "You are direct and no little bit abrupt."

Yan wanted to keep matters friendly as yet. "If so, I apologize, Löm Kerandiri. Life in the coastal kingdoms follows a different rhythm than in the empire. Yet I am most curious to know how I may be of service to you."

"I ask no service for myself. As the gods' plans have unfolded, I travel upon a service myself." Adding portentously, "A service for Church and empire at the bidding of his Most Holy Eminence."

Said aloud, and by a man of Kerandiri's considerable presence, the concept took on a reality Yan had hitherto been able to ignore. The unlooked-for delegation had brought its business to Yan's doorstep. He tried not to let his nervousness show in his voice. "Church *and* empire?"

Kerandiri nodded solemnly.

"Ah," Yan said, pretending to think while he checked the newcomers for signs of political allegiance. With what the holy man had said, Yan expected them to be wearing a mix of Church party and Imperial tokens, but almost all wore the yellow and blue colors of the Church party. Even the scholar wizard had blue and yellow feathers in his cap. The only exceptions among the newcomers wore signs of affiliation with the Solonite sect, leaving the only Imperial tokens in sight those worn by Schell, his aide, and his clerk. If there was Imperial interest here, it was in the minority.

Or was it? Schell's position as a *staliarm* man made him an important player, even if he was pretending to be no more than an escort for the priests. There were hidden issues here, matters for later thought. For the moment, Yan had best deal with what was before him. "I am but a backwoods magician. What business could the primate of the Triadic Church have with me?"

"I believe that to be a matter best discussed in more private circumstances, Master Magician."

Circumstances unlikely to be favorable to Yan. "I would prefer any business between us be open."

Kerandiri's eyes narrowed; Yan guessed that the holy man wasn't used to being argued with. "My instructions say that it should not be so."

"Then it may be that you have no business with me," Yan said nonchalantly. His attitude was all pose, but he couldn't resist trying the ploy as a way to avoid whatever it was they wanted. A matter that drew the attention not just of the primate but also of the emperor was beyond what he wished to be involved in.

"Think not to test my resolve, Master Magician. We have come a great distance on no slight errand."

"I never thought otherwise."

Kerandiri offered a conciliatory smile. "Let us speak in close conference, then. You will understand the import of my mission when you have heard what I will say."

Yan might understand, but he was growing sure that he would not like it. "I have no desire to offend, but I wish to point out that I am bound neither to the Church, save for the bindings on any gods-fearing man, nor to the emperor. Any demands you make of me are no more than requests, to be granted or denied at my will."

"There are matters in which the Church may compel," Kerandiri said. Yan saw at once where the holy man was heading; he didn't need the löm's next question. "Do you work in light or darkness?"

The question was the opening of the Ritual of Clarity, a special procedure developed centuries ago to catch out a magician who had fallen to the lures of the darker aspects of magic. The ritual was the heart of the Church's certification for magicians, their way of ensuring that a magician worked only the magics allowed by the Church. Such certification was something every magician must regularly go through if he practiced anywhere that the Church held sway.

Yan didn't think the holy man was expecting to conduct the ritual here and now, but he answered with the formal response nevertheless. "I work in Horesh's light. May that light sear me if I lie."

"May I inspect your *claviarm*?" It was an order rather than a request, which Kerandiri emphasized by holding out his hand.

Part of the compact between a magician and the Church was that, upon duly authorized request, a magician would surrender his *claviarm* to be examined by a cleric. Kerandiri, as a löm, carried that authority. Yan removed the chain from around his neck and handed over his *claviarm*.

Kerandiri took the focus, turning the talisman in his

hands as he studied the symbols engraved in the metal. Finishing his visual examination, the holy man cupped the talisman in his hands and closed his eyes. Yan felt a tingle as the air grew still.

Something was suddenly present.

In his trance, Löm Kerandiri smiled a guileless, almost beatific, smile.

Yan was uncomfortable. He had never denied that there was a power beyond the natural, a power that only priests and saints seemed able to tap. How could he? He did not understand such power, for it did not fit into a magician's understanding of the way the world worked. But it existed; its presence could sometimes be felt, and its effects were documentable. Undeniable. Some piece of that power was present now, come at the call of the holy man.

As suddenly as the *something* had come, it was gone. Kerandiri opened his eyes. His face held the expression of someone fondly remembering a lover. The holy man held the *claviarm* out to Yan, and Yan took it back.

"Your *claviarm* is interesting, Master Tanafres. Though I felt no taint of the dark in it, I must confess that I have never seen its like. I believe that it will bear further investigation." Kerandiri's interest was unlikely to improve Yan's standing with the Church; the Church liked magicians little enough, and liked troublesome magicians even less. Kerandiri was placed highly enough that his word could brand Yan as a troublesome magician. Kerandiri struck again. "What priest has administered the ritual for you?"

Yan was not surprised that the question had come up. The Imperial Church hierarchy was not renowned for its faith in the competence and good judgment of clergy outside the empire, an attitude based more on conceit than reality. Kerandiri could make even more trouble for Fra Bern than he could for Yan.

Yan looked to Fra Bern, expecting him to speak for

himself, but the priest stood with his head down, eyes fixed on the dirt. So Yan said, "Fra Bern examines my *claviarm* each year as the Church prescribes. He has been diligent in his duty." Of course, Yan had never felt a *something* come when Fra Bern examined the *claviarm*.

"I know this priest, Löm Kerandiri," the Baaliffite announced, pointing at Fra Bern. "Though a servant of the Lord Einthof, he is but a country man, little versed in the duplicities of wizards. Moreover, he was with this wizard in the wilderness when his Majesty's wizard Fasolt died under suspicious circumstances. The priest returned from that misadventure in a fevered state during which, it is said, he babbled of a dark place of evil."

"Many men speak of imaginary things when they are in a fever," Yan pointed out.

"Some men speak secrets when they are in a fever," the Baaliffite countered. To Kerandiri, he said, "We have no way of knowing what might have occurred in the wilderness."

Kerandiri was thoughtful for a moment. "Other than the priest's fever, do you have reason to suspect impropriety, Fra?"

"Until such time as Fra Bern is certified pure and free of dark influences, his word must be considered suspect. His work as well."

Yan gave the Baaliffite a hard look. There was something familiar about the man's scarred features, and Yan felt sure he'd met this priest before, but he couldn't quite place where or when. Whoever the Baaliffite was, Yan was sure that he didn't like him.

"Good Fra," Yan said mildly, addressing himself to the Baaliffite, "why do you go on so about Fra Bern? Has not the löm himself tested my *claviarm* and found it untainted? Who are you to cast shadow on the löm's judgment?"

The Baaliffite stood stiff as a pikestaff. "I call no doubt on the judgment of his Holiness. The dark may not be involved, but that does not mean that there is nothing amiss." The warrior priest smiled harshly. "If all were well, would not your country priest remain among us?"

Yan looked. Fra Bern was gone.

"He must have had duties to attend to," Yan said lamely.

"Religious devotions?" asked the Baaliffite.

"I wouldn't know."

"As you would not know where he directs his devotions?"

Yan didn't like the direction in which the questions were leading. "To the Beings Above and to his patron Einthof, I would expect."

"And to no other?"

"Enough, Fra Zephem," Kerandiri said curtly.

Zephem! Yan knew now where he had met the warrior priest. Zephem had commanded the Baaliffite contingent in the Imperial force sent to King Shain's aid at the beginning of Yellow Eye's invasion. Yan thought the man had died along with most of his Baaliffites in the battle by the Tersrom River. Clearly he had not.

Kerandiri was still speaking. "Such matters are not to be spoken of lightly."

"Fra Bern is a good priest," Yan said.

"I have not questioned Fra Bern's devotion," Kerandiri said.

Something about his tone suggested that he could easily have added, "yet." The löm left unspoken the possibility that others had questioned Fra Bern's devotion. Zephem had asked, "And no other?" Had Yan heard an emphasis on the last word? Did these priests know something of Fra Bern's theory about the Other, a deity outside the Courts? Questions about the Other would be no small part of their reason in coming. *Was* the Other their reason for coming? It could not be all of their motivation because they said they had come to speak with Yan, not Fra Bern. How did they think Yan was involved in this?

"Our meeting has not gone as I hoped," Kerandiri admitted. The conciliatory smile was back. "We did not come here to set ourselves up as your enemies, Master Tanafres."

"Then tell me why you *did* come."

Kerandiri sighed. "Sir Kopell, Master Tanafres is proving a most obstinate man. Since he will not allow us to retire to a better place for our discussions, I pray that you help make this one more suitable. Please send your folk back to their places and to their chores."

"As you wish, Löm Kerandiri."

The knight started giving orders, sending his soldiers and people away. Captain Schell nodded to Captain Namsorn, who led the Imperial soldiers away as well. Peyto glared daggers at Yan as Teletha dragged him away; with Schell sending his clerk away, and Kerandiri dismissing all his attendants but the wizard and the two warrior priests, there were no grounds for having Peyto remain. Yan didn't let the clerk's anger bother him. Peyto would hear all about it later when Yan asked for his advice; the old man wouldn't die from not hearing for himself what the priests had to say.

Yan asked that Sir Kopell remain; he wanted at least one witness present who wasn't a member of the Imperial delegation. Kerandiri agreed. Sir Kopell didn't look happy to be included, but then Kerandiri didn't look happy to have him included, either.

"Satisfactory?" Yan asked Kerandiri.

"It seems that this must suffice."

"Tell me then, what part do I play in Imperial and Church schemes?"

"That is in the hands of the gods."

Yan was getting tired of the mystery game. Having played it himself, he knew how often it was used to conceal a lack of knowledge. Just what did these people know? Just what brought them here? "Let me try again. Why have you come to see me?"

Kerandiri hesitated a moment. "There is the matter of the magic used at the Battle of Rastionne."

"The Serpent's Eye," said Zephem.

"Such a thing could be of great help to the empire should the drakkenree menace come again," Schell said.

So, there it was. More than enough reason to drag them here. Between the power the Eye had shown and its connections to the Baansuus, reasons for both emperor and primate to be interested.

"The Eye no longer has power," he told them.

"That is not the truth, Master Magician," Kerandiri said.

Could the man tell, or was he just guessing?

"What are you hiding?" Kerandiri asked.

"Are you denying that you can control the Serpent's Eye?" Zephem asked.

"I *can't* control it."

"You did," Zephem accused. "You used it at Rastionne."

"What matter if I did?" Yan snapped. "I can't use it anymore."

Kerandiri silenced Zephem's retort with a gesture of his hand. "Master Tanafres, surely you understand our concern about this matter. Many within the Church and the empire were disturbed to hear of the drakkenree invasion of this land. We know that in ancient times, the drakkenree were great wizards, greater perhaps than any magicians since; but until the invasion, none of their magicians had taken the field for a long time. Many among both Church and civil councils want to know why. What has changed? Where did the wizard come from?"

"Are you expecting me to have the answers?"

"You were seen in the close company of the drakkenree wizard. It has been suggested that you have knowledge of his secrets."

"I was a captive."

"You wore no chains," Zephem said, his tone making it an accusation.

"No visible ones."

Zephem wouldn't leave him alone. "Do you claim that you were held in magical bondage by the creature Yellow Eye?"

To claim that he had been held by coercive magic would brand Yellow Eye as a magician tainted by the dark—at least by the Church's beliefs. "Not exactly."

"That is not a clear answer," Kerandiri said. "This is a grave and important matter, Master Magician. Surely you understand that we must have clear answers. We know that you have studied the drakkenree lore. While no one has accused you of anything, there are those who think that something, shall we say, improper must have occurred. Prove to us that such is not the case. Help us to understand what happened. Show us that there is no heresy to be rooted out and cleansed with Horesh's purifying fires."

How could he do that?

"We wish to help you," Kerandiri said.

"It's your duty as a citizen of the empire," Schell added.

"I'm tired," Yan said. It wasn't a lie. Not exactly. His head hurt from maintaining his concealment spells and from fencing with these people. He needed time to think.

Kerandiri nodded. "I understand. We have traveled far and are tired, also. Yet we must speak with you at length on these matters and many others."

"Tomorrow? Tomorrow, I shall make myself available at your convenience, Löm Kerandiri."

"Tomorrow it shall be." Kerandiri smiled broadly. "Will you join me for morning service to greet Horesh?"

Still testing? "I would be honored."

"I am encouraged by your devotion to the gods, Master Tanafres." He turned to Sir Kopell. "Good knight, if you would be so kind as to show my fellows and me where we may take our rest?"

Sir Kopell led the priests away. Schell went with them, but the scholar wizard lingered, eyes locked on Yan.

"And you are?" Yan asked. He hadn't been around for the introductions, and no one had bothered to correct the situation.

"Handrar, a magician," he replied, bowing deeply and making an unusual gesture with his hand.

No mention of his title? Modesty wasn't an attribute Yan associated with wizards connected to the Imperial court.

"You do not seem surprised to see me, Master Tanafres."

"Should I be, *Ser* Handrar?"

Handrar smiled slightly when Yan used the honorific. "I see some measure of my reputation has reached you."

"Some measure."

"A cautious answer, Master Tanafres. By which I take you for a cautious man. That is good. A cautious man is a wise man, and a wise man lives to pass his wisdom to his grandchildren. It is a crime before the gods when wisdom is lost." Handrar leaned closer and whispered, "Be careful of the priests."

"Why?"

Handrar shrugged. "As magicians, we both know that they do not understand the calls of the Great Art."

"If they are dangerous to magicians, aren't you at risk as well?"

"At no more risk than any practitioner. You know as well as I how secrets call to a true practitioner."

What *is* this man's game? "Do I?"

"Would you be so coy otherwise?" *Ser* Handrar smiled. "I, too, am a cautious man. If the gods will, we shall speak again."

"Do you know of some reason why we might not speak again?"

Handrar's voice dropped again to a whisper. "I will say only that there are those who think your soul already beyond redemption."

"Fra Zephem alone, or do you think Löm Kerandiri has given up on my soul as well?"

"I name no names." Returning his voice to a normal level, Handrar said, "But I do wish you good health, Master Tanafres. It would be a shame if all you have learned were lost."

"And what do you know of that?"

But *Ser* Handrar only smiled, bowing his good-bye and leaving Yan standing alone in the middle of the common.

7

JERR SAT QUIETLY IN THE DOORWAY of Master Tanafres's house, where the light was best. She was almost done with repairing the skirt she had torn rushing down to tell of the riders coming to the village. Had it been only two days ago? The village's peace and quiet had vanished like dew in the morning. Faintly the strains of angry, arguing voices drifted to her from within the long hall. There was more turmoil to come, of that she was sure.

"Jerr, go to the cabinet over the worktable and get out the white jar with the green stripes."

"Yes, Master Tanafres."

Jerr was pleased by Master Tanafres's casual tone. Though it hadn't been her intention, staying out of his way must have been the right thing to do. The unseen servant is rarely scolded, the grannies always said. She must be back in his good graces if he was trusting her to get something from his cabinet. Untangling herself from her work, she gladly went to do his bidding.

Master Tanafres had just fetched a mug of hot water from the kettle on the firegrate. She heard him rejoin Master Lennuick at the table; the clerk was working on accounts while Master Tanafres read. The last of the light was fading. Jerr hoped that Master Tanafres would call his magelight soon; she liked its glow far better than a candle's.

"Headache?" she heard Master Lennuick ask.

"Intense," Master Tanafres replied.

He must have sent her to get something to ease the pain. She wondered if he used the same herbs the grannies used. She guessed that she'd know soon.

To Jerr's surprise, when she turned back the latch the cabinet door started to open of itself. Something grated inside, rough pottery against wood. The door swung wider and a jar, the very one Master Tanafres had asked for, rolled out. Jerr was quick. She caught the jar before it struck the worktable. Her grip was not good. Something inside shifted, and she lost her hold. The jar tumbled to the floor. It struck hard and shattered.

Jerr looked down, terrified. She had failed Master Tanafres's trust yet again. The nature of her terror changed when she realized what lay at her feet.

A long-necked, long-bodied animal writhed among the shards, scattering dried herb in all directions. A sisstrecht. She took a step backwards. Sisstrechts were little larger than weasels, but they were dangerous nonetheless. All the grannies said that a sisstrecht's bite was a sure and painful death. The sisstrecht's ringed tail switched jerkily in agitation, and it grumbled to itself as it scrambled to its feet. The beast raised its head and fixed its beady eyes on her. Hissing, it bared sharp yellow teeth. Jaws agape, the sisstrecht leapt at her.

Jerr threw herself back, shrieking. Her flailing arm caught the beast behind its head and knocked it aside. Even so, she heard its teeth click together and felt a tug on her arm as claws ripped at her sleeve.

The sisstrecht dropped to the floor.

While it was gathering its wits, Jerr stumbled back toward the door. She was almost out when she backed into someone and felt hands on her arms, holding her. She struggled, desperate to escape.

"What's going on?" It was Mistress Schonnegon.

Unable to think of anything more than escaping from the sisstrecht, Jerr struggled harder.

"Stand still and be quiet," Master Tanafres ordered.

He repeated his order for quiet in a strange, yet compelling voice as he stepped toward the sisstrecht. The beast turned to look at him. As he advanced, the sisstrecht humped its body around to face him and crouched low. Jerr wanted to scream a warning, but she had no voice. Master Tanafres crouched and, crooning soft words, held out his hand to the sisstrecht.

Jerr nearly swallowed her tongue.

The sisstrecht stared intently at Master Tanafres. Its whiskers quivered, and its lean body tensed, ready to attack.

But it didn't.

Master Tanafres continued to speak to it, softly, quietly.

The sisstrecht relaxed and stretched out its neck. Its nose wrinkled as it sniffed at the magician's fingers.

Jerr relaxed, too; she understood that there was no need to run now. Mistress Schonnegon released her grip.

Master Tanafres coaxed the sisstrecht closer until he could take it by the loose skin of its neck and lift it from the floor. The beast didn't struggle as he held it. The magician stood and brushed past her on his way to the door. The sisstrecht lay in his arms as calm as a sleepy kitten. Once outside, he crouched and put the beast down gently. The sisstrecht looked up at him, blinking its dark eyes. It made a tentative chittering sound.

"Go," he told the beast, and it did.

Master Tanafres remained crouched just outside the doorway, watching the beast scamper into the woods. Over his head, Jerr could see the back of the long hall and the drakkenree lying where she had seen it in the morning. If it had lain there all day, it would have seen whoever had entered Master Tanafres's house, whoever had brought the sisstrecht.

The skin around the drakkenree's eyes was so dark
that its emerald eyes seemed to glitter from deep pits as it
stared unwinkingly at her. She felt very cold.

Master Tanafres stood and turned to come back into
the house. She knew she should move, but she felt para-
lyzed by the lizard's glare. He looked over his shoulder,
then back at her.

"Go sit down. It's all right now," he told her.

She did go sit down, but he went back outside and
closed the door after him.

Yan closed the door behind him. He didn't want any
of the others coming with him; their presence would
only make the conversation more difficult. He crossed
the space that separated his house from the long hall.
The drakkenree watched him come, and, when Yan
stood before the saurian, he did not rise, a sign of his
contempt that no one in the steading but Yan understood.

Nervous about being so close to the saurian again,
Yan looked down at him and reminded himself their situations were reversed now. Yan was free and the
drakkenree was property. Yet, it was hard standing still
with those teeth and claws so near. But the drakkenree,
by his own sworn word, was harmless. Most of the time
Yan believed that.

"You are amused?"

The drakkenree looked up at him and clicked its teeth
once.

"Not your doing, though."

The saurian said nothing.

"You have been here all day, haven't you?"

The long snout turned away as if the saurian had no
interest in Yan's words. Yan could see from the darkness
around the drakkenree's eyes that he continued to find
the situation amusing. Yan didn't. Jerr had come close to

being bitten by the sisstrecht, but Jerr was likely not the one intended to find the animal; the beast had been hidden in *Yan's* cabinet. Someone had intended Yan to find the angry beast. Yan had used herbs from the jar last night, and Teletha had slept beneath it all night; the sisstrecht had not been there then. Whoever put the sisstrecht into the jar had to have entered the house during the day. Yan wanted to know who, and he was in no mood to play games.

"You forget your place," Yan said. "Tell me who you saw enter my house, slave."

The darkness around the saurian's eyes faded, but he still remained silent.

"You need not pretend that you don't speak this language. We both know better than that, Khanke—"

The drakkenree cut him off with a hiss. "I have no name," the saurian said vehemently. "And I *never* forget my place."

"Then tell me who you saw entering my house this day."

"Some come, some go. They all look alike. How can I tell one from another?"

"You are not so unobservant."

"Truth." The dark flush returned around the drakkenree's eyes. "I will tell you nothing."

"I demand that you—"

"I am not *your* property."

"No," Yan agreed. "You are Sir Kopell's slave. But his charge is to protect me. In aiding me, you aid him."

"Property has no will of its own."

"Then I will have Sir Kopell order you to speak."

"Do so. I will speak, but I will say nothing."

Yan glared at the willful saurian. "I will remember this."

"Good. I remember, too."

* * *

Teletha was confused by the turmoil to which she had returned. The animal, Yan leaving without a word, Jerr trembling and pale, and good old Peyto right back to his accounts. In short, no one willing or ready to explain. That wouldn't do, not when she wanted to know what had happened. She stepped over to the table and blocked his light. "What was that thing?"

"How should I know?" Peyto snapped. "Some kind of weasel? I've never seen anything like it before."

"Neither have I. What about you, Jerr?"

"It was a sisstrecht."

The name didn't mean anything to Teletha. "Some kind of local house vermin?"

"They never come into houses." Jerr was clearly appalled by the idea.

"Well, that one was certainly inside." Peyto pointed across the room to a pile of pottery shards and herbs. "It was in there." He told Teletha how Jerr had opened the cabinet, and the jar had fallen, releasing one very vexed animal. The conclusion was obvious. "Someone crammed the beast into the jar."

"Why would someone have put a sisstrecht into Master Tanafres's jar?" Jerr asked.

"For him to find," Peyto answered. "So, Teletha, who do—"

"But they're deadly!" Jerr exclaimed.

Dangerous, yes—Teletha had seen the beast's teeth and claws—but deadly? "So small a beast?"

"They have a poison," Jerr told her.

Poison! If Peyto was right that someone had placed the sisstrecht in the jar for Yan to find, someone had intended him to be bitten. And Jerr said that sisstrechts were deadly. "This is more than a prank."

"Obviously," Peyto said.

"Who do you think might have done it?"

Yan opened the door as Teletha asked her question.

"Someone who knows the nature of sisstrechts," he

said. "Their poison is almost always fatal. The sisstrecht was a gift from someone who would prefer me dead."

"Taking it personally, are you?" Peyto asked.

"Who else could be expected to find the beast? I am the only one who opens that cabinet in the normal course of events."

"So you think someone wants to kill you?"

"It seems that way," Master Tanafres said calmly.

Teletha couldn't believe he was taking it so lightly. "Why?"

"That is a question more easily answered once we know who."

"You don't have any idea, do you?" she asked.

Yan ignored her question, instead speaking to Jerr. "See if you can scrape up some of that chamomile, will you, Jerr. My headache is getting worse."

8

THE NEXT MORNING, Yan opened the door to his house to find *Ser* Handrar seated on the bench outside. The mage closed the cover on the tablet he held, but not before Yan saw that the wax inside was nearly filled with minuscule writing. Handrar looked up at Yan and smiled.

"Good morrow to you, Master Tanafres. On your way to Löm Kerandiri's morning service?"

That had been Yan's intent, before he found a wizard ensconced on his doorstep. Too many people were making free with his hospitality of late. "*Ser* Handrar, what are you doing outside my door so early in the morning?"

"Why, I am studying the drakkenree, of course. I have not had the chance to be so close to a live one before. A most extraordinary opportunity. The old records and few artifacts remaining in the empire offer such a limited view. How fortunate you are to have one of them so readily to hand. It must be a very useful supplement to your experiences among them. But I must admit that I find it curious that you feel no need to restrain it. I see no chains, and I sensed no arcane constraints."

Yan looked over at the drakkenree, who was, of course, watching them. "He is bound by his word."

"Ah, yes. Sir Kopell tells me that you were instrumental in taking the drakkenree's parole. He says you vouch for the creature's docility. It understands oaths, then?"

"*He* understands.

"You know that it is a male, then?"

"He is a male." Yan wondered why Handrar refused to grant the drakkenree a human pronoun, but decided that Handrar's attitude was not Yan's to correct. At least Handrar didn't insist on calling the drakkenree a lizard, as the locals did. Besides, was Handrar's dehumanizing pronoun any worse than Yan's compliance with Khankemeh's insistence that he no longer had a name? And hadn't Yan once thought of Khankemeh as an "it"? "If you're so interested in him, why don't you go over and talk to him?"

"I was given to understand that it speaks no known language—ah, excuse me, Master Tanafres, I meant to say no *generally* known language, I meant no disrespect to your achievements—and I was also told that it only understands the most basic Kolvinic."

"He understands better than most think."

"Indeed." Handrar looked thoughtful. "I observe that it watches us. Does it hear us as we speak?"

"He might. Your voice is deep. Had you a higher voice, he would need to be closer."

"Most interesting. I shall speak softly, then. Or perhaps it would be best to speak of other things for the moment. I understand that you experienced some trouble with the local wildlife yestereve."

"What do you mean?" Did he know something about the sisstrecht?

"The young girl, your apprentice, has a piercing voice. This is a small village, and there are, as there always are, rumors circulating among the servants. I had hoped that you would be able to supply me with the true story."

There seemed no harm in telling the tale. Yan related last night's encounter with the sisstrecht. "So you see, the jar was set to fall and release the animal in such a way as to anger it and incite it to attack. Sisstrechts are known for their pugnacious nature and the ferocity with which they will attack anything that annoys them."

"And you are sure that there was no way this sisstrecht could have gotten into the jar on its own?"

"None. And if there had been, why should it have done so? The animal did not enjoy its confinement."

Handrar nodded agreement. "So you believe that someone placed it there and intended to anger the beast, expecting that it would attack and bite whoever discovered it. Didn't you say the beast's poison is fatal?"

"Almost invariably."

"Your apprentice seems an unlikely target for such a ploy."

"I agree."

"Meaning you think that someone else was meant to find the sisstrecht. Yourself?"

Yan shrugged. "It was placed in a cabinet in which only my things are kept."

"Most distressing." Handrar shook his head. "I would not have expected such a thing out here. But then, magicians are rarely liked, wherever they work. The culprit is surely one of the locals."

The locals were Yan's *last* suspects. "Why do you say that?"

"Only a local would know that the cabinet was for your exclusive use, though loose lips could certainly spread such information, given careful questions. It is the beast itself that incriminates. You tell me that sisstrechts are local creatures, and quite rare. Who but a local would know how to obtain one?"

Yan didn't see Handrar's proposal as the only answer. "Someone could have learned of sisstrechts from a book, as I did."

Handrar conceded the possibility and added another. "Or someone could have been told of them by a local who knows the beasts. That same local could have provided the beast itself. I think that it would take some experience to handle such an animal safely, don't you? In any case, I think that you will find a Kolviner involved in this matter. You should search for someone from hereabouts who wishes ill to you and yours."

"But why? There has been no trouble before this."

"Perhaps someone does not wish you to talk with the priests." Handrar leaned closer. "Or to talk with me."

It was a possibility, but Yan couldn't think of anyone willing to take such drastic measures. On the other hand, he didn't know any of the Imperial delegation. "Your earlier warning suggested that I have enemies among the priests and their followers. Are there Kolviners among them?"

"They are islanders all."

Handrar did not have an islander's color. "And yourself?"

"I am not a Kolviner," Handrar said, though he did not say where he *was* from. "But you do not suspect me."

That was true, and Yan saw no reason not to say so. "You're right."

"Of course I am. You know as well as I that no magician would use an animal against another. Not without a compulsion on the beast, anyway. If you had sensed anything arcane about the animal, you would have suspected me at once and taken an accusation to Sir Kopell. Had you thought me the culprit, we would not be having this friendly conversation. Am I right?"

"Again."

"So." Handrar stroked his beard. "But have you considered that a magician, knowing what we as magicians know, might choose to place the animal anyway—without a compulsion—counting on the beast's sudden appearance to catch you off guard, and hoping that the beast might act so swiftly that you would be bitten before you could charm it? No need to answer; I see from your face that you did not. Well, you need not have thought of it. It is bootless speculation only, a passing thought of no importance. You and I are the only magicians here, and I would have no part in seeing you gone and your knowledge lost. Others, now: others do not understand what you seek. They do not know the importance of your studies with regard to the ancient enemy."

Why was Handrar trying to waken suspicions of him in Yan's mind? Handrar's mention of Yan's studies drove his mind to other concerns. "What do you know of my studies?"

"Little enough." Handrar spread his hands wide. He smiled. "But you will find that I am an eager student."

Yan was not looking for a student. "And if I say that I am not a teacher?"

"Then I will say that you may consider me a fellow scholar. Surely two minds are better than one at deciphering the secrets of the drakkenree?"

The last Imperial wizard Yan had met also wanted to know his secrets. That wizard had known more than he had been willing to tell Yan. How much did Handrar know? Was he as willing to share with Yan as he was for Yan to share with him? "Scholarship flourishes in the light of many minds."

"Armiacodi," said Handrar, identifying the quote. "He also says 'Knowledge unshared is soon a lost secret.' I think that there would be many lost secrets, should you meet an untimely accident. Given the incident with the sisstrecht, perhaps you should consider what would happen to all that you have learned, should something untoward befall you."

Meaning that I should tell you everything I know about the drakkenree? "The sisstrecht is gone, the danger is past."

"You don't truly believe that."

No, he didn't.

Handrar sighed. "You do not trust me. No, no, I take no offense. After your experience with Gan Fasolt, why should you trust a strange magician who shows up on

your doorstep and says he wants to help you in your
research? Why, indeed? I have given you no reason to
trust me, nor have I presented any credentials to you.
Perhaps, though, I have something that will make you
see that I am not the self-seeking exploiter you suspect I
may be." Handrar drew a sparkling talisman from the
folds of his gown. "Do you recognize this?"

"It is a *claviarm*." Every magician had one, but this one
was dead. His inner eye told him at a glance that it was
obviously not Handrar's.

Handrar looked disappointed at Yan's response.
"Nothing else? Perhaps your memory will improve if I
tell you I had it from Hebrim Tidoni."

Gan Hebrim Tidoni had been Yan's master, and Yan
had not seen or heard from Gan Tidoni since leaving
Merom years ago. "What do you have to do with Gan
Tidoni?"

"I have the honor of being acquainted with him,
although I wouldn't say we are old friends." Handrar
tapped the talisman, making it swing on its chain. "This is
a matter of business. Tidoni brought this item to the
attention of *Ser* Arun Vernasur. It came from his hands
into mine."

Arun Vernasur. The name was vaguely familiar. The
name of a magician of whom he'd heard? Perhaps a
name that Gan Tidoni had mentioned while Yan was an
apprentice. "I'm afraid that I don't know the gentleman."

"You *have* been out of the empire for some time,
haven't you? *Ser* Arun is the emperor's own wizard."

The emperor's wizard! But Gan Tidoni had abandoned Imperial politics. What would have motivated him
to contact such a man? What connection did Handrar
have to Vernasur?

"And how do you figure in this, *Ser* Handrar?"

"As an emissary, and as a seeker of knowledge,"
Handrar said, with a bow of his head. "Were it not for *Ser*
Arun I would not be here. I was—I am pleased to say—

the first person he consulted in the matter of this *claviarm*. I told him what I could, which was very little, but enough to convince his master that this"—Handrar hefted the *claviarm*—"was connected to other matters. Because of my interest in certain obscure but related subjects, *Ser* Arun recommended me to this commission. The recommendation was accepted, and here I am, bearing this artifact.

"Look closely at it, Master Tanafres, particularly at the inscription along the rim. Certain of the symbols seem to me to be in the drakkenree script. Unfortunately, I do not know the meaning of these symbols, but you, I am told, can read some of the drakkenree script."

"Who told you that?"

"Word of your ability has come to the emperor's ear through the account of Iaf Smyth, a respected general, whom I believe you know well. An honest man, is he not?" Handrar held out the *claviarm*. "Please, take a look at it. Can you at least confirm that there is drakkenree script among the sigils?"

Yan looked at the sigils. Most were standard protections, formulae, and invocations. One of the charms was, without a doubt, in drakkenree script. Once he would have had no idea what those symbols meant, let alone that they were in drakkenree script. Even now, most of the sinuous markings were beyond his understanding, but he recognized the form of an invocation. He also recognized the being addressed, as well: the Baansuus.

"Can you read it?" Handrar asked anxiously.

"Not completely," Yan temporized. Something about the *claviarm* was very familiar.

"But some. You *can* read some of it. What does it say?"

"The structure of the words is familiar to me. It is an invocation."

"An invocation?" Handrar seemed to turn the concept over in his mind. "Theurgic?"

Enthralled by the concept himself, Yan said yes before

he realized that answering might not be the wisest course. Handrar wore the favor of the Church party. Inscriptions invoking deities and asking Their protection was common magical practice. However, the Baansuus was not part of the Celestial Court; someone invoking the Baansuus *could* be considered heretical by the Triadic Church.

Handrar caught some of Yan's discomfort. "Something about the invocation troubles you. Could it be that the named deity is not one we know as a member of the Celestial Court?"

"How could such a deity be a member? Drakkenree do not follow the Triadic faith."

"But you, as a good Imperial citizen, do follow that faith. You are just as surely aware of the Doctrine of the Analog and how it might apply to the drakkenree. This, I think, is something else, isn't it?"

Yan didn't know what to say. He noticed that Handrar did not suggest the invocation might be to a member of the Under Court. Did the Imperials already know about the Baansuus? And how much could Yan reveal of what he knew and guessed, without being branded a heretic? Handrar sat waiting for him to say something. Unfortunately, Yan couldn't read anything from Handrar's schooled expression. Yan had to respond in some way. He needed to say something safe.

"I can only be sure that the charm is an invocation form."

"I see," Handrar said, nodding. "Well, time presses, if you wish to honor your promise to Löm Kerandiri and join him at his morning service. Horesh will soon be over the trees. I think that attending the service would be wise." Handrar stood and tucked his tablet under his arm. "We can, and should, talk more on this matter later. Magician to magician. For now, keep the *claviarm* as sign of my goodwill."

"But—"

"We seek the same knowledge, Master Tanafres. I see no reason that we should not work together. Now we had best go. Löm Kerandiri will be wondering where we are. The löm is a man who takes his beliefs very seriously. You would do well to remember that."

Yan didn't think that he would be allowed to forget.

9

TELETHA WALKED BACK to Yan's house after Löm Kerandiri's morning service, thinking about what Yan had said during their all-too-brief conversation after the ceremony; the priests hadn't waited long before dragging Yan off to the long hall. Putting their short conversation together with what she'd overheard of Yan's talk with *Ser* Handrar left her very confused about the priests' business with Yan. She might not understand what was going on, but she was confident that this visitation was at least part of what Iaf's letter had tried to warn about. It was serious. It would have to be, if Yan wouldn't let her in on it.

Wouldn't it?

Maybe not. Yan had left her out of his business before, usually for what he thought were good reasons. Most often he was trying to avoid trouble for her. A kindly impulse but one that bothered her nevertheless; she was fully grown and capable of handling trouble. Hadn't she fought in a war, stood siege, survived her share of duels, and risen to captaincy of an airship in Imperial service— no mean feat—before she ever met him? And they'd seen a deal of trials since they'd met on that damned Scothic adventure, too! One would think he'd have learned by now that she could handle trouble, but he still tried to protect her.

Just what was he protecting her from this time?

It seemed to her that he was the one needing protection just now. Putting aside the priests and their mysterious errand, there was the matter of the sisstrecht. Religious doctrine and magic might be things beyond her understanding, but an attempt at murder was something she could deal with. And deal with it she would—once she found out who was responsible.

The identity of the villain was exactly the issue she brought up when she returned to Yan's house. She hoped Peyto might have some better ideas than she'd had.

"Yan said that if we knew *who*, we'd know *why*," Peyto said. "However, since we seem to have little hope of having the *who* come up and tell us he was responsible, we have to consider the *why* as the way of finding the *who*. The two are inextricably intertwined. So we must ask ourselves, who would have a reason for wanting Yan dead?"

Teletha had already gotten that far. "The wizard Handrar thinks it was someone from around here. A Kolviner."

"Handrar thinks? How do you know what he thinks?"

"I heard him talking to Yan."

Peyto shook his head. "And you chide *me* for listening in on other people's conversations."

"I didn't do it *deliberately*."

"But you learned something, didn't you? Long ears are more valuable around courts and courtiers than armor is on a battlefield. Well, how the information is come by is not important. What matters is the reliability of the information. You say you yourself heard him express this theory?"

Teletha nodded. "He sounded quite certain. He said it would take a local to know the sisstrecht was deadly. He said that even if the villain wasn't a local, there would still be a local involved because nobody else would know how to catch one of the beasts."

"Hmm, so he thinks that our culprit is a Kolviner or had the aid of one. That leads to interesting thoughts. In all the time we've lived here, I've heard none of the usual grumbling about a resident magician. I do not think *Ser* Handrar's Kolviner could be a resident."

"Everyone here likes Master Tanafres," Jerr said.

The girl had been so quiet that Teletha had forgotten she was present. Naturally she would have an interest in the matter. She had nearly been bitten by the sisstrecht.

"No one in the village wants to kill him," Jerr claimed.

"You have a somewhat biased view, girl," Peyto told her.

"But I think I agree with her," Teletha said. "Any local with a real grudge against Yan would have acted sooner. There are those who might not like him for being a magician, but I don't think anyone here has a strong enough dislike for magicians to try to kill Yan just because he's a magician. As far as I know, he hasn't made any enemies for being himself in this steading. Even if someone from the steading did want to kill him, why strike now? It doesn't make sense."

"Perhaps the timing is not so strange," Peyto said. "Now that we are leaving, this someone might have decided that he must strike at Yan now or never have the chance."

"Leaving?" Teletha was confused. "Who said anything about leaving?"

"Captain Schell's clerk made mention of ships waiting at Brandespar," Peyto told her, smiling.

"Why do you think that has anything to do with us?"

"The matter seems simple. The waiting ships mean that the Imperial delegation intends to return to Brandespar forthwith. A serious investigation into Yan's doings would be a prolonged procedure and one that—if I am not mistaken in my understanding of Church procedures—would require someone with more regular Church authority than that carried by Löm Kerandiri.

Therefore, this delegation is here for another purpose. A purpose that—as the waiting ships testify—is expected to be accomplished with relative dispatch. An interview, followed by an invitation to the Imperial court, seems the most likely mission. You will see. When Yan returns from his interview with Löm Kerandiri, he will have the word."

Peyto's conclusion didn't seem right to Teletha. It didn't seem to match the mood among the Imperials. She'd listened to enough of Peyto's complaints; she knew that the clerk hated the wilderness even more than he hated the "uncivilized" culture of Kolvin, and that he longed to return to the empire. Was he seeing what he wanted to see in the Imperials' presence?

Rather than arguing the point, Teletha wanted to get back to the issue of who had tried to kill Yan. "Then you think that Handrar may be right in believing that the villain is a local."

"He could be. Consider. King Shain is a popular ruler, well loved. Most here consider Yan a member of the king's affinity, so Yan's departure might be presumed to be an affront to the king. Kolviners are a prickly lot when it comes to matters of honor. Perhaps some Shain loyalist, a misguided one of course, was trying to avenge what he perceived as an insult to his king."

The leaving again. And how like Peyto to assume that the matter was related to standing at court. "If you're thinking to name Sir Kopell, think again. He would no more kill by stealth than mate with a drakkenree. His men would not act without his leave, either. Or did you think one of the craftsmen, or the cook, or one of the apprentices or servants, or maybe a member of one of their families did it? All the Kolviners are here, and prospering, *because* of Yan. Why would they want to kill him? You must see that your speculation goes too far. Even if Yan were sworn as a king's man, leaving the kingdom is not a crime worth death. It seems to me that the villain must be among the newcomers, for the trouble arrived with them."

Peyto frowned sourly at her. "If they came to kill him, they'd hardly be talking to him."

"You assume that everyone in the delegation has the same motives. When was the last time more than two islanders thought the same way?"

She saw from the flicker in Peyto's expression that she'd slipped her point through his guard.

"Then let us consider them individually," Peyto suggested. "Perhaps *Ser* Handrar is the villain? Magicians have a way with beasts; no doubt he could have handled the sisstrecht as well as Yan did. In my experience magicians are often less tolerant of other magicians than ordinary folk are, though I think it more from fear of rivalry than from simple fear."

Teletha found it easy to distrust Handrar; he *was* a magician. But . . . "Yan does not think Handrar guilty, and told him as much."

"I see. Kerandiri then?"

Teletha was a little shocked that even the cynical Peyto would consider the holy man a possibility. "Kerandiri is a löm. He is beyond such things."

"Priests are men. They are prey to ambitions and flaws as are all men."

Teletha had witnessed the morning ritual and felt the radiance that Löm Kerandiri reflected. His holiness was no false face. She had to protest Peyto's vilifying of Kerandiri. "Löm Kerandiri is beyond earthly ambition. He has no murder in his heart."

"Perhaps you are right," Peyto conceded, though his next words showed that he didn't equate sanctity and innocence. "I suspect that had Kerandiri the desire to be Yan's end, he would find a means more legitimate than murder. Over the years the Church has burned more than one innocent accused of trafficking with the dark powers. But since Yan says that Kerandiri found no trace of dark taint in Yan's *claviarm*, Yan should be safe from that fate. Still, Churchmen always seem to find ways to dispose of those who get in their way."

Peyto's bitter tone made Teletha wonder if the clerk had once gotten in the way of a Churchman. She decided not to ask.

"Before you rule out all the priests, I suggest that you give some thought to Fra Zephem the Baaliffite," Peyto said. "Yan said that he had a very belligerent attitude in the conversation yesterday. Baaliffites dislike magic in any form. Perhaps Fra Zephem believes that Löm Kerandiri will not act against Yan, and has decided to take matters into his own hands. He has been in the kingdom before; therefore, he might well know of sisstrechts and their habits."

Teletha had been preparing to say that religious doctrine wasn't a reason for stealthy murder, but Peyto's last statement caught her off guard. "How do you know he's been in Kolvin before?"

"Didn't you recognize him?"

Recognize? With scars the man bore he'd be memorable. If she had met him before, she would have easily recog—Scars? She thought about how Zephem's face might have looked without the scars. "He's *that* Zephem?"

"Most assuredly," said Peyto.

Zephem had commanded the Baaliffites during Yellow Eye's invasion, although it was clear by the way the other priests treated him that they no longer considered him anything more than an ordinary priest. Teletha knew what demotion could do to soldiers in the Imperial forces, and didn't think that it would be much different for those in the Church's forces. Could the man's hostility arise from his loss of position? Did Zephem think that Yan was in some way responsible? If he did, he might well be contemplating revenge. Baaliff's justice was bloodier and more immediate than Vehr's.

Peyto looked satisfied. "Ah. I see from your furrowed brow that you don't believe *all* priests are above the desires of ordinary men."

So it seemed. Still, she disliked the idea that the villain was a priest. She told herself that there were good reasons for her attitude. It wasn't just because murder was a sin as well as a crime, and priests were supposed to be beyond sin. There were everyday reasons to conclude that the priests, even Zephem, were innocent. Surely there must be. It took her a moment to think it through, but she found one. "It seems to me that none of the priests would have had time to find a sisstrecht."

Peyto had an immediate counter. "The culprit might have carried it in his baggage."

She hadn't thought of that. "If he did, that would mean he had been planning to kill Yan since before he arrived. Löm Kerandiri would not have countenanced that."

"If he knew."

Wasn't a löm supposed to be able to sense sin in those around him? Could anyone conceal murderous intent from a holy man? What a holy man could or could not do wasn't the sort of thing Teletha was used to thinking about. She was used to more practical, earthly things. Like carrying around hidden animals. She knew that animals confined too long became listless; the freed sisstrecht had been anything but that. "I don't think that the sisstrecht had been caged long."

"I thought you knew nothing of the beasts."

"I know other animals. None like being confined, especially in small places. If the sisstrecht had been hidden among the baggage, its cage would have had to be small. The beast would not have been able to leap and move so easily after such a confinement."

"Hmm." Peyto nodded. "Well reasoned. Which means, of course, that the beast was either captured almost immediately before being placed in the jar or that it was held somewhere nearby in a more spacious cage."

"None of the priests or their escort had time to hunt the beast down," Teletha stated confidently. There had been too little time between their arrival and the time that the house had been occupied.

"Which, since you eliminate all of the Kolviners, leaves us with the members of the Imperial delegation, who arrived earlier." Peyto looked at her out of the corner of his eye. "Are you considering Captain Schell? We know that he is attempting to keep at least one thing secret. Could he be the culprit?"

"No," Teletha said without thinking. "Not him."

"I see. Do you have reason to declare him innocent, other than your attraction to him?"

Did she? Teletha thought about it and found that she didn't. She tried to remember whether he would have had an opportunity to enter Yan's house and realized that there were several times yesterday for which she did not know Schell's whereabouts. Any one of them would have allowed him time to place the animal in the jar. But it couldn't be Arun. Could it? What reason would he have? Zephem, at least, might believe that he had a reason to wish vengeance on Yan. Why would Arun wish to see Yan dead?

"What reason could he have?" she asked

"I know of no personal reason," Peyto answered. "But politics move many men to acts that they would not undertake for personal reasons."

"Politics." She said it like the dirty word it was.

"If we knew more of current conditions in the empire we would have a better idea of how reasonable such a supposition is. Lacking such information, we can only guess. Nevertheless, we must be aware that factionalism in the empire could result in the captain having secret orders that run counter to his official mission."

"But he wears the token of the Imperial party."

"And he is too honest a man to do otherwise? Yes, well, so he *does* show his faction openly. Who is to say that the emperor himself might not send one of his *stal-iarm* men on a mission that, to all appearance, is another sort of mission entirely?"

"Like Janden?"

"Janden was a rogue who hid his affiliation with the Coronal Empire, something your Captain Schell does not do."

"Then you don't think Captain Schell is the one."

"I said nothing of the sort." Peyto looked affronted. "I merely say that while we have no firm basis for suspecting him, we have no basis for dismissing him, either. And since the captain is worth suspicion, what about his aide, that Martello boy? Servants often work while the master is at his ease."

"Galon is innocent," Jerr said, startling Teletha.

Once again the girl had faded into the background, but mention of someone near to her interests had brought her to life.

"And how would you know that?" Peyto asked dismissively. "I suppose you were by his side all day until you returned to the house."

Jerr flushed and stammered, "No, Master Lennuick. It was not that way, not that way at all."

"And what way was it, girl?"

"Leave be, Peyto." Teletha softened her voice when she spoke to Jerr. "You were watching him when you were not at your chores, weren't you?"

A nod. Jerr was clearly too embarrassed to explain herself. Teletha had been as young as Jerr once, and knew what it was to have longings for a young man; she tried to make it easier for the girl. "So you know that Martello had no opportunity to enter this house. Since he was never in the house, he couldn't be the one who put the sisstrecht in the jar."

Jerr nodded again, a grateful expression on her face. Teletha gave her a reassuring smile and turned her attention back to Peyto. "Since you brought up the possibility of servants, what about Captain Schell's clerk? Didn't you spend some of the day with him?"

"He had no opportunity to do mischief, unless he could be in two places at one time. He was in my sight or nearby all day; but even if the man had reason, he would not have acted." Peyto shook his head disapprovingly. "He is a mouse."

If anyone knew the measure of a clerk, it was Peyto. That left only one of the Imperial advance party. "And Captain Namsorn?"

Peyto laughed. "You cannot be thinking that he is our villain? The man is pompous and annoying and thoroughly disagreeable, but he is a Solonite. Those of his sect find even the strictest of ordinary Triadics to have loose morals. Good Captain Namsorn would find murder a most grievous sin, one too great for his soul."

She'd seen the use-worn grip on Namsorn's sword; she wasn't so sure. "He is a soldier. Are you telling me Solonite soldiers won't kill?"

"In war, Teletha. War is another matter all together. I'm sure the good Captain Namsorn would gladly smite the unrighteous given the license of a just war. I haven't inquired, but you will surely have heard; has he fought against the Essarin Kalfate, or the Quatsallans, or maybe even the nomads of the Nalat? Yes, yes, I can see from your face that I am right. The specifics of whom he has campaigned against don't matter. I have no doubt that for him they are all saü infidels, with no noteworthy differences among them; any war against them is just, and no matter for his conscience unless he failed to do his part."

"Then we have found no likely villain."

"I don't seem to recall exonerating Schell." A trifle maliciously, Peyto added, "He speaks Kolvinic well, does he not?"

"So do I," Teletha snapped. "That doesn't make me the villain."

"I did not say that he was a villain. To further our speculation, I am only considering points that might be relevant. I think we must consider how well Schell might know this country."

Teletha remembered noticing how well Arun had sat his Kolviner saddle when he arrived. Could Arun Schell be the villain? Could he be following orders from the emperor, advancing some nefarious scheme for some obscure political end? She didn't want to think so, but she remembered Raff Janden. He had been a *staliarm* man, like Arun, and had been fully capable of murder by night—and devious enough to hide a poisonous beast in a man's cabinet. Arun wasn't like Janden. He couldn't be.

"Perhaps some judicious questions about the whereabouts of certain persons during certain hours will shed some light on the matter," Peyto suggested.

It was a good suggestion, but putting it into practice brought Teletha little success. Most of the folk in the steading had been busy; too busy to keep close track of their visitors. By midafternoon she knew no more than she had in the morning. She kept at it. As Horesh touched the trees on the western side of the clearing, she returned to the house, where Jerr had been keeping watch all day to ensure that no one entered uninvited. The girl was relieved to be given a few hours to be elsewhere, and ran off in the midst of her thank-you's. Teletha had a good idea of where Jerr was headed, and hoped that she wouldn't be getting herself into trouble. Martello was older than Jerr, and apparently a good bit more worldly. Teletha hoped that Jerr would keep her head on her shoulders and her skirts down; she was too young yet to be burdened with a mother's cares and responsibilities.

Teletha sat on the bench in front of the house and let her mind drift. She was dozing when Peyto joined her. He was pleased with himself, having discovered that Fra Zephem had been unaccounted for during a short period of time on the previous day. Teletha wasn't so happy; she found herself forced to consider that the priest might be the villain. She still didn't like the idea that a priest might do murder.

They compared what they had learned, sifting through the inferences and arguing over the significance of what each had been told. Nothing that they had learned really clarified the situation. They were still arguing as dusk gathered and a haggard Yan emerged from his meeting with the priests. Yan's exhaustion was unsurprising; he'd been closeted with them for the whole day.

Yan shuffled past them and into the house with the barest of greetings. He went straight to the central table, pulled out a chair, and sat down with a sigh. Teletha and Peyto followed him in, exchanging worried glances. Yan hauled a silver talisman from some hidden place in his gown. Laying the amulet on the table, Yan rested his head in his hands and stared at it.

Teletha sat down across from him. "Yan, we need to talk about who put the sisstrecht into your cabinet."

He didn't look up. "Not now. I have other things on my mind."

"Other things!" How could he be so uninterested? *What could be more important than figuring out who was trying to kill you?* "If whoever tried to kill you succeeds next time, you won't have *anything* on your mind!"

Yan looked at her. His brow was furrowed, his expression distracted. "What do you mean, next time?"

"Well, someone made an attempt to kill you, and he didn't succeed. Do you think whoever it was has stopped wanting you dead?"

"No, I guess not."

"He'll try again," said Peyto. Teletha and the clerk were agreed on that much.

Yan shrugged. "I dealt with the last attempt. Whoever it was does not understand what a magician can do, so I see no reason to think that the next attempt will be more successful."

Was Yan being willfully stupid? Couldn't he see the danger? "Maybe next time he'll use a gun," Teletha said. "You can't charm a bullet!"

"You have the only guns in the steading," Yan said quietly. "None of the Imperial soldiers brought any."

She knew that! Guns weren't the point! "What does *that* matter! *How* he tries to kill you doesn't matter. What matters is that he *will* try again, and *you're* his target!"

"I know that," Yan said. "But I think I ought to be more concerned with Löm Kerandiri and his delegation. Our talk did not go well."

"Your talks with priests won't matter if you're dead."

"Don't be so sure."

What in the name of the Celestial Court did he mean by that? "We need to do something about figuring out who wants you dead. I'm not willing to stand back and let some nameless stranger kill you."

"You'd prefer I be killed by someone you know?" Yan asked with a trace of his old humor.

"What I'd *prefer* is to see you die in bed of old age."

"Old age . . ." Yan's voice was suddenly far away. "Yes, that's it!" Yan snatched up the silver talisman and thrust it under her nose, shouting, "This is Adain's *claviarm*!"

"Who's Adain?"

"Long ago, back on Merom, I went on an errand of mercy to aid a dying man. That man was a mage, and his affliction was magical. I had only been licensed for a few weeks at the time, and there wasn't anything that I could do for him. He spoke a little before he died, said that his name was Adain."

Teletha was lost. "So?"

"He wasn't a saü."

That didn't clarify matters. "So?"

"Adain is a saü name, but he wasn't a saü. He was a

stranger, and so is Handrar who brought this *claviarm* to me. There was magic at work in Adain's death. He died in bed of old age—old age that came upon him with unnatural swiftness."

"That wasn't what I wished on you!"

"I know. But it reminded me. Adain talked of great changes to come. I think I may be beginning to understand what kind of changes he was talking about."

"So tell me."

Yan started to speak, then seemed to think better of it. He cleared his throat. "I don't think I should."

"I don't need your protection, Yan."

"In this, you might."

"Yan!"

"Give me some trust, Teletha. This is a matter you're better off not being involved in."

Cutting off Teletha's angry retort, Peyto asked. "Has this got something to do with the priests?"

"I'm afraid so," Yan answered, but it was all he would say on the topic.

10

AFTER THE PREVIOUS DAY'S INTERROGATION by Löm Kerandiri and his priests, Yan was not really interested in attending the löm's morning ritual. Although he didn't think it wise to miss the ceremony he did so. His absence might be misconstrued. Too bad. He needed time alone.

He no longer doubted that the priests knew of the drakkenree deity. They never called it the Baansuus, referring to it as "the curious deity revered by the drakkenree" or, more simply, "that deity." The tenor of their talk suggested that some of them believed, at least tentatively, in the existence of "that deity." An interesting situation, that; Fra Bern had been afraid that *he* had stepped into heresy when he'd accepted the existence of the Other, the Baansuus. With their veiled references and hypothetical statements, the interrogating priests had come close to the edge of heresy themselves. Where did these priests stand? The matter was clearly under investigation, yet there were no inquisitors among the priests. Did that make Fra Bern safer, or did it put him more in peril? Fra Bern had feared a Church investigation of his "fall into error." In many ways, Fra Bern's fears had materialized in the form of this Triadic delegation and its probing questions about "that deity."

In one way, Yan was glad that he was the target of the

priests' attention. Had Fra Bern been subjected to such intense scrutiny, the country priest would have told all he knew about the Baansuus, even to his own detriment. Yan's guess was that the Imperial priests did not know much about the Baansuus and its religious significance; they were probing for information. Their ignorance was something that he was trying to use to his advantage.

As a magician, Yan believed in what he could sense, either mundanely or arcanely. He knew that the Baansuus was real. What place the deity held in celestial hierarchies was of considerably less interest to him than to priests. As far as he was concerned, the deity held whatever role it held; nothing he could do or believe would change supranatural reality. But the priests' interests drove this situation, and "that deity's" supranatural nature was of great concern to them—as was evidence that Yan adhered to the deity in any way. So far their questions had been sufficiently roundabout and obtuse that Yan remained unsure whether they were trying to learn if he had stepped over the edge into heresy or whether they were trying to push him over into it. Peyto—if he'd known about the situation— surely would have chosen the latter, given his opinion of the clergy.

Though Yan had been fearful that the Triadic priests had come because of the Baansuus, he was a little surprised that his fears had been correct. Yan knew how he had learned of the Baansuus, and knew that his sources were not available in the empire. Yan hadn't spoken of the Baansuus to any but Fra Bern, and Fra Bern was so absolutely terrified of being accused of heresy that he wouldn't have told any mortal soul about it. *How* had the Imperial priests come by this knowledge? Perhaps more importantly, what else did the priests know? Yan found himself longing for their secret knowledge as much as they apparently wanted his.

Though Handrar seemed to have no care for the

Baansuus, the scholar wizard was desirous of Yan's
arcane knowledge. And Captain Schell wanted to know
all there was to know about the Serpent's Eye and
drakkenree battle magic. Once Yan had wanted to be
sought after for his knowledge. Reality was turning out to
be something less than the respect and adulation of his
dreams. In his dreams, there had been no peril in knowing things others did not, and there had been no concern
for the trouble such knowledge might bring.

Right now, all he wanted was to be left alone. Which
was not to be; he was expected to spend another day
with the priests. Wearily he drained his mug and left the
house. The bench outside was empty. At least this morning Handrar wasn't sitting on his doorstep.

Instead the scholar wizard was waiting just outside the
door to the long hall. "You're looking poorly this morning," Handrar said after he greeted Yan. "You look as if
you haven't slept for a week."

Yan hadn't gone a week without sleep; he only felt
that way. Maintaining the spells on the cavern was taking
a toll. "I have a lot of things on my mind."

"Why not make it easier on yourself, and drop the
concealment spells on your cave? I know it is there."

Yan looked sharply at him. Someone had been in the
decoy cave last night; Yan had felt the thrum of his
arcane trip wire. "You're the one who was in the little
cave."

"The little cave? No, I know a decoy when I see one.
Besides, as a fellow magician, I would be rude, at the
very least, not to honor your wishes for discretion.
However, I would be most happy to receive an invitation
to visit the real site of your discoveries."

"Perhaps after the priests have gone."

"Or perhaps not," Handrar said, looking disappointed.
"I would also like to speak with you concerning the
elaviarm."

"I have some questions myself."

"Good. This evening, then? Assuming the priests don't consign you to Horesh's purifying fires."

Yan caught a twinkle of amusement in Handrar's eye, but he didn't find the joke funny.

"Come now," Handrar chided. "Things are not so grim. You'll see."

Just then Captain Schell emerged from the long hall. "Master Tanafres, Löm Kerandiri just sent me to find you."

"I'm not lost," Yan said.

"So I've told him," said Handrar. "But Löm Kerandiri listens little to my counsel."

Yan noted the eyebrow that Captain Schell raised at Handrar's comment.

Schell stepped aside and indicated the doorway with his hand. "The löm awaits you, Master Tanafres. You too, *Ser* Handrar."

They went inside. As he had yesterday, Yan took a seat at a table set in the center of the hall. Löm Kerandiri, Zephem the Baaliffite, and Serent the Vehrite sat on the other side of the table; they did not rise in greeting. The other priests stood behind the three, while Handrar and Schell took their places near the walls on either side of Yan, almost out of sight in the dimness of the hall. Löm Kerandiri began without preamble, speaking more slowly and deliberately than was his wont.

"Our discussions yesterday were necessary, Master Tanafres. I hope you did not find them too uncomfortable. We needed to ascertain your—well, let us just say that we needed to know where your beliefs and loyalties lay. Having spent some hours in debate concerning your answers, we have given the matter before us hard consideration and prayed for enlightenment."

This sounded like a speech preceding a judgment. Could the inquisition be over so quickly and so simply? Kerandiri looked solemn but not grim. Had Yan managed to avoid condemning himself? Could they have decided that he was no threat to their faith? Yan was too impatient to wait for Kerandiri to plod to his conclusion. "And now you are satisfied that my soul is untainted?"

"Are any of our souls truly untainted? We are all fleshly beings, after all, and prone to temptations of many sorts. However, in all that you said, I heard nothing that forced me to conclude that you had fallen into idolatry concerning that deity. Let us say that I shall keep an open mind in the matter of your soul."

"Wonderful."

"For now," Kerandiri said ominously.

Not so wonderful.

"I think it only fair to tell you that some of my brothers feel differently."

Yan wasn't surprised. Given the sour frown on Zephem's face, Yan had a good idea of which of the brothers was chief among the dissenters. Yan wanted to leave, but Kerandiri wasn't finished with him.

"Now that the necessary preliminaries have been concluded, Master Tanafres, we may move on to the reason why we have sought you out." Kerandiri raised his hand, and one of the priests stepped out from behind the table. "We have brought something with us that we wish you to see."

The priest carried a leather case big enough to hold a man's head. Whatever the case contained, it was heavy; it thumped solidly when she laid it on the table near Yan. She unlocked the case, opened it, and fumbled out an object covered in folds of soft leather. Yan was a little unnerved that the object appeared to be the size and shape of a man's head. He caught the white gleam of bone as she stripped away the last of the wrapping. A skull? To his relief, the object she placed before him was not a skull, although it was, in fact, bone.

A hemisphere of gleaming bone, intricately carved, layer upon layer. The outer surface was worked into arches and apertures that revealed an inner layer of more

arches and apertures. Beneath the second layer was a
third, and beneath that a fourth; Yan estimated that there
were at least six levels. Among the struts of each layer
were figures, the sinuous saurian shapes of drakkenree.
The craftsmanship was of such skill that he could detect
no seams where pieces of bone were joined together, nor
could he tell how inner layers were suspended within the
outer; they seemed free enough to move although they
did not. It was a superb piece of work. And fascinating.
Yan had never seen its like, although some of the decorative motifs on the struts reminded him of other drakkenree carving he had seen.

Awed, he asked, "Where did this come from?"

"Let us consider other questions for the moment,
Master Tanafres," Kerandiri said. "Please, examine it
closely."

Yan was more than happy to do so. He leaned closer,
but did not touch it as yet, satisfied to study it with his
eyes. Seeing it closer, he noticed drakkenree script
carved in tiny letters along the struts.

They must certainly want him to decipher the writing,
but with an object of such intricacy, there might be other
reasons why they would want him to examine it. "Do
you wish to know if it is magical?"

"We already know that it was prepared for arcane pur-
poses," Zephem answered testily.

Handrar's voice drifted in out of the darkness. "But it
was never invested with power."

Kerandiri said, "Note the delicacy of the carving."

"It is quite fine," Yan agreed.

Leaning forward, Kerandiri said, "You have told us
that you have made a study of drakkenree art. Would
you say that this piece is of such an origin?"

"Are you asking me if I think this was carved by a
drakkenree?" Yan asked.

"*Do* you think so?"

"Well, I have never seen anything quite like this piece,

but some of the decorative elements are much like those I've seen on certain old friezes."

Kerandiri raised his head and tightened his expression. "An antique style, then, not a recent one?"

"I would say so." Yan's comment caused a buzz of hushed conversation among the priests.

"Look at the carving carefully, Master Tanafres. Note the sharpness of the detail and the sheen of the bone. It appears not to be worn in the least."

It was as the löm said. Yan decided that a cautious comment was in order. "What you say is true."

"I find myself thinking that it is new," said Kerandiri. "What do you think, Master Tanafres? Is this a recent work?"

"I see little sign of age," Yan said, staying cautious.

"You do not think that it is an imitation or a copy of an older work?" Serent the Vehrite asked.

"I am no critic of art," Yan stated.

"But you are steeped in the lore of the ancient enemy," said Zephem.

Kerandiri sat back, looking troubled. "This carving is why we are here, Master Tanafres. All else revolves around it."

They clearly knew something about it that worried them. "It *is* new, isn't it?"

Kerandiri met his eyes, but didn't speak for a moment. Then, almost to himself, he said, "I had hoped you would say that it was false."

Yan looked at the carving again. It looked new, and it looked like a true drakkenree artifact, one carved in an ancient style. Yan was beginning to be afraid of where the priests were leading him.

"We are bidden to learn the true origin of this item," Kerandiri announced.

Something Yan himself would like to know. "How do you expect to do that?"

"We have a guide."

Oh, really? "A guide? Certainly you do not refer to me. I have no knowledge of where this carving came from."

"No, not you, Master Tanafres. Our guide is another," Kerandiri said.

Stepping close to the table, Schell said, "But your counsel could be invaluable in this matter. The emperor would be grateful for your aid, Master Tanafres."

Yan had been promised the emperor's gratitude for his aid against Yellow Eye's invasion. Yan had seen nothing of such gratitude. King Shain had been far more forthcoming in material support. "The empire has had little to do with me before now."

"Times change," Schell said.

"I fear that there are even greater changes in the wind," Kerandiri said. "Great powers are stirring."

Kerandiri's words brought a flash of memory into Yan's mind. Adain, the mage whose *claviarm* Handrar had given to Yan, had spoken of great powers stirring in the depths of the world. Yan stared at the bone carving, and saw for the first time that deep within the layers, at its heart, lay a ring of six drakkenree carved nose to tail. *Coincidence?*

Practitioners of the Great Art knew that coincidence was just a word to be used when a matter was not fully understood.

"You will come along with us," Kerandiri said. "I call upon you as a faithful son of the Triadic Church, to lend your aid in this matter."

"The empire needs all its loyal citizens," Schell said.

Yan didn't want to get involved in Imperial intrigues, but he did want to know more about the carving. He had seen nothing of such delicacy among the goods of the drakkenree he'd known. Not even Yellow Eye's finest instruments showed such a delicate hand. The only similar work he'd seen had been in the oldest of drakkenree places, specifically the guardian chamber beneath Laird Gornal's keep, the place where he had encountered ancient drakkenree mages preserved by a strange and powerful magic. Could it be a coincidence that the figures in the bone resembled those wizards more closely than they did the drakkenree who had invaded Kolvin? He didn't think so. A fake was unlikely; as far as he knew, he, Teletha, and Peyto were the only living people to have seen those ancient wizards. Could this hemisphere of bone have come down through the ages in a similar way, preserved by a timespell as those wizards had been preserved?

Or was the truth something more dire?

Once he'd feared that Yellow Eye was a drakkenree mage come from the past to wreak havoc on the world. He'd been wrong about Yellow Eye, but now he feared that the past could indeed intrude into the present.

He didn't think it was a coincidence that the bone carving had been prepared as an arcane receptacle, either. Whatever magic was at work here, he didn't understand it.

"I must think on this," Yan said.

"What thought is required?" Zephem asked. "Your hesitation reveals your unrighteousness."

"You speak out of turn, Fra Zephem," said Serent.

"You both speak out of turn," Kerandiri said. "Master Tanafres understands the import of what is at stake here. A request for time is not untoward. I am sure he will see where his interests lie and make the right decision."

Which would be the decision you want me to make, wouldn't it, Kerandiri?

But could he afford *not* to learn the secret of the bone carving?

Yan stood, offering what he hoped was a suitably polite parting. Handrar followed him out of the long hall. Yan decided to take advantage of the opportunity that the wizard's presence offered.

"What do you think the hemisphere is?" he asked.

"A ritual object," Handrar replied casually.

"That much is obvious."

"It is all that is obvious about the thing."

Yan had been hoping Handrar would have something informative to say. "Have you compared the *claviarm* to the hemisphere?"

"Do you mean, have I noted that some of the drakkenree symbols on the *claviarm* are repeated on the hemisphere?"

Exactly. The invocation to the Baansuus, for one. "And you still say that you cannot read what is written there?"

"It is not kind of you continually to point that out."

Handrar sounded truly aggrieved; Yan decided that the wizard was being honest about his lack of ability. It seemed that only Yan knew of the connection between the Baansuus and the two artifacts. While he was considering what such a connection might mean, Handrar caught him off guard by changing the subject.

"What about the man who made the *claviarm*? Do you remember anything about the mage that might be helpful?"

Yan remembered that he hadn't been able to help Adain. "I remember very little."

"Perhaps I can help you to remember more. There is a spell to invoke the past that I know. Using the *claviarm* as a focus, I might be able to help you to relive the day. In your memory, of course. Not even the legendary Arkyn could truly turn back time."

"Memory evocation? That is not a magic familiar to me." It sounded intriguing, though.

"It is an obscure magic, but I do have some facility with it," Handrar said modestly. "Would you be willing to give it a try?"

Knowing *anything* more about the merin mage whose *claviarm* bore a drakkenree invocation might shed some light on an increasingly murky situation. Yan agreed. But instead of taking Handrar to the cavern to perform the spell as the wizard wanted, Yan insisted that they try his memory evocation in Yan's house. Before long, and with Jerr looking on, Yan was seated by the firegrate, with Handrar standing before him.

"Relax," Handrar told him. "Find *præha* and let yourself drift. I will guide you."

Yan let himself slip into *præha*. He felt Handrar's presence solidly beside him. Jerr was a whisper of existence.

"Do you see the *claviarm*?" Handrar asked.

Yan held the amulet in his lap. Though his eyes were closed, he raised the *claviarm* before his face. "Yes. I see it."

"Steady its image in your mind. You see it now as it is. Remember it. Remember it as it was years ago. Remember where you were then. See the *claviarm* as you first saw it."

Because of its nature, Yan was able to see the *claviarm* in the *præha* state. Its image was clear, as sharp as he would have seen it with his eyes. The silver disk was studded with flecks of gemstone that he now knew were metron, a magically efficacious stone which he had not encountered before he met Adain. Tiny sigils in Nitallan and the drakkenree script were engraved around the edge. And in the center of the disk, under the glass dome, lay an enigmatic dark object. The *claviarm* glowed for a moment, then faded a little, becoming almost transparent. Yan realized that his hand no longer held the amulet. He was still staring at the *claviarm*, but now he saw it lying on worn wooden boards.

The floor of the inn!

Yan seemed to stand again in the sickroom. In one corner lay a rolled blanket, a hat, a sack, and a traveler's staff: Adain's goods. On the stool by the bed lay a disarrayed pile of clothes; the *claviarm* lay on the floor beside the stool. Behind him stood a shadowy presence, the terrified innkeeper. Before him lay the preternaturally aged Adain, and the man's raspy breathing was the only sound.

Yan remembered how he had feared a wasting spirit or a curse, and how he'd been reluctant to examine Adain magically. He hadn't wanted to contract a magical curse. But he had examined the *claviarm.*

Which was in his hand again. The innkeeper was gone, and he was alone with Adain. Yan sat by the bed, listening to the man's ravings. They were so disjointed that they made no sense at all. Even the words that were not mumbled were as often as not in a language unknown to Yan. Then there were the hissings, sibilant sounds that seemed out of place in a human throat, sounds that Yan now knew to be a language: the drakkenree language. Adain spoke it with an accent that Yan found hard to follow, but now with the words refreshed in his memory Yan understood some of what Adain had said. The mage spoke of a gathering of drakkenree, by which he might have meant Yellow Eye's invasion, but somehow Yan didn't think Yellow Eye's small army of drakkenree fit the saurian concept of *hiss'laktatun*: the whole or the all. And *hiss'laktatun* was the word that Adain used. Most of the rest was garbled, but Yan understood a few more words and phrases: night and dawn and long periods of time. But Adain said another word, a word that sent chills down Yan's spine: *ka-slekrak.* Yan didn't understand the drakkenree concept clearly, but he knew that it was connected to the Baansuus. The nearest meaning he had been able to assign to it was "great awakening."

"Good greeting to you, brother in the Art," the memory of Adain said. "I had hoped the man here would have sense to summon a mage. I knew you when you came, but for so long I was unable to do anything about it. What is your name?"

"I am Yan Tanafres."

"And your master?"

"Hebrim Tidoni."

"Will he come if you call?"

"If the matter is of import." At the time the answer had been honest.

Adain spoke. "Import? Oh, yes. Can you not tell? Can you not feel it?"

Yan heard himself ask the man's name.

"I am beyond names now," Adain said with his sad-eyed smile, but he gave Yan the name by which Yan knew him. Yan again insisted on his intention to help Adain. He had more questions now than he'd had then, but he found he could only ask those he had asked at the inn. The answers were no different, no more informative. Adain's faraway voice once again said, "There are great powers stirring in the depths of the world. A shift in the wellspring of magic is upon us."

Adain paused, then said the words that hurt as much now as they had then.

"Any true mage would feel it."

Again Yan endured Adain's suspicion when he denied feeling what the mage had spoken of. Yan had felt better later when he had learned that Gan Tidoni had felt nothing. But now, his own doubts about his progress in his chosen profession echoed the old hurt and amplified it. In memory, he did as he had done; he tried to reassure Adain that he was getting better.

"Tomorrow you will see things differently," Yan said. Certainly *he* had seen things differently.

"No," Adain denied. "The wheel of the universe turns, and we all have our place upon it. All in its order, each in his place. Our wheels have intersected. I have come here, and you have come to me. I go, and you must go. That is the order that is, the order that shall be. You must share this burden with me."

Adain closed his eyes and lapsed into the silence from which Yan knew he would never return. Adain had never explained what the burden might be, and Yan still didn't understand what it might be, but the wheel of the universe had turned and come round again. Once again Yan held Adain's *claviarm* in his hand.

And he looked upon it not with his memory but with his eyes. His hand shook as he realized that not all was the same. There was power in motion.

Great powers stirring in the depths of the world.

Handrar stood before him, looking anxious.

"Are you all right, Master Tanafres?"

Adain's *claviarm* was quivering under his hand, vibrating with a power that was not just an echo of memory. Shakily, Yan laid down the amulet on the floor.

Yan had seen Adain's body burned before his eyes. The power he felt throbbing in the *claviarm* couldn't be Adain's. It had to come from somewhere else. Yan touched his own *claviarm* and felt something there as well, something unusual. It seemed an echo, distant and exotic. But an echo of what? There was a shape to it that reminded him of the carved hemisphere. There was also a taste of the transcendence he had experienced when he had controlled the Eye of the Serpent. Yan scratched at the itch in his palm.

"Tell me, *Ser* Handrar, magician to magician, where does the carving come from?"

"Magician to magician, I do not know its ultimate source. I know only that it was brought to *Ser* Arun and through him to the emperor himself. It was the emperor who involved the priests and complicated the matter. I wish that I could tell you more, but I cannot. I had hoped that you would look upon it and understand all, but I see that I held a false hope. You do not have the answer in your cavern or in your books, do you?"

"If the answer is there, I cannot read the riddle of it." But the origin of the carving was not something that Yan could let go unsolved.

"Perhaps I can read what you cannot," suggested Handrar.

"By your own admission, you could not read the sigils

on the *claviarm*. How can you expect to understand an arcane text or a half-effaced inscription?"

"Given time I can—"

"Time seems to be the commodity that we do not have."

"What are you saying?"

"You want an answer? Touch Adain's *claviarm* now!"

Handrar's face contorted at Yan's preemptory tone. He snatched up the amulet. With a gasp, he dropped it nearly as quickly, staring at it in shock.

"It is active! How can that be? The mage is dead!"

"Now touch your own *claviarm*. Can you feel anything?"

Handrar did as Yan suggested and said quietly, "I do feel something. The sensation is . . . singular. Like a faint echo of what I felt in Adain's *claviarm*."

"Have you ever felt anything like it?"

Handrar just shook his head.

Yan understood the man's reluctance to speak. There were aspects of the Great Art impossible to put into words. Beautiful things, dreadful things. The feeling he got from the *claviarm* was both beautiful and dreadful at once.

Was this the *ka-slekrak* that Adain had spoken of?

If it was, Yan wanted—needed—to know more. Adain was dead and gone and could offer no answers, but whoever had carved the bone understood something of this strange magic. Yan had questions for that carver.

Löm Kerandiri was withholding information, awaiting Yan's agreement to go along with the priests. Very well, then, Yan would go along—as long as cooperation brought him closer to unraveling this mystery. But he wouldn't be going along to earn the gratitude of the emperor or the thanks of the Church. There were mysteries to understand. The strangeness that Yan had felt was something that no magician could leave unexplored.

11

JERR WAS AT ONCE HAPPY and scared at the prospect of leaving the village and going with the priests. Other than her harrowing trip to the village from the farm where she'd been born, she'd never traveled anywhere. Well, if she wished to continue to learn from Master Tanafres, she'd be traveling soon. She was bursting with the excitement of it, but she didn't know whether she would burst out laughing or crying.

However, this was no time for daydreaming; she had an errand to perform. She found Sir Kopell, right where Master Tanafres said he would be. She also discovered that she was too late to deliver her message—Sir Kopell already knew Master Tanafres would be leaving. And by the tenor of his argument with Captain Schell, the knight was not happy about the situation. Jerr couldn't remember hearing Sir Kopell shout at anyone before, other than his soldiers, and his dreadful lizard.

"I don't care if you still consider him an Imperial citizen!" Sir Kopell's face was dark with his anger. "He left your empire years ago! He is of King Shain's affinity now. I cannot allow you to drag away one of the king's men."

"We are not dragging him away," Captain Schell protested. "He is leaving of his own accord."

"Not without the king's permission!"

"Neither you nor your king has the authority to forbid him to travel where he wills. He is an Imperial citizen."

"Master Tanafres has lived here in Kolvin for years; his Imperial citizenship is a thing of the past. He is of the king's affinity," Sir Kopell said again. Jerr didn't exactly understand what that meant, but she understood what the knight said next. "He goes or stays at the king's will. If you insist on taking him, you threaten the old alliance."

They couldn't do that. The old alliance was what kept the lizards from stealing good merin lands. Everyone knew that! How could these men consider an end to the old alliance? Jerr was relieved to hear Captain Schell say, "We have no wish to end the alliance."

"Very well, then," Sir Kopell said with a smile. Seeing the knight relax let Jerr relax. "Master Tanafres stays."

Captain Schell frowned. "He goes." Jerr's relief went. Captain Schell stood up straighter. "If the alliance comes to an end, it will be because your king chooses to end it. I think that, upon sober consideration, King Shain would find that an unprofitable course."

The two men glared at each other. It looked as if they might come to blows; but after a long time, Sir Kopell unclenched his jaw and relaxed a little. Captain Schell relaxed, too.

Was it safe to relax this time?

"You are determined to do this," the knight said.

"Absolutely," Captain Schell said in a firm voice.

Sir Kopell's narrowed eyes seemed to take the islander's measure. "If this matter is as grave as you say—"

"It is."

"*If* it is, then Kolvin is threatened by the vague danger you claim, maybe even more threatened than your empire. King Shain does not like unknown dangers. If you are going to take our wizard away, you must tell me more about this matter."

Jerr was eager to hear; most of what Master Tanafres said about the situation had never been clear to her, but she remembered him saying that the Imperials knew more than they were telling.

"I cannot tell you," Captain Schell said.

"You mean that you *will* not," Sir Kopell said.

"Actually, I said what I meant. The nature of the danger is as much a mystery to us as to you."

Sir Kopell spent a moment thinking about that. "Yet you are sure that it touches on the ancient enemy."

"Yes. I think it's safe to say that the drakkenree are involved."

Sir Kopell spent some more time thinking. Captain Schell waited, watchful. Jerr waited, too; but where the captain was calm, she was not. The drakkenree were the ancient enemy. The monstrous lizards were the villains of goblin tales, eating young children who didn't listen to their parents. But the drakkenree were real, too, and they did other things than eat misbehaving children, terrible things. When Sir Kopell spoke, his words carried solemnity.

"The drakkenree are very dangerous, as we know from olden times. Long have Kolvin and the empire stood shoulder to shoulder against the ancient enemies of our peoples. We should stand together against this danger as well."

Captain Schell smiled, the sort of smile she'd seen a horse trader smile when he'd gotten the price he wanted. The islander said, "I could not agree more wholeheartedly."

"Then you will understand that if Master Tanafres goes with you, some of the king's men must go with him," said Sir Kopell.

Captain Schell's expression changed. He looked as if he had bitten into a sour fruit, but he recovered quickly. "There is but little room in the ship."

Ship? Jerr hadn't realized there was a ship. She'd

never been on a ship. Fear of the unknown started to overtake her excitement about the trip. Maybe it would be better if Master Tanafres stayed. Maybe Sir Kopell had been right in the first place. What about Master Tanafres's dignity? A great magician needed a suitable escort. Surely Sir Kopell could point that out. Master Tanafres *was* of the king's affinity, was he not? If a suitable escort couldn't fit on Captain Schell's ship, Master Tanafres couldn't go. Sir Kopell could tell Captain Schell *that*!

Sir Kopell disappointed her. "A little crowding is a small matter. Kolviners are used to hardships, Captain."

"Just how many men did you have in mind?" Captain Schell asked.

"I would think a number of men-at-arms sufficient to match the soldiers escorting Löm Kerandiri would be suitable."

"Too many," Captain Schell said quickly. "Besides, you do not have half that number here."

"They need not come from here. The king will soon know of this plan. He will choose men, and they will meet us in Brandespar." Sir Kopell smiled. This time *he* was the horse trader. "You said that the danger was great, Captain. Surely you would not refuse good fighting men of whom you might have great need."

"This is not a military expedition."

Sir Kopell looked over to where his warriors and the Imperial soldiers were practicing. There were nearly twice as many islanders as Kolviners. "No? Maybe it should become one."

"War is not my master's will. Emperor Dacel desires information before all else. So, since we are not ready to march off to war, a single envoy should be sufficient to keep your king informed of all that happens."

"A single envoy?" Sir Kopell sounded surprised, but Jerr knew he wasn't; he was horse trading again. "Besides the ordinary warriors under Captain Namsorn, Löm

Kerandiri travels with yourself, two warrior priests, and a wizard. Surely if your master thinks that our Master Tanafres is a wise man of whom he has need, then Master Tanafres is worthy of a more suitable honor guard."

"As I said, the ship is small."

"Myself and my lance then," Sir Kopell suggested.

Captain Schell nodded. "Agreed."

"Good." Sir Kopell called for his servant, who nearly bowled Jerr over in his haste to respond to his master. The knight started giving orders before the man reached him.

"Tell Myskell to pick two of the archers and prepare to travel. Pack full harness, and don't forget the oils against the sea air. A dozen sheaves for each archer, and whatever else Myskell thinks proper. Oh, and see that we have enough dried meat for the lizard."

"No," Captain Schell said. "We will not take the drakkenree."

Take the lizard? The prospect horrified Jerr. Captain Schell said the ship was small. Would there be anyplace to get away from the lizard?

Sir Kopell turned slowly to face the captain. "Why not? He is little trouble, and he might prove useful."

"It is a drakkenree."

Which is to say, a monster. Jerr held her tongue; it was not her place to join this conversation.

"I know what he is," Sir Kopell said. "That is why I think it wise to have him along. Surely you have traveled enough to know that it is wise to have someone who speaks the tongue of the land."

"I never said that we sailed for the drakkenree lands."

Mannar's mercy! Jerr had never thought that might be their destination!

"You did not say otherwise, either," Sir Kopell said. "And you do not deny it now."

"Sir Kopell, you are a difficult man."

"So my enemies say."

"I would not like to be one of them."

"Then we are agreed?"

"We are agreed."

Agreed on going to the land of the drakkenree? Jerr felt sick. It couldn't be!

No, she realized with relief, it *really* couldn't be. Captain Schell had said that he was not on a military expedition, that he was not going to war. How could one go to the land of the ancient enemy and not be going to war? And with only one ship. They couldn't possibly be going to drakkenree lands.

Sir Kopell's voice shook her out of her thoughts. "What is it, girl?" Jerr couldn't find her voice. "Come now. You've been hanging about. Is it me or Captain Schell you want to see?"

"Uh, you, Sir Kopell."

"Well, what is it?"

"I'm, uh, well, I suppose it doesn't matter now."

"What doesn't matter?" he asked with exaggerated patience.

"Nothing, sir." Gods, she sounded stupid!

Sir Kopell sighed and shook his head, dismissing her as an empty-headed girl, no doubt. "Well, since you have nothing to do, run an errand for me. Go tell your master that I will be traveling with him."

She ran off on her new errand, trying to outpace her embarrassment.

Teletha sat on the corral fence, contemplating the news. She'd gotten the word about Yan's impending departure from Jerr when the girl ran into her, literally, on her way to bring Yan Sir Kopell's message. Teletha had gone with Jerr to Yan's house, but he hadn't been there. Peyto had been present, packing and babbling about how wonderful things were going to be once they got back to the empire.

Peyto had known what was going on, so why hadn't Yan bothered to tell her?

If he thought he could leave her here while he ran off to the gods knew where, he had a lot more thinking to do! He couldn't claim it was too dangerous if he was dragging Peyto and Jerr along.

Of course, the empire might not be the safest destination for her. There was still the unresolved matter of her unintentional desertion while in the emperor's service as an air captain. Unintentional or not, desertion was desertion, and the explanation for her actions wasn't the sort to satisfy a military court. She had expected trouble when the Imperial expeditionary force had arrived during Yellow Eye's invasion, but her old friend Estem Honistonti had been in charge of that force. Estem had promised her he'd taken care of the problem, but she'd never actually seen a writ of pardon. She didn't feel comfortable not having seen the writ. She had no reason to doubt Estem's word, but there had been treachery in that campaign, and some of it had come from people with court connections.

Gods! She was starting to think like Peyto, seeing intrigue and duplicity everywhere.

What did it really matter where they were going? Yan needed her to look out for him. Anyone so wrapped up in scrolls, old caves, and priestly inquisitions that he couldn't be bothered to think about someone who was trying to kill him definitely needed to be watched over.

She was going along, and that was all there was to it!

Well, not all, but she *was* going along.

She didn't like the idea of traveling with a group that might include a person who was trying to kill Yan. Though she and Peyto were still arguing about whether the villain was a Kolviner or an islander, she couldn't assume that the trouble would be over once they got on the road. Yan might need a good and trustworthy blade defending his back.

She couldn't think of anyone else better qualified than herself.

And she'd tell him so, as soon as she saw him.

12

TRIADIC PRIESTS RISE TO GREET the dawn, so Yan woke Fra Bern well before the sky began to lighten. Yan wanted to limit the potential witnesses who might see them enter the cavern. Even though the sleepy priest stumbled a bit, he had little trouble following Yan up the path to the cave, making Yan wonder how effective his efforts at concealment were. Had he been giving himself a constant headache for the last few days for nothing? Whether he had or not, the spells weren't the answer, even if he stayed. Other solutions were needed.

Once they were inside the cavern, Yan said, "Since you will be staying here, I want you to have charge of my workroom while I am gone. There are no experiments which will need tending, so the task should not discommode you much. Just check in now and again to be sure everything is as it should be. However, there is one thing I need you to arrange. I want a door emplaced to close off the passageway here. A door with a strong lock."

Fra Bern had not been seen much about the steading since the Imperial priests had arrived, and when Fra Bern was about, he had spoken little. His uncustomary quietness continued as Yan explained his plan, but Yan could see the plan disturbed the priest. Yan could not let that deter him.

"I believe that the work should be started today," he said. "As soon as I leave, in fact. You are the only one I can trust to see that the work is done right."

Fra Bern looked even more unhappy at Yan's expression of confidence. "Löm Kerandiri intends to leave two of his priests here. They will object if they are not allowed access to the lower caves and to the worship chamber."

"All the more reason to see that the carpenter and the smith do their work quickly. I don't think it wise to let those priests have free access to this place."

"Perhaps not," Fra Bern fretted. "But they will see the locked door as a deliberate attempt to keep them from learning about the drakkenree temple."

"It is," Yan said. But it was more than that, too. If allowed access to the temple, the priests would have access to Yan's workroom. They could meddle with Yan's things. Not that he was planning on leaving anything behind that their suspicious minds might find incriminating. Nothing unhidden or unprotected anyway. But hiding places could be discovered by diligent searchers, and protections could be overcome. He didn't want to take the chance.

"They will see our efforts to interfere with them as clear evidence that we have fallen into heresy," Fra Bern said.

Yan suspected that he was right, and did not intend the good-hearted priest to be implicated. "Not our efforts, Fra Bern, my efforts. Should they ask, as they will, tell them that the door is made at my order. Warn them that I have threatened the workmen. Say even that I threatened you. But do not let them prevent the work."

"To say that you threatened me would be a lie," Fra Bern said.

"Would you rather tell them I compelled you?"

The priest blanched. Yan could see him considering the possibility that Yan *had* compelled him. After all this time, he still had some of the suspicious awe most people felt toward magicians. Yan waited for the priest to recover his faith in his colleague. He was pleased to hear Fra Bern say, "But that would be even more wrong and dangerous for you. You did not compel me."

"Of course not. I trust you, Fra Bern. These foreign priests I do not know. Löm Kerandiri seems open to new things, but not all of his followers are like him. I fear that it would be all too easy for these priests to misunderstand what we have discovered down below. You know how easy it would be for them to misinterpret our researches."

"Very well," Fra Bern said in a low voice.

"Good." Yan smiled reassuringly. "Keeping them away from the lower levels is only a temporary measure, anyway. Just until I return. I would rather not have anyone other than you poking around down there. There's no telling what a stranger might destroy." Knowing it was wicked, since he hadn't actually seen any signs of danger, Yan added, "Or unleash."

"You haven't—"

"I haven't done anything truly dangerous," Yan reassured him. "But you know as well as I that much is strange down there. You don't understand it, and I don't understand it. In truth, there *may* be real dangers."

"Lord Einthof as my witness, I have feared it."

"Not without justification," Yan said, though he thought such hazards unlikely. "These priests may be brought to understand the wisdom of the precautions that I wish undertaken. If anyone can convince them, it is you, my friend."

Fra Bern looked as if he envisioned the task as a heavy burden, but he said, "I will try."

"Good. Now there are a few things that I want to show you."

Yan showed Fra Bern several places where he said he had placed enchantments—which he hadn't; there hadn't been time—and told the priest how to avoid their nonexistent effects. It was a deception, but Fra Bern need never know. It was for the better, actually. Belief in such spells would encourage Fra Bern to ensure that no one should enter the cavern; he would not be burdened by duplicity when he tried to keep others out, and would thereby be more convincing. It was not the kindest use of his friend, but time denied Yan other avenues. He was sure that Fra Bern would understand.

They departed the cavern as the sky was graying and were the first to arrive at the place Löm Kerandiri had chosen to perform his morning rituals. Captain Namsorn was the next to arrive and, after polite greetings, the three of them stood in silence until Löm Kerandiri and the other priests came. Teletha attended, too. "Begin a journey as you would a new day, by greeting Horesh, and you will come safely home," she said, quoting the old proverb. She was still making a point of having invited herself along on the journey.

After the ritual the steading grew steadily busier, as more and more of the folk bustled about getting ready to leave or helping those who were leaving. Yan had little to do, having already made his preparations. While helping Jerr harness the horse that she would be riding to Brandespar, Yan noticed Fra Bern conferring with the smith and the carpenter.

The cavalcade was ready well before noon. Good-byes were said and last-minute instructions and admonitions given. With Captain Namsorn and a handful of his soldiers leading, they set out.

The first day's travel took them only as far as Baron Yentillan's steading, where they spent the night. Yan spent some time with the baron, learning just what King Shain expected of him, but otherwise he spent the night undisturbed in the private quarters the baron provided for him.

On the following day, just before crossing a river in full flood, Yan checked his horse's harness and discovered that someone had slit the stitching on his girth strap. Not enough to make the strap fail immediately, but enough to weaken it so that use would make it fail. The threads holding the strap together were almost entirely gone, and the strap was nearly ready to part completely. A little magic strengthened the remaining threads and allowed him to cross the flood safely, but he restitched the strap that night; being a shoemaker's son had some advantages. He managed to keep the incident to himself. Why bother anyone about it? There was no way he knew of identifying the culprit, and he'd had enough of Teletha and Peyto's attempts to guess. Besides, he had handled this as easily as he had handled the last attempt.

The rest of the trip to Brandespar took the better part of three days, but was uneventful. They could not ride at any great speed because of Sir Kopell's drakkenree, but the saurian's pace seemed acceptable to Captain Schell and the priests; they made no complaint. But there was a sense of urgency in the way Captain Schell saw to the breaking of camp each morning and his small tolerance for lingering on rest breaks. Upon arriving in Brandespar, Captain Schell led the cavalcade directly to the quays and to a ship flying a long blue streamer powdered with golden stars.

The lettering on the ship's sterncastle named her *Mannar's Handmaiden,* and the flag fluttering on her mainmast proclaimed her to be sailing under Imperial command. *Mannar's Handmaiden* was the biggest of the vessels warped to the quay, but not the only one flying Imperial colors. Teletha pointed out two other vessels anchored in the harbor that, she said, were flying the star-studded streamers. Yan squinted but he couldn't convince himself that the blurry shapes on those flags were the same as on the one nearby. The flags had similar shapes and colors, though, so he decided to take Teletha's word for it; she saw better over distance than he did.

Yan followed Captain Schell's lead and dismounted. Most of the others did so as well, but only Yan, Teletha, Kerandiri, and Namsorn followed Schell and his aide down the wharf toward the ship. The rest of the travelers stayed with the horses to begin the work of unloading them.

A heavyset bregil, his wide shoulders exaggerated by the winged jerkin he wore over his white linen shirt, clumped down the gangway to meet the advance party. A broad-brimmed hat shadowed the bregil's face so well that Yan did not recognize him until Captain Schell began the introduction.

"This gentleman is Master Threok, our sailing master. Master Threok, this is—"

"We've met," interrupted Threok. He drew back his bifurcate upper lip to show his strong, straight teeth. The expression would have been a snarl for a merin, but it was a smile for a bregil. Not a pleasant smile, but a smile. Threok pointed over his shoulder with his thumb, indicating the seaward horizon. "You do anything about this foul weather, Master Magician?"

"I'm not a weather mage," Yan said.

"Too bad. Maybe it's a sign. They do say it's bad luck to take a mage to sea."

"A superstition."

"If you say so. But even with personal blessings from Mannar, Theris, Mardian, Baaliff, and a full dozen of maritime saints, we'll not be putting to sea on the next tide. That would only put us in the way of the storm. Screaming up from the Sea of Storms, she is, and a right monstrous blow by the color of those clouds. She'll be storming hereabouts for a day at least, and that's weather heavier than I care to chance, by Mannar's grace."

"Are you planning on weathering the storm in harbor?" Schell asked.

"Safest place I know of."

"Then we had best get everyone and everything

aboard quickly. You'll be wanting to get away from the wharf."

"Tied to the wharf's no way to take a storm, for a truth. Your people may not want to board as yet, though. I don't think we'll get the worst of it, but the sea will run heavy enough. Anyone unused to the sea will not be wanting to be aboard." Threok stared at the priests gathered by the horses. "Not a good start for those without their sea legs."

Schell followed Threok's gaze and nodded. "A good thought. We'll take lodging ashore for the night. See to the arrangements, Master Martello."

"Aye, sir," the boy said, and ran off to do as he was bidden.

Schell didn't bother to watch; he stood, gazing at the horizon while the rest of the advance party started back toward the horses. Yan didn't go with them; he wanted to speak with Threok.

"You never said you were a sailing master, Threok."

Threok shrugged in the bregil way. His tail curled up until the tip was at a height with his hunched shoulders and the gripping pad coiled and uncoiled twice in rapid succession. "I am better than many, though not so good as some." In Captain Schell's direction, Threok said, "The magician and I met while I was on a holiday from my regular business."

While the captain seemed to pay Threok no heed, Yan was intrigued by the bregil's choice of words. A holiday? Not the word that Yan would have chosen. Like Yan, Threok had been a slave among Yellow Eye's drakkenree. Threok had been responsible for Yan's surviving his first encounter with the drakkenree. Yan had returned the favor, saving Threok's life during the tumultuous end of the Battle of Rastionne. Yan hadn't seen or heard from the bregil since. Was it not strange that Threok should turn up now?

"Are you part of this because of your holiday?" he asked.

"I'm thinking that you would know better than I, Master Magician." Threok spoke more politely than Yan remembered, but seemed determined to remain a difficult source of information.

Yan could be determined, too, and he wanted to know more. "Have you fared well since last we met?"

"I'm a merchant, Master Magician. A trader." Threok shrugged again, then surprised Yan by speaking freely. "I gather goods in one place and sell them in another. It's a good life, if you're lucky. And smart. But even the smartest fellow can fall afoul of bad luck. While I was away from my business, some rivals took advantage of the situation. The time I spent on holiday cost me quite a bit. I've been working to regain what I lost and had been doing fairly well. *Mannar's Handmaiden* here is mine." He pointed to the mainmast with his tail. "The flag up there flies by Imperial writ, with a promise of all debts against the *Handmaiden* forgiven if I discharge this service. Not an insignificant reward. The gods my witness, I've never much cared for being impressed into service. But I've survived it before, and I will again. Your being here tells me that they have impressed you as well."

"I came of my own will," Yan said, knowing that it was almost true.

Threok's dark eyes glittered in the storm's growing gloom. "And what reward were you promised?"

"The matter wasn't actually discussed."

"So you still have more curiosity than sense," concluded Threok.

"And you have more impertinent bluntness than wisdom," Yan returned.

Threok frowned for a moment, then burst into a sudden, deep laugh. "All the changes and still the same, eh? I think we're in for an interesting voyage. But not until the weather shifts, eh? Go to the nice hostel Captain Schell's boy will arrange, sleep, rest. I think you still have time to be sensible; we will not sail until tomorrow, or maybe the next day."

Yan wished Threok good luck in weathering the storm in the harbor; Captain Schell had some business to attend, so Yan went off to follow the others to the place they would spend the night.

Captain Schell joined the travelers at the hostel for the evening meal, and announced that they would have to split up. "Master Threok refuses to have too many passengers aboard any one ship," he said.

Yan requested that Threok's ship carry him, Teletha, and Peyto.

Löm Kerandiri agreed at once. "Since Master Threok's ship is not sufficiently large to carry the whole delegation as well as all of our new additions, I suggest that Sir Kopell and his men and servants travel aboard *Mannar's Grace of Avsenkor.*"

"I am charged with warding Master Tanafres," Sir Kopell said. "Such an arrangement is not acceptable."

Sir Kopell's objection sparked off intense debate regarding the disposition of the passengers. A split among the travelers was necessary. The Kolviner knight was not mollified until the Imperials agreed to split their party if the travelers from Kolvin were split. The compromise, reached after a night of argument, was that Yan, Teletha, and Peyto would travel on the *Handmaiden*, accompanied—and guarded—by the two Imperial captains and a third of the Imperial soldiers. Sir Kopell and his men were to travel on the *Grace*, but so would Löm Kerandiri, the other priests, and a third of the soldiers, with Galon Martello as their commander. The remainder of the soldiers were consigned to the third and smallest ship. Kerandiri raised another objection.

"There must be a Church presence aboard *Mannar's Handmaiden.*"

"I see no reason for such," Peyto said. Sir Kopell agreed.

The final arrangement, equally unsatisfactory to the heads of both the Imperial and Kolviner groups, was to have Serent and Zephem sail on the *Handmaiden*; Sir Kopell was willing to accept the warrior priests as additional soldiers to guard Yan.

"They are more warriors than priests," the knight said.

It was two days before the weather at sea cleared sufficiently for the ships to sail. Threok's messenger came to the inn on the morning of the day the clouds broke, carrying the word that they would sail on the evening tide.

Yan spent the afternoon concluding arrangements for Master Gannedan, a Brandespar alchemist with whom he had corresponded, to undertake Jerr's care. The cost was nominal, though Peyto complained that it overly depleted their traveling funds. Yan didn't care. Jerr could learn some valuable skills from Master Gannedan, and Yan wouldn't have to worry about whether she was getting into trouble, either back at the cavern or on the voyage.

"Keep working on your exercises," he told her as he departed Master Gannedan's shop.

"Why?" she asked sullenly.

Jerr seemed to have taken an immediate and irrational dislike to Master Gannedan. Yan was sure she would get over it. Master Gannedan was a good man; Yan was sure he would be a good master for her. She would understand that in time. It was a part of growing up to learn how to adapt to changing circumstances. Everyone had to do it, especially those who had dreams of becoming great magicians.

"I don't want to be an alchemist," she said. "I've always dreamed about being a magician."

"Dreams don't always work out," he told her.

He wouldn't listen to any more of her complaints or arguments. She would be safer here, especially if the Imperial priests changed their minds about Yan's purity, a possibility that still seemed too likely. Horesh's purifying fires burned as brightly for disciples of heretics as for the heretics themselves. Jerr was better off staying in Brandespar. She knew very little about the Baansuus, and she most certainly hadn't fallen into heresy regarding that deity. There was no need for her to be involved in any unpleasantness that might arise.

When the travelers arrived at the wharf, they found the two larger vessels of the three-ship flotilla tied up and loading supplies. As Yan walked down the wharf, he noticed many bregil among the seamen. Though the men were clearly not wild tribesmen of the Kolvin hills—they wore islander fashions and spoke Empiric—Yan still felt a little uncomfortable; he'd not seen so many of their kind in one place since the invasion. Yan kept his discomfort to himself; it was an unworthy feeling.

Yan, dressed in his fancy robes, garnered some sidelong glances from the sailors. Magicians were not considered lucky among sailors. Such furtive looks were nothing compared to the reaction Sir Kopell's drakkenree received when he strode down the wharf. Heads turned and whispers raced along the pier and across the ships. Sailors and dockworkers stopped their work and stared. Some aboard the ships climbed up the lines for a better look. Out in the harbor, watching sailors hung in the rigging of the other Imperial ship. Yan saw several of the nearer sailors and workers, horror on their faces, make the sign of the Triad. The saurian ignored the commotion that he caused and boarded the *Grace*. Stopping briefly at the top of the gangway, he looked around as though inspecting the ship. He set his clawed feet on the deck and strode toward the sterncastle companionway. But instead of climbing to the upper deck, he ducked underneath the companionway and lay down; he'd chosen a position that would keep him out of the way.

Captains and ships' officers shouted and cursed, urging their men back to the work of preparing the ships for travel. The tide had already started to turn by the time loading was complete. More curses and orders were shouted. Seamen hastily cast off lines. Freed of their bonds, the *Handmaiden* and the *Grace* wallowed away from the wharf and hurried to catch up with *Theris's Breath of Sharhumrin*; their sister ship was already making her way out of the harbor.

Yan, a privileged passenger aboard the *Handmaiden*, stood on the quarterdeck, Threok's domain, and watched the town dwindle behind them. Peyto joined Yan as the ships made their way past the headlands. The two of them leaned on the railing and looked out at the sea. No words passed between them. Yan wondered whether Peyto was thinking about the last sea voyage they had shared. That voyage had ended in disaster, especially for Peyto; it had cost him his left arm.

Surely this voyage would have a better end.

At length Peyto gave off looking at the sea and looked to the sky. He turned to Threok and said, "Good Master Threok, it appears to me that we are sailing south and to the west."

"Are you a navigator, Master Lennuick?" Threok responded without taking his eyes from the horizon.

"I know which way the sun travels."

"Then you know which way we are sailing," Threok said amiably.

"Insufferable man," Peyto mumbled in Nitallan. He switched back to Empiric to say, "Sessandir and Sharhumrin lie to the north of Kolvin."

"So they do," Threok agreed.

"Then why do we not sail in that direction?"

"Because we sail in this one. If you do not care for the direction we travel, speak to Captain Schell."

"I will."

"Have a nice talk," Threok said in Nitallan as Peyto left the quarterdeck.

Yan doubted that Peyto heard because the clerk never faltered in his progress. If Peyto had realized that Threok spoke Nitallan, he would have been embarrassed at having his remark overheard; Peyto was always embarrassed at having his judgmental comments overheard. Not that he found any shame in making them; rather Peyto enjoyed the superiority he demonstrated in being able to comment in a language unknown to a listener, especially when the comment was about the listener, and Peyto hated to be wrong about his listener's linguistic ability.

Peyto got no satisfaction from Schell that day, but he persisted, bothering the captain whenever he could get him alone. Captain Schell contrived to avoid such occasions as the days wore on. The ships sailed under increasingly clouded skies. Yan was content to wait and let Peyto try to pry out the information; now that they were traveling, he felt little need to press for information; he was content to wait upon new developments. Even had he felt a need to ask questions, those who might have the answers of most interest to him were aboard the *Grace*, and there was no communication among the ships except the thrice-daily reports between their captains; and those used coded horn blasts, not designed to convey subtle information. There would be time enough for questions and answers when they reached their destination. Now was a time for peace and reflection.

But someone had a different idea of the opportunities of the voyage, as Yan learned when a spar came crashing down through the rigging and nearly crushed him. Someone had pulled a belaying pin and loosened a crucial line, but none of the crew had seen anyone near the vital pin and knot. Had it not been for the previous attempts, Yan would have thought it an accident.

"The attempt with the sisstrecht was contrived so that—in the absence of immediate witnesses—the beast's attack might have appeared to be a chance occurrence," Peyto pointed out.

A point, Yan conceded. The slit stitching on Yan's saddle girth would have looked like an accident as well.

Yan was discussing the latest attempt with Teletha when Peyto burst into the cabin that they shared with Captain Namsorn and Captain Schell.

"Schell has as much as admitted it," Peyto announced breathlessly. "Our destination is *not* Sharhumrin! It never was!"

Peyto sounded mortally insulted. Teletha smiled surreptitiously at Yan. Peyto's announcement was not a surprise; Yan had never developed expectations concerning their destination the way Peyto had. Peyto's outraged attitude might have angered one or both of the captains, so Yan was glad neither was present. He was even more glad of the captains' absence when Peyto made his next breathless announcement.

"Kerandiri and his gaggle of priests have lied to us!"

13

"HOW HAVE THEY LIED TO US?" Yan asked. Certainly the priests had withheld information and shaded the truth, but Peyto was acting as if he had uncovered deliberate and bold untruths.

"I certainly never heard them say that we were bound for Sharhumrin," Teletha said. "You've been counting too hard on your wishes being real. Wake up! There haven't been any lies."

"Haven't there?" Peyto sniffed. "They got Yan to agree to go with them by promising to tell him where the bone artifact came from." Peyto turned his attention to Yan. "Would you be surprised to learn that the artifact is more of a mystery to them than it is to you?"

Yan frowned. "Are you saying that they have no idea where it came from?"

"They had it of a bregil trader who refused to tell its origin," Peyto announced. "We should have known from the start that they meant to deceive us. Would Schell hide the fact that he is a *staliarm* man if they did not harbor some evil intent?"

"First of all, there is no reason to think that there is evil about," Teletha said. "Even if there were, why assume it is directed at us?"

"They have tried to kill Yan."

"Now you *know* that the villain was an islander?"

"The only Kolviners who accompanied us are Sir Kopell and his men, and they are aboard the *Grace*. They could not have arranged the falling spar from there; therefore, the villain must be one of the islanders. He is probably acting under orders from Schell."

"Now hold on there!" Teletha shouted.

"No, you hold—"

"Be quiet, the both of you!" Yan demanded. A ship was a small place, and sound carried far. They didn't need the kind of trouble Teletha and Peyto's argument could bring. "If you wish to discuss the matter, discuss it quietly."

Teletha and Peyto both found that sulking was a more suitable course of action. Yan decided that the air on deck would be fresher and more congenial. The confinement and uncertainty of the voyage were making everyone testy.

But being on deck did little for Yan's mood. The seamen went out of their way to avoid passing near him, and often he saw them making the sign of the Triad in his direction when they thought he wasn't looking. Yan retreated to the quarterdeck, telling himself that the view was better up there.

The skies were clouded, as they had been for days now. There was a foreboding feel to those lowering clouds, something like what one felt when a storm was passing in the next valley over. Threok showed no distress or expectation of bad weather. Yan was willing to grant that the bregil sailing master had a better knowledge of the ways of the sea than he did; so if Threok was not expecting a storm, Yan shouldn't have any cause for concern. But the clouds still troubled Yan; there was something about them that just did not seem right. He stared at them for hours, the subtle agitation that they caused growing within him.

As the light grew less, he puzzled over the bruised

look that the sky had taken on the horizon. Too dark for sunset. Too solid for a storm. He didn't understand what he saw, but found that it inspired dread in him.

"Master Threok, what is that on the horizon?"

Threok didn't answer, even when Yan asked again.

"It's the Wall," said a seaman standing at the foot of the companionway.

The Wall. Yan had never been much interested in the lore of the sea, but he had heard of the legendary Wall at the heart of the Sea of Storms. He had never expected to see it, though; prudent sailors steered clear of the Wall. The tales said that the Wall was a place of darkness from which came all the tempests that ravaged the sea. The sky before them certainly looked menacing enough to be such a thing.

"Is that where we are bound?" Yan asked the seaman. The man looked up at Yan with frightened eyes, then glanced at Threok. He seemed to want to say something, but didn't have the courage for it. Yan went to the bregil sailing master. "Well, Master Threok, do we sail to the Wall?"

Threok took his eyes from the horizon and turned them to Yan. For a moment he said nothing. Then, "No ship I've ever heard of has sailed to it and returned. One can't rely on sun and stars under these skies. The Wall makes a good mark for navigation, though, eh?"

And with that remark, Threok started shouting orders to bring the ships about. They turned away from the dark horizon and sailed away from the Wall for the rest of the day and on into the night. Sometime near morning, Yan felt the *Handmaiden* change course again. Yan had become accustomed enough to the ship's feel to know that they hadn't turned completely around; no doubt, Threok was making some adjustment.

The day dawned brighter than the last; the sky ahead seemed freer of clouds; they had a good wind on their starboard quarter. By the time Horesh's cloud-dimmed glow was overhead, the sky on the horizon ahead was clear.

Not long after the midday meal, the lookout cried that he saw land. Seamen and passengers crowded the rail, straining for a sight of the land, but it was hours before the distant coast was visible from the deck. Threok ordered the flotilla onto a course running along the coast, well out from the shore. Squinting at the distant shoreline, Yan saw nothing of note. The excitement among those at the rail wore off, and they began to wander away to their work or to other amusements. Clearly, the drabness of the shore was not due simply to his weak eyes.

The lookout called something that Yan did not understand, and, before he could ask Threok what it meant, the bregil was past him and headed for the rigging. Threok joined the lookout in the topcastle and scanned the water ahead of them with his spyglass. When Threok returned to the quarterdeck, he called for an adjustment in the ship's course. All he would say to Yan's questions was, "You'll see."

What Yan saw was a current of dirty-looking water making a separate stream in the ocean.

Threok turned the ships into that stream, and for three days they crept along the coast, moving slowly against dark, brownish water that seemed to hold them back. The air grew hot and damp. Most of the seamen discarded their shirts. The soldiers were not quite so barbaric, though they did leave off their coats to go about the ship in their shirts. In deference to the heat, Yan abandoned his magician's robe, borrowing shirt and trousers from Schell.

It felt strange to be dressed in islander style again. Schell's shirt drooped from Yan's narrower shoulders and the captain's pants were too short in the leg, leaving an expanse of bare shin between pant cuff and boot tops. Aside from the boots, the only items Yan retained from his somber magician outfit were the gloves; despite the way they made his hands sweat and itch, he thought such a small discomfort better than displaying his scars. The ensemble gave him a scarecrow appearance, and he knew it, but he was more comfortable than he had been in his imposing but confining robes.

Schell paced the quarterdeck each day. He, too, had doffed his coat, and the dark sweat stains on his linen shirt were signs of his discomfort. The slight sea breeze offered little relief from the heat. Like most aboard, Captain Schell's mood had grown darker, his temper shorter. "Well, Master Threok?" he asked at noon of the third day of creeping along the coast.

"There," said Threok, pointing.

"What am I to see?" Schell asked.

"A river mouth," Threok said.

Yan squinted in that direction, but he could see nothing except a solid line of rocky shore. Only when he borrowed Threok's spyglass did he see what he was supposed to be looking for: a darkness, hinting at an opening in the wall of vegetation that crowned the top of the rocky shore. He saw a sparkle of stone that suggested something more than a minor undulation in the rock walling the shore. But a river mouth?

Yan handed back the spyglass. "Are you sure?"

"You'll see," Threok assured him.

They sailed closer, and Yan saw that his eyes had played him tricks. The coastline curved away and then back, bringing a more distant bluff in line with a nearer one so that they appeared to be a continuous wall of rock. In reality, the rock formations were far apart, bastions guarding a bay. At the head of the bay, the mouth of a great river emerged.

At Threok's direction, the ships turned into the river. *Mannar's Handmaiden* led the way, as she had throughout the voyage. As the ships progressed up the river, the steep walls of rock stood less tall, their summits coming closer to the water. Their crowns of plants and trees grew denser away from the ocean wind. When the bare rock dwindled away, the dense vegetation huddled at the river's edge and obscured the banks. The ships might have been traveling on a wide road through a forest, save that it was water beneath the ships' keels and not dirt. At the prow, a seaman called out the water's depth in a slow rhythm as he cast forth the lead line and the weight pulled the knotted line through his hands.

Yan didn't know the ships' draft; that was the sailing master's business. The river would be navigable. Threok knew what he was doing. At least, Yan hoped he did.

The passengers grew nervous, many making the sign of the Triad. A few of the soldiers dug out and donned their buff coats. More gathered their weapons to hand. Even Teletha donned her sword and tucked a pistol in her belt.

"You never know," she said. "It's a strange place."

It *was* a strange place. Most of the lush vegetation was new to Yan's eye, and he was intrigued by the few tantalizing glimpses he caught of creatures by the shore or flitting through the trees. Once he saw a leathery-winged shape flap explosively from a tall tree, and was suddenly grateful that the soldiers had armed themselves. The flying creature had looked much like one of those terrible lizard bats the Kolviners called mortfleigers. Such beasts had attacked Baron Yentillan's keep during the assault that had opened Yellow Eye's invasion.

The river narrowed and twisted back on itself, but never did it become so tight that the shore came closer than a hundred yards. The call from the prow varied, yet the depth of the water seemed sufficient to Threok; he rarely called for the steersman to modify course and seek a deeper channel.

Rocky outcrops began to appear, thrusting through the greenery on the starboard bank. Before long, a new wall rose from the river edge, and they sailed past banded rock half as high as the *Handmaiden*'s mainmast.

"Spire ho!" came the call from the topcastle.

The lookout pointed ahead. Some of the seamen climbed the lines for a better look, leaving places at the prow open to the curious passengers, who rushed forward and jostled for a place at the rail. Though Threok remained on the quarterdeck, Yan and the rest went forward. What had prompted the lookout's shout was in plain sight: some kind of structure sat atop the cliff.

"It's a tower!" someone shouted.

The tower sat guard at the sharpest bend in the river they had yet encountered. The shape of the tower was disturbingly familiar to Yan; he had seen pictures of others like it. The dark, smooth stone gleamed in the light.

"I see no one," said someone.

"Is it deserted?" Peyto asked.

Yan hoped so.

Teletha pointed. "Something flashes upon it."

"Weapons?" asked Namsorn. "Armor?"

"A signal of some sort, I think," Schell said. He was studying the tower through a spyglass.

"A signal?" Yan had thought it might be; there was a rhythm to the flashing. "To whom?"

No one had an answer, but Captain Namsorn made sure that any soldier who had not put on his buff coat or gathered his weapons did so now. Namsorn even unlocked the chest that he kept in the cabin and distributed the arquebuses therein to the soldiers. To each arquebusier, he handed a belt from which dangled a powder horn and a dozen stoppered, wooden tubes; each tube contained a lead ball and enough firepowder to propel it. Soon the acrid smell of burning slow match hung in the heavy air.

On the quarterdeck, Threok gave the orders to bring *Mannar's Handmaiden* around the bend of the river. Much to Yan's relief, they passed the tower without incident. A more general feeling of relief spread when the river widened a bit; having the river wider somehow felt safer.

To starboard, the cliff face grew taller, making a wall of rock. Ahead, there was a smaller channel bearing off to port while the main channel bent away around the cliff to starboard.

"Look there," a soldier shouted, beating the lookout's cry by half a heartbeat.

Yan saw what had been screened by the trees on the cliff top as the *Handmaiden* moved forward. A fortress-city stood upon the summit of the cliff. Crenellated walls ran along the edge of the rock face. Dark embrasures pitted those walls at regular intervals, suggesting a lower gallery beneath the parapets. The roofs of buildings could be seen above the tops of the walls and towers that guarded each of the angles in the outer fortification. No standards or banners flew from the towers, and no one was visible on the parapets.

Who would build such a fortress-city here in the wilderness?

"What do you make of it, Master Tanafres?" Schell asked, handing Yan his spyglass to use.

Yan looked. The architecture was not what he expected, especially after seeing the first tower. The walls and the buildings didn't look at all like those pictured in the drakkenree cave paintings. "The roofs have strange cants and decorations. And those sloped towers. I've never seen the like," Yan replied.

"I have," Peyto said. "Those towers look like the bastions at the gate of the bregil mine on Merom."

"They do, don't they?" Schell said. "But that place is little more than a village, and built under the mountain at that. This place is large enough for hundreds, maybe thousands, to live."

"I thought bregil never built towns open to the sky," Teletha said.

"Not in the empire," Peyto said. "But these towers are bregil work."

"A wonder," Teletha said.

A wonder indeed. But was it a wonder that Threok had brought them here?

"Master Threok," Schell called as he strode toward the quarterdeck.

"We're here, Captain," Threok called back. "No need to fret."

"We need to have words, Master Threok."

Schell didn't sound pleased. Yan guessed that the ever-informative Threok hadn't told Schell the nature of their destination.

"First things first, Captain," Threok said. He gave orders to his crew. The *Handmaiden* hove to and dropped anchor. The *Grace* slid up into the *Handmaiden*'s shadow and did the same. The *Breath* drifted a little farther from the cliff before dropping her anchor.

Just as Schell and Threok began to have their words, men along the rail began to point. Like everyone else, Yan looked.

At the base of the cliff upon which the fortress-city sat, a stone wharf thrust out into the river. From behind that construction a small boat emerged. Oars dipped in unison, propelling the craft toward them.

So the fortress-city was not deserted.

"They're all monkeys," one of the soldiers said.

The insulting soldier's eyes were good, even if his tact was deficient. All of the dozen or so people aboard the boat were bregil. And all wore armor. It was perhaps only because a dozen bregil seemed to offer no threat to three ships that no one opened fire on them.

Or it might have been the round, dark snouts of cannon that now showed in most of the embrasures of the fortress walls.

14

YAN STARTED WHEN A LOUD BANG resounded from the port side of the *Handmaiden*. To his relief, it was not the report of a gun, but the slam of wood on wood. A gangway, run out from *Mannar's Grace*, had landed on the rail of the *Handmaiden*. Several of *Handmaiden*'s seamen scurried to secure the gangway. They hadn't finished their job before Ley Nensk, captain of the *Grace*, was across, eager for his own look at what was captivating the attention of the *Handmaiden*'s crew and passengers. Captain Nensk elbowed his way to the starboard rail. He took one look at the crew of the small boat approaching the *Handmaiden* and turned suspicious eyes on Threok.

"Your friends?"

Abandoning the rail, Threok chuckled. "Not my friends. Not these."

Yan thought he caught a hint of resignation in Threok's voice. Could the bregil be hiding something? Of course he could. The real question was: what was he hiding? Namsorn and Schell were speculating about the bregil on the boat and about the nature and ownership of the city; clearly they were as much in the dark as Yan. But Threok was showing very little curiosity—a curiosity in itself, under the circumstances—and most of the other bregil aboard were looking to Threok as if they were expecting something.

By Einthof, Prince of Knowledge and Lord of Secrets, Yan wished he had spent more time studying bregil! Yan knew very little about the tailed men. Bregil were a minority in the empire, even more so in the coastal kingdoms, and Yan had little experience with them. His greatest contact had come through Yellow Eye's hillmen allies, who were barbaric primitives and quite unlike Threok and the bregil sailors. Or were they so different? Yan remembered how easily Threok had blended in among the drakkenree's hillmen bregil slaves. On the other hand, the bregil of Yan's home island of Merom were renowned as miners of great skill and as artisans of surpassing craft. They took little part in the governance of the island or of the empire as a whole. He vaguely remembered something about independent bregil kingdoms somewhere that were allies of the empire. A kingdom allied with the empire would hardly be primitive, and its people certainly not barbaric. The bregil of the empire were civilized. But what were bregil like when there were no merin around? Was a bregil's civilized manner only appearance? Or worse, how much of such civilized manner was false assumptions on the part of a merin like Yan?

This was not the time for pondering the nature of bregil. Kerandiri, Sir Kopell, and their entourages began to file over the gangway from the *Grace*. And among them was someone who was not supposed to be present: Jerr. Young Martello, looking more personally than professionally proprietary, crossed at Jerr's side, steadying her.

For a moment, Yan wasn't sure he was seeing correctly. Surely he had to be mistaken. But he wasn't. Jerr avoided his stare, apparently finding the deck of the *Handmaiden* intensely interesting.

Yan yielded his place at the rail to one of the newcomers eager to see what was attracting so much attention. There was time to investigate other matters before the bregil-crewed boat reached the ship.

Handrar did not join the crowd at the rail. Giving Jerr a gentle shove in Yan's direction, he said, "I believe this is yours, Master Tanafres."

The wizard's smile and frivolous manner only increased Yan's annoyance. How could Jerr have been so stupid? "Would an explanation be too much to ask?"

Jerr stood silent.

"Stowaway," Threok said for her.

Yan turned on him. "You knew about this? Why didn't you tell me?"

"There seemed little to be gained in telling you except argument. We were a full day out when Nensk signaled that she was aboard. We were not going to turn back."

Which was what Yan would have requested. Threok was right, Yan would have argued. How was it that Threok knew him so well?

"Come here, Jerr," Yan ordered.

Slowly she did, but she still refused to meet his eyes.

"For now, tell me one thing," he said. "Did you go aboard the *Grace* of your own will?"

Jerr struggled to speak but seemed unable to find the right answer. Martello stepped up and spoke for her.

"Jerr stowed away out of concern for your welfare, Master Magician. She knows that she is only an apprentice, but she wanted to do what she could to help you in this adventure. It took a lot of courage for her to do as she has done. She had never been aboard a ship before. She meant no defiance."

"How is it you know her mind better than she does? No, don't bother answering, Master Martello." Yan reached out and laid a hand on Jerr's shoulder. "Go to the cabin with the red door and wait. We will have words later."

She said nothing, just swallowed, nodded, and did as she was told. Yan supposed that was for the best. Had she said anything, he would have told her then and there what he thought of her stupidity, likely embarrassing her before her champion. And she would have cried; he could see that she was ready to. They both would have embarrassed themselves before everyone.

To Martello, Yan said, "You had best see Captain Schell. He'll likely have need of you soon.

Sir Kopell had been standing nearby. "Don't go too hard on her. I did something similar once to follow my knight on campaign. He was right to leave me behind, but I didn't know that at the time. I learned. The learning itself was hard enough without any hard words, and he was wise enough to know that. She's a good girl, just young. She'll learn."

Sir Kopell's defense was surprising; Jerr had clearly ingratiated herself with more than Martello during the voyage. "I will take your words into consideration, Sir Kopell."

"I am honored, Master Tanafres." Sir Kopell bowed his head. "I would also be honored if you would have a look at my drakkenree. The priests won't go near him, and I can't talk to him, so I don't know what's wrong, but he's not been eating. He looks sick to me."

Realizing that he hadn't seen the drakkenree cross over to the *Handmaiden* with the rest, Yan looked over to the *Grace*. The saurian stood on the nearboard side, his hands gripping the rail so tightly that his claws dug into the wood. His head was cocked to the side and his snout was raised, his jaws slightly open, as if he listened to the sounds drifting in from the forest. Something about the way the saurian stood seemed brittle and feverish. His skin was dull and his flesh loose. Certainly something was wrong with the drakkenree.

But now was not the time to deal with it. Pointing at the approaching boat, the lookout in the topcastle called something down to Threok. Yan didn't recognize the language, but Threok must have; he smiled, and his tail gave a twitch.

"They're coming alongside," a seaman shouted from the rail.

"Throw down a ladder," Threok ordered.

The rope-and-wooden-rung ladder went over the side. Seamen and passengers moved away from the ladder to make room for the new arrivals. The first bregil aboard wore a mail shirt, and over it a harness of straps and elaborately cut enameled plates. His helmet was a low-domed prawntail design with elaborate swirls of gold inlaid into its surface; Yan recognized a Triadic sun disk and several chalices of Baaliff among the decorative motifs. The harness was the fanciest among the boat's bregil, marking him for their leader, but the hilts of his sword and tail dagger were the plain, worn, leather-covered grips of a longtime campaigner.

The bregil was an ox of a man, bulky and broad-shouldered even for one of his race. Scars on his bare arms and legs showed that he'd clearly seen his share of action, but Yan's eyes were drawn to one particular wound; the bregil's tail was only half the normal length. Yan's trained eye recognized the mark of a cauterizing iron in the scars at the amputation point. The man had a harsh face, consistent with his soldierly manner, and he was not much for the fine points of courtesy and etiquette; he started demanding answers as soon as his booted feet hit the deck.

"Tell me who are you and what brings you here," he said in accented Nitallan. His voice was gravel ground against steel, as harsh as his face.

The abruptness of the bregil sent a round of exchanged glances through the Imperial delegation. The seamen and soldiers who did not speak Nitallan whispered to each other, trying to learn what was happening. Yan was surprised that no one was answering the bregil. Just as he decided to take it on himself, Kerandiri stepped forward and spoke.

"I am Geroy Kerandiri, a priest. At present traveling under the command of his Most Holy Supremacy,

Primate Komall the Fourth. Whom do I have the honor of addressing?"

Kerandiri presumed to know the bregil's religious leanings and offered his ring for the bregil to kiss. The bregil warrior looked at the ring and twitched his tail, but he made no move to kiss it. While the tableau held, two more bregil came over the rail to stand at the first's back. They wore prawntail helmets and mail shirts, but not the plate and leather harness. One, who wore enameled vambraces, was likely a lieutenant. That one took in the scene and whispered something into the first bregil's ear.

"I am Captain-general Lorm," the first bregil said, naming himself commander of *someone's* military forces.

Kerandiri withdrew his hand without comment and made a formal bow of greeting. "And to whom do you give service, Captain-general?"

"That is not important." Two more bregil came over the rail as Lorm said something, in a language unknown to Yan, with a vehemence that suggested an oath of some kind. It wasn't an order to action; his soldiers remained where they stood. Lorm pointed at Kerandiri. "I do not come here uninvited. *You* do. You do not belong here. You will leave if you do not answer me well."

"We will be happy to answer the questions of the rulers of this land, Captain-general. But you must understand that we have many questions of our own. Indeed, it is questions that bring us here."

"What questions?" Lorm asked.

"They are as varied as they are many. The first, however, is one that you could answer if you were so kind. Pray, in the name of Great Horesh, by what name do you call this place?"

Lorm eyed Kerandiri suspiciously. "How can you be here and not know that?"

Threok stepped from the back of the crowd. "I had something to do with that."

"You!" Lorm snarled.

"None other." Threok's bregil smile, which looked so much like a snarl, was on the edge of becoming a real snarl.

Lorm spat on the deck. "We should have taken your head instead of—"

"Should have," Threok interrupted, "could have, but you didn't. Too late now."

"Not too late at all." Lorm turned to one of his men to give an order, but before he could express his wishes, Kerandiri spoke.

"Master Threok is under our protection."

"Imperial protection," Namsorn added.

Aborting his intent, Lorm gave Kerandiri a sideways glare, then swept his gaze across Namsorn and the soldiers. He nodded like a man making a decision. He glowered at Threok. "I see you've found someone to believe your lies."

"I have told these folk no untruths, although I suppose I could start, by telling them that you are trustworthy. You say that I lie. Well, then, is it a lie to say that the name of this place is Jor Valadrem and that people here trade with the drakkenree?" Threok repeated his accusation in Empiric, bringing oaths from the gathered merin.

Lorm barked a scoffing laugh. "I see no drakkenree here, save the one that you are trying to hide aboard the other ship."

"We hide him not," Sir Kopell objected. The knight's Nitallan was atrocious, but he made himself understood.

"Hidden or not, the drakkenree is with you, not me," said Lorm.

"Löm Kerandiri," said Threok. "*Handmaiden*'s mast is tall enough for one to see the top of the cliff. Send aloft someone you trust and ask what he sees before the gates of Jor Valadrem."

"I'll go," Martello offered. At Schell's nod he ran for the lines and scrambled upward.

Threok barely gave the boy time to clamber into the topcastle. "Well, boy, what do you see?"

"I see a gate and stalls. Like at a fair. I see bregil, but no drakken—Wait! I see one! No, two! Yes, two of the lizards. They have a bigger lizard with them, all strapped up and burdened like a sumpter mule."

"Thank you, Galon," Schell shouted. "Stay there and keep a good eye out."

"Aye, sir."

Attention on the deck returned to Lorm. Arching his eyebrow, Kerandiri asked, "No drakkenree?"

"So there are drakkenree here. What matter? This is not your place," Lorm asserted, stone-faced. "You have no business here."

"We wish to speak with the ruler of this place."

"He doesn't want to talk to you."

"Who are you to say?" Threok asked. "Who is running things, anyway? Gessilarm? Krodak? Or did Choshok come out on top?"

Lorm glowered at Threok. "Factor Choshok holds this place."

"Choshok, eh?" Threok turned to Kerandiri. "Offer the emperor's coin. Choshok's attention, among other things, can be bought."

Lorm said something under his breath.

Kerandiri spoke in a placatory tone. "Surely bribes are not necessary to convince Factor Choshok to grant audience to a legitimate emissary from the primate. Factor Choshok is surely a reasonable man and a devout son of the Church. He *is* a follower of the Divine Triad like yourself, isn't he, Captain-general?" Kerandiri didn't wait for an answer. "And as a man of good and honest faith, he could hardly refuse a few moments of time to an emissary of the primate, who has traveled so far on matters of spiritual import."

From Lorm's expression it was clear that he understood some of Kerandiri's veiled threats; refusal would be tantamount to declaring the people of this place to be apostates or worse. Still, Lorm hedged his bets.

"I will ask if Factor Choshok will speak with you, but do not expect an answer you will like."

Kerandiri smiled. "I will give you a letter to carry to Factor Choshok. In it, I will explain our presence and thank him in advance for the privilege of an audience."

Lorm and his men stood silently where they had come aboard while Kerandiri wrote his letter. Lorm accepted the letter and handed it to his lieutenant. The bregil warriors went down the ladder one after another, until only Lorm remained. He had a last demand.

"Do not leave your ships to go ashore."

Captain Namsorn bristled at the peremptory order. "You have no authority to—"

Lorm interrupted the Solonite. "It would be dangerous for any of you to go ashore. There are very dangerous beasts in the jungles. Very dangerous."

"We have faced the great *terriserpens* of the drakkenree unafraid," Zephem said, referring to the giant saurians Yellow Eye had unleashed as beasts of war. "We have no fear of any skulking forest animals."

"Terri—what?"

"Drakkenkain," Yan said.

"Ah," Lorm said. He stepped over the rail and prepared to lower himself. "There are worse things that the drakkenree control. Stay aboard your ships."

15

INSTEAD OF GOING TO MASTER TANAFRES'S CABIN as she had been told, Jerr hid in the shadows of the underdeck, where she could listen to what was happening. She saw the bregil come aboard and heard what was said. She began to think that she had been stupid in wanting to come along—too stupid to think straight and too frightened to believe what she had been told. She'd been afraid that Master Tanafres was abandoning her, going back to the empire where he had come from and leaving behind a stupid girl who wasn't good enough. Why hadn't she believed him when he'd said he was coming back? Why? Because she knew that's what you told people you didn't want to hurt when you were leaving them; because that's what her brother had said before the battle at Rastionne. He had never come back, and she'd been sure that while Master Tanafres wasn't going off to a battle, he wasn't coming back either. And if he never came back, she'd know she was nothing more than a stupid, bumbling farm girl.

She wasn't going to be a farm girl again.

But stupid? Oh, Bright Lady Mannar, she could still be stupid. Why had she believed Master Lennuick when he'd said that the Imperial ships were sailing back to the empire? *Why?* Because Master Lennuick had said what she wanted to hear. Everyone knew that the Coronal

Empire was a place of wonders, where they had boats that flew in the sky, where they made the awesome and terrible firepowder, and where there were wizards that made even Master Tanafres's amazing command of magic seem as poor as Jerr's. Going to the empire would have been an adventure. But they hadn't gone to the empire. Instead they had sailed to a hot and smelly land where tailed apes traded with lizards. Jerr wasn't having an adventure; she was having a waking nightmare.

And she was in trouble for disobeying Master Tanafres again.

She wished she were dead.

She should have stayed with Master Gannedan in Brandespar. She should have known when she was well-off. She didn't need Master Tanafres to scold her; she already knew how stupid and foolish she was.

Of course, it was too late now.

Make light of what you cannot change, or it will drag you down, the grannies always said.

Nothing was the way she thought it would be.

Not that it was all bad. There was Galon Martello. Gallant, handsome Galon, who had rescued her from the bregil seaman who found her stowed away aboard the ship. Brave, dashing Galon, who had stood up to Sir Kopell and Captain Nensk, and kept her from being tossed overboard. Dear, sweet Galon who—

Who was coming toward her, along with many of the people on the deck. The meeting had ended. She shuffled backwards toward the cabin door. No one pointed her out. As best she could tell, even Master Tanafres hadn't noticed her. She couldn't believe her luck. *Thank you, Merciful Lady.*

Jerr slipped into the cabin and found a place to sit, trying to figure out how to look as if she had been there all along, awaiting Master Tanafres's return.

*   *   *

Captain-general Lorm did not return.

Yan took Sir Kopell's advice and said little to Jerr about her foolishness. What was the point? The harm was done. The thing to do now was to see that no more harm was done, and the best way to do that was to keep the girl close, where she could be watched and kept from trouble.

Yan had Jerr carry his satchel across to the *Grace* when he went to examine the drakkenree. She refused to go near the saurian, despite Yan's assurances that there was nothing to fear. Yan gave up and went to the drakkenree by himself.

Illness was something drakkenree warriors found embarrassing; to spare the saurian's honor, Yan spoke to him in the drakkenree tongue. That language involved posturing as much as it did sound. From the corner of his eye, Yan could see Jerr watching with avid eyes as Yan posed and asked, "Are you well?"

The saurian turned dull eyes on him and spoke in Kolvinic. "You still mangle the language, magician. Sew a tail to your ass; it'll improve your talk."

If Khankemeh was going to be that way, Yan saw no reason to spare his feelings. In Kolvinic, Yan said, "You didn't answer my question. Are you sick?"

"Sick of *maah'nn'kun'yee* like you. Sick of bregil. Sick of stink. Sick of boats. When do we get off boats?"

The hostile attitude was nothing new. "I don't know. Sir Kopell said you have not eaten for most of the voyage, and that you could not hold down what you did eat. Is there something wrong with the dried meat?"

"There is no pleasure in it." The saurian's gaze drifted away from Yan, toward the shore. "Do we get off boats soon?"

"I've already told you, I don't know." Forgetfulness was not something Yan associated with Khankemeh. He might truly be ill. "Is something aboard making you sick?"

"Sick? No matter if property is sick."

"If you are sick, I want to try and help you."

The drakkenree's glittering green eyes returned to Yan. "Not sick, hungry."

"Come away, Master Tanafres," Jerr called worriedly.

Yan wanted to dismiss Jerr's concern. He believed that hunger would not drive Khankemeh to attack. The drakkenree had abandoned himself to the role of a slave, or "property" as Khankemeh would have it; the saurian was sworn to attack no one. Honor was important to Khankemeh, too important for him to break his vows. But Yan's convictions weren't enough to overpower his natural reaction to the saurian's toothy jaws. He backed away.

"Go." The drakkenree's eyes were ringed darkly in amusement. "Let me die undisturbed."

Yan gave Khankemeh one last look before recrossing to the *Handmaiden*. The saurian lay on the deck, his muzzle pointed toward the shore. Tail twitching, the drakkenree muttered in his own language. What words Yan understood seemed out of context. Was Khankemeh slipping away from rationality? And if he was, was he going to become dangerous?

Yan sought out Sir Kopell and suggested that the drakkenree be force-fed and that he be watched at all times. The knight listened carefully to Yan's reasoning, but seemed disinclined to go along.

"Will you be the one to stick your hand into the lizard's mouth?" Sir Kopell asked.

Yan conceded that he wouldn't. Sir Kopell promised to do what he could to get the drakkenree to eat and to inform Yan of any changes in the saurian's manner or condition.

Schell suggested that Yan take advantage of the wait by observing the drakkenree and bregil from the ship's topcastle. The captain even offered Yan the use of his spyglass. It sounded like an excellent opportunity, but

Yan took nearly an hour to work up the courage to make the climb. Once he had, and had made his way to the precarious perch high above the *Handmaiden*'s deck, he knew almost immediately that he'd made the right decision.

The scene before the city gates might have been a fair back on Merom. There were merchant tents and craftsmen's stalls and beast pens and stacks of cages for smaller animals and racks of butchered meat. Hawkers wandered about, carrying their goods on poles or in packs and offering sale to passersby. Yan saw pots, both metal and crockery; trussed birds and small mammals; knives; decorated cloth bands; and shiny trinkets exchanged for coin as well as for other goods. For a while he watched a dancer perform for a small knot of onlookers. Yes, it might have been a fair on Merom, save that no fair on Merom had ever been peopled exclusively by bregil and drakkenree. And it was all so peaceable. He wished that he could hear what was said.

Through the glass, Yan could tell that the drakkenree of this place were so like those he had known in Kolvin as to be indistinguishable. He wasn't sure whether to be relieved or not. These drakkenree were not as strange as he had feared.

Had he really been expecting to see the slighter, smaller forms of the ancient saurian wizards that he had encountered in Scothandir? Weren't their kind gone from the world forever? Once, learning that the drakkenree invading Kolvin had a wizard among them, Yan had feared that such creatures had somehow pierced the veil of time to renew their threat to the world, but what Yan had found was Yellow Eye. To be sure, Yellow Eye was a wizard and a drakkenree, but not one of the ancient stock; Yellow Eye's hide was as black as night, but otherwise he looked no different than the saurian warriors who fought for him.

Black scales, it seemed, was a mark of a magician

among the drakkenree, much as mismatched eyes like Yan's often betokened an affinity for magic among the merin. Yan watched carefully for black-scaled saurians among those outside Jor Valadrem, but he saw none. He did see several gray saurians, recognizing them as keepers, the drakkenree who had an uncanny rapport with other saurian creatures. These keepers had no beasts with them that Yan could see. No dangerous beasts, anyway. Yan did observe a keeper among a group of dome-headed saurian pack beasts similar to, but larger than, the beasts that Yellow Eye's minions had sometimes used.

Horesh sank toward the horizon while Yan observed in fascination each new set piece before Jor Valadrem. Darkness gathering on the river forced Yan to abandon his watch. Slowly and carefully he climbed down, his mind full of the sights he'd seen.

Captain-general Lorm had not returned.

That evening, the leaders of the Imperial expedition and the captains of the ships gathered aboard the *Handmaiden* to discuss the situation. Yan attended, as did Sir Kopell, though neither of them said much. There didn't seem much for them to say; the priests and captains talked though. At length. At last they concluded that, for now, they would await developments.

What other course made sense?

After the others had gone to their beds, Yan talked long into the night with Handrar. The scholar wizard had been unwilling to climb into the *Handmaiden's* rigging, so he was dependent on Yan's observations. Yan was impressed by Handrar's astute questioning, especially by the way Handrar had of bringing Yan to clearer remembrances regarding the details of what he had seen. The longer they talked, the more Yan began to believe that he had at last found someone with whom he could discuss his speculations about the drakkenree. Still, Yan's enthusiasm over his new observations, and not just the habit of years of caution, kept the conversation focused

on the drakkenree who traded with the bregil of Jor
Valadrem.

Teletha sat in the outer circle of the evening conference
between the passengers and the captains, as she had for
two days, listening to Threok holding forth on the dangers of the connection between the drakkenree and these
fortified bregil. Each day he grew more eloquent, and
more persuasive; each day she saw more concern and
fear on the faces around her. But for all Threok's
rhetoric, he was a little short on firm facts; all his information seemed to be "it is said" and "or so I've heard."

Did anyone else wonder how he got his information?
Or was he considered a knowledgeable and reliable
source simply because he'd piloted the ships here?

To most of those gathered to discuss the situation, her
opinion was of little import; she was no more than a mer-
cenary bodyguard in hire to Yan. After all, she wore her
Sword Guild band on her sword arm to show she was
employed.

There was, in fact, no contract between her and Yan,
but she was content to have others think differently.
She'd seen all the trouble Sir Kopell had gone through to
go along on the voyage. The pretense of employment
had been the easiest way to ensure her own inclusion
among the travelers. All it had taken was tying on the
band, standing near Yan a lot, and dropping a few choice
words where they could be overheard and misunder-
stood. She doubted Yan had noticed; he had been
absorbed in his own worries and, in any case, he would
just have assumed that she would be included. For all his
knowledge, Yan could be woefully ignorant of the real
world.

Peyto was aware of her deception but, although he
had done nothing to aid her, neither had he betrayed her
secret. Nor would he. She and the clerk had little per-

sonal liking for each other, but they shared a mutual desire to see Yan safe. Each knew the other could offer aid toward that goal. They could and would work together. Over the years, she had learned to respect the clerk, and he her—she hoped.

Being a simple bodyguard, she wasn't asked for her counsel. She was almost an outsider here; only her connection to Yan let her hear what was said. She might have been a pot on the shelf—but then, pots knew all the secrets of the kitchen. She liked knowing secrets.

Threok was supposedly advising Arun Schell and Kerandiri, but the bregil was pitching his words to reach all within earshot. He actually got a few cheers as he concluded, "Sack Jor Valadrem, I say. Root out this nest of dangerous plotters before their villainy hatches and flies across the sea on the dark wings of war."

"Strongly stated," Arun said. "But since we have seen no evidence that the bregil here plot war, the course you suggest may be overly rash."

"Is it rash to crush a known enemy while he is weak?" asked Zephem. Of the priests, the Baaliffite was the only one who had openly sided with Threok in earlier discussions.

"We do not know these bregil to be our enemies," Serent said.

Trust a Vehrite priest to disagree with whatever one of Baaliff's followers said. But in this case, Teletha thought that Serent might be expressing his honest opinion. The bregil of Jor Valadrem weren't hospitable, but enemies? There wasn't any proof.

Zephem looked at Serent with contempt. "These bregil trade with the drakkenree as the empire trades with the coastal kingdoms. They show the ancient enemy the soft silver of coin rather than the hard steel of swords. The actions of these bregil damn them!"

"Metaphorically, I assume, and not theologically," Yan said. "Drakkenree are ordinary beings, not members of the Under Court. It is trade with demons that damns a man, is it not, Löm Kerandiri?"

"As you say."

Yan continued. "Destruction is not the answer. We came with questions, questions that remain unanswered. And I, for one, have found more questions. The drakkenree here are as different from those who invaded Kolvin as a Kolviner is from an islander, perhaps even as different as a merin is from a saü. We need to learn more about the drakkenree with whom these bregil are trading. Attacking the city will not help us learn what we need to know."

Zephem was not content to let it drop. "Who cares if these drakkenree wear different clothes from other drakkenree? All drakkenree are the ancient enemy, foes to all who are unlike them. What more do we need to know?

"A good deal," Handrar answered. "I begin to suspect that this land is more the home of the drakkenree than that of the bregil. Consider, no bregil visitors have been seen to come to Jor Valadrem, only drakkenree. It is the bregil who huddle within the walls and the drakkenree that roam the countryside."

"This might even be the ancestral lands of the drakkenree," Yan added. "There would be much to learn if that is so."

"You have too fine a liking for the lizards," said Zephem.

"Information is what we came for," Arun pointed out.

"Yes, we know, Captain. We did not come for war," Zephem said with a sneer. "How is it that a captain in the Imperial forces is so afraid of fighting?"

"Enough, Fra Zephem," Kerandiri said. "Captain Schell is right to remind us of our principal mission. One learns more with words than with swords."

"How much longer do you intend to wait?" Threok asked. "We've sat here for two days, letting Choshok snub you."

"That is true," Kerandiri agreed. "But Factor Choshok is the legitimate ruler of this place. We are guests in his lands. Without his permission to go ashore, we can do naught but return to the empire and report our failure."

"You cannot mean that, Löm Kerandiri." Namsorn looked appalled. "You know what they are doing in that godforsaken fortress. How can we not punish them for consorting with the enemy?"

"We have the means," said Zephem. "Between them, these ships carry nearly three dozen guns. I count no more than a dozen apertures on any face of the fortress walls." Zephem went on to detail the possibilities for attack. Namsorn backed him up; clearly the two had conferred. "We need only the will to show them they cannot defy us."

"This is a sovereign land," Kerandiri objected.

"It is not ruled by our sovereign," Namsorn said.

"But we are ruled by our sovereign's wishes," Arun Schell said firmly. "The emperor wants answers, and we will get them. If Factor Choshok won't give them to us, we'll get them some other way."

Could Arun have been swayed into taking a belligerent stance? Teletha had thought Zephem and Namsorn's plan chancy at best. They might have more guns, but the bregil probably had heavier guns; they wouldn't know until they were committed, and then it might be too late. She'd thought Arun had a good head for tactics. Was she wrong? Was he now thinking that taking the fortress was a reasonable alternative?

Kerandiri appeared worried by the apparent change in Arun's attitude. "Captain Schell, are you suggesting that we defy Captain-general Lorm's orders and go into the jungle to ask our questions directly of the drakkenree?"

"Something like that," Arun said.

"What about Lorm's threat?" Nensk asked. As captain of the *Grace*, he would be worried about the vulnerability of his ship. "Their cannon are very real."

"Too real," said the captain of the *Breath*.

Clearly Zephem and Namsorn hadn't consulted the ship captains about the assault plan.

"The cannon are very real," Arun said. "But we do not know if Lorm's threat to use those cannon is real. Our ships have cannon as well, and he must know that we will use them to defend ourselves."

"Had he no fear of good Imperial cannon, he would have fired ere now," said Threok. "If we were to strike first, we could silence half his batteries in our first volley."

Arun looked at him. "Are you a master artilleryman, as well as a sailing master?"

"I know how to lay a gun," Threok said. "And I can count."

"The number of guns is not the issue," said Arun. "We did not come here to make war, and I do not yet see a reason to provoke one."

"Going ashore would provoke the captain-general. He hates defiance," Threok said.

"Yes, Lorm warned us against going ashore, but the Nitallan phrase he used literally means 'setting feet upon the ground.' There is much that we can learn without setting foot on the shore."

Arun's strange remark brought frowns of consternation and confusion from those listening. Teletha herself wasn't sure what he meant. Did he mean to sail on up the river?

Arun Schell, secret holder of the emperor's *staliarm*, looked at Teletha and smiled. "In her hold, *Mannar's Handmaiden* carries all the parts of a small airship. And we have an experienced airship captain among us."

All Teletha could do was stare at Arun. An airship?

"What say you, Teletha? Are you ready to take to the skies again?"

Her head was spinning. No one but the Imperial forces had airships. No one but Imperial soldiers used them. If Arun knew that she had been an air captain, Arun knew that she wasn't under service to the emperor anymore. She had left that part of her life behind. Or had she? She realized that she was already considering the technical problems of dealing with launching the airship in the heavily overgrown landscape that lined the river. She saw an immediate obstacle to his plan.

"We'd need a clearing big enough to lay out the bag before it's inflated. That means going ashore."

"Not necessarily," he said almost before she finished speaking. "We can unstep the mast on the *Breath*. There should be sufficient space on the deck to do what is necessary."

"Madness," she said. An airship? Flying again? Madness; all behind her. "It won't work. It's never been tried."

"Some said the very concept of an airship was madness before it was tried."

Could she fly again? With the opportunity being offered to her, she realized just how much she wanted to fly again.

"Want to give it a try?" Arun looked at her expectantly.

Behind him, she could see Yan studying her, watching for her reaction. Did he look disapproving? So what if he did?

"I'll need to see this airship," she said.

The meeting adjourned. Martello brought a lantern, lighting it and closing the horn window before handing it to his master. Arun led Teletha to the hold, and they descended the ladder into darkness, where the glow of the stars and moons above was lost to them. She let Arun lead the way.

Arun held the lantern up so that it shed its light on the lumpy jumble of shapes he said was the airship. Together they pulled back the canvas covering. Teletha's heart skipped at the sight of the wood-and-wicker boat that was the crew compartment of a six-man ship. She ran her hand along the coaming, thrilling at the smooth feel of the varnished drilm wood. The screw hub and crankshaft were swathed in cloth through which grease stains showed black in the lantern light.

"The burner is broken down in the two barrels over there," Arun said.

"She looks wonderful," Teletha said. "But—"

"But there's more to a ship than the hull. The bag's in this case." He kicked the waxed leather shape at his feet, then tossed her a key. "Go ahead, open it."

He held the light for her to set the key in the lock. The mechanism was stiff, but yielded to her pressure. She pulled the hasp free, and with his help shoved up the lid. The smell of oiled silk filled her nose.

Teletha ran her hand along the surface of the fabric. Delight turned to dismay. Grabbing a double handful of the stuff, she heaved out a fold. Scraps of silk and a puff of powdery stuff drifted down.

"Look," she said, poking her hand into the holes in the fabric. Dreams crumble easily. "The bag is ruined."

"What?"

Arun leaned closer to see for himself. The sallow light shining through the horn panel made him look like one of the fierce guardian statues on the citadel gate in Sharhumrin. Teletha had always thought those statues looked as if the models had been half-demon. Arun's expression frightened her a little, but she hoped to be there when he caught whoever had done this.

"It was fine when it was packed aboard in Avenskor," he said.

"It's not fine now. The rats have seen to that." Teletha rubbed at the gnawed edge of the silk. There would be no patching it; the damage was too extensive. "You'll have to find another way to do your reconnaissance."

The fabric's surface felt gritty, and that wasn't right at all. Whatever she was feeling wasn't part of the bag; it shifted away from her touch like sand. She found a drift of the stuff piled against a fold of the silk, scooped some up, and sniffed at the stuff. To try its taste, she licked a bit of it.

"Grain flour," she said with disgust.

"That explains why the rats found it so attractive."

"But not how they got into the case. Waxed leather usually holds them at bay during a voyage, when there are so many other easier things for them to despoil."

Arun nodded. "If the rats had been put into the case, we would have found them when we opened it."

"Unless someone let them out after they had done their work."

"I've the only key," he said.

"There are those who can open locks without needing the proper key."

"Why bother with the flour, then? Locked in, the hungry rats would have eaten the silk without such incentive."

"Attracted by the smell of the flour?"

"Can rats smell so well?"

"I don't know," she admitted. Yan would know. But she had another idea. "Let's take a look at the case."

They did, finding a rat-sized hole in the back, near the bottom. There were dark stains, sticky to the touch, in a couple of spots around the edge of the hole. By smell and taste, Teletha knew this substance, too.

"Honey. No doubt of it now; someone deliberately arranged for the airship's bag to be destroyed."

"And wanted to make it appear an accident," Arun concluded.

Teletha wondered if the someone who had done this was the same someone who had tried to kill Yan. That someone had wanted his villainy to appear accidental. But if this was another attempt to kill Yan, why cripple the airship before it flew?

16

"NO SOLDIERS," the guard said in heavily accented Empiric.

Yan didn't recognize the accent, but he did recognize the attitude; the guard seemed ready to back up his prohibition with action. Teletha echoed Yan's suspicion by slipping her hand onto the butt of the pistol tucked in her belt.

Löm Kerandiri protested at once, arguing with the captain of the detachment which blocked their way. Beyond the dozen armed and armored bregil lay an ironbound door, the only entry into the cliff face that Yan could see. There were other openings, to be sure: narrow slits in the rock overlooking the stone wharf. Yan felt eyes watching from those apertures.

A hundred paces behind the visitors lay the boats they had come in. Yan looked back at them along the open stone quay; the ships' boats looked far away.

Though Horesh was barely above the trees, the day was already hot. Sweat trickled down Yan's flanks beneath his robe. When he'd gotten dressed aboard ship, his magician outfit had seemed appropriate; the priests were in their habits, and Handrar wore his scholar's robes. It was a formal visit, after all. But the skirts of the robe would hinder him should he have to run. He looked again at the slits in the rock. Would he have to?

Could the invitation from Factor Choshok be a ruse?

Kerandiri waved the parchment that a bregil messenger had brought under the nose of the guard officer. The man didn't bother to look at it. "No soldiers," he insisted.

Was the summons to audience a device to get all of the delegation's principals together? If it was, it had almost succeeded. All the priests had come, as had Handrar. Threok represented the captains of the little flotilla; he was accompanied by a pair of armed seamen and a half dozen more waited at the boats. Teletha, Sir Kopell, and his man-at-arms Myskell had come, as had Schell, his aide Martello, and Namsorn. Namsorn had brought ten soldiers, all in buff coats and helmets and carrying arquebuses, as an honor guard for the löm.

Certainly, they were a large group, but a threat to the town above them? With fewer than half of them in armor, and most of the rest unarmed, hardly.

Why this provocation?

"This could be a trap," Teletha whispered.

She was not the only one to think so. One of the Imperial soldiers, using his fellows to screen him, lit a slow match. He passed it around surreptitiously, allowing the others to ignite their matches. The smell of the burning cord was very recognizable, and ten small trails of smoke were impossible to ignore.

The bregil soldiers shifted uneasily and whispered among themselves, while Kerandiri continued to berate the stubborn bregil captain.

Yan felt exposed. They stood in the open, under the dark, unwinking eyes of the slits in the rock wall, easy targets for whatever weapons the watchers held. Yan felt the heavy weight of his *claviarm* against the damp skin of his chest. He was a magician; an enemy could expect him to have a spell capable of blasting any threat. Such an assumption would make him a target. But would they know he was a magician? His *claviarm* was hidden; could they guess from his clothes? Suddenly his elaborate costume did not seem a good idea. He knew no spell to stop arrow or shot.

A harsh grating sound began to emanate from beyond the gate.

"Steady," Namsorn warned his men.

The valves of the gate started to swing inward, to the harsh sound of iron moving across iron. From the darkness within, Captain-general Lorm appeared. He strode up to Kerandiri. Abrupt as before, he spoke.

"You said you came in peace, and in peace Factor Choshok agreed to see you. He has nothing but goodwill for Emperor Dacel, yet you bring soldiers armed for war. Do you show bad faith already?"

"An honor guard is customary," Kerandiri protested.

"Unnecessary here." Lorm grinned. "You may choose. Keep your soldiers and sail away now, or leave them behind and enter Jor Valadrem to speak with Factor Choshok. There are no other choices."

"We will leave the soldiers here to await our return," Kerandiri said. Namsorn started to object, but Kerandiri silenced him. "Our desire to speak with Factor Choshok is greater than the need for an unnecessary honor guard." He turned back to Lorm. "However, I am sure that the provision against soldiers does not extend to the officers and their aides. Such would be a breach of custom so ancient that the denial would offend the gods."

Lorm's half-length tail twitched as he made the sign of the Triad. "The gods have sway where mortals do not."

"Very well. The soldiers shall remain here on the wharf to await our return. Horesh shines upon us, Captain-general. He sees all. We shall entrust our honor to your care."

Yan heard Threok mumble, "Horesh doesn't shine under a mountain," but Threok didn't object when the bregil guardsmen barred the passage of his seamen. He simply nodded to the sailors; they stepped aside and joined Namsorn's soldiers.

Twenty or more armored bregil awaited them inside. An exact count was difficult, for the only light came from the open gate, and most of the chamber was wrapped in shadows. Lorm urged the visitors forward, clearing space for the valves to close, which they did with a screeching clash of machinery. The space around them was darker, but they were not enclosed in total darkness. Burning lamps hung at intervals along the walls. A massive iron bar began to slide across from the left of the gateway, fitting itself into brackets mounted on the doors. As Yan strained to discover the mechanism at work, Lorm leaned over to him.

"You would like to know how the gate operates, wouldn't you?"

"Yes, I would."

"I thought as much." He turned and walked away from Yan, calling for everyone to follow him.

Lorm led the group through a corridor hewn from the native rock of the cliff. The bregil warriors fell in behind. Yan's magesight made good use of the faint lamps, but their dull glow did little to help the ordinary folk, who stumbled and groped in their efforts to match Lorm's pace.

They went up a stairway. Polished wooden railings allowed those unable to see well to feel their way and gauge the steps. Another corridor. Another set of stairs.

All around them there was a faint herbal scent, something in the lamp oil. Was the fragrant odor a normal feature of the corridors or was it something done to disguise recognizable scents?

More corridors, and more stairs, until it seemed that they were making their way through a maze. Generally they progressed upward, but Yan noted that some of the passages sloped downward. Time passed. Yan estimated they still had far to go to reach the level of the clifftop city.

Lorm stopped before a great curving arch. Lamps lined the upper portions, offering more illumination than in any portion of the complex they had seen so far. Beneath the arch, the wall was polished mahogany rather than the hewn stone of the corridor. A double door carved and painted with an elaborate interlaced design stood in the center of the arch. Lorm stepped up to the doors, turned the handles, and shoved the panels open. No light flooded through; the chamber beyond the doorway was no brighter than the corridors they had traversed. They were still deep within the rock of the cliff. Lorm stepped aside from the now open doorway.

"What is this place?" Kerandiri asked.

"This is where Factor Choshok will see you."

Kerandiri did not look pleased. "We are not sneak thieves or pernicious conspirators, to be met in the dark. Why do we not meet him in his palace?"

"You were not asked to come to Jor Valadrem," Lorm reminded him.

"Choshok doesn't want you to see the city," Threok said.

Lorm ignored him. "However, Factor Choshok has graciously consented to a short audience and, in his wisdom, decided to hold that audience here. If you wish to speak with him, it will be here."

"This is inappropriate," Namsorn said.

"You can always return to your ships and sail away," Lorm told him.

"We will speak with Factor Choshok," Kerandiri said, walking past Lorm.

The other priests followed the löm. Lorm stood at the door until all of the visitors entered. He closed the doors behind him, leaving the honor guard outside.

But Factor Choshok was not there to see them. They stood in the great bowl of the chamber and waited.

Yan noted the curving walls of dark stone, smooth here and not rough like the halls through which they had passed. A path of the same dark stone led from the door-way to a dais at the center of the chamber. On the dais sat a throne, unoccupied.

A handful of bregil entered the chamber from the corridor. They were not warriors, but were dressed in clothes of strange cuts, though no one of them looked any more distinguished than another. They hurried past the visitors without a word and took up places behind the throne. Lorm made no introductions, and none of the new bregil offered any. Kerandiri apparently decided to go along. They waited some more.

Something about the construction tugged at Yan's memories. He stepped off the dark stone onto the mosaic of tiles that made up the rest of the floor and looked past the throne. The dark path did not extend past the dais; it ended at or under the elevated area.

"Such precision," Handrar mused, gazing at the domed ceiling. "Have you ever seen its like?"

Once or twice, Yan realized, although in those cases the curve had extended below as well as above the level of the tiles. To Yan's knowledge, only drakkenree ritual chambers achieved such precision of curving form.

The double doors to the chamber opened again, and this time a procession of warriors entered. They wore elaborate armor much like that worn by Captain-general Lorm, though not so fine. In their midst walked a bregil who, by the deference shown him by the other bregil, could only be Factor Choshok.

"Look, they haven't got any armor on their backs," Martello observed.

It was true. The bregil warriors' armor of mail and plates only protected their fronts. Only the necessary straps crossed their backs.

"They must not be worried about getting stabbed in the back," Schell commented in a whisper.

"Have we the same luxury?" Teletha whispered back.

Yan thought that they should have been more concerned

with Choshok than with his warriors' armor; the scowl on
the factor's face reminded Yan of the one his father wore
when interrupted from his work. Choshok seated himself on
the throne and arranged his robe. Lorm positioned the
guards and took a place to one side of the throne while
Choshok exchanged a few words with one of the bregil nearest him. As the factor settled into his seat, that bregil drew
himself up importantly and bawled, "The worshipful Factor
Choshok of Jor Valadrem grants audience. Draw near, you
who would speak, and make plain your cause."

Kerandiri stepped forward and began a flowery introduction, but Choshok cut him off. "I read your appeal,
Löm Kerandiri. There is no need to repeat yourself. Shall
we get down to the particulars?"

"It is not our intention to inconvenience you, Factor
Choshok," Kerandiri said mildly. "To the particulars,
then." At Kerandiri's gesture one of his priests advanced,
carrying a wrapped object. "We carry with us an object
that has raised concerns among many in the empire. We
have been advised that you might know something about
this."

Yan didn't have to see beneath the covering to know
what it was; he kept his eyes on Choshok's face to gauge
the bregil leader's reaction when the package was
opened. He was rewarded by seeing Choshok's surprise,
quickly covered. The factor made a show of examining
the carved bone dome before speaking.

"An exquisite carving, but hardly cause for trouble.
From the skull dome of one of the *vekkanconday*, I think."
Choshok returned the artifact to the care of the priest.
"Do you wish to sell it? I can give you a fair price."

"It was not our intention to sell this artifact," Kerandiri
stated. "However, we do wish to determine its origin and
its maker. You seem to know something about that. Pray,
what is a *vekkanconday*?"

"A beast that the drakkenree use to carry burdens.
Stupid and fractious, especially in rutting season, but

quite strong and able to bear loads that would crush a mule. Being a mass of solid bone, *vekkanconday* skulls inspire many carvers to exercise their talents. But if I say more, you will think me too enamored of this piece, and I will not get a good deal. Will you take a quarter of its weight in silver? There is a certain cleverness to the design that I find mildly intriguing."

"As I said, it is not our intention to sell the artifact." Kerandiri sounded a little irritated; the löm did not like being diverted from what he thought important.

Choshok continued with his dickering. "Actually you said 'was.' Knowing as I do that there is little market in the empire for the eccentric carvings of primitives, I assumed that, having discovered an opportunity to dispose of this piece, you had changed your mind. A mistake on my part. Forgive me if I offended. Still, it is clear that you set some store by this thing you have brought with you. How, pray, did you come to possess it?" Choshok pointedly looked at Threok. "From dishonest hands, I expect."

Kerandiri responded, "Master Threok did bring it to our attention, but he found it among the goods of a curiosity dealer in Learth on Merom."

"He is a liar," said Choshok.

"You are most wise and ever honest, mighty Choshok," Threok said, sounding not at all insulted by Choshok's accusation.

"You will keep silence here," Lorm thundered. "Your word means nothing anymore, so be silent. Baaliff as my witness, under other circumstances we would be meeting in the challenge pit."

"Good dog, Lorm. Nice teeth," Threok said, baring his own teeth.

Lorm snarled and surged forward, drawing his sword. Choshok raised a hand and several of the guards leapt to restrain Lorm. In their grip, he subsided, slamming his sword back into its scabbard. He shrugged off the hands and tails holding him and returned to his place by Choshok's side. Factor Choshok drew himself up and spoke.

"We suffer the presence of this thief and liar only owing to his association with you, Löm Kerandiri. We must believe that you are instructing him in the error of his ways and opening the gods' path of forgiveness to him. However, if *you* cannot curb his tongue, *I* shall see it done."

Kerandiri's eyes narrowed. "Master Threok travels on behalf of our emperor. He is not subject to you at this time."

If he ever was. Threok's bearing had nothing in it of a thief returning to the scene of the crime. It seemed to Yan that Lorm and Choshok were more concerned about Threok's presence than Threok was worried by their insults and threats. Yan wasn't sure that he would have had the courage to walk into the hands of people who were so clearly his enemies, even *with* the emperor's protection. The emperor was very far away.

"Your pet was never subject to me," Choshok said. "Greater pity, that. I could have taught him manners, at the least. I might still teach him some things."

Threok started to reply, but Kerandiri cut him off. "Factor Choshok, we did not come to discuss Master Threok. There are other matters, far more important matters, that concern us."

"Yes, yes. You want to know where your bone trinket came from? In all likelihood, the thing came from the wild lands upriver. I have seen its like before. Things like it are carved by naked lizards, using their own claws because they do not have knives. Once, I think, such things served as signs of the carver's devotion; they were an offering to the gods. Now, they have no purpose."

"What gods would they be offered to?" Kerandiri asked.

"The Celestial Court, of course. What others are there?"

Kerandiri didn't answer. Yan had debated with Kerandiri enough to recognize that the priest was considering his next question. Choshok didn't give him a chance to ask it.

"I know why you have come, hiding martial concerns behind priestly robes, and I tell you that there is no threat here to your emperor or his empire. The drakkenree of the forest are not your ancient enemy. They are primitive creatures, debased from the ancient ones, and their ambition is as decayed as their greatness. They are a stagnant backwater in the river of history. There is nothing in this country for you to concern yourselves with."

Kerandiri pounced on the opening Choshok had left. "Then you can have no objection to our making contact with them."

"No," Choshok snapped. "That is not allowed. It is too dangerous."

Kerandiri feigned confusion. "But you said the drakkenree are no threat."

"Not to the empire, no. But to foolish folk wandering in the wilds hereabouts, there are many dangers. I do not choose to explain to Emperor Dacel how his ambassadors were eaten by the local wildlife."

"We can protect ourselves," Zephem asserted, earning a sour look from Kerandiri for his interruption.

Choshok did not react to the shift in speakers. "You have no idea of what you would encounter out there."

"Exactly why we must see for ourselves," Kerandiri said.

"No," Choshok said.

"We don't need your permission," Namsorn said.

"Be careful, soldier," Choshok said. "Your emperor's writ does not run here. This realm is under the protection of King Pasturm of Salsanadect."

"Who?" Teletha whispered to Yan.

"I've never heard the king's name, but I seem to recall

Salsanadect from an old chronicle. It's not one of the coastal kingdoms. One of the Jelnorek Fiefs, maybe?"

"Either way, the king is no more here than is the emperor."

"Meaning?"

"Your king's writ is only as strong as those who enforce it," Namsorn said, answering Yan as well as responding to Choshok. "The empire is where its captains go."

"A threat, Captain Namsorn? You are in no position to make threats." Choshok turned to Kerandiri. "Since your folk express their hostility so freely, I think that there is little more to be gained by speaking with you. We will see that your ships are reprovisioned. Go home. Tell your emperor that he has nothing to fear from this place or from the rulers of Jor Valadrem. We are not your enemies, but we do not desire your presence. I tell you now that, should you remain within our realm and defy our request that you leave, we will hold you responsible for the consequences. Any unpleasantness that might arise will be the result of your own stubbornness and foolishness. All the gods as witness, you have been warned."

Schell bowed to Kerandiri. "Most holy löm, perhaps it would be wisest to withdraw and consider the wisdom of Factor Choshok."

Kerandiri nodded. It seemed that the audience was over. Were the voyage and all the waiting going to be for nothing?

Threok tapped Yan with his tail and whispered, "Ask the fathead on the throne about the bone wizard."

Zephem was close enough to overhear. "What is this of which you speak, Threok?" he asked "Who is this bone wizard? Is he a necromancer?"

Zephem's voice was louder than Threok's. When the Baaliffite said "necromancer," several heads turned in their direction, including that of Löm Kerandiri. Factor

Choshok was in conversation with his advisors; apparently, they took no note of Zephem's words. Kerandiri, however, did.

"What is this, Fra Zephem?" he asked in a hushed tone. "Who speaks of the forbidden?"

"The sailing master bid the wizard Tanafres to inquire after a necromancer."

"The Wizard of Bones. It's just a name," Threok protested.

"A descriptive name?" Kerandiri asked.

"I suppose so. I really don't know."

"Bones and magic have old and infamous associations," Kerandiri observed.

The löm referred to the regime of corrupted wizards who once had ruled most of the known world with their necromantic magic. The rule of the necromancers had been so terrible that the memory still lingered after nearly a millennium, fueling the Church's distrust of magicians.

"We could do as Master Threok suggests and ask Choshok about this bone wizard," Yan said. "The reference may have nothing to do with necromancy."

"How can you say that without evidence?" Zephem asked. "The name is plain enough."

"As easily as you can accuse this unknown magician without evidence." Yan found Zephem's narrow-mindedness disturbing; if the rest of the priests took the same view, they might stir themselves up into a fervor, ready to find any magician a dark magician. It had happened before. He tried to sound calm and reasonable as he spoke. "Look. The artifact is bone and attuned magically, but it has no hint of the dark about it; Löm Kerandiri said so himself. Maybe the carving is one of this wizard's creations. Maybe this bone wizard earned his name because he crafts his artifacts in bone. No more, no less."

"Perhaps it would be wise to inquire, most holy löm,"

Serent said. "Factor Choshok seems a man with a firm belief in the gods. He cannot begrudge us an inquiry into this matter."

Choshok did, in fact, begrudge further talk, an attitude he went on to explain at great length. Neither had he cared for the delegation's sudden hushed conference in the middle of his audience room. He went on at length about that as well. However, eventually he did speak of the Wizard of Bones, dismissing any attempt to associate the wizard with necromancy. He concluded, "The Wizard of Bones is a myth, a goblin story to frighten small children. No more than that."

Choshok's denial was strangely fervent for something he claimed trivial.

"Are you saying that there is no connection between the artifact and this Wizard of Bone?" Kerandiri asked.

"Fathead Choshok never said any such thing," Threok said under his breath. "He's not utterly stupid."

By which statement Yan inferred that Threok believed that there *was* a connection.

Choshok clarified his statement. "What I said was that you would waste your time were you to chase such a phantom. And I have wasted my time speaking with you. We have no more business. Return to your ships, determine what provisions you need, and bring the list to my victualler, who shall wait for your list on the wharf. Once you have the supplies, I expect you to sail away. Is this understood?"

"Your wishes are clear, Factor Choshok." Kerandiri bowed, beginning the formal ritual of departure.

They were escorted back to the wharf, where they emerged into the heat of the day. The soldiers and seamen they had left behind were plainly relieved to see them all returned in safety.

They rowed back to the ships.

17

LITTLE WAS SAID ABOUT THE WIZARD OF BONES until everyone
was back aboard the ships, but it turned out that Yan was
not the only one who didn't believe Choshok's protesta-
tions that the wizard did not exist. The factor had been too
quick to deny the wizard's existence, too hollow in his
mockery of the concept. Handrar found Choshok's
attempt to buy the bone artifact suspicious and suggested
that Choshok had recognized something about the carving.
To him it was clear that there was a magician who worked
in bone, even if that person was not the fabled Wizard of
Bones. Fra Serent pointed to the *vekkanconday* and said that
unless such beasts roamed elsewhere, the artifact had to
have been made nearby, leading him to believe that the
Wizard of Bones must reside somewhere nearby.

"All supposition," Schell said.

Since Threok had brought up the existence of the wizard, he was questioned. He told them that the Wizard of
Bones was supposed to be a drakkenree mage who lived
in the upriver country. The wizard had long been a legendary figure hereabouts, and stories about him had been
the reason Threok had connected the bone artifact with
Jor Valadrem. The bregil had brought them here because
he believed that the artifact came from somewhere
nearby.

"Where exactly, I can't say," Threok admitted with his tail-curling bregil shrug. "I'll wager Choshok knows. Why not knock Jor Valadrem's walls down on Choshok's head and beat the truth out of him?"

Attacking the fortress-city seemed to be Threok's answer to everything. Schell said, "We did not come here to attack the city."

"Which does not preclude other choices of action," Kerandiri said.

The trend in the evidence was undeniably pointing inland or upriver. That seemed to be where the answers would be found. Unfortunately, they were being denied permission to seek those answers, and Schell was apparently in agreement with that prohibition. Kerandiri began an argument against Choshok's demand that they return at once to the empire. The other priests stood with the löm—as did Handrar and Namsorn. Yan felt sorry for Captain Schell, but that didn't keep him from joining the others in urging the flouting of Factor Choshok's order to leave.

The arguments over what to do if they *didn't* leave went on. Handrar bowed out of the discussion and disappeared for a while. He returned and announced that he had sensed a link between the carving and a source of magical energy somewhere upriver.

"Is that enough for you, Captain Schell?" he asked.

Schell wanted Yan to confirm Handrar's findings. Yan assessed the artifact anew, concentrating on associational and contagious resonances, but what he sensed was ambiguous.

"There is something, but I'm not sure what," he said.

"But you can sense enough of the nature of the magic in the carving to know that it needs to be explored," said Handrar.

Yan nodded. "I think it does need to be explored."

"Then the wizard must be sought out," Handrar concluded.

Namsorn was willing to take his soldiers into the wilds to do so. "We need not let a jumped-up mountain monkey command our actions. We are servants of the empire."

"More importantly, we must stand to our duty to the gods," Zephem said. "Having caught the scent of necromancy, we must determine the guilt of the unknown wizard. We cannot look the other way. We have uncovered a connection to a festering evil. It must be traced to its source and eliminated!" The Baaliffite remained unswayed by arguments that the reference to bone might be coincidental. "This drakkenree evil must be stamped out!"

"The necromancers fought the drakkenree," Yan pointed out. "According to some legends, those we call dark wizards turned to necromancy to combat the saurians. It is said that they hoped to use a magic unknown to the drakkenree to defeat them. The wizard who made the carving is almost certainly a drakkenree. Doesn't that seem to you to be contradictory?"

"Corruption spreads," Zephem insisted.

Zephem's statement spurred the other priests to press their arguments on Captain Schell. Kerandiri held back from the discussion. Yan noted that the priests directed their arguments to Schell; now that they had come to a sticking point in the expedition, there was no longer any pretense about who had the final say in where the expedition went.

Schell listened until the storm of words blew itself out, then made a pronouncement. "We will test Factor Choshok's resolution."

"I'll have the firepowder kegs opened," Threok said, grinning.

"You will not," Schell snapped. "This is not yet a matter for cannon. I want you to take us up the river, Master Threok."

"We won't get far," Threok predicted.

"Before Factor Choshok orders the guns to fire on us?" Handrar asked.

"He just might do that," Threok said.

"And he might not," Schell said. "We'll soon know. Master Threok, prepare to sail."

"As you order." Threok turned away sullenly and went to give the orders.

Namsorn addressed Schell. "Should we not be prepared to return fire?"

"They can see our decks from the walls. Preparing the guns might provoke them. If guns are necessary, we can be ready in short order; the ships' crews are good."

"Still, I think—"

"*I* think your authority concerns the foot soldiers, Captain Namsorn."

Namsorn appeared taken aback by Schell's abruptness.

"Excuse me," Kerandiri said, stepping away from the two captains. "If we are to travel on the *Grace*, we must go across before they stow the gangway."

Kerandiri departed, followed by his priests. Namsorn was not finished, however.

"The safety of the troops is my concern in this matter. As is the safety of all three ships. Sorigir Renumas will not take kindly your endangering his resources, nor will he condone your placing the holy person of Löm Kerandiri in unnecessary danger."

"As to Löm Kerandiri, he knows the dangers as well as you and can speak for himself. As for the 'resources' you mention, Sorigir Renumas may have paid the cost for much of this expedition, and he may be responsible for *your* position on this expedition, Namsorn, but *I'm* here by the emperor's command, and by that command those 'resources' are mine to use in the emperor's service. I answer to the emperor. Ultimately you do as well, and you would be wise to remember that."

Namsorn stiffened and spoke in a cold voice. "Ultimately I answer to no *man*, Captain Schell. My accounting is to the Great God. *Him* alone, Captain Schell. You would be wise to remember *that*, and your own ultimate accounting as well."

"Thank you for reminding me, Captain Namsorn. I hope you take your command and its responsibilities as seriously as you take your religion."

"Nearly, Captain Schell, nearly. May you be guided by Horesh's light to the wisest course."

"As the god*s* will, Namsorn," Schell said, emphasizing the plural noun, deliberately spurning the Solonite's monotheistic creed. Schell turned his back on the Solonite's glare.

Yan decided that he was overdue in following the priests' lead in leaving. He found Peyto waiting for him at the companionway.

"So the good Captain Namsorn is beholden to Sorigir Renumas," Peyto said. "Interesting."

If Peyto found the connection interesting, there had to be some political slant involved. "Renumas is chancellor to the Emperor Dacel, isn't he?"

"I'm surprised you remember."

"I may not be much interested in palace doings, but I do have a good memory."

"For things you care to remember." There was no malice in Peyto's gibe. "Memory can be a slippery thing. I myself am reminded of an old saying. 'The truest agents are mirrors of their masters.'"

"Meaning?"

"The traditional meaning is that the best service is given by one who acts as the master would himself. In the present case, if these two are true servants, it would seem all may not be well in the empire."

"Hardly a matter of immediate concern to us."

"The empire is wherever its captains go."

Yan had heard the phrase before, but Peyto's use of it

in this context suggested meanings different from the norm. Something to think about.

"Chain ahead!"

The lookout's call brought Jerr's head around in a futile attempt to see what lay before them. Her place in the waist of the *Handmaiden* let her see the jungle and rocky shore that slid past, without offering any view of what lay ahead on the river. And until that shout, the walls of Jor Valadrem had seemed a more important thing to watch anyway. That was where the cannon were. Despite the fears of the sailors and soldiers, none of the city's guns had fired upon the ships as they moved upriver, for which Jerr gave prayers of thanks. She had thought that, with Jor Valadrem behind them, they were beyond threats. Yet now. . .

"Full up?" Master Threok bellowed at his lookout.

"Full up," came the reply. "And a guard tower."

"If there's a chain, we be blocked. We won't be going no farther," one of the sailors grumbled. He hurried off toward the bow.

Jerr wanted to go, too. She wanted to see what sort of a chain could block a ship, but a look toward the bow told her there was no room for even as slight a girl as she to squeeze through the sailors and soldiers crowded there to see the chain. She could see the top of a forti- fied tower, though. Whatever the chain was, it was guarded.

A perch on the mast or any number of places in the rigging would be high enough to see over the crowd, but she didn't dare climb while the ship was moving. Maybe the quarterdeck? It might be high enough for her to see over their heads, and she was allowed there when Master Tanafres was present. Was he? He was. She hurried toward the stern. As she climbed the companionway, Captain Schell was asking, "Can we break it?"

"Moving against the current?" replied Master Threok. "Are you crazy? These are merchantmen, not rams."

Captain Schell was not so easily daunted. "*Ser* Handrar, Master Tanafres, do either of you have a spell to open the way?"

"Nothing timely," Handrar replied, speaking for both magicians. "Such magics take preparation."

Master Threok ordered all the canvas struck. He turned his steady gaze from the weed-festooned chain stretching across the river's width. He shook his head. "Too fast, still." He ordered out the anchor.

Mannar's Handmaiden slowed to a stop, her prow scarce a dozen yards from the barrier. The other ships were stopped more handily and lay at rest behind the *Handmaiden.* Löm Kerandiri and his priests crowded the foredeck of *Mannar's Grace* and shouted anxious questions across the water. Master Threok and Captain Schell started to explain the situation, but all talk halted at a shout from the fortified tower.

"Your ships may not pass."

"Lower the chain, you misbegotten spawn of baboons," Master Threok yelled back.

The insult didn't bother the hidden person in the tower. "You are denied passage by order of Factor Choshok. Turn about, or you will be fired on."

"Ready to fight now, Captain Schell?" Threok asked.

"No," he replied, staring grimly at the chain as if he might sunder it by an act of will, but Captain Schell was not a magician to do such a thing. "We'll have to go back."

Ser Handrar or Master Tanafres might break the chain, but *Ser* Handrar had said that such magic would take time. Master Threok did not seem to think that there was enough time.

"Back?" Master Threok laughed; it wasn't a pleasant sound. "You've shown Choshok the way your sails are set. He won't take such defiance lightly. Don't be thinking

Choshok will be eager to let us sail away now. You've insulted him; he's got a habit of striking out at those who insult him. We should strike first, before he realizes that this is his best chance to sink us. We're still in range of the guns from the city, you know."

Jerr hadn't realized that. She looked toward the city perched on its cliff top. It seemed so far away. Could the guns reach so far? Why would Factor Choshok shoot at them, anyway? "I thought he wanted us to go away."

"Don't be foolish, girl." Master Threok turned from her to Captain Schell. "Are you as foolish as she, Captain? You don't believe Choshok when he tells you that there is no Wizard of Bones, but you believe that he will let you sail away."

"If they intended to sink us, they'd have fired on us by now," Captain Schell said.

"Maybe." Master Threok didn't sound as if he really believed it. "Choshok's a little slow to act sometimes because he doesn't like to be wrong. Well, you've shown him that he's not wrong to be worried about us. If he would have let us go before, he won't now."

"You speak as if you know him very well."

"Not well enough, but then again, well enough to know he'll want to see the *Handmaiden* and the *Grace* and the *Breath* on the bottom of the river."

Löm Kerandiri shouted over from the *Grace*. "Perhaps if we turn about as they ask, we can depart unmolested. Later we can—"

"Look there!" Master Threok pointed at the fortified tower. "You see that flashing signal? It is too late." To Captain Schell he said, "Your temerity will be the death of us all."

"Do not speak to the Captain in that tone of voice," Galon said.

"I'll speak to him as I please, Martello. There's little reason to be polite to fools."

"Whom are you calling a fool, Threok?" Captain Schell's voice was soft with anger.

"Did you not see the signal?"

"I saw."

"Remember the tower we sailed past on our way up the river? Look over there." Threok pointed at the tower again. "Looks a lot like that one, doesn't it? The tower downriver has a chain barrier as well. The chain will be rising to block passage as soon as they get that signal. What do you think will happen when we reach *that* chain? The *Handmaiden* is the biggest of our vessels and even under full sail she wouldn't be able to break the chain. We will be brought to a stop there, and the current will keep us hard against the chain. We'll get in each other's way. That's when the guns will start from Jor Valadrem and from the tower."

"Why then? Why not now?"

"Since Choshok hasn't ordered his men to open fire on us yet, I'd guess that he thinks he has a better chance of sinking us there. We'll have a harder time replying with our own guns with the current forcing us up against the chain."

"We don't even know this second chain exists," Captain Namsorn said.

"You calling me a liar?" Master Threok asked.

"I wouldn't be the first."

Ser Handrar cleared his throat to gain attention. "Captain Schell, it seems to me that we operate in darkness, so to speak. While there is little I can do about the barrier before us, there is something I might be able to do to shed some light on our predicament. I may be able to determine whether Master Threok's assertion about another barrier is correct."

"That would be useful," Captain Schell said.

"I thought it might." *Ser* Handrar turned Jerr. "Run to the cabin and fetch up my satchel. Don't try to open it; just bring it here."

Jerr looked to Master Tanafres. He nodded. She ran.
She knew the satchel *Ser* Handrar meant; he had carried
it aboard from the *Grace*. When he hadn't gone back
aboard the *Grace* with the priests, he'd had Galon put it
in Master Tanafres's cabin. She knew right where it was.
She wasn't quite as quick coming back as she had been
going; the satchel was heavy. It clanked slightly when
she put it down in front of *Ser* Handrar.

He knelt before the case and mumbled something.
Jerr couldn't tell if it was "thank you," or if the wizard
scholar was saying the cantrip necessary to safely open
the satchel's wards.

"Give the man room, Jerr," Master Tanafres said.

As *Ser* Handrar rummaged through his bag, he said. "I
need a pitcher of water. River water would be best."

Captain Schell sent Galon. By the time he returned
with a dripping jug, soggy rope trailing behind him, *Ser*
Handrar was seated on the deck with a silver bowl, a real
glass mirror, and a wax-sealed pottery flask.

Ser Handrar poured the river water into his bowl, filling
it near to the rim. Unstopping the flask, he poured something oily onto the water. He looked up at the fortified
tower, down at the bowl, and back at the tower. In his left
hand he picked up the mirror, breathed on it, and whispered something to it. Holding the mirror in both hands,
he pointed it at the tower. His gaze shifted between the
tower and the bowl as he adjusted the angle at which he
held the mirror. Finally he seemed satisfied. He closed his
eyes and started an invocation of protection.

Jerr saw a tiny image of the tower reflected on the surface of the water in the bowl.

"Master Tanafres, what is he doing?"

"It's a farseeing ritual," he replied. "He is using the
image of the tower and the river water to set up a similarity. The water is also connected to the river, being a part
of it, and the river connects the sites of the two towers. It
will be interesting to see if it works."

Jerr was fascinated. She'd asked Master Tanafres once if he could see what happened at great distances, and he'd said that wasn't a magic he could do. She had thought he had meant that no one could do such a thing. Clearly she had thought wrong, but being wrong didn't bother her a bit. She watched every move *Ser* Handrar made and tried to remember every word of the chant he sang as he stared into the bowl.

The onlookers waited in silence, listening to *Ser* Handrar's chant. The priests crowded against the rail of the *Grace*, listening even harder. Were they all trying to learn the secret of *Ser* Handrar's magic, as she was? Or were they just in awe of the magic happening before them?

At the last syllable, *Ser* Handrar's shoulders slumped in exhaustion.

Jerr couldn't contain her excitement. "What did you see?"

"I saw the other tower." *Ser* Handrar's voice was dreamy and far away. "I saw a cord of iron stretched across the flow of the river."

"Then it's true," one of the priests aboard the *Grace* wailed. "They do intend to kill us!"

18

"THIS IS INFAMOUS," Kerandiri said.

Treacherous was the word Teletha would have chosen, but as usual no one asked her. She kept her peace since most everyone else seemed to be finding it necessary to offer his own solution to the problem. When the first flurry of panic died down, Namsorn spoke. He was calm and sounded confident.

"We must appear to be unknowing of this perfidy and willing to follow the monkeys' arrogant orders," he said. "Our best chance is to open fire on Jor Valadrem as we approach it. The cowards don't know we are aware of their plan to destroy us; if we stand in the God's favor, they will think us meekly sailing away. We can sail close and catch them unawares. We'll show those monkeys what our good Imperial guns can do. We can blast open their gates and take the city by storm."

Arun Schell shook his head. "We are not here to make war."

"Even if war is made on us?"

"Denying us passage on their river is not an act of war."

"The magician says they are denying us exit as well."

Namsorn glared at Arun when he didn't bother to respond. Namsorn's calm started to crack. "This provocation is an insult to our honor."

"I don't feel my honor insulted."

"Really? I suppose I should be surprised, but I am not. I should have understood long before now that you, too, had hidden loyalties. Woe to the worldly ruler who puts his faith in those who serve his enemies."

You, too, *had hidden loyalties?* To whom was Namsorn referring? An image of the treacherous *staliarm* man Raff Janden leapt to Teletha's mind. Were all the *staliarm* men corrupt? They couldn't be. *Arun* couldn't be. She just couldn't believe that the Arun Schell she knew and joked with was a hidden traitor. But while Teletha was denying to herself Namsorn's implied accusation, the Solonite was still talking.

"You say that your honor is not insulted. What about your emperor's honor? Are you not sworn to uphold that? The burden of your oath weighs lightly on you, if you can stand by and allow the monkeys to thwart the emperor's desire. If you will not think of the emperor's honor, think of the God's honor. These apostate monkeys who dwell among the drakkenree threaten the person of an anointed löm!"

"No one's been hurt yet, have they?"

"Your actions make disaster only a matter of time! Do men have to die before you will take another course? Or is it your intention that men die? Is that the end you seek? Are we all pawns to be sacrificed in some plot between you and the enemy?"

"Lying dog!" Galon Martello shouted as he surged forward.

Teletha, standing near the boy, was not surprised; she had noticed his growing agitation during Namsorn's attack on Galon's master. Teletha grabbed the boy's left arm and swung him around, then caught his sword arm before he could clear his blade from its scabbard.

"Well meant," she whispered to him. "But he has to deal with this his way."

"His honor has been impugned," Galon complained as he struggled against her grip.

"It's his honor, boy, not yours. Leave it to him." Easy words. Not so easy to follow. Teletha wanted to shove Namsorn's tongue down his throat as much as Galon did. "He doesn't need your help."

More easy words. Teletha hoped they were true. The boy seemed to believe them; he stopped struggling.

Arun Schell *did* have an answer for Namsorn. He dug into his shirt and pulled out the *staliarm*. "Look at this, my sign of service. I am as loyal to the emperor as I was the day I took the oath of service. I say this now and call upon the *staliarm* as my witness."

Several men gasped as the fleck of metron in the center of the talisman flared to life. Few Imperial citizens ever got to see a *staliarm*, but all knew of their existence and the people who wore them. The *staliarmati*, the men and women of the *staliarm*, were the servants of the emperor, answerable only to him. By their *staliarms*, such people could command in the emperor's name, and the folk of the empire could obey without doubt; for the magical affinity between the talisman and its bearer was absolute and unbreakable. The *staliarm*'s glow was the sign that the bearer was the true bearer, and could mark the truth of his words.

Namsorn was not cowed. "I heard not your oath. A clever man can craft words that hide his heart and—"

Arun's patience ended. His fist lashed out, taking Namsorn in the belly. The Solonite whuffed and went down. Arun stood over him.

"A clever man knows when to shut up," he said. Namsorn had no reply; he was too busy gasping for breath. "It's time for you to be clever, Namsorn. You like to remind me that the empire is where its captains go. You may be one of those captains, but so am I, and I hold the *staliarm*. Where the empire is, the empire's law runs. That law has provisions to deal with those who

desert their officers in the face of the enemy. You point at
the bregil of Jor Valadrem and call them the enemy, and
you want me to believe that they are the enemy. Shall I
grant your desire? What then? How then shall I see your
actions? Shall I be obliged to call you an insubordinate,
troublesome, mutinous viper? Shall I then be obligated to
speak in the emperor's name—to preserve his honor, you
understand—and call for you to be beheaded as a
traitor?"

Namsorn started to speak. "Sorigir Renumas—"

"Sorigir Renumas is powerful, and his family is more
powerful still, but they are subordinate to the emperor.
Even Renumas cannot save you from the emperor's justice."

Getting slowly to his feet, Namsorn said, "I do not fear
man's justice."

"You should, Solonite. For you do not live in your
creed's Paradisical Garden Hereafter; you live in man's
world. Your life is at hazard, as is every other man's."

Arun might never have spoken. Namsorn began to
quote, Teletha guessed, from the Book of Solon. "I am
armored by the God; I have no fear of death. The God
favors those who walk in His light, and they shall walk
with Him in the Paradisical Garden Hereafter. Our lives
are a test of our faith and trust in the God, and He will
cherish those who honor Him."

"Enough!" Arun shouted. "Enough! We need none of
your sectarian preaching. You have demonstrated that
you cannot accept the lawful commands of your superiors. I will give you time to reconsider your mutiny.
Threok, have some of your men take this man below and
put him in his cabin. Galon, see that he stays there."

After the unresisting Namsorn had been led away,
Löm Kerandiri spoke from the other ship. "Captain
Namsorn's challenge was unseemly, yet one must won-
der about the wisdom of submitting meekly to Factor
Choshok's dastardly plans."

"I do not plan to submit," said Arun. "Perhaps it is time to let them know that they are dealing with the emperor's personal representative. We may be able to convince them that they have made a mistake. But if we open fire first, there will be no more negotiations. There will be a battle, and I little like the thought of a battle confined by this river."

"Your *staliarm* will make no difference now," Threok said. "With both chains up, Choshok has chosen his course; he won't turn his back now. There'll be a fight. The best we can do is make it on our terms."

"I would prefer terms to cannonballs," Arun said.

"As would we all, Captain," Kerandiri said. "But I fear that Master Threok may be right. I am not generally in favor of violence, but Fra Serent and Fra Zephem are in agreement that it is the only course, and I must take note of the harmony between two who serve the Warrior Siblings. We seem to have had the alternatives taken from us."

Teletha didn't think that pitting the guns of the ships against those of the fortified city was a good roll of the dice. There was too much they didn't know about the city's guns and her troops. Fighting blind was often worse than fighting outnumbered. Vehr help them if they were outnumbered and didn't know it. She could only hope that the warrior priests had been given some sort of divine inspiration, and that they had a chance of succeeding in their upcoming struggle. But sitting under the guns of both the tower and the city wasn't the way to use their resources. Arun showed he was thinking along similar lines when he spoke.

"Master Threok, you say that Factor Choshok intends to open fire on us when we reach the downriver barrier and not before."

Threok nodded. "A smart man would have taken us under his guns already, but we are talking about Choshok here; he would rather be safe than smart. He'll

wait until he thinks he has us where we have the least
chance of harming him. I'd stake my life on it."

"You may well be doing just that."

"I know him," Threok said.

"I hope you do. Now tell me, is that tributary across
from Jor Valadrem navigable for our ships?"

Threok looked puzzled, but he answered readily
enough. "Not far for the *Handmaiden* and the *Grace*; a bit
farther for the *Breath*, for she has a shallower draft."

The answer seemed to satisfy Arun. "Could we get far
enough up that branch that the jungle would screen us
from the city?"

Threok was slow to answer. "I think so."

"And can we bring the ships around fast enough? Can
we get into the tributary before they understand what
we're doing?"

"That will depend on how long it takes Choshok to
realize that we're not falling into his trap. It will be a hard
turn, and then we'll be fighting the current. We'll be
slow. If he's put Lorm in charge of the artillery, we will
likely take a shot or two."

Arun considered Threok's words. "But even with
Captain-general Lorm watching, we have a chance."

Threok didn't seem to like the plan. "A damn small
chance."

"Better than none at all," said Arun. "That's what we'll
do, then. We'll take the ships up the tributary for now."

"To what end, Captain Schell?" Kerandiri asked.
"Master Threok says we cannot travel far on that river.
We'll be no less trapped."

"Chains don't get tired," Threok said. "They'll still
be blocking the main channel. Trying that course will
only tell Choshok that we know his plan. When we
come out of the branch—and we'll have to, sooner or
later—we'll be back under the city's guns and they'll be
ready for us."

"We'll deal with that when, or rather if, we have to. In

the meantime, we will have bought some time to consider our situation and we won't have paid any blood for it. I don't see how we will be any worse off, and we might find a way to better the situation."

"How do we know that they will be content to let us do as you suggest?" Sir Kopell asked.

"We don't," Arun said. "But then, they don't know our plans."

"Do *we* know our plans, Schell?" Threok asked sarcastically.

Arun frowned at Threok's tone. "Sailing Master Threok, give the necessary orders."

Threok didn't move. "The *necessary* orders include opening fire on Jor Valadrem."

"Perhaps you'd like to join Captain Namsorn below," Arun suggested, steel in his voice.

Still, Threok defied him. "Lock me in a room with him, and only one of us will come out."

"And I'd have to behead the other. At the moment, that would seem to be no loss," Arun said. "Give the sailing orders, Master Threok. Just those orders and no others. Take us up the tributary."

It was a long moment before Threok said, "As you order, Captain." Threok's tone made his disagreement plain, but he did give the orders.

Teletha hoped that Arun knew what he was doing.

Jerr stood in the waist of the *Handmaiden*, leaning her back against the rail and watching the walls of Jor Valadrem draw nearer. Galon stood by her side, making her feel less uncomfortable among the rough soldiers and seamen. She would have preferred being on the quarterdeck with Master Tanafres, but he had told her no. Galon caught her looking back that way.

"The Captain said we'll be safer here." Captain Schell, he meant. *The Captain* was always Captain Schell. "Once the ship makes the turn, the quarterdeck will be exposed to the enemy fire."

"Will they shoot their guns at us?" she asked.

"The Captain doesn't think so. Not until we've turned, anyway."

Jerr turned and stretched over the rail to look ahead. She could see that the river was wider just ahead. The trees thinned out, and she caught a glimpse of another line of trees, farther away. "Is that where we're going?"

Galon looked where she pointed. "That would be it."

She watched the point where the two rivers met; it was a less menacing sight than the walled city with its guns. Not that she could forget about the guns. Who could? It was all anyone talked about, when they weren't talking about the dread Wizard of Bones. They might not be any nearer to finding out about the wizard, but they would soon know about the guns. *Mannar's Handmaiden* was passing the point.

And still sailing downriver.

"What's gone wrong?" she asked.

"Nothing's wrong. We're just getting room to make the turn," he said.

She felt like an idiot. Ships needed room to turn, even more room than carts did. She knew that. She did! She'd just forgotten it because she was worried about the guns. Galon must think her an idiot. She turned to stare at the shore so he wouldn't see her embarrassment.

"There," he said, tapping her on the shoulder and pointing astern. "See. *Theris's Breath* is turning. With her shallower draft, she can run closer to the point."

It was true; the *Breath* was turning. Jerr could see sailors aboard the *Grace* starting to move about, preparing to turn, too. But no orders had been given aboard the *Handmaiden*.

Jerr looked to the quarterdeck. Master Threok stood by the hatch over the wheel on the underdeck below. Captain Schell stood beside him. Each man's attention was focused on a different thing. Master Threok looked ahead at the river, and Captain Schell watched Jor Valadrem through his spyglass. Both men were intent; she could see Master Threok's grim expression and could imagine Captain Schell's.

Master Tanafres and *Ser* Handrar were on the deck as well, at the stern rail. Like Captain Schell, they looked toward Jor Valadrem. Unlike Captain Schell, they sat upon the deck. Only when the ship pitched, and *Ser* Handrar's hand rolled from his lap and stayed where it fell, did Jerr realize that they were in trance.

They were attempting a magic of some kind!

Master Threok shouted out, giving the orders to turn. Men leapt to do their jobs. Jerr was nearly trampled by a bregil seaman heading for a ratline near her. Master Threok told his steersman to lean hard on the wheel.

The *Handmaiden*'s sails sagged as she turned. Men chanted as they hauled lines. The ship wallowed through her turn, drifting farther downstream in the pull of the sluggish river current. Slowly, slowly, her bow came about. Above Jerr the sails slapped. Lines sang as the sails began to catch the wind again.

"Too slow," Master Threok called out. "Too slow!"

"How long till we're out of their sight?" asked Captain Schell.

"Too long," Master Threok answered.

Captain Schell lowered his spyglass. "They are standing to one of the guns. Have your gun crews stand ready to return fire."

"Now? Not long enough for that," Threok said. "Unless they hole us, then we'll have all the time until we sink. Of course, had we readied the guns before . . . "

"We'll just have to hope they miss, then, Master Threok." Captain Schell raised his spyglass again and looked toward the city. He didn't see the obscene gesture Master Threok made in his direction.

Through it all Master Tanafres and *Ser* Handrar never moved.

Thunder rumbled over the river, and Jerr looked up. No storm clouds. Was this the magic Master Tanafres and *Ser* Handrar were doing? Something whistled through the air above her head and landed with a splash near the shore. A cloud of smoke was drifting away from one of the apertures in the walls of Jor Valadrem. Not the magicians. The dreaded guns.

Mannar's Handmaiden plowed for the mouth of the tributary.

More guns spoke from Jor Valadrem, several this time. Most of the shots fell short or went wide. One tore away some of the rigging. A bregil sailor fell, streaming blood; his hand had been torn away with the lines. He hit one of the shrouds and tried to grab a ratline with his tail, but failed, bouncing away from the ship. He landed in the water.

"Man overboard," Jerr yelled, but no one listened.

The *Handmaiden* was nearing the point. The *Grace* had already gotten the trees between her and Jor Valadrem, and the *Breath* was well up the tributary. The *Handmaiden* was the only target for the guns. They spoke again.

There were no more hits, but splashes of water washed across the deck. A fish, thrown up from its home, flopped helpless on the wood.

Only a little farther.

The guns fired again. Branches showered down on the point of land between the *Handmaiden* and Jor Valadrem. Birds and mortfleigers burst in shrieking confusion from their roosts. One tree, caught by a cannonball, cracked and crashed to the earth in a splintering roar. Along the banks of the point, many of the great lizards that Master Tanafres called crocodiles, and other, stranger beasts, crashed into the water to escape a terror they could not understand.

But now the trees protected the *Handmaiden* and all still aboard her from the guns of Jor Valadrem.

They were safe.

Master Tanafres joined the ship's surgeon in treating those with minor injuries. Jerr helped. The bregil sailor had been the only fatality.

"We were lucky," Master Threok said, more than once.

After the evening meal, there were more discussions. That's what Master Tanafres and his friends called them; Jerr thought they sounded much more like arguments. Everyone kept saying the same things over and over until Jerr got bored.

She went down into the waist of the *Handmaiden.* It wasn't such a bad place with all the sailors and soldiers bedded down for the night. She stood by the rail and looked out at the jungle.

What a strange place it was, so different from the forest she'd known back in Kolvin. Back home. Home was so far away now; she hadn't the slightest idea how far, but she knew she could never walk there. For one thing, the jungle was between her and Kolvin. She listened to the noises, so few were familiar. Most were strange and a little scary. The animals here were strange, too; so were the plants. Everything was strange. But wonderful, too. Hadn't she wanted to see things she had never seen before? Well, here she was, seeing things she had never seen before.

So why was she so scared?

Something splashed in the river. A fish? There were a lot of them here, some very large, many with teeth. Maybe it was one of those crocodiles. Jerr usually saw fairly well at night; but this night was dark, and, though she looked, she didn't see anything.

She leaned on her folded arms and stared at the deep darkness that was the shore. The night sky made silhouettes of the treetops and a mystery of the land below. The thin sliver of V'Delma's Moon was low in the sky, not offering enough light to reveal anything of the land. There would be more light later when V'Narra's Moon rose, but for now, there was only V'Delma's silver sliver and the stars, hardly enough to see by.

If she was a magician, she could make her own light. Master Tanafres said that making magelight was simple. For him, maybe. Though she'd tried, she hadn't mastered the trick of it.

There was another splash, nearer this time. Softer, too. Through the wood under her arms, Jerr felt a soft thump. Something had bumped up against the *Handmaiden*'s hull. It was the sort of sound one of those crocodiles might make if it bumped into the ship.

And if it had, what of it? The big lizards were water dwellers. Master Tanafres said that they could not come aboard the ships.

She stopped leaning on the rail.

She took a step back when she heard a soft, scraping sound, like a claw on wood. It was the sort of sound that a lizard's claws might make as it crawled up a tree. Or a ship's hull. But crocodiles weren't really lizards; Master Tanafres said so. They didn't climb as lizards did. The noise couldn't be a crocodile crawling out of the river and climbing aboard the ship. *It couldn't be. Could it?*

She wanted to know, but she was terrified to look. She thought that she heard the slithering scrape again, but she wasn't sure. The ship was never quiet; it had a lot of odd noises. Couldn't this just be a sound that she had not yet noticed? No, there it was again, and it was definitely coming from the outside of the hull. Should she interrupt the discussions and tell them of her fears? Would they listen? And what if they did listen?

There was the sound again!

She could run and get the man on watch, but she would feel a fool if there was nothing to be seen. But if there was something, she would be the one to warn everyone.

Was that breathing she heard in the darkness beyond the rail?

She had to know, and to know she had to look. Taking a deep breath, she leaned over the rail to look. She found herself staring into the face of a bregil. She let out a bleat. It was a strangled sort of sound, hardly audible; she'd meant it to be a scream.

"Sshh!" the bregil hissed.

He was near enough to get one of his hands on the deck. Something shiny dangled from a thong on his wrist. His tail curled up and wrapped around one of the stanchions. He heaved himself up and got his other hand on the rail. He clambered over. He was dripping, and he was naked, but somehow that seemed to make him more menacing, like some night-stalking beast risen from the river. He was not a crocodile, but possibly something worse. Jerr thought about soldiers from Jor Valadrem. No more came over the railing, but she backed away anyway.

"Where Threok?" asked the bregil.

She stopped, stunned by his question. "You know Master Threok?"

The bregil lunged forward and grabbed her arm. It hurt. "Take me to Threok," he demanded.

19

JERR THOUGHT AGAIN about trying to scream. She decided against it when the bregil laid his tail on her shoulder. She could feel the callused, leathery gripping pad against the bare skin of her neck. This man would not be happy if she screamed. His grip on her arm hurt; he would hurt her more if she did something he didn't like.

She took the bregil to Master Threok's cabin at the back of the afterdeck. Master Threok had left the quarterdeck discussion before Jerr had grown bored; from the light leaking through the cabin door's slatted window, Jerr guessed that Master Threok was there and still awake. She could hear the discussion still going on, just one companionway up. So near.

The bregil rapped on the door with his tail, making a softer thump than a hand would make. Master Threok opened the door nearly at once. He took in his visitors at a glance and stepped aside. The dripping bregil released Jerr and entered the cabin.

"Go about your business, girl," Master Threok said as he closed the door.

Jerr ran for the quarterdeck.

The group was smaller now than when she had left; most of the priests were gone, back to the *Grace*; only

Löm Kerandiri, Fra Serent, and Fra Zephem remained. There were others still talking, but she looked for Master Tanafres. He and his friends were where she'd seen them last, and she ran to him. She gasped out her story of the arrival of the bregil, jumbling up the account with the fears the noises had awoken in her before she knew it was the bregil. By the time he had gotten a straight story from her, the rest of the group on the quarterdeck was listening as intently as he had from the beginning.

"He must have come from Jor Valadrem," *Ser* Handrar said.

"But why?" asked Löm Kerandiri.

"Did not you say that he asked to be taken to the sailing master?" Fra Zephem asked Jerr.

Jerr nodded.

"This stinks of a plot," Fra Zephem said.

"Everything stinks of a plot to you, brother," Fra Serent said. "It is not unnatural to seek out the master of a ship when one comes aboard. Who else would be in command? Perhaps this bregil brings good news."

"Skulkers in darkness seldom bring *good* news," Fra Zephem said.

"We do not know that he brings *any* news," Master Tanafres said. "But we can find out. Let us go and ask."

By the time they reached the afterdeck, Master Threok and the bregil were standing before the cabin door. The newcomer was wearing a pair of Master Threok's trousers. Dressed—at least partly—he didn't look so menacing. He was still wet, though.

"This is Gissel," Master Threok said. "He's come from Jor Valadrem. I would say that he brings news, but I don't think any of you would be surprised to hear that Choshok is not happy with us."

"You came alone?" Löm Kerandiri asked of Gissel.

"Hard swimming any other way."

"You swam?" Löm Kerandiri sounded amazed. For an answer, Gissel ran a hand down his furred arm, then with a flick of his wrist sent a spatter of water to the deck. "Yes, I see now that you must have, or you wouldn't be so wet. Why brave the crocodiles? Why not come in a boat?"

"Choshok guards boats night and day," answered Gissel.

"Are you saying that you have not come as Factor Choshok's messenger?" asked Löm Kerandiri.

Gissel chortled. "Not everyone in Jor Valadrem willing to spit in face of Coronal Emperor."

"So there is dissent in Jor Valadrem," said Captain Schell.

"Have you ever known a city without it?" asked Master Threok. "Tell them why you're here, Gissel."

"I heard you came here in name of Coronal Emperor and of primate. You came to see Wizard of Bones. This is true?"

"We do wish to meet this wizard," Löm Kerandiri said.

Gissel nodded as if satisfied. "I take you to his camp."

"Camp?" several voices asked.

"I thought he lived around here," *Ser* Handrar said.

Shrugging a bregil shrug, Gissel said, "Sometimes. Drakkenree not stay in one place much more than one season. It is their way. They be moving on soon, or they already on move. None of wizard's people at city for two days. You want to meet wizard, you go to his camp now. "

"Why are you doing this?" Fra Zephem asked suspiciously.

Again the shrug. "Choshok not wanting you to see Wizard of Bones. Choshok not telling you wizard going soon. I came to tell. I came to show."

Fra Zephem apparently didn't believe in simple good deeds. "What do you gain?" he asked.

"Even in Jor Valadrem we have heard of Coronal Emperor's gratitude." Gissel smiled. "And of emperor's generosity."

"If you can take us to the Wizard of Bones, there will be a reward," Captain Schell promised. "But tell us, Gissel, why do you think we should see the wizard?"

"As I say, Choshok not wanting you to see wizard. Choshok is not right always. We not always getting along."

"What does it matter what his reasons are?" *Ser* Handrar asked. "The wilderness is wide, finding someone in the greatness of it would be an impossible task without help. Master Gissel offers us a service that we can hardly do without. I think we should take advantage of his offer."

"We can't trust him," Fra Zephem stated. "He is of Jor Valadrem."

"Trust me or not. You decide," Gissel said. "Not blame all of Jor Valadrem for what Choshok do."

"I believe Master Gissel," *Ser* Handrar said. "Time is clearly an issue, given our current situation. We must take this opportunity to reach the Wizard of Bones. We certainly can't expect success on our own if we go blundering blindly about in the upriver jungle. This is an opportunity that we cannot ignore. Don't you agree, Master Tanafres?"

"A guide to the wizard's camp would be invaluable," Master Tanafres said.

To Jerr, he didn't sound as if he were wholeheartedly endorsing *Ser* Handrar's position, but *Ser* Handrar seemed to think so. He said, "The practitioners of the Art are agreed. What about you, Löm Kerandiri? What say you?"

"Having learned how this wizard is called, we cannot ignore the implications. As we cannot ignore the implications of how this wizard chooses to embody his magic. These are secrets which cannot remain secrets. We cannot return to the empire without answers. If this man can take us to the wizard, we must go."

"Very well," Captain Schell said. "We will go in the morning."

"*Who* will go?" asked Master Threok. "We cannot leave the ships unguarded."

"Jor Valadrem remains a threat," Fra Zephem said. "It would be unwise to abandon the ships."

Captain Schell said, "I had not expected to do so. They need a guard."

"A strong guard," Master Threok said.

"Who goes and who stays?" Sir Kopell asked.

"My priests must go, as must the magicians," Löm Kerandiri said.

"*All* your priests, Löm Kerandiri?" asked Captain Schell. "I would suggest that we leave the clerkly ones aboard the ships. They will not take the hard travel well."

"All of them must go, Captain," Löm Kerandiri said firmly. "They will bear whatever hardships befall. This matter we pursue comes closer to my sphere the more we learn about it. We must be prepared to deal with whatever we find. I can spare none of them."

"If Master Tanafres goes, my men and I will go as well," Sir Kopell said.

"And I," Mistress Schonnegon said, echoing Jerr's thoughts.

"And I," Master Lennuick said.

"No, you won't," Master Tanafres said.

The three of them fell into an argument. Sir Kopell ignored their bickering and addressed himself to Captain Schell. Jerr had heard Master Tanafres's arguments before, so she listened to Sir Kopell.

"We will need soldiers. There are dangerous animals out there."

"Not needing soldiers," Gissel said. "One man be afraid. Much danger one man. Animals not bother many men."

"I am not worried about animals," Sir Kopell said. "If Choshok might make a sally against the ships, so might he send troops into the wilderness after us, if he learns we are going to the wizard's camp. Gissel says that Choshok does not want us to see the wizard. We will need warriors to defend the löm and his priests."

"Don't forget the ships," Master Threok said.

"We will have to divide the soldiers," Captain Schell said.

"What about provisions?" Fra Serent asked.

"If there are animals, we can hunt," Sir Kopell said.

"It will slow us down," Captain Schell said. "We do not know how long we have before Factor Choshok reacts. To move quickly, we will have to carry our provisions with us. Some of the sailors can serve as porters."

"Not my seamen," Master Threok said. "Not on this foolishness."

Captain Schell's voice was cold. "Do I have to remind you again whom you serve?"

"Apparently I have to remind you of what the contract stipulates," Master Threok said. "My men and I provide sea transportation, which means delivery to a site. No overland treks. As I see it, you have been delivered."

"And a return, Master Threok. The contract specifies a return."

"I'm not planning on abandoning you. If it's within my power, you won't be without a ship to go home. But I can't defend the ships single-handedly, and that's why none of my seamen will be going ashore. Every one of them is needed to assure that the ships remain safe. Give me some of the soldiers to make it more likely that we'll still be here if you return from your trek."

Captain Schell looked unhappy about Master Threok's objection, but he didn't dispute it. "Gissel, how far away is this camp?"

"I make journey in one day. You not know way and there are many of you, you slow. Two days." He passed his gaze among the islanders. "Maybe three."

"That far?" *Ser* Handrar sounded dismayed.

Gissel shrugged. "Is where it is. Camp is near this season. Not like last. Maybe wizard knows you come."

"It's not so far," Captain Schell said. "Each person can carry sufficient food to feed himself on the way. There is water, isn't there?"

"Enough. Your kind not caring for taste maybe," Gissel answered.

"We are not expecting the sparkling waters of Lirinis," Captain Schell said. "We'll manage."

"Captain, do you not think we should go ashore under the cover of night?" asked Sir Kopell.

"Dark not good time to travel," Gissel said.

"The morning should be fine," Captain Schell said.

"After morning ritual," Löm Kerandiri amended.

"I still say that this adventure is ill-advised," Threok said. "The jungle is dangerous."

"You sound like Captain-general Lorm," Master Tanafres said.

Master Threok snorted in indignation. "There is no need to insult me because I tell you that you've made a bad decision."

"And there is no need to spend any more of this night in fruitless argument," Löm Kerandiri said. "The decision is made. If any of you have doubts, pray to the gods that They will guide us safely, for what happens is at Their wills, not ours."

Jerr didn't have any doubts that Master Tanafres would have gone whether there was danger or not. She intended to do a lot of praying.

Yan stood on the quarterdeck and looked out at the night-shrouded jungle. The others had retired to get some rest before tomorrow's journey, but he was still unready for sleep.

Was he ready for what was to come?

When he agreed to take this journey, he had not been thinking of the possibilities that had come to light with the name of the magician they sought.

The Wizard of Bones.

A strange name. Was it a magician's trading name, such as was sometimes used in the empire—did the drakkenree follow that practice?—or was it just an appellation hung on the saurian magician by others? If it was a trade name, it wasn't one that would have garnered him a following in the empire; the reactions of the priests had been clear evidence of that. If it was an appellation, did it—as Fra Zephem asserted—say anything more about the wizard than his preference in ritual materials? The drakkenree knew many strange and unusual magics. Did they know necromancy? Did they keep the dark art alive?

Yan had been more worried about the connection between the carving and the Baansuus, the drakkenree deity. The priests didn't know the Baansuus by name, but they had seemed concerned about such a possibility as well. Now, that question seemed forgotten. Fear of the dark art dominated the priests' talk now.

He supposed that such a strange turn should not have come as a surprise. Had he ever set out on a journey that had taken him where he expected to go?

That was an exaggeration, of course. He'd taken many journeys that ended where he had intended, but those had been ordinary journeys such as ordinary people took. Yan was a magician; maybe not a great magician, as he had dreamed of being while Gan Tidoni's apprentice, but a magician nonetheless. He was not an ordinary person. It was the journeys that touched upon magic that always seemed to go awry. And what had motivated his going on this one if not his fascination with the magic of the drakkenree?

He looked up into the sky. He knew that all three moons were there. Part of the sliver of light that was

V'Delma still remained above the trees. V'Narra had risen to take her place, and her golden light limned the tops of the trees. He had to look for the darkness that was V'Zurna, smallest of the three and, it seemed, more often in her dark phase.

Some made of V'Zurna a patroness of the Great Art. Those same folk called the Art just one of the many secrets that the old crone held, one of the mysteries that she administered. V'Zurna was supposed to be secretive, wise, jealous, knowledgeable, and chary of those with whom she shared her gifts and secrets. Yan had always taken Einthof as his patron of the Art, preferring the scholar god's love of learning and its sharing as a paradigm for the Art.

The dark jungle was a paradigm, too, but a different kind. It was like the drakkenree magic: strange, foreign, and difficult to comprehend. Both the drakkenree magic and the jungle seemed to partake more of V'Zurna's way than of Einthof's. Maybe that was why Yan lost his way so often with the magic. Was he walking the path with his eyes closed?

Soon they would be on their way to confront a drakkenree wizard. Of all of those who would be going, only Yan had ever met and talked with a drakkenree magician. He was supposed to be the expert, the knowledgeable one. The expert on drakkenree magic? He could barely speak or read their language. The thing that he knew best was how little he knew.

What would this wizard be like? Yan couldn't accept that he was a dark magician, despite his appellation. Bone was a material like many others that came from living beings. Bone could be made into tools, shaped into useful things. Craftsmen in the empire used bone tools all the time, yet no one accused them of the dark art. Did the priests suspect the drakkenree magician to be a dark magician simply because he was a drakkenree?

What would Fra Bern think of that? Likely, no more

than Yan did. Armiacodi was one of the most respected thinkers in the history of the empire, and Armiacodi thought that what made a race human was the ability to touch the Great Art. By that philosophy, the drakkenree were human.

Being human meant that they could embrace the gods. One thing Yan knew for sure was that the saurians had a religion, even if he did not know that religion's validity. But if the drakkenree were human, they were as capable as anyone of embracing the dread philosophy of the dark art. They would be as open to temptation as any merin, saü, or bregil.

All of which meant that he had almost no idea of what they would face out there in the wild. They were going to meet a drakkenree wizard. Yan carried the scars he'd gotten in his last encounter with a drakkenree wizard. But he knew that even if someone told him that he would be facing the same sort of pain and humiliation, he would go to meet this drakkenree magician. There was too much to be learned. How could he not go?

20

TELETHA FOUND ARUN SCHELL standing by the rail, watching the efforts to get Sir Kopell's drakkenree down into the landing boat. The saurian wasn't making the task any easier by struggling in his improvised sling.

"You'd think it didn't want to go," Arun mused.

"Maybe he knows something we don't," she said.

He looked at her. "So you call it 'he,' too."

Why not? But, by Vehr, she wasn't even consistent herself, calling the lizard a "he" sometimes and "it" others. "He *is* a male."

"It's a drakkenree. They're not like us."

She'd often thought so. "Yan would argue against that."

"I know. And he has, but he hasn't convinced me. Just look at it. Look at those teeth. Look at the tail. Look at the serpent eyes. How can anyone seriously believe that lizard is human?"

"Bregil don't look like us, and they're human."

"I said I've heard the arguments."

"If he bothers you so much, why did you agree to let Sir Kopell bring him along?"

"Back in Kolvin, I didn't think the point worth arguing. I guess I didn't really believe that we'd be going into the wilderness with it." He drew in a deep breath.

"You've spent time around it. How much do you think it can be trusted once we are among its own kind?"

Who really knew the answer to that? "Yan says the drakkenree will keep his word."

"And he should know, having lived among them." Arun didn't sound convinced.

"Yan's a better authority about them than you or I," she said. "I trust him."

"Trust who? Tanafres or the lizard?"

"Yan, of course." Teletha shook her head bemusedly. Clearly Arun was still worried. "Look, if you are worried about taking the drakkenree along, why not leave it here? I'm sure you could convince Sir Kopell."

"Leave it behind? Don't you think Threok was serious about killing it if we left it aboard?"

She hadn't really thought about that. Threok had been making a lot of violent promises. "Maybe. I don't know. Reading a bregil is hard, and Threok's harder than most."

"Glad you think so. I was beginning to think I was slipping."

"Don't let Galon hear you say that. You'll shatter the boy's illusion that you're perfect."

"Don't worry about Galon; he knows I'm not perfect, just very good."

"But too modest."

They laughed. She was glad to hear him. He hadn't so much as smiled since they had discovered the sabotaged airship.

The crew of the *Grace* managed to get the drakkenree down into the boat. The saurian immediately folded his legs and settled to the bottom of the craft. The others boarding had to step around him—or on him, which some did. Uncharacteristically, the drakkenree did not react to such abuse. Arun watched without comment, still staring contemplatively over the rail. Something was still worrying him.

"Arun, how wise is this expedition?"

His voice was far away and soft. "It's never been wise. Just necessary."

Had he answered the question she had asked? "I meant the trek into the wilderness."

"Ah." A moment later he said, "Well, what I said applies to that, too."

Those going ashore from the *Grace* were nearly all loaded onto the boat. Namsorn was giving final instructions to his soldiers, both those who were to go and those who were to remain aboard the *Grace*. Despite his confrontation with Arun, Namsorn was still the commander of the military contingent; she hadn't agreed with Arun's decision to keep it so, but Arun refused to discuss it. Namsorn had proven himself hostile to Arun's goals. How could he trust the man any longer? Teletha couldn't help but wonder what Namsorn was telling the soldiers.

"Arun, is it wise to leave Namsorn with the ships?"

"Threok won't let him do anything foolish."

"Is this the same Threok that you think might murder the drakkenree?"

"The same. Namsorn may well be the best choice to leave behind."

"They both want to attack the city. Without you to tell them otherwise, might they try?"

Arun shook his head. "Namsorn won't risk that while Löm Kerandiri is with us. In fact, I'm counting on Namsorn to make sure Threok doesn't try it. We need the ships here and waiting for us when we get back. Namsorn won't desert the löm; he'd never be able to square that with his god. He'll see that the ships remain safe and our retreat route secure."

"I could see him deciding that taking the city was the best way to make things secure." Eliminating all threats was the safest way to stay secure.

"He's a good enough soldier to know when the risks are too high. Don't worry about it."

Why shouldn't *she* worry? *He* was worried. "I'm supposed to leave that to you?"

"It's my duty."

She understood that, but . . .

"Arun, I'd like to help. I used to be an officer and—"

"I know what you used to be, and I know what you're going to offer, but I think it better that you not. In this, I think you might serve the emperor better, if you are not serving the emperor. Just go on doing what you've been doing. Keep Tanafres safe, if you can; we need his knowledge. There shouldn't be any more accidents now, but there will be other dangers in the wilderness."

Any more accidents? "What accidents?"

"The sisstrecht, the saddle, and the spar. Were there others?"

Saddle? "What saddle?"

"He didn't tell you about that? It was the first day out of Yentillan's steading. Someone had slit the stitching on his saddle's girth strap. I saw him repairing it that night."

She'd be asking Yan about the saddle and giving him a piece of her mind about not telling her. For the moment, though, she was with Arun, and he knew about the so-called accidents. He might know other things. "Do you know who arranged these things?"

"No more than you." He tapped his chest, where the *staliarm* hung under his shirt. "If I *knew*, I'd have to act on it."

From his tone, Teletha knew that he *would* act on it. She felt relief. She hadn't wanted to believe that Arun might be the villain, and now she was satisfied that he wasn't. Maybe together they could discover the cowardly knave.

It was good to know that justice would be near to hand when they found the cur.

Jerr made her way down the ladder and dropped into the *Handmaiden*'s boat. The craft rocked under her feet, but not so much that she felt in danger of falling into the crocodile-infested water. There were other dangers in what she was doing, though, and she knew that one was near. She could feel Master Tanafres's eyes on her without having to turn around. Slowly, she turned to face him.

"You told me to stay out of trouble," Jerr said, pre-empting his admonition.

He scowled at her. "That's why I expect you to climb back up that ladder and stay aboard the ship."

Jerr launched into the arguments she had prepared. "You said that the best way for me to stay out of further trouble was to stay in *your* sight. You hain't going to be in sight of the ship for long. Besides, what makes the ship any safer than the land? Captain Schell is leaving soldiers and taking soldiers. He thinks there could be danger anywhere. Why would I be safer aboard ship than going along with you?"

"Master Lennuick is staying aboard."

As if the old clerk could protect her. "And Mistress Schonnegon is going with you. I won't get into trouble," she stated in what she hoped was a decisive manner. Master Tanafres appreciated decisiveness.

He looked at her for a long time without saying anything. She didn't look away; not looking away was part of being decisive. She had to show him she knew she was right. At last, he spoke.

"Perhaps it would do you some good to get away from Master Lennuick. You are starting to argue like him, entirely too well."

Jerr hadn't thought she was doing well at all, but she wasn't going to contradict Master Tanafres. At least not when he was apparently agreeing with her.

"I will carry your satchel," she said. That was an appropriate duty for an apprentice; if she didn't go along, Master Tanafres would have to carry it himself, along with the provisions that Captain Schell had decreed each person would carry. Not having been issued any, she'd had to beg hers from the ship's cook.

"I'll carry the satchel," he said, to her relief. She hadn't been sure she could handle the extra load, but she had been sure she needed to make the offer. "You can carry my provisions. Perhaps the extra burden will teach you something about going out of your way to make work for yourself."

"A lesson that needs to be learned well," said *Ser* Handrar, inserting himself into the conversation. "She may carry my provisions also."

He handed her his sack. She took it; she couldn't let it drop into the sloshing water in the bottom of the boat. The three sacks of provisions weighed as much as or more than Master Tanafres's satchel. Could she object to this added burden? *Dare* she object? Master Tanafres didn't object; she dared not.

The sailors pushed the boat away from the *Handmaiden.* Master Tanafres made no objection to that either. She had succeeded in getting him to let her go along. She'd prove his decision wise; she'd carry any load he cared to place on her. She wouldn't disappoint him.

The expedition went upriver. Captain Schell ordered the seamen to make for a small open space in the heavy growth at the river's edge. The two crocodiles occupying the space turned their heads toward the oncoming boats and watched their approach. When the boats came within a dozen feet of the shore, the reptiles splashed into the river with a sudden rush and disappeared beneath the murky water. Yan was glad to see them go; he had begun to fear that the crocodiles were going to contest with them for the space on the shore.

Schell was the first ashore, his aide Galon no more than a few heartbeats behind him. The two of them sur-

veyed the immediate area while everyone else waited in
the boats. Schell seemed satisfied; he gave the seamen
orders to secure the boats. The sailors found stout trees to
which they lashed lines. Threok had been convinced to
allow a few of his men ashore; they were to stay with the
boats, holding them ready for a quick return to the ships.

Yan found that the lush and tangled growth that
walled most of the river was little more than a few yards
in depth; beyond that barrier the forest floor was much
more open. The trek would not be as arduous as he had
feared. He saw that it would take time to unload all the
boats and sort everyone out, and decided to use that time
to gather samples of the local plants. There was so much
around them that he did not recognize. He found something that looked a lot like hagweed, but had differently
colored buds. Would it have different efficacies? He was
pondering the possibilities when he felt a tug on his
sleeve, a sharp pull like a thorn caught in the fabric.

How could he have caught it on anything? He was just
standing still.

When he turned to free his sleeve, he saw that the
thing his sleeve was hung up on was one of Khankemeh's
claws. The drakkenree bobbed his head and slipped his
claw free. He backed up a step and raised his torso to
submissive erectness.

"Magician, great and powerful, there is meat among
the trees." The saurian cadences and posture made it
clear that this was not simply an observation.
Khankemeh had never used the honorific salutation with
Yan before. Something was up.

"I don't understand," Yan said.

"Worthless property that I am, I still hunger." The
drakkenree pointed his snout toward the deeper woods.
His nostrils flared, and his fingers flexed.

Yan thought he understood. "You want to hunt?"

"Wise you are, magician, great and powerful. This one
basks in your light. There is no other I can ask."

So much for understanding. "Ask what?"

"To be my mouth. To speak to *kedja'k'krr*, the master. To ask what I cannot. *Kedja'k'krr* would lose little for his generosity. *Kedja'k'krr* would gain. A short hunt, a small meal. His property would be stronger." The drakkenree paused, perhaps gauging Yan's reaction to his plea. Not knowing how to respond, Yan said nothing. In a strained voice, the saurian added, "More loyal would this property be."

Khankemeh was making a reasonable request. Drakkenree much preferred freshly killed meat; all that the saurian had been fed aboard ship had been dried, and he'd only been able to keep any of that down for the last day or so. Khankemeh's color was coming back, but his flesh was still weak. Fresh meat would be good for him. "I will speak to Sir Kopell."

"One who was not property would owe you a debt."

Gratitude? From Khankemeh? Yan decided to seize the opportunity to deal with something that had been bothering him since he had first recognized Khankemeh. "If you believe that you owe me something for speaking to Sir Kopell, allow me to use your name when I speak to you. I find your insistence that you are no longer human to be unsettling."

The drakkenree looked away before he spoke. "Worthless property that I am, I cannot prevent you from doing as you will."

"I'll take that as a yes, Khankemeh."

"You are crueler than Kopell's men," the drakkenree said so softly that Yan almost didn't hear.

But though he heard it, he didn't understand it. How could recognizing Khankemeh as a fellow human be cruel? Cruelty came from all the people who insisted on referring to Khankemeh as an "it," an object, something less than even a beast. Even ships had gender to those who sailed them.

"I don't understand," Yan said.

"You said you would speak. Take me to *kedja'k'krr*. Be my mouth."

Yan shook his head. It wasn't easy trying to fathom the peculiar mind of a warrior drakkenree. When they stood before Sir Kopell, Khankemeh placed himself at Yan's side, standing as erect as he could. The drakkenree stretched his neck out, offering his vulnerable throat. "Speak as asked, honored magician," Khankemeh said in his own language. Khankemeh held his posture.

Sir Kopell frowned. "What is this?" he asked. "I have not seen him do this since the day I captured him. What does he say?"

"Sir Knight, your drakkenree is hungry and requests your permission to go hunting."

"Is that all?" Sir Kopell laughed. "I feared some more dire thing. If he can be quick about it, he can go. We will leave soon."

"I can follow the trail," said Khankemeh, letting Yan translate the boast for Sir Kopell.

"I'm not surprised," Sir Kopell said.

"You are not going to let it go, are you?" Schell asked.

"Certainly. He can hunt food for himself better than we can."

Schell shook his head, disbelievingly. "All this way, and you just let it go. You cannot really expect that it will come back."

"Why wouldn't he? He has given his parole, and he is an honorable bastard—in his own way."

"It won't come back," Schell said

Sir Kopell disagreed. Schell could not be convinced. And while they talked, Khankemeh vanished into the forest.

21

THE HEAT WAS THE WORST THING about the journey through the jungle. Or maybe it was the insects. The combination left Yan with only unhappy choices. The clothes that protected from the insects, sagged damply, chafed, and made the heat seem worse; but without the protection of those clothes, the insects' stings and bites bid fair to drive a man mad. Yan made the same decision as almost everyone else; he put up with the heat in order to be spared from being eaten alive. Only Gissel seemed unbothered by the tormenting bugs; he still wore only trousers. His indifference to the insect torture might have been because he was a native to the parts and was thus inured to pests, or it might have been because he was a bregil—the only one in the party—and somehow unattractive to the insects that found merin flesh so tasty.

Though Gissel showed no personal concern for the discomfort of their situation, at least he did not expect the same of the others. The bregil guide did not press the group to travel as quickly as he could. Yan didn't think that the bregil was making allowances for Khankemeh to catch up; Gissel seemed to believe that they had seen the last of the drakkenree. Still, Gissel made no effort to force the pace, though he did complain about the lack of stamina among the merin.

As they moved inland, the scourge of the insects lessened. Yan noted the drier, firmer ground. It seemed that the tiny creatures of the air had an affinity for water; he doubted that they had left simply because they had eaten their fill. The matter was a curiosity for another time. Still, if the pests did have an affinity for water, Yan felt sorry for the soldiers and seamen who had remained with the boats. Those poor men by the river would have no relief from the voracious little monsters.

The annoyance of the insects was replaced by a less tangible worry. All about them, the jungle reached toward them in a smothering, suffocating closeness. A man more than two places before or behind in the line of march was invisible, swathed in green or gloom. Not being able to see very far made everyone nervous.

Horesh was almost at zenith when their progress was interrupted by a half dozen small beasts that burst from a clump of feathery fronds. Squealing, the furry animals scampered among the group and disappeared into the brush again. Clearly the animals posed no threat, but men scanned the surrounding vegetation that hemmed them in on all sides; something had disturbed the animals.

One soldier raised his arquebus and fired. The shot boomed in the jungle air, startling birds and mortfleigers out of the trees in raucous, complaining flurries. "Drakkenree!" the soldier yelled, explaining his action. Unseen animals crashed away through the brush in all directions. The soldier stabbed a finger in the direction he had fired, then fell to reloading.

"Hold fire," Schell shouted, forestalling a fusillade. His eyes roved over the jungle. "But stand ready."

Men clumped closer together in the sudden silence. Nothing emerged from the surrounding jungle. No attacking drakkenree. No more squealing beasts. Nothing.

Yan looked where the soldier had pointed. All he

could see was a sapling's limb, dangling on shredded fibers. The soldier had shot a tree.

Then something *did* move, stepping from behind a tree a man's length nearer the group and barely the same distance from the nearest soldier. And it *was* a drakkenree, a drakkenree who held his arms wide, the claws of one hand outstretched. The other hand gripped the tails of three animals, of the same kind that had run squealing among the group. "Hold fire," he said, sounding uncannily like Schell.

It was Khankemeh.

"Ha! Put up your weapons." Sir Kopell smiled. He walked toward Schell, passing in front of the soldiers and slapping up any arquebus muzzle still pointed at Khankemeh. "I told you he'd be back."

"It nearly got itself shot," Schell pointed out.

"If that man's shot is an example of your men's marksmanship, there seems to have been little enough danger." Sir Kopell turned to the drakkenree. "Why didn't you call out before you approached?"

The saurian didn't answer the question. Lowering himself on his haunches, he tied the tails of his catch together. When he completed his task, he slung the bundle of beasts around his neck like a bizarre necklace.

"Master Tanafres, ask him the question," Sir Kopell said.

"He understands," Yan told the knight. "He just doesn't want to answer."

Sir Kopell harrumphed. "Well, it's done and nothing harmed. He's had his hunting, though. He'll stay with us from now on."

Khankemeh made no objection. In fact he seemed to take Sir Kopell's pronouncement literally; when they resumed their march, the drakkenree strode along only a step behind the knight.

The ground over which they traveled grew uneven and became a series of ridges and vales. The trees were more widely spaced here, less confining; the forest less oppressively close. They often crossed old stream channels, mostly dry. Rather than move along the relatively clear and level channels, Gissel seemed determined to take them up and down each of the hillocks that separated them even when the streambeds seemed to go in the direction Gissel was leading them. Kerandiri and his priests wilted under the heat. If asked, Yan would have had to admit that he was not doing well himself. The cooler morning—even with its bugs—began to seem attractive.

While the hillocks often offered views some distance down one of the streambeds, they themselves were choked with bushes, vines, briars, and ferns. Gissel grew cautious, spending much time scanning the jungle. His nervousness soon infected everyone. It was easy to recall how close Khankemeh had come to them without being seen.

As they came down the bank of one hillock, Kerandiri asked for a chance to rest. As Schell was about to order it, Gissel said, "Climb one more hill before stop. Leave open place, eh? Too open, eh? Dangerous. Big animal move too quiet out here; get close too fast."

Schell agreed and they toiled up one more slope. The hillock on which they took their rest would be an island if water ever filled the channels. It was one of the larger ones they had climbed and supported a substantial grove of trees, which offered shade and a space somewhat clear of the vegetation through which they forced their way as they had climbed. When Gissel proclaimed the spot satisfactory, worn-out priests, tired magicians, and footsore soldiers gratefully took their rest. Jerr sat at Yan's side and began to dig in the bags for something to eat.

Gissel started out of the clearing. When Schell asked him where he was going, he answered, "See where we are, I will. I look around, eh? Make sure we on right path."

"Marefinn, go with him," Schell ordered.

Gissel looked glumly at the soldier who was wearily hauling himself to his feet. "I return faster alone."

"Speed isn't everything," Schell said. "Considering all the talk we've heard about how dangerous the jungle is, I think it better that you be protected. We wouldn't want to lose you."

Gissel made a grimace that Yan guessed was supposed to be a smile. "Honor to me. You think of my health."

Not long after Gissel and Marefinn left the clearing, Yan heard a distant, unfamiliar coughing sound, so slight that he wasn't entirely sure he had heard it. Listening to hear if it would repeat, he realized that the sounds that had surrounded them during their trek had changed. The noise had abated. Distant sounds—far more distant than the cough—continued, but the jungle in their immediate vicinity had grown quiet.

Troubled, Yan thought to ask Teletha about it; but when he turned to find her, he noticed that Khankemeh had taken off his improvised bundle of provisions. The drakkenree wasn't taking any interest in the furry corpses at his feet; his gaze was turned toward a point among the trees. Anything that focused the warrior drakkenree's attention so fully must have significance. Forgetting about the coughing sound, Yan followed the line of the saurian's stare.

He saw it nearly at once and swallowed hard.

The creature had an ocher hide striped with darker markings, making it almost invisible against the brush in the dappled light of the jungle. For a moment Yan thought that it might be one of the ancient drakkenree; but only for a moment. Calming himself, he looked more closely and saw that its neck was shorter, and its snout longer, and its three-fingered hands bore larger claws. There were other subtle differences in shape, and, although he couldn't be sure at this distance, he guessed that the beast was even smaller than the ancient drakkenree; he thought it no bigger than an elkhound.

Jerr noticed the beast and gasped.

"Master Tan—"

"Quiet!" Yan shushed her. Startling the creature seemed like a bad idea. "What is it?" he asked Khankemeh in a whisper.

"*Shrr'kch'kain*," the drakkenree said, lifting a foot.

Yan didn't recognize the word, nor had he seen a drakkenree use that particular foot gesture before. The gesture seemed connected to the beast. Yan checked the creature's feet and saw that each bore a huge scythelike talon curving up above the weight-bearing toes. Seeing the claw jogged his memory of drakkenree sounds; the word that Khankemeh had used meant something like "fang or claw hunter." *Sharkkain* was the closest Yan could come to saying the name.

"Are *sharkkain* dangerous?"

Khankemeh didn't bother to answer; the question sounded foolish to Yan even as he asked it. One need only look at a *sharkkain* to see that it was capable of mayhem. But would it attack them? Well armed it might be, but there were many of them and only one of it.

"Yan, is it some kind of drakkenree?" Teletha asked.

So she had seen the beast, too. At least she had enough presence of mind to keep her voice soft. Yan turned to answer her, and saw that most of the group were looking toward the beast. Several soldiers were blowing up the matches and uncovering their priming pans.

The *sharkkain* made a coughing sound, several short barks in rapid succession. Though breathy and soft, the noise didn't sound at all like what Yan had heard earlier. The beast's stuttering call was repeated from somewhere in the brush to Yan's left.

Another one!

"Ready arms," Schell ordered.

Few of the soldiers had waited to be told. The warrior priests had taken their guard. Teletha held sword in one hand and pistol in the other. Sir Kopell and his men had their swords out as well. Everyone watched either the visible *sharkkain* or the brush where its companion could be heard.

Lacking a weapon, there was little Yan could do; he caught Jerr's arm and dragged her closer. Beasts were beasts, and he might be able to calm them or distract them. He wished he'd had more practice establishing a rapport with reptiles.

The visible *sharkkain* gave its call again. This time there were several responses from the brush on its right.

"How many, Captain?" one of the soldiers asked.

"Stay steady," Schell replied.

There was a rustling in the brush near the source of the cries. Something was moving toward the clearing. Several somethings.

The tension shattered as one soldier discharged his arquebus. Three more fired after him and sent bullets into the jungle. More arquebuses banged.

Several of the soldiers had chosen the visible *sharkkain* as their target. It lay writhing on the ground.

With an earsplitting screech, a dozen *sharkkain* burst out of the jungle behind them. The creatures leapt into the clearing and immediately threw themselves into the air, feet and hands extended. Sunlight sparkled from their talons. Each *sharkkain* pounced upon a victim.

One landed on Sir Kopell's back, and he went down under its impact. So did other victims, Handrar among them; he had been standing in back of the soldiers and was fully exposed to this ambush attack. The scholar mage was bowled over. He and the *sharkkain* went tumbling out of the clearing in a tangle of flailing limbs.

Like many of the men, Yan was shocked and confused by the rush from an unexpected direction. He stood slack-jawed, unsure of what to do.

More *sharkkain*, those who held the soldiers' attention by their response to the first one's call, burst into the clearing and leapt upon victims. Yan watched, stunned, as man after man was gutted by the creatures.

But some of the merin fought back.

Sir Kopell was struggling to get from beneath the beast that had leapt upon him. The *sharkkain* gripped him, finger claws caught in the links of his mail, while it raked across his stomach with the dagger-sized talon on its foot. Only the mail he wore saved Sir Kopell from being disemboweled. As it was, the claw slipped from the armor and gouged a furrow along the knight's thigh.

Khankemeh exploded in a leap that smashed the *sharkkain* away from Sir Kopell. The larger, stronger drakkenree sank his fangs into the *sharkkain*'s neck and snapped its spine with a shake of his head. He tossed the body toward a trio of *sharkkain* headed in his direction. They stopped their advance. Khankemeh roared at them. They backed away, heads low and threatening. But they did not stay intimidated for long. They advanced again, starting to separate, each taking a different angle toward Khankemeh. The drakkenree charged toward them, and the *sharkkain* scattered before his rush. Khankemeh didn't chase any of them. Instead he plunged into the brush, abandoning the clearing and the furious battle within it.

Yan thought that the drakkenree had deserted them until he heard Khankemeh roar again. A second roar answered him, cut off as a violent thrashing erupted among the plants. Two heavy saurian bodies crashed through the undergrowth. In flashes of gray and green, Yan caught brief glimpses of the combat. He saw enough to recognize that Khankemeh's foe was a gray drakkenree: a keeper.

The keeper's presence explained the deviousness of the ambush. This was more than an attack by a hungry hunting pack. The *sharkkain* must have been ordered into attacking the merin by one or more keepers. Such drakkenree could control certain beasts through an uncanny rapport; Yan had seen keepers send the giant drakkenkain into battle in Kolvin and keep them fighting longer than any uncontrolled animal would.

Somewhere out of sight, Khankemeh bellowed his victory.

But the *sharkkain* fought on.

More than one keeper, then.

"Yan, behind you!"

He spun around at Teletha's warning. One of the *sharkkain*—it looked to be the first one they'd seen; the stripe pattern was distinctive—was charging him. The beast was stumbling, bleeding from several wounds. One of its arms dangled uselessly at its side, but it came on, seemingly oblivious to its wounds. More evidence of the keeper's unseen influence.

Yan shoved Jerr hard, toward the trees and out of the *sharkkain's* path. As he'd hoped, she stumbled and fell, leaving the beast only one standing target; he noticed that they preferred an erect victim over one on the ground. Jerr would be safe.

For the moment.

He, on the other hand—

The *sharkkain* launched itself into the air, stretching all of its claws toward him. The sickle-taloned feet were curved swords aiming for his heart.

22

THERE WASN'T MUCH TELETHA COULD DO—she wasn't close enough. She yelled to alert Yan. He saw the danger, shoved Jerr to safety, and faced the beast alone. What did he think he was doing? He had no magic to blast the beast. If only she had not already discharged her pistol! She could have shot the creature.

But her pistol was still a weapon. She dropped her sword, took the gun in her steadier hand, and hurled it like an ax. The heavy butt struck true, just behind the creature's eye. The deadly, hooked fingers and toes spasmed open. The creature hit Yan, but it didn't disembowel him. The two of them smashed, entangled, into the ground. Yan was the first one up, fighting to free himself from the thrashing *sharkkain*. He managed, and scrambled toward the trees.

Good man! They can't leap so easily there.

The *sharkkain* got to its feet slowly. It had already been wounded; otherwise, Teletha doubted that it would have been so slow. Vehr's precepts against butchering the wounded didn't apply to animals. Teletha snatched up her sword and headed for it, intending to gut it while she had the chance.

Another *sharkkain* cut into her path. She wouldn't be able to shoot this one. She took her guard, sword arm leading and sword point well before her to put as much distance as possible between her and the beast's claws.

Over her attacker's back Teletha saw the wounded one rise and follow Yan into the trees. There wasn't anything she could do to help Yan now; she had her own problems.

The *sharkkain* that faced her had learned to respect a sword point. But though wary of her point, it was still aggressive. Teletha was forced back by its attack. The *sharkkain* was damned fast, and, though it was smaller than she was, it had the feral strength of an animal; she felt that strength every time it batted away her blade with its hands. Steadily, the *sharkkain* forced her back and back.

How far could she go before she backed into a tree, or lost her footing, or tripped over something?

The worry distracted her. The beast dodged past her point, ducking low. It kicked out with one taloned foot. She swept her leg out of the way—barely. The sickle claw ripped through the skirts of her buff coat. She knew it must have scored her flesh, but she didn't feel anything.

Yet.

The price of distraction. She found herself wonderfully concentrated on her defense.

But still she was forced back.

And back.

Her foot slipped as the ground crumbled away beneath her. A sinkhole? An animal den? It didn't matter. The *sharkkain* saw an opening. It tensed, crouched low, and sprang. She knew that she would not be able to interpose her point.

She let herself go with the fall, slamming her sword hilt up as she did. The guard caught the creature's shin and the shock wrenched her shoulder. Talons swept past her nose. The *sharkkain*'s tail slapped against her arm.

Intent on their duel, neither of them had realized where they were. The *sharkkain* discovered its error as it

hurtled past. It twisted in the air, trying to change its
course and slash at her at the same time. They were at
the edge of the hillock, at the brink of a steep overhang.
There was no more ground behind Teletha. There was
nowhere for the *sharkkain* to land except on her. Had she
not dropped, the *sharkkain* probably would have taken
both of them over the edge.

Arcing over Teletha, the beast tried to recover its balance, to ready itself for the fall. But the distance to the
dry streambed below was too short. The *sharkkain* was
still twisting, trying to right itself when it landed. Teletha
heard bone snap. The *sharkkain* shrilled its pain. Teletha
could only smile at the gleaming white bone poking
raggedly through its calf muscle. This *sharkkain* was out
of the fight.

But there were more.

She listened for the sounds of fighting, but heard nothing. Was that was good or bad?

From her vantage at the edge of the hillock, she could
see several of the streambeds and the elevated mounds of
jungle-covered earth around which they threaded. In one
of the channels ran several *sharkkain*, racing away from
the hillock where she stood. A black-and-gray drakkenree ran with them.

So it *was* more than a simple attack by hungry animals. She had guessed as much, but it was good to know
for sure. Drakkenree were behind the attack. Why did
drakkenree want the members of the expedition dead?
Or was the intent of the attack one of lethal finality? The
attack might only have been intended as harassment.
Either way, the question remained: who had ordered the
attack?

The *sharkkain* and their keeper were moving quickly.
Were they retreating, their deed done, or were they chasing down survivors? She couldn't see any merin down in
the flat areas, but everyone had scattered when the
sharkkain attacked. As she watched, the *sharkkain* left the

channel and clawed their way up onto another of the
hillocks, disappearing into the vegetation. The drakkenree followed its charges without stopping to look around.
They were in pursuit, Teletha decided; if they had been
retreating, the master of the pack would have wanted to
know if he was being followed.

Someone other than herself had survived the attack.

For the moment, anyway.

But the moment was all one had. This was no time to
daydream. There might be other survivors as well, and
some of them might need help. She needed to know who
had survived. Yan? Jerr? Arun? She prayed that they had
all managed to fight off their assailants as she had, or had
found a safe place to hide. She knew Yan could hide better than most, when he had wits enough to use his
magic—but he hadn't seemed to have all of his wits
about him when he'd bolted from the *sharkkain.*

She made her way back to the place where it had all
started. She had no trouble finding it; she could smell the
stink of blood and death. The scavengers would arrive
soon; if she could smell it, so could they.

The clearing looked like a battlefield. No, not a battlefield, more like a city turned to sack, for those killed by
the *sharkkain* reminded her more of the helpless victims
of maddened pillagers than the honestly slain warriors of
a battlefield. There was blood everywhere, already soaking into the earth. The carnage wrought by the *sharkkain*
when they tore a victim apart made it difficult to assess
how many had died. She set herself to the grim task.

She did not find Yan or Jerr, or any part that she
could confidently recognize as belonging to either of
them, but she did find Myskell. The man-at-arms lay
with his dagger buried in the rib cage of a *sharkkain* and
his burly arms wrapped around the beast, hugging it to
him. The *sharkkain* had a foot buried in Myskell's belly,
having slid the taloned paw up under his mail. They had
slain each other.

Sir Kopell's archers were dead as well, but at the spot where the knight had gone down, she found only blood and a track, as if something had been dragged away. Had the *sharkkain* taken him? None of the others she had seen fall were missing. Hoping that she wasn't wasting time following the trail of a wounded man who had crawled off into the bushes to die, she left the clearing.

She found Sir Kopell holed up with his back against a tree. Another tree grew close by the first and protected his left. A third tree, toppled, blocked much of his right flank. Clearly he had intended to make a stand. The blood-soaked bandage wrapped around his thigh told why he didn't run; he couldn't. But no *sharkkain* had come for him. The knight lay on the ground, eyes closed and sword hilt resting in his open palm.

But he breathed!

As she approached, his eyes fluttered open and his hand closed convulsively on his sword hilt. He struggled to rise, shouting, "You'll not take me!"

"Easy, Sir Knight. I'm no lizard." She was careful to hold her sword low and stay out of his reach.

"Teletha?" He sounded confused. "Are we the only ones?"

The knight's eyes were bleak with despair, but she couldn't lie to him. "Maybe. I don't know."

"Myskell?"

"Dead. He took at least one with him."

"He was a good man. Dav and Chanz?"

They would be the archers. "Dead, too."

"Master Tanafres?"

"Missing."

"The king will have my head."

Sir Kopell's king was not their greatest worry at the moment. "King Shain's not here; he can't have your head unless we get out of here. We need to find out who else survived."

Sir Kopell agreed, but they had to retie his bandage

before he could walk. Teletha cut down a sapling for him to use as a crutch, and they started their search. Progress was slow, but she didn't dare get too far from the knight; there were just the two of them.

They came upon a trail mashed through the foliage by someone or something moving in a hurry. There was blood on some of the leaves, and some of them had been cut. There was *sharkkain* spoor in the loam. The beasts had pursued someone through the area.

The trail led to a small clearing; in it were three dead *sharkkain* and Arun Schell, wounded unto death. Teletha ran to his side, carefully not looking at the organs that spilled from beneath his tattered buff coat. To her amazement, she found that he was conscious.

"How is it with you?" she asked

"Now I know how the stag feels when the dogs catch him." He smiled weakly. "I don't think I'll do much hunting anymore."

"You'll be fine," she told him, hoping it wasn't the lie that she feared it was. "As soon as we get one of the priests over here. Vehr won't refuse to aid such a warrior."

"Much as I love my Lord Vehr, a god's mercy can only do so much. Besides, the priests are all dead, aren't they?"

"We don't know."

"You don't know otherwise."

"Let's get you under some shade," she said, temporizing.

"If we move him, he'll die," Sir Kopell whispered in her ear.

"Then we'll stay here," she said. If Arun was going to die, she wanted no part in hastening it.

"They'll come for us." There was no need for Sir Kopell to specify what *who* he meant; his eyes, roaming the surrounding jungle, said it all. The *sharkkain.*

"They're gone." Arun's voice was weak. "A drakken-ree came and called them away."

"Mine?" Sir Kopell asked.

"No. Another."

"How could you tell?"

"Gray," Arun mumbled.

"A keeper," Teletha said.

"A keeper," Arun agreed. "It said the work was done. The price earned."

"You speak the drakkenree tongue?"

Arun tried a laugh, but it was smothered in a coughing fit. When he recovered, he said, "Hardly. It spoke bad Empiric. It was talking to Gissel."

Sir Kopell exploded. "That traitorous hill monkey bastard! By Vehr, I'll kill him and take his tail for a belt!"

Teletha knew Sir Kopell would keep that oath, given the chance. She wasn't planning on giving him the chance; she wanted Gissel's tail—and head—for herself.

"Threok must have ordered it," Sir Kopell said. "I'll take his tail as well."

"Choshok," Arun said. He grimaced at the pain it cost to lift an arm and pull the *staliarm* out from beneath his shirt. "There must be other survivors. Look for them, Teletha. Give Handrar this."

"Handrar went down in the first rush," she told him.

"Dead?" Arun asked disbelievingly.

"I don't see how he could have survived."

He closed his eyes and was quiet, for so long that she thought he had slipped away. But he hadn't.

"Teletha?" He sounded much weaker.

"I'm here, Arun."

"I can't see you."

"I'm here, Arun. I'm holding your hand."

"Oh."

Vehr, be merciful, she prayed silently.

"Teletha, take the *staliarm.* The emperor knows your loyalty," he said. The gem in the *staliarm*'s heart flickered, testifying to Arun's words. "I'm sorry that I couldn't be the one to let you fly again."

"It doesn't matter."

"Ah, it's a fine standard," Arun said. "Glorious as the sun."

He died with his eyes set on a sight only he could see. Teletha reached out and gently closed the lids. She put Arun's sword in his hand and closed his lifeless fingers around the grip.

"Vehr, protect a soldier," she whispered. Stifling tears, she rose. She kissed her sword blade and saluted Arun's corpse with her weapon. "Honor to Lord Vehr. Honor to those who march with His standard."

23

YAN RAN FROM THE *SHARKKAIN*. What else could he do? The vegetation whipsawed him as he passed, tearing cloth and skin. It didn't matter. He had to lead the *sharkkain* away from Jerr.

He couldn't hear anything over the shouts and roars from the clearing. Was the *sharkkain* close?

Risking a look back, he immediately tripped over something. He saved himself from sprawling by slamming into a tree. A frightened lizard scampered away up the bole.

Yan looked down to see what had caught his feet. A body. One of the soldiers. Why was he lying there? There was no blood on him that Yan could see. Yan bent to help the man; the *sharkkain* would be on them soon, and they couldn't stay here.

"Come on, man. Get up!"

The soldier didn't get up, would never get up. He was dead, strangled. It was the man Schell had sent with Gissel.

Somewhere nearby the *sharkkain* gave its coughing call.

Yan's eyes fell on the soldier's sword, still resting in its scabbard. The man had no more need of it. Yan drew the sword. He was no swordsman, but having a weapon made him feel better. Against a *sharkkain*, any weapon was better than none.

The *sharkkain* pursuing him was wounded. Perhaps he could lure it close and strike it down. No, that wouldn't work; rapport could not be achieved with murderous intent in your heart.

The *sharkkain* coughed again.

Yan wouldn't need rapport to bring it to him.

Bringing the beast to him suddenly didn't seem like a good idea. What did it matter that he had a sword in his hand? He didn't know how to use it.

Should he run again? Some predators proclaimed their presence in order to flush their prey from hiding. Perhaps the *sharkkain* was doing that, having lost his trail. If so, running was the last thing he should do.

Quiet and inconspicuousness might serve better for the moment. Calling upon his magic, he cloaked himself in stillness and willed himself to be a part of the world around him, no more noteworthy than a fern or a vine. Within the stillness, he opened his senses, listening for the approach of the *sharkkain*.

At his hip, his satchel felt warm. The sensation grew more intense as he exercised his *præha* senses and strained to become fully aware of his surroundings. His understanding of the jungle around him became greater, but so did the incandescence growing from within his satchel. He could not ignore the phenomenon. He looked down and knew the source: the Eye of the Serpent. Within the satchel, within its box, within its wrappings, the talisman glowed. How and why, he didn't know; it frightened him. Had he made a mistake in bringing it along?

Quickly he retreated from *præha*.

The heat died instantly, gone as if it had never been, but the fear remained. The Eye was no longer inert. Why? What did it mean? With a saurian predator hunting him, he had no time to investigate magical phenomena. Yan's curiosity about the Eye rose to new heights, but he had to ignore its call. If he thought too hard on the Eye, he might not survive to unravel its secrets; the *sharkkain* was still out there.

And so was someone else. Though he had been barely conscious of it at the time, overwhelmed by the revelation that the Eye was active, he had heard something while he was in *præha*: the sound of someone murmuring in Nitallan, praying. The prayers hadn't sounded like those of a wounded man; Yan had heard such prayers too often and knew their kind too well to mistake them. The fervor was similar, but these prayers were a far more eloquent plea for deliverance.

The same sense that had let him hear the prayers gave him a feel for the direction from which they had come. As quietly as he could he moved in that direction. Soon he was hearing the prayers with his ears. He recognized the voice; the praying man was Löm Kerandiri.

Yan found Kerandiri in a small tree-ringed hollow, kneeling in plain sight and still praying. Unfortunately, the *sharkkain* had found the priest as well; Yan saw it moving through the brush, eyes set on Kerandiri and jaws already agape. While Yan believed in the gods, he didn't expect that They would protect Kerandiri from all harm, as the man asked. Unless Yan did something, Kerandiri was doomed. And if Yan tried, they both might be doomed.

Yan ran forward, shouting.

"Run, priest! This way! This way!"

They might have a chance if they were not in the open. Who was he fooling? He held the sword out before him in the hope that it might intimidate the *sharkkain*. He need not have bothered.

Kerandiri ignored Yan's shout and continued praying. The *sharkkain* only increased its pace toward the hollow. Yan had started out closer than the *sharkkain* to Kerandiri, but the beast moved faster. Yan was still several yards

from Kerandiri when the *sharkkain* burst from the brush
and launched itself at the priest. The löm was as insensi-
tive to its piercing scream as he had been to Yan's warning; Kerandiri remained kneeling, praying, oblivious to
his danger.

Yan was too distant to do anything to save the priest.

One moment the *sharkkain* was moving through the
air, arcing toward Kerandiri, claws outstretched; the next
the beast hung suspended in the air, shrieking and
writhing. Something invisible supported the *sharkkain*
and prevented it from reaching Kerandiri.

Running full tilt, Yan was unable to halt himself
before he came as near to Kerandiri as had the *sharkkain.*
Surprisingly, he struck nothing. Nothing impeded him.
He skidded to a stop by the side of the oblivious priest.

How long would the *sharkkain* hang there? The barrier
did not seem to be hurting it; its screams were of rage,
not of pain. It was hard to be sure, but the beast seemed
to be pulling itself free. The weight awkward in his hand,
Yan thrust with the sword. He felt the shock in his arm as
the point dug into the *sharkkain.* The creature screamed,
thrashing more violently and tearing the sword from
Yan's hand. It crashed to the ground. Somehow Yan had
managed to strike well; the animal lay writhing.

Yan looked down at the dying *sharkkain.* He watched
its struggles lessen and still. It died. The sight of the dead
saurian reminded him of another time, another place. He
had used a sword then, too. He told himself that this was
nothing like that time; that this *sharkkain* was not an intelligent being, let alone a fellow magician. His assurances
to himself didn't make his stomach any less sour.

In the ground beside the dead *sharkkain,* Yan could
see other *sharkkain* tracks. He wasn't much of a tracker,
but even he could see the story in the forest floor. Other
sharkkain had been here; they had circled Kerandiri.
Perhaps one of them had tried to reach the priest, as this
one had. The tracks showed that none of those other

sharkkain had come any closer to the priest than a few yards. Clearly the beasts were gone; if they were not, they would have appeared in response to the dead one's noise. Something beyond Yan's understanding had happened here. There seemed but one conclusion: Kerandiri's prayers had been answered; the löm had been spared by the gods.

Kerandiri's deliverance raised an immediate question in Yan's mind. He shook the priest until the man's eyes focused on him.

"If you could have turned them away, why didn't you do it sooner? Men died while you withheld this power!"

Kerandiri shook his head, his expression bleak. "How many?"

"I don't know. There was still a lot of fighting when the *sharkkain* chased me away from the clearing. Last I saw, half or more of the soldiers were down with their insides ripped out. The beasts chased others, like me, into the jungle." Yan thought about Teletha; she'd warned him, and he'd been too busy saving himself to see her fate. Could she have escaped? "They may all be dead by now."

"Horesh greet their souls with light." Kerandiri wept as he made the sign of the Triad.

"You could have saved them."

Kerandiri wouldn't meet his eyes. "This protection is the work of Horesh and His Court. It is not anything that I did."

Yan almost objected, but Kerandiri's protest didn't sound like the usual perfunctory clerical denial. There was a solemn seriousness to the man's tone. He let the priest speak on.

"The gods require asking before they interfere in the affairs of the mortal world. It is the rightful way of the world. Yet you are correct to rebuke me. I should have asked sooner. Lady Mannar grant me mercy. I am but a mortal man, as much prey to surprise and terror as any other. When the beasts came out of the jungle, I was frightened, and only the quick thinking of my brethren saved me. They dragged me from the clearing, using their own bodies as shields. Though several paid with their lives, they took me from the immediate danger. I would not have asked such action of them, Vehr's just sword strike me down if I lie; I would not have asked such sacrifice. I did not come to my wits until we were here. I thought that only my brethren and I had survived the attack, and I saw that all was not over; the beasts remained. There were more of them coming. We were in the hands of the gods. There was nothing to do but pray that the Court intercede. I tried to convince my brethren as well, calling upon them to pray with me, but they had insufficient faith. They ran before the beasts. Woe to their souls; where are they now?"

Dead, Yan thought, but he didn't say it. Another voice answered from the brush.

"Gone to serve their patrons."

It was Zephem. The Baaliffite priest was battered, wounded, and bloody, but alive. His sword ran red with blood and his shield was battered into near uselessness.

"Where have you been?" asked Yan.

"I have not been hiding, if that is what you imply," Zephem replied. "I did what I could to protect the others. It was not enough. I do not know why, but the beasts retreated. Had they remained, they would have had me, though I would have opened a few more of them for Lord Baaliff to drink their blood."

"You're the only one spared?" Kerandiri's voice was cracked as he spoke.

Zephem nodded. "The fight took me back toward the clearing. When the beasts ran away, I went there and searched for others who survived the attack. I saw none there alive."

"Some may have escaped into the jungle as we did," said Yan.

"May Horesh and all the gods protect them if they did," Zephem said. "The jungle is thick with the abominable beasts. And we are at the mercy of the ancient enemy."

"What do you mean?" Yan asked.

"Did you not think the beasts unnaturally clever? I did. Until I saw that these creatures attacked at the order of the drakkenree."

"You saw a keeper?"

"You would know better than I what it is called," Zephem said with a sneer. "I saw a drakkenree, all gray and black. It petted the beasts as if they were faithful hounds."

"This bodes ill," Kerandiri said.

An understatement, Yan thought.

"We must return to the ships," Zephem announced. "If we can. Then we must break free of Factor Choshok's trap and sail back to the empire. We will return with an army and raze Jor Valadrem around Choshok's ears, and scour the jungle clean of the drakkenree and their abominations."

"What about the Wizard of Bones?" asked Yan.

Zephem spat. "Likely it was he who set the beasts on us. We must burn him and all his issue. Even with the blessing of the gods and Their strength in us, we are too few to deliver the necessary vengeance."

"There are still questions unanswered," Kerandiri said.

"I see none," Zephem said. "Our path is clear. We must return to the empire and gather sufficient force to serve as Baaliff's cleansing sword. Our course is clear. We must deal with this problem as we should have from the beginning."

"We must know—"

Zephem interrupted Kerandiri. "We do know! We know our enemy! And we know that we must destroy them!"

"You said there are creatures all around us," said Yan. "What makes you think we can escape?"

"The gods will protect us. We do Their work," Zephem said.

"No," said Kerandiri.

Zephem turned shocked eyes to him.

Kerandiri continued, "The gods set us on this journey to learn the answers to questions that vex us. We have not learned those answers, and have only found more and troubling questions. Master Tanafres is right; we have little hope of going back. We must go on as we have and pray that the gods will protect us, as They protected me when I did not flee from the beasts. That protection was Their sign, brother. They do not wish us to turn back from this path. We must face and overcome the trials They place before us."

"You're wrong," Zephem said.

Kerandiri's expression hardened. "You speak beyond your role, Fra Zephem."

"I say what is necessary."

"And *I* say that you are bound to obey. Your oath to the gods demands it. Or are you prepared to deny that as well?"

For a moment Yan thought that Zephem was ready to send Kerandiri to the gods, that the löm might get his answers directly from Them. The Baaliffite's rage was visible. Slowly the tremor in his hands subsided.

"As Baaliff serves Horesh, so shall I serve," he said at last.

Kerandiri nodded, accepting the response. "We must find the Wizard of Bones. I feel sure that our answers and our fates lie with him."

Yan could agree that the Wizard of Bones would have answers, but didn't care for the suggestion that the wizard controlled their fate. It was too likely to be true.

Jerr fell when Master Tanafres shoved her, but she didn't stay down. She scrambled to her feet and ran as fast as she could. Away from the clearing. Away from the beasts, and away from the death.

It was worse than the battle at Rastionne.

Her eyes darted about as she sought the easiest, fastest passage through the undergrowth. But in her mind, all she could see were the terrible claws and snapping jaws of the creatures that had burst out of the jungle around them. The creatures were awful. Though they were smaller than drakkenree, they were somehow more menacing. They seemed all teeth, claws, talons, and a terrible, mindless desire to kill. And there were so many of the creatures. They had come from everywhere. For all she knew, the jungle was full of them. Each time she burst through a screen of vegetation, she expected to run right into one. She couldn't stay and let them catch her. She had to get away.

So she ran.

As fast as she could.

Her heart hammered. Her lungs seared her with each breath. Her face ached, itched, and burned, sore from the beating it was taking from the vegetation through which she plowed.

Still, she ran.

She had to.

She ran down the hillock and into the flat openness of the old streambed. It was easier to run in the open. *Open*? She was in the open! In the open, it was easier, too, to be chased.

This channel still had water in it, a broad ribbon of murky brown. Who knew what lurked under the surface? But she didn't see any crocodiles basking anywhere nearby. She splashed in and made her stumbling way down the stream. She'd heard a hunter once complain about a deer losing his hounds by running through the water. She was being hunted now; maybe she could escape from the creatures by doing what the deer had done.

Behind her, someone called her name. She almost stumbled. The creatures knew her name! The thought terrified her. They were coming for her! For *her*!

She ran harder.

And was betrayed by the water she'd hoped would help her. Her foot slipped on something that squirmed away. Flailing, she fell.

Lying in the water, she knew she couldn't run anymore. She was too tired. Her lungs felt scorched, as if she had taken a deep breath too near a fire. Her limbs were trembling, as much with fatigue as with fear.

She was doomed!

There was nothing to do but wait for her death, anticipate what was to come. Think about what was to— Think?

No longer running, she could think. As much as the creatures looked like drakkenree, they were not. They had attacked with animal screams, not human shouting and yelling. They were beasts. How could they call her name?

Someone had, and it couldn't be one of those terrible creatures. She dared to look back the way she'd come.

Not someone, two someones. The more distant figure wore the green, black, and gold of a Vehrite and carried a two-handed sword. It could only be Fra Serent. The nearer figure was dressed in the tattered remnants of islander clothes. She recognized him at once.

Galon!

"Jerr, wait!" he called. "Don't run!"

She wouldn't run. Not from him.

She picked herself up. When he was close enough, she threw herself into his arms. She heard his sword splash into the water, its hilt clanging against a rock. Not that she heeded it much. He paid it no heed, too. They clung to each other in a wet embrace, and she felt his warmth, especially where she could feel his skin through the rents in his clothes. He was warm, alive! And so was she!

Their mouths met, their kiss confirming how glad each was that the other had survived.

"Why did you run from me?" he asked, when they came up for air.

"I didn't know it was you."

"Who else would have called you by name?" Fra Serent asked, shocking Jerr back to the awareness that she and Galon were not alone.

Jerr felt acutely embarrassed and relinquished her hold on Galon. This was no time for such intimacy, but her fears that such a time would never come had vanished.

All they had to do was live long enough.

It was time to think of other things. "Where is the löm?"

Fra Serent looked nervous. "I do not know. The first attack separated me from Löm Kerandiri. I saw Fra Zephem and the other priests take him from the clearing. I also saw a pack of the beasts follow them. Fra Zephem is a devotee of Baaliff, and he can fight, but the others . . ." Fra Serent shook his head sadly. "These beasts are murderous and have great numbers. I fear that we must pray that Horesh has taken all my brothers into His light."

"They can't be dead," Jerr protested.

"I fear that they are," the priest said.

"But what about Master Tanafres?" She could see him standing there, the creature leaping toward him. She felt ashamed that she had run. What danger had there really been? He had not been afraid. He had been ready to stop the creature with his magic.

"Jerr." Galon's eyes were sad. She knew what he was going to say; she didn't need his words. "I saw Master Tanafres go down. I'm sorry."

She didn't want to believe it. Wouldn't she know somehow if Master Tanafres was dead? Magicians' apprentices in goblin tales always knew when their masters died. "He can't be dead."

Fra Serent squatted next to her and put a comforting hand on her shoulder. "Everyone dies, Jerr. It is a part of the cycle. Take heart. Perhaps Lord Einthof now shares with your master all the secrets he sought to learn in his life."

"No. I won't believe it!"

But this was real life, not a goblin tale. And she was no real apprentice. She started to cry. If Master Tanafres was dead, so were her dreams.

"There was still fighting when I ran after Jerr," Galon said.

She supposed he meant the statement to offer hope. Jerr only cried harder. Dreams could be replaced, especially if she had Galon. But no one could replace Master Tanafres.

"And when I went after you," Fra Serent said. "But it was not going well. I hold no hope for any of the others."

"You don't *know* they're dead," Jerr argued, but Fra Serent was a Vehrite. If anyone understood battles, it was the soldiers' god's priests. All too likely he was right. Master Tanafres was dead. He'd died saving her. Was that fair?

"I don't know they're not," Fra Serent said. "But I have seen battles, and I know when they are lost."

"The battle won't be lost as long as the Captain is alive," Galon boasted.

The words sounded a little hollow to Jerr.

Clearly Fra Serent didn't believe them either. "Your Captain Schell was pursued from the clearing by a half dozen of the beasts. No man would be a match for such a ravenous pack."

Poor Galon looked as if he were facing the end of the world. Jerr wanted to hold him, but he looked so fragile that she didn't dare try. His voice, when he spoke, was tiny.

"You think the Captain is dead?"

Fra Serent nodded solemnly. "I think that he must be.

He was a good man and a good soldier. Though he no longer carries his sword in Lord Vehr's service in this world, I feel sure that he marches by my Lord's side in the world beyond ours."

Galon's attitude visibly changed. His troubled look changed to one grim and determined. It frightened Jerr a little.

"We must avenge the Captain," he said.

Fra Serent shook his head. "What we must do is try to get back to the ships."

Sailing away sounded wonderful to Jerr. Galon stared into the jungle and just kept shaking his head.

"Galon Martello." Fra Serent's stern tone clearly caught Galon's attention; Galon turned to the warrior priest. Fra Serent spoke earnestly. "You and I are soldiers. We have a duty."

"A duty to avenge our comrades. Vehr says so."

Fra Serent had to acknowledge the truth of that. "You speak truth. Lord Vehr honors those who stand by their comrades. But among those who understand the true path of our Lord Vehr, vengeance is a right, not a necessity. Vengeance is to be taken as time and chance permit, and most certainly not when the cost of that vengeance is too high. A soldier who loses a battle to avenge a friend is no true soldier. Would Captain Schell abandon his duty?"

"You said the battle was over! What's left of duty but vengeance?"

"You sound like one of the more odious followers of Lord Baaliff," Fra Serent said sadly.

Galon's jaw clenched at the remark. He balled his hands into fists and flung himself at Fra Serent. Jerr didn't know the warrior gods well, but she knew that their followers disliked each other. Galon was a professed follower of Vehr; Fra Serent knew that. Why had Fra Serent insulted him?

Galon's assault was furious, but Fra Serent avoided

most of the blows. The warrior priest was a grown man and an experienced fighter; he did not let the fight last long. Through strength and skill, he wrestled Galon to a halt, holding him fast. Galon slumped in Fra Serent's grip. Jerr could see the despair in Galon's eyes as their gazes met.

"Do you not see a need that vengeance wait?" Fra Serent asked.

Galon looked deep into Jerr's eyes. He clenched his jaw. "Let me go, Fra Serent."

The priest released him. Galon straightened his clothes, as if by smoothing the wrinkles he could smooth his dignity. Fra Serent handed Galon his sword. Galon accepted it gravely, gave it a shake to shed water droplets, and checked its condition before sheathing it. Having done that, he faced Fra Serent, standing straight and tall.

"We must see that Jerr is safe," he said.

"A gallant decision."

"Dutiful," Galon corrected. "The Captain was under orders to protect the magician and his party. It seems that we have failed in that mission, and I will answer for it. Yet there is still someone needing protection. If I fail to protect her by my foolishness, there is no answer I can give. I will have no honor."

"Captain Schell would be proud of you," Fra Serent said.

"It's what the Captain would have done."

"You honor him."

"I always have. And I *will* avenge him," Galon said. "But not today. Today we must get Jerr safely back to the ships. Then we can go after the Captain's killers. Tomorrow—"

"Tomorrow we must break through the barrier on the river and begin our journey back to the empire."

Galon started to protest, but gave up when Fra Serent said, "It is our duty."

Galon drew in a deep breath. All the while he glowered at Fra Serent. Just when Jerr thought Galon would burst, he let his breath out in a sigh. "Then let us be about it."

"Better to travel where we will be less likely to be seen," Fra Serent said. He pointed toward one of the hillocks. "It will be harder going, but safer, I think."

Jerr took Galon's hand. She felt the tension there; he did not return her clasp at first. "We must go."

He nodded, squeezing her hand.

They left the streambed, crossed the dry part of the channel, and began to climb the bank. She was grateful for Galon's help; the bank was steep. After Galon had gotten her safely up, he turned back to help Fra Serent up the slope.

She was pleased. As she had once she stopped running, he'd come to his senses. There really was only one reasonable course, and they were taking it by heading back to the ships. She was glad that Galon had accepted it so quickly. She hadn't wanted to see him go running off into the jungle to die. There was enough trouble looking for them; they didn't need to go looking for trouble.

Jerr turned around to start walking and saw that trouble was no longer looking for them. It had found them. Standing before her was a drakkenree, a bloody sword in its hand.

She screamed.

24

TELETHA FELT CONFIDENT that the saurians Yan had called *sharkkain* had left the area. Knowing that the beasts were controlled by drakkenree keepers, she could predict their actions by reason rather than trying to guess at animal thought processes. At least she hoped so. The beasts that the keepers had commanded during the invasion of Kolvin had been under the tight control of the keepers, but those beasts had been as foreign to Kolvin as the keepers. If, as Yan believed, the drakkenree were native to these parts, so might the *sharkkain* be, and there might be wild ones. Animals often behaved differently in strange places than they did in their native haunts; the local beasts might not need a keeper's urging to attack people. Most hunting animals avoided healthy, well-armed prey. Would wild *sharkkain* do so?

She hoped that they wouldn't have the chance to find out.

Having found Sir Kopell a safe place to rest, she returned to the clearing where the attack had started. She wanted to recover her pistol and maybe add a pair of arquebuses to their armament. Some provisions would be nice, too.

She hadn't been prepared to find fresh merin footprints in the clearing.

She located her pistol—still usable, she was relieved to see—and loaded it. She found an undamaged arquebus, readied it, and set a slow match asmoldering before checking out the trail. Whoever had come back had been making his own survey of the clearing. Looking for gear, as she was? Nothing seemed gone since the last time she'd been through. Maybe he was looking for survivors?

There weren't any here.

She searched the perimeter of the clearing and a bit beyond. She couldn't find anything of the man's trail to follow. Whoever it was had taken precautions to conceal his trail out of the clearing. Fear of the *sharkkain* could motivate such caution.

She did find Yan's trail out of the clearing, and that led her to Marefinn, dead, and not by a *sharkkain*. He had been strangled. His sword was gone, but nothing else. There were two sets of tracks near the body, Yan's and a bregil's. Gissel, she expected. Yan wouldn't have killed Marefinn, so it must have been Gissel. She looked for a trail and found that the bregil had concealed his departure. Was it worth trying to pick up?

Not with Yan wandering around out there.

Yan had left the site of Marefinn's murder the way he had arrived, at a run. For once, Teletha was glad of Yan's lack of woodcraft. Yan's trail led her to Marefinn's sword, stuck in a dead *sharkkain*. There were several sets of *sharkkain* prints, but no sign of a fight beyond the dead beast. There were merin footprints as well, three sets. Yan's was one of them. One of them was the man who had revisited the clearing; some blood nearby suggested that the man had been wounded. The third was connected to impressions suggesting that someone had been kneeling in the small clearing. Löm Kerandiri? Could the gods be so kind?

All three men had set out together, but as near as she could tell, they weren't headed back for the ships. Were they confused?

No, she thought, and shook her head bemusedly. Yan had to be in charge; no one else would be so foolish as to go deeper into danger after the disastrous attack of the *sharkkain*.

No one?

So why was she thinking about going after Yan?

Zephem's warning had been timely; the drakkenree seemed unaware of their presence. Yan, Kerandiri, and the Baaliffite crouched in the concealing brush at the edge of what appeared to be a logging cut, waiting for the saurian to pass. The drakkenree moved slowly, walking along the sunlit space that seemed almost a river of sunny brush and debris between banks of dense jungle.

This drakkenree was a warrior; his mottled green coloring readily apparent in the sunlight of the cut. He carried a knobby-shafted spear and wore a harness very similar to those of the drakkenree who had invaded Kolvin. An assortment of bags, sheathed knives, and a hand ax hung from the straps. A cap made of interwoven leather straps adorned his head. Light glinted from the metal studs on the leather and gleamed from the iridescent feather that streamed back from his cap like a heron's crest. From what Yan knew, the feather suggested rank.

Was the drakkenree searching for them? Or was he about some other business entirely?

A terrific crash echoed down the lane between the trees. Yan started, as did the priests, but the drakkenree paid the sound no heed even though it came from the direction in which he was heading. To Yan's surprise, the saurian stopped to examine one of the fallen trees in the cut. Finishing his examination, the drakkenree clicked his jaws, expressing his satisfaction with something. Yan took a closer look at the tree; the bole was shattered, not cut.

This was not a logging cut.

The drakkenree took up a branch and began to poke into a greenish brown mass, much the way a herder would prod the stool of his charges to ascertain their health. Stool? Yan's eyes swept the cut. Yes, there were many such masses. They were so large that he had not connected them with the heavy, rank odor hanging in the air; such piles were too large to be the leavings of animals. Or were they? Something had smashed down the trees and trampled the vegetation. Something very large.

Somewhere out of sight another tree shattered and made its crashing way to the ground.

The drakkenree tossed down his stick and started on.

He was about to pass them by. They remained unseen; they also remained without any idea of where they were going. The drakkenree did not look bellicose, and he was an inhabitant of these parts. And he was alone, and so perhaps not a great threat to them. It seemed too good an opportunity to pass up.

Yan stepped out into the cut, and the drakkenree spun to face him. Fighting down the urge to run from the spear-wielding saurian, Yan said, "*Hachni, seskegriften. Nak yakweeni.*"

Yan did not bow since such a gesture might be misconstrued. Conforming to the alien etiquette was difficult after years of formal Kolvin etiquette. Yan did tilt his face toward the ground, though, because he didn't want to undermine his statement.

I greet you, honorable warrior. No challenge is offered.

Hoping he had said the words correctly, Yan nervously watched the drakkenree from the corner of his eye. It was hard to remain still and wait. For a long moment, the saurian did not alter the stance that he'd taken when Yan had stepped from the concealing brush. His body remained tilted down, his head held back on the S-curve of its neck. His spear remained pointed in Yan's direction. The drakkenree's posture was somewhat hostile, though not openly aggressive. Yan's words did not cause the drakkenree to shift into a more belligerent stance; Yan took that as a positive sign.

He tried again. "*Hachni, seskegriften. Gifni* Yan Tanafres."

No response.

"*Ye drakkenree kaini. Nak yakweeni.*"

"*Gifni ye drrr'hak'n'rr'ee. Y'kk'wee? Ne?*" The skin around the drakkenree's eyes darkened with amusement. "*Ye maah'nn'kun'yee shess n'k y'kk'wee.*"

Yan didn't expect that one merin would be a challenge to a drakkenree warrior. In fact, he'd been counting on the drakkenree seeing things that way. "*Nak Yakweeni.*"

"*Shess ssess.*" *I accept that as truth.* The drakkenree remained amused. "*Ka'a* Yan Tanafres *maah'nn'kun'yee kem dja'krr rr'ee?*"

In the uncanny way of his kind, the drakkenree spoke Yan's name almost exactly as Yan had, a distracting ability, but Yan couldn't afford to be distracted. The warrior was asking who Yan was to speak the drakkenree language. Yan didn't want to give the honest answer; saying that he had learned the language while a slave in a drakkenree camp would not stand him well. He decided to ignore the question, pressing his own interests.

"*Kaini—*" he started before realizing that he didn't know how to name the Wizard of Bones. All he knew was the term for a master of magic that Yellow Eye had used. Hoping that the Wizard of Bones was the only magician in the area, he used that term to say whom he sought. "*Kaini sestraka kedjaka.*"

"*Ssess'trak'ka?*" The drakkenree's body dipped lower, his stance more guarded. It seemed that like warriors everywhere, he distrusted magic.

Here perhaps was an opportunity. "Yes, *sestraka kedjaka*. A magician. Like me." Yan conjured his magelight, letting the small sphere of cold green light float over his outstretched hand.

After an initial flinch, the drakkenree's attitude became more polite. It was clear that Yan had impressed him. Or frightened him. In any case, when Yan again stated that he sought the drakkenree magician, the warrior agreed to lead him.

The drakkenree warrior's name was Gresshannak, as near as Yan could pronounce it. When Kerandiri and Zephem emerged at Yan's call, Gresshannak asked if the priests were Yan's property. Watching the way the drakkenree fingered his spear shaft when he looked at Zephem—the only one of the merin carrying a sword— Yan thought it wise to confirm the drakkenree's impression. Drakkenree warriors were a fractious lot and very conscious of their position relative to other warriors. If Gresshannak thought Zephem a free warrior, the saurian might find it necessary to challenge Zephem. Nothing good would come of that. If they fought, Zephem would likely be killed. If, by the grace of the gods Zephem won the fight, they would lose their guide and perhaps the goodwill of the Wizard of Bones. Better Gresshannak think the priests were Yan's slaves; the priests need never know, and the pretense might save their lives.

Gresshannak led them along the cut. They traveled back the way the saurian had come, away from the source of the splintering crashes. Yan felt a little disappointed. He'd wanted to know what sort of creature could force such a path through the jungle. It would have to remain a mystery for another day.

After several miles, the drakkenree led them into the jungle along a game trail. As before, they saw little wildlife other than birds and the occasional mortfleiger flitting among the overhead branches. They heard other animals on occasion, calling or crashing away through the brush. Nothing and no one challenged their progress. Yan was relieved.

"How much farther?" Kerandiri asked.

Yan translated the question, and Gresshannak replied, "Near."

A hollow crashing sound punctuated the remark. The noise reminded Yan a little of the sound made by bones struck together. He felt chill despite the heat. Could the accusations of necromancy be true? He asked Gresshannak the source of the noise.

"*Ah'taumk'rroan,*" said Gresshannak, with a dismissive flip of his tail. *Mating season.*

The reply took Yan off guard. Mating season? He remembered reading a work of natural history which spoke of the rutting behavior of certain deer, who clashed their antlers together to determine which buck would rule the herd. Clashing antlers might make such a sound, though not so loud. The theory seemed far-fetched; they'd seen no deer. Then what had made the sound?

He soon learned.

They emerged from the trees onto a rocky slope that led down to a river valley. A herd of *vekkanconday*, the pack beasts used by the drakkenree, milled on the slope, while a pair of keepers watched them. Gresshannak bobbed a greeting to the keepers, who returned his greeting, but only after several moments of staring at the merin. Gresshannak led them around the *vekkanconday* herd.

On the far side of the herd, two of the largest *vekkanconday* stood facing each other, a little distance from the rest. Those two held their bodies low and horizontal in the manner of challenging drakkenree. But unlike drakkenree, these dome-headed beasts held their heads with their snouts pointing to the ground. Each turned its head slightly that it might eye its opponent, shifting from side to side to give each eye a good view. As if by common agreement, they simultaneously took three rushing steps forward and hurled themselves at each other, their

heads coming into line with their bodies in the way a
jouster tilted up his helm just before impact. And what an
impact it was! The thick-boned skulls slammed together
with a resounding crack, the sound that they had heard
more than a mile away.

No dead bones here. Live ones, within living bodies;
bodies working to make more life.

"*Ah'taumk'rroan*," Gresshannak said, pointing at the
contending *vekkanconday* with his spear. "It will be
decided soon; the young bull is tiring. It is not yet his
time."

So it was true. These bulls were dueling like buck
deer. Yan was fascinated.

Kerandiri was not content to allow Yan to study the
vekkanconday; he took Yan's arm, forcing Yan to turn.

"What make you of that place?" the löm said, pointing.

That place was a village of huts situated on the floodplain of the river valley. A stockade of logs enclosed the
village, and a ditch enringed it. The ramshackle structures
contrasted oddly with the sturdy palisade. Despite the fer-
tile ground of the floodplain, there were no crops to be
seen. Unusual for a settlement of such a size. Unless . . . By
squinting Yan could just make out that the inhabitants of
the village were drakkenree. As carnivores, the drakkenree
would not need crops.

"Is it the place of the Wizard of Bones?" asked
Kerandiri.

Yan wondered that himself. He hoped so; they had
walked far enough. Gresshannak led them down the
slope toward the stockade. It was easier walking on the
floodplain, but Yan found himself reluctant to take
advantage and increase his pace. Was this the end of
their journey? And if so, what sort of an end would it be?

Like scavengers from a battlefield, squawking mortfleigers rose on flapping leather wings from the stinking
midden heap as the travelers passed.

Now that they were closer, Yan could see that the logs making up the palisade were not wood but stone columns in the shapes of tree trunks. The columns were too realistic to be carvings; they must be transmuted wood! His old master had owned a small fragment of such stuff, a valuable curiosity in Talinfad; here, that artifact would be no more than a waste chip from one of the stone logs. A wonder, but a strongly protective one. The protective aspect was enhanced by the sharpened wood stakes set at intervals in niches cut into the stone trunks and planted at an angle along the base of the stockade wall. Such a defense would deter even the great drakkenkain, which, in this land, it might have to do.

Drakkenree warriors watched their approach from the parapet behind the wall. Gresshannak stopped and spoke to them. His words came forth faster than Yan could follow, and most of his postures were strange to Yan. The guardian drakkenree did not grow agitated, for which Yan was thankful. Gresshannak motioned Yan to proceed. All seemed well. Perhaps Yan's fears of disaster were unfounded.

The gateway into the village was guarded by nothing more than a massive log through which other, smaller logs had been driven, making two lines set at right angles to each other. The ends of the lesser logs were sharpened. Yan had seen similar, less massive, barricades in military camps. For the moment, the barrier sat at an angle to the opening in the palisade, allowing free entrance.

No one challenged them as they entered.

Drakkenree appeared, standing beside the flimsy huts or in the doorways of the structures. They watched curiously, silently. Some began to follow the little procession, though none came within a man's length of the merin. The saurians whispered among themselves and, more than once, Yan heard himself identified as a magician.

He wasn't sure whether that was good or not. The little he knew of drakkenree postures left him undecided as to the mood of the village drakkenree.

The village seemed infested with small creatures. Tiny long-necked and long-tailed saurians scurried about, getting underfoot in the same nonsensical way that chickens got underfoot in the village where he'd grown up. But for their long tails and their lack of feathers and beaks, the creatures might have *been* chickens, or at least the drakkenree equivalent. Did the drakkenree eat them as merin ate chickens?

There were other small saurians around the village as well. Yan spied some that at first glance appeared to be smaller versions of the *sharkkain*, though they lacked the dreadful claws of those beasts; their coloration was different, too: ocher spots within dark rosettes instead of stripes. One of the spotted creatures ran across their path, clutching something small and furry in its hands, a half-eaten rodent of some kind. A second spotted saurian chased the first, trying to snatch away the prize.

Nowhere did Yan see any signs of the murderous *sharkkain*. Or any keepers, for that matter. Though not all were as large as the saurian warriors with which Yan was familiar, all the drakkenree of the village had the green mottled scales of warriors. However, none were so small as the ancient mages he'd seen in Scothandir, and none had the black scales of those mages. Yan wished he knew more about drakkenree society.

Gresshannak led them to the center of the area enclosed by the wall. There stood a hut with substantial wooden walls—real wooden walls, the first that Yan had seen here. Clearly an important structure. But it was not the building that drew the eye, for a ring of stakes surrounded the hut, and upon each stake was balanced a drakkenree skull.

"*Kkss'Kedjaka'trak che ff'hoss k'ne,*" Gresshannak announced, backing away.

"What did it say?" Zephem asked.

The Baaliffite was nervous; his hand rested on his sword hilt. Yan was grateful that Zephem had enough restraint not to draw. Yan tried to give him the best answer he could.

"I'm not sure. I understand the construction, but some of the exact words escape me. He says the righteous and honorable master of something or other who works with or through something else is here. I think he means the magician lives here. Whoever lives in this hut is an important personage among the drakkenree."

"The Wizard of Bones?" asked Kerandiri. He seemed both eager and frightened. Yan understood that.

"Possibly," Yan said. "Let us hope so."

"In *that* hut?" Zephem asked.

"So it would appear."

"This wizard is a necromancer," Zephem said grimly.

"We don't know that," Yan pointed out.

"You ignore the evidence of your eyes," Zephem said.

Yan wasn't ignoring anything; he was just trying to be fair. Those skulls worried him, worried him greatly, for even without entering *præha* he could feel the power in this place. There was something alien about that power. Once he had thought that he'd know when he encountered dark magic, but after years of studying the Great Art, he was less sure that he would instantly know dark magic by its feel; recognition, he'd found, came with familiarity. Was this dark magic, or just some unusual form of drakkenree magic? He couldn't be sure. He *was* sure that what he felt here was not quite like anything he'd ever felt before. And he *was* sure that this magic dealt with bones. But was it something as malignant as necromancy?

They had come to find out, and now they stood on the edge of learning the answers to so many questions. Standing affrighted was not doing any good. Forward was the direction to go. Forward Yan went, into the darkness of the hut.

The interior was dimly lit and smoky, and smelled of decay, musk, and burned vegetable matter. The floor was covered in several inches of brown, crumbling plant matter and the walls were undecorated save for niches filled with skulls. A carved stone brazier held dull-glowing coals. Next to it stood a great table-sized block of marble carved with the symbol of the Baansuus; it might have been an altar. Stretched upon that slab lay a drakkenree unlike any Yan had seen before.

This saurian was of a size and shape with those ancient mages Yan had encountered in Scothandir, but where those had been armored in scales the color of deep night, this one's scales were as pale as a cave-dwelling fish. The drakkenree's flesh seemed shrunken and wasted under its scaly hide; its bones punched up through its skin like poles on a badly pitched tent.

The drakkenree wore a harness festooned with fetishes and amulets and talismanic bags as had Yellow Eye, a magician's harness. Unlike Yellow Eye's harness, this saurian's rig had a theme, an ominous theme. The buckles of the harness straps were carved bone, and bones dangled individually and in clumps from thongs tied to the harness. A helmet built of bone plaques covered the drakkenree's skull, and long ivory plumes projected from a tiny skull set upon the brow of the helmet; that tiny skull was too small to be a merin skull, but Yan thought it looked uncomfortably like one. Everywhere that Yellow Eye had worn metal, this drakkenree wore bone. Bone buckles, bone strap ends, bone decorative plates, bone rings, bone fetishes. Bone. Bone. Bone.

Who could this be but the Wizard of Bones?

The right honorable *Kedjaka'trak che ff'hoss k'ne.* The right honorable Wizard-Master of Bones.

And now—what?

The wizard did not stir when they entered, not even to open an eye. Yan could not tell if the saurian breathed. Could they have come all this way to find the Wizard of Bones dead?

25

GALON WAS AT JERR'S SIDE an instant after she screamed. An instant more and he stood, sword ready, between her and the drakkenree. Her fear that he should place himself in such danger almost overwhelmed her thrill that he had done so to protect her. Galon was a good swordsman— even Mistress Schonnegon said so—but to stand against a drakkenree warrior? The saurian's teeth, claws, and bloody blade offered only death.

Yet it did not attack; instead it spoke.

"I see not Sir Kopell Mastillan with you," it said in Kolvinic.

How did it know Kol—Of course, this was Sir Kopell's captive drakkenree. She'd never heard the lizard speak Kolvinic before, and the sound of the language in the saurian's mouth bothered her. It was wrong somehow.

More wrong was the sword the saurian carried. It hadn't had a sword the last time Jerr had seen it. This drakkenree wasn't supposed to have weapons. It was a beaten lizard, a harmless enemy, wasn't it?

There was a difference about the drakkenree now, and it wasn't just the sword. She'd always been afraid of the lizard, but now it looked more menacing. There was something about the way it watched them, something restrained and hungry. Jerr realized that she had only *thought* she had been afraid of it before; she hadn't known what *real* fear the creature could raise in her.

The drakkenree repeated its statement.

"What's it saying about Sir Kopell?" Galon whispered to her.

She had forgotten that he didn't speak Kolvinic well. She started to stutter out a translation into Nitallan, but she was too nervous. Galon understood less of what she said than what the lizard had said. She was sure that the lizard would grow impatient and attack them. She looked to it, to see if it was about to attack, and saw that its attention was elsewhere. Fra Serent had completed his climb up the bank of the hillock. The Vehrite warrior priest advanced, his great two-handed sword held low but ready. He seemed calm, unworried by the lizard or the lizard's gory sword. The priest stopped by Galon's side; now two warriors stood between her and the drakkenree.

"You are Sir Kopell's drakkenree, are you not?" Fra Serent asked.

The drakkenree glared at him. "Where is Sir Kopell Mastillan?"

"As you can see, Sir Kopell is not with us," Fra Serent said.

"Dead, then?"

Did the drakkenree sound eager?

Jerr, Galon, and Fra Serent exchanged glances, silently asking each other whether they had seen the knight's fate. Jerr hadn't. Galon gave the tiniest tilt of his head to indicate his lack of knowledge. Fra Serent looked grim. Earlier they had answered the question for themselves with their decision to return to the ships. Was that the same answer to give the drakkenree?

Fra Serent spoke for them. "We do not know Sir Kopell's fate."

The drakkenree said nothing for a moment. "Sir Kopell Mastillan died in the attack." The lizard didn't sound completely sure.

"You like he dead," Galon accused. His Kolvinic was poor, but his disgust was evident.

"Warriors die in battle," the drakkenree said.

"Not battle. Attack by animals," Galon said. "Not dead in battle."

"Warrior *shrrk'kain*, not wild ones," the drakkenree said. "Even your kind know that ambush is a legitimate battle tactic."

Sharkkain? That was the word that the drakkenree had used when Master Tanafres had seen the creatures before they attacked; he'd asked the lizard what they were, and the lizard had known. Known and not spoken a warning. The lizard had looked into the forest and seen the creatures; it would have said nothing if Master Tanafres hadn't seen the creatures as well. But Master Tanafres hadn't known the *sharkkain* for a threat; the lizard had. Outrage helped her find her voice.

"I saw you looking into the forest before the attack. You knew those creatures were going to attack. You knew before Master Tanafres did."

The lizard didn't deny it. "I saw the *shrrk'kain* and their keepers, yes."

"If you knew there was an ambush, why didn't you warn us?" Fra Serent asked. "Are you not pledged to Sir Kopell?"

"As property, not as warrior."

"Jerr says that you knew that the *sharkkain* were there. You could have given warning." Fra Serent looked grim.

The drakkenree gave a short hiss. "The bregil Gissel went to speak to a keeper. I *might* not have understood. It *might not* have been an ambush."

"But it *was* an ambush," Fra Serent said.

The drakkenree said nothing.

"You gave not warning, but you fought animals," Galon said.

"I killed a keeper and scattered his pack, with no more than the god gave me. I fought, yes." The drakkenree clicked his jaw, and added, "As honor demanded."

"If honor so much to you, why not warn?" Galon asked

"Honor does not demand that property advise its *kedja'k'krr*. Defense was necessary, warning was not. I fought. Honor is satisfied."

"You let innocents die," Galon accused. "You have not honor, craven spawn of bug eaters."

The drakkenree bent low and thrust its head forward, jaws open. Jerr took a step backwards and tripped over something. She landed hard on her butt. No one looked at her. Not Galon or Fra Serent, for they were on their guard and intent on the lizard—she was grateful. Not the drakkenree, for it was taking the measure of the merin warriors before it and ignoring the sprawled, harmless girl—for which she was even more grateful. She scrambled away from what she feared was an impending fight. The brush offered little safety, but little was better than none.

Yet the drakkenree did not attack as she expected.

Why? What was holding it back? She had seen it tear into the *sharkkain* without a weapon; she didn't think it held back through fear of the prowess of the sturdy Vehrite and brave Galon.

"You do not understand *grrff'tn*," the drakkenree said, relaxing its stance and easing the tension of the confrontation slightly. "Why would you? Many of my own kind do not understand true *grrff'tn*."

"What is *griften*?" Fra Serent asked.

"The closest you know of it is your code of honor. Your cult, priest, knows some of the demands of *grrff'tn*. For you, I ignore the youngling." Dark rings of amusement flashed around the drakkenree's eyes. "For the moment."

"You'll regret that remark," Galon said. The tip of his sword sketched a cross in the air.

"Anger will not serve you here," Fra Serent said to him. "Remember your duty."

Galon subsided, but Jerr could see he was not mollified; the drakkenree's words vexed him. They bothered Jerr as well, but, she suspected, in a different way. For a long time Jerr had thought the drakkenree a simple brute, but here was the lizard again speaking of honor; its actions seemingly guided by this honor it professed. A strange sort of honor, perhaps, but such a belief made it more than an animal, more than the brute she had always conceived it to be. It seemed that Master Tanafres had been right—no, *was* right! She wouldn't believe he was dead—Master Tanafres was right; the lizard was almost human. How strange to think of one of the ancient enemy as human! She understood that she must do so, but she wasn't sure that she was ready to accord the lizard a human's pronouns; this drakkenree would remain an "it" to her for a long time.

If she lived a long time.

The drakkenree waved its sword in the air like a new knight testing the balance of his first blade.

"There is a custom among your kind concerning property," it said.

"There are many customs," Fra Serent said. The warrior priest's cautious tone rang like a warning to Jerr. Fra Serent must think that there was more to the drakkenree's remark than appeared on the surface. Fra Serent's sword remained at ready; clearly, the trouble was not over. Jerr huddled down in the bushes.

"Many, yes. But what fate to property after the death of the *kedja'k'krr*, the owner? Death of owner ends all rights in property, yes?"

"Goods, chattels, and lands pass to the heirs," Fra Serent said.

"But the *kedja'k'krr*, he owns no more, yes?"

"The dead own no more than the glory or torment they have earned in their life."

"You say that it is so among your kind." The drakkenree snapped his jaws together. "And Sir Kopell Mastillan is dead."

"I told you that we do not know his death is certain." Fra Serent shifted his position, placing himself slightly in front of Galon. Galon, clearly annoyed, took a step back and began to move to the priest's left, where there was more room for swordplay. The drakkenree continued to speak.

"You know. You know well. I smell certainty on you. On all of you."

"We have not seen his body," Fra Serent said. "We cannot know he is dead."

"*Kedja'k'krr* is dead," the drakkenree insisted. "Sir Kopell Mastillan has no more property. Glory or torment is all that is his. So you say, yes?"

Fra Serent shifted to block Galon's attempt to stand at his side. "Stay with Jerr."

"But I—" Galon started to protest.

"Duty," Fra Serent said. Pivoting swiftly, the warrior priest planted his foot in Galon's midsection and shoved. Flailing, Galon tumbled backwards toward Jerr. He landed near her, and she rushed to his side. He was winded, disoriented. She knelt by his side, torn between worry for him and dread concerning the confrontation between Fra Serent, standing alone, and the drakkenree.

"You understand *grrff'tn*." The dark rings of amusement made the drakkenree's eyes pools of emerald fire. The lizard saluted with his sword. *"Ja'kk'k n'k'rr'ni kedja'hreff!"*

"I do not understand your words." To Jerr, the priest sounded incredibly calm.

"*I am no longer property*," the lizard said. The darkness

faded from around the drakkenree's eyes. "You understand what that means, yes?"

Fra Serent brought his sword up. "I believe I do."

"Hachni, k'grrff'tn, rr shess grrff'tn. Gifni Khan'kmm'eh!"

Master Tanafres had told Jerr that magicians understood languages easily because they understood nature and the nature of mankind. Jerr didn't know if the knowledge came from magic or some other ability, but she understood that the drakkenree was speaking again of honor, this time offering honor to Fra Serent. She also recognized that the drakkenree was referring to itself as Khankemeh, the name Master Tanafres had used for the drakkenree, a name the drakkenree had refused to acknowledge. Until now.

Sword raised, Khankemeh attacked Fra Serent.

Galon, though still dazed, wanted to go help the priest. "He is lost if I don't aid him. Only the greatest of warriors stands a chance in single combat with a drakkenree."

"You'll be killed."

"Fra Serent will die if I don't help."

"You'll both die if you go. He's trying to give us time to get away."

"I must go."

"He didn't want you to fight."

Galon took up his sword. Despite her continued protests, he got to his feet. But he didn't go running into that hopeless fight.

A scream ripped through the trees. Jerr looked; she couldn't help herself. It was awful and she nearly gagged. Khankemeh had severed Fra Serent's arm. The priest was doomed.

Jerr tugged on Galon's sword arm, pulling him back into the brush. He let her.

"We've got to run," she said.

"We can't outrun him."

"Then we'll hide."

Behind them Fra Serent screamed again. This time the sound cut off with a horrible gurgling noise. Jerr wouldn't look. She threw herself into a dense clump of fronds, hands locked on Galon's arm to drag him with her. They landed in a tangled jumble, and the vegetation swayed back, closing over them.

"I am Khan'kmm'eh again!" roared the drakkenree.

Merciful Mannar, protect us. The lizard would come for them now. She dared a peek through a gap in the vegetation. Already Khankemeh was looking for their hiding place.

If it found them—

She didn't want to die, she didn't want Galon to die, especially not at the hands of the lizard. The only way they could survive was to remain hidden. Galon trembled at her side; he wasn't really afraid, not like she was. He was trembling with anger. He'd defend her. To the death. They would both die.

No! It wasn't fair! The lizard had already killed, what were they to it? Why did it need to kill them, too? Hadn't there been enough killing?

It had to pass them by. It *had* to! She clutched the talisman that Master Tanafres had helped her make. It was only supposed to be a tool to let her sense the magic, something for her to use until she was advanced enough to make a real *claviarm.* It wasn't intended to focus the magic. She didn't care. She needed magic, and she needed it now. With all her heart she willed the lizard to look elsewhere, to turn aside from them. Will was stronger than craft; Master Tanafres had said so. Once blood had been spilled, will was the most important element of sorcery; if the will was strong enough, the magic would happen.

Pass us by. See us not.

She wanted to be hidden. She'd never wanted anything more in her life. Her will had to be strong enough. It *had* to be!

We are not here. Pass us by.

She didn't want Galon found; he would fight and die. She didn't want to be found either; she wouldn't be able to put up a fight worthy of the name, but she'd die just the same. She wanted to live, she wanted Galon to live, and the only way was to be hidden from the murderous Khankemeh. Her head spun from the intensity of her wish. She held her breath; it was too much effort to breathe and will the lizard to go away at the same time. She felt light-headed.

We are no more than another bush. See us not.

Was the magic working? Flashing colors hung before her eyes, obscuring her sight. She'd seen such lights once when she'd struck her head hard against a table. Was she losing consciousness? She set all her will to making them hidden.

Nothing but jungle to be seen.

Through narrowing vision, she watched as Khankemeh sniffed the air. The lizard's head turned this way and that as it surveyed the area. For one awful moment the lizard seemed to be looking right at Jerr. But only a moment. The fanged snout turned away from their hiding place.

Just jungle. Plants. Trees. No merin. Not one. Just jungle.

"I know you are out there, younglings," Khankemeh said. "The hand of the *kedja'k'trrk* is upon you. Thus, does he betray that he lives. Let him hide you. You are of no importance to me; not when I know his heart still beats. I will hunt him. I will find him. Tell him, if you can; tell Yan Tanafres that I, Khan'kmm'eh, will eat his living heart before his eyes."

The threat shattered Jerr's concentration; she felt the magic slip away. But it didn't matter; Khankemeh was gone.

Was the drakkenree right about the source of the magic? Was it Master Tanafres's magic and not hers? If it was his magic, he was alive! But then she didn't understand how he might have cast such a spell, and if he had, why he hadn't let them see that he was all right. Whether the magic was his or hers, Khankemeh was hunting him now.

If Master Tanafres was alive, he might not be much longer.

26

KERANDIRI ENTERED THE HUT with obvious trepidation. Without magesight, Yan knew that it would take the priest's eyes some time to adjust to the dim interior. When they did, and he saw the honorable Kedjaka trak chay Foss Kenay, the holy man began to mumble a prayer in Nitallan. Zephem was less circumspect concerning the Wizard of Bones.

"It is worse than a necromancer," he said. "It is undead itself."

The Baaliffite warrior priest advanced past Yan, ignoring Yan's protest and shrugging off the hand Yan put on his arm. Kerandiri, absorbed in his prayer, made no effort to stop Zephem. The priest's sword cleared its scabbard with a soft rasp that was loud within the confines of the hut. Yan feared that Zephem's actions would condemn them all, but he couldn't think of how to stop the Baaliffite.

He didn't have to.

A man's length from the slab, Zephem came to a sudden halt as if he had walked into a wall. Looking a little dazed, Zephem took a step back and shook his head. He tried to advance again, recoiled again. Angrily, he struck at the hidden wall with his sword. The sword made no sound as it rebounded, but sparks flew as they did when steel struck stone.

"Abide," Kerandiri told him. Glowering, Zephem halted his assault on the invisible barrier. Kerandiri turned to Yan. "It is a wall of power, but its nature is strange to me. Is it born of the Great Art?"

Yan had been about to ask the holy man if the barrier was a thing of the gods.

"God protects his servants from those who seek to harm them," said a creaking voice in stilted, archaic Nitallan.

Yan looked to the altar. The wizard had lifted his head and pointed his snout in their direction. The wizard's eyelids were open, revealing two milky orbs. Those eyes looked blind, but somehow Yan knew that the wizard saw them. The wizard spoke again.

"Che'mn'drr and his *tr'nr'che* said they had met and killed a band of *maah'nn'kun'yee* invaders. Their *shrrk'kain* had feasted well, he said. Ever boastful, Che'mn'drr. He was wrong, yes?"

That was obvious. Yan wondered if they were the only survivors. He hoped not.

"We have walked into the jaws of the lion," Zephem told Kerandiri. "I warned you." To the wizard he said, "Your Chaymender is a skulking coward to send animals to do the work of warriors."

"My Che'mn'drr?" croaked the wizard. "Were Che'mn'drr mine, he would have died young."

"Are you saying that you did not order the attack on our group?" Kerandiri asked.

"I did not say that, but, yes, it is true."

"Do not believe its lies, Eminence," Zephem said.

To Kerandiri, the wizard said, "Much like Che'men'drr, this one. Unfortunate that we cannot put them together in the pit? It would be a good fight, yes?"

"We did not come here to fight," Kerandiri said.

"He did." The wizard's snout pointed at Zephem.

"Fra Zephem is obedient. He will not fight unless ordered to do so." Kerandiri's words seemed more directed to Zephem than to the wizard; a hidden order. Kerandiri returned his focus to the wizard. "Can you say the same for this Chaymender, who led the attack against our peaceful party?"

The wizard twitched his tail in a drakkenree shrug. "As I cannot speak for Che'mn'drr, you cannot speak for this one. Do not deny. I know."

Wisely, in Yan's opinion, Kerandiri did not protest. Kerandiri said, "We came in peace, to seek counsel."

"Yes, yes. To see *Kedjaka'trak che ff'hoss*," the wizard said impatiently. "Your dream is fulfilled. You see before you he who the *bray'kk'll* call the Wizard of Bones. Che'mn'drr did not think that you should. Was he right?"

Without awaiting an answer, the wizard reached behind the slab on which he lay and dragged a drum around to the front. The fittings on the drum were, of course, bone. The wizard dipped a clawed hand into one of the pouches swinging from his straps. His hand emerged in a smooth motion and cast something onto the drum. The sound of the falling, pale objects was magnified into a strange, arrhythmic beat that pattered off into silence as the objects stopped their bouncing and came to rest.

Bones carved with drakkenree glyphs.

"Necromancy," Zephem said under his breath as if intoning a curse.

The wizard ran his fingers delicately across the bones. Mouth open, he hummed a delicate, airy tune that seemed totally out of place in the darkness of the hut. His fingers slowed in their course over the cast bones. Selecting one, he raised it to his snout and sniffed.

"Yes, yes," he said. "The past, the future. A connection." The wizard snapped his jaws in satisfaction and turned his milky orbs on Yan. "You who stand so silent, you who spoke your name to my children, you are the egg that holds the youngling who will grow into the

answer to my question. You knew Ock'kmm'dey'ahmm.
I catch Kmm's scent upon you."

Ockemdayum? Yan was confused until he realized
that his puzzlement came from the fact that he had only
rarely heard this name, and then it had always had an
honorific attached. He knew who the wizard meant.
"Yellow Eye."

"Yes, yes. By your tongue, near enough." The wizard
snapped his jaws. "You knew my child."

Child? Was the wizard saying what Yan thought the
wizard was saying? "You are one of Yellow Eye's parents?"

"That is surprise, yes?" Gray tinged the skin around
the wizard's eyes. "We make children, too."

"I never doubted it."

"With eggs. Did you know that?"

He had suspected, and he said so.

"Bloodlines are important," the wizard said.

Yan had suspected that, also. Were they so important
that the wizard would demand that Yan pay for what he
had done? A merin would have, so would a bregil.
Would a drakkenree demand a blood price? Strangely,
the wizard seemed to have something else on his mind.

"There were so few touched with the glory," the wizard said. "Their blood was weak, and they were heavy
with the weight of the world, dull as a snake before molt-
ing. A distraction, it was. Such a cost you understand,
brother in the Art. A cost paid to a greater end. Do you
have an heir, brother in the Art?"

Did the wizard mean an heir to the body or an heir to
the Art, an apprentice? As to the first, there was none
that Yan knew of. As to the second—Yan thought about
Jerr. He hadn't seen her body; she might have survived.
Chaymender had been wrong in boasting that his
sharkkain had killed everyone; he might be wrong about
Jerr, also. And Teletha. And—Yan stopped; it wasn't a
profitable line of thought. Not here in front of the wizard.

"I had an apprentice before the attack," he told the wizard.

"Lost?"

"So it would seem."

"You do not *know*?"

Something in the way the wizard asked embarrassed Yan. He wished that he did know. Knowing was always easier than not knowing, even when the news was bad. "She wasn't a formal apprentice."

The answer seemed to satisfy the wizard; he clicked his jaws.

"Kmm had passed through the circles well before he left us. But always it is difficult to see a student go." Despite his words, the wizard's posture suggested indifference. The contradiction confused Yan; he wasn't used to such inconsistency among the drakkenree. "Kmm went past the place where the *t'hn'pah* and the *ah'nss'pah* summer, beyond the great mountains and out into the lands where the cold comes. Often rash, Kmm was. I do not like cold. I told him, 'Do not go.' I said that, I did. But Kmm did not listen. Often deaf, Kmm was. Visions, he said he had. A call like unto that the *t'hn'pah* hear, he said he heard. The right honorable masters of *ssess'trak'ka* said there was no call, but Kmm said there was."

Ssess'trak'ka was a drakkenree term concerning magic. Yan didn't know the exact meaning; the term contained the sense of magic-as-the-Great-Art and seemed to be most often used that way, but it also encompassed *præha*, the mana flow, and a host of other related concepts. Here, he guessed, best to consider the term in its broadest sense and to translate it simply as "magic."

"Kmm did not listen to the Masters of Magic," the wizard said. He did not appear distressed by the observation, just resigned. "Often deaf, Kmm was. He is dead now."

Yan's cool, analytical attitude collapsed as the issue of Yellow Eye's demise came around again. He found himself sweating. Just how did the wizard know that Yellow Eye was dead? More importantly, did the wizard know *how* Yellow Eye had died? Yan wanted to know the answers, but he didn't dare ask the questions.

"Death comes," the wizard said. "One must raise one's head when B'han'ssu'uss challenges. There is no challenging God."

Yan felt the sudden tension in the priests. They had clearly caught the singular nature of the wizard's expression of deity.

"What is this about challenging God?" Kerandiri asked. In the Triadic religion a god's will was supreme within His or Her area of influence, save only when overruled by a god standing higher in the Celestial Court. Even ruling Horesh was not supreme in every sphere.

The wizard showed no offense at Kerandiri's abrupt question. "Only the foolish think they can challenge God. Often foolish, Kmm was. He is dead now. B'han'ssu'uss has ripped his throat."

Yellow Eye was dead, all right, but not because some deity had acted. Yan had stuck a sword through Yellow Eye's heart while the drakkenree mage lay helpless before him. Yan had thought it a mercy. How did one explain to a father that you had slain his son? Yan couldn't think of a way.

"This Baansuus is your god," Kerandiri asked. "Your only god?"

"B'han'ssu'uss is God," the wizard said with a posture that said there could be no contradiction. "He is the all, She is everywhere. The eye of B'han'ssu'uss is upon the world. He knows, She stirs. I have felt this. Do you think Kmm truly felt the stirring of God? The right honorable Masters of Magic thought that Kmm was foolish. Often foolish, Kmm was. Yet often wise." The wizard turned to Yan. "You touched Kmm. Is B'han'ssu'uss speaking? Have you heard the voice of God?"

"I don't know," Yan answered honestly, earning a glare from Zephem. Yan suspected that anything short of absolute denial of anything regarding Baansuus was heresy in the Baaliffite's eyes.

The wizard hissed a sigh. "To know when you do not know is wisdom. Yet I sense that you wonder. I wonder, too, but I am old, and the old hear things that no others do. Are the whispers I hear imaginings? Were I *grr'drrr'hak'n* there would be no question. Yet I know that the Magic is strong in me. The Magic has my heart. I listen. How can I not? I listen, I listen to the bones. They speak to me, they do. And they have spoken with the voices of the ancestors."

"Only those tainted by the Dark Art speak with the dead," Zephem said. "You condemn yourself with your own words. You are shown to be corrupted and possessed by evil."

The wizard dismissed the condemnation with a huffing laugh. "You are more limited than your master, Frazephem. Your eyes see only the toe claw of God. He is greater than you think, She encompasses more than you can imagine. The ancestors will walk Aelwyn again. This is the truth in my heart."

"You call the dead to walk?" Kerandiri's voice trembled. Yan couldn't tell if the source of the tremor was anger or fear. He suspected both.

"God will make it so," the wizard answered firmly. "This is the belief in my heart."

"Then your heart is a void at the center of your soul," Kerandiri snapped. The anger had won, as his red-faced scowl clearly showed. "Your god is false, an abomination in the light of Horesh."

"You do not understand, priest who gives no name."

"I understand better than you think. I had sought to believe that there might be other explanations for the evidence before me. I was willing to listen, and what did I hear? *Not* what I wanted to hear. Your words con-

demn you for the false follower of the dark way that
you are. In my foolishness, I ignored the warnings and
did not pay heed to good counsel. But as day always
dawns after night, I have come to see the truth. Horesh
is my Lord, and His light feeds my eyes. I see your evil
for what it is."

"Your Horesh is not master here," the wizard warned.

"Blasphemer!" Kerandiri screamed. "Horesh is Lord
of All!"

Yan flinched back, as much from the distinctly hostile
tilt of the wizard's head as from Kerandiri's impassioned
tone. The confrontation had arisen as swiftly as a summer thunderstorm and was likely to be as unstoppable
and violent.

Kerandiri began to chant. Almost immediately, he
began to glow. Horesh, it seemed, was listening.

The wizard raised himself from the slab. In two steps
he was free of his resting place. Pivoting to face
Kerandiri, he dropped into a warning crouch; the wizard's blank orbs reflected the golden light emanating
from the löm. "Do not do this, priest. Do not make your
wisdom match your courtesy. B'han'ssu'uss will not be
mocked in His nest; She will not be tolerant of a fool
who knows not his place."

"The light of Horesh will show your dark-crawling
worm for what it is," Kerandiri shouted back. He flung
up his arms and the roof of the hut whirled away as if
captured by a tornado. Daylight flooded into the hut.
Kerandiri turned his face upward. "Come, great Horesh!
Fill Your willing vessel! Guide me! Take me! Fill me with
the smallest part of Your self. Give unto me Your might,
that I may lay low those who are Your enemies. Give
unto me Your power, that I may smite the godless dark
worshipers. Let Your will be known! Let Your will be
done! Make me Your hands!"

Yan saw the golden shaft of sunlight in which
Kerandiri stood. He saw how the edges of the beam rip-

pled like the air over rocks on a hot summer's day. Yan
trembled. This was not a power he understood.

Zephem, shielding his eyes against the sudden light,
stumbled toward Yan. "Run, magician. You are impure.
Get away, lest you be burned by His fire."

If Yan left, he would not see what happened next.
"What's Kerandiri doing?"

"Löm Kerandiri calls upon Horesh." There was awe in
the Baaliffite's voice. "He offers himself as a vessel of the
god."

Yan gasped. Was that possible? Wasn't that sort of
thing just the imagery of legends? Yan's senses suggested
otherwise. His mouth dropped open as Kerandiri
appeared to grow in stature. The löm shone with light
that seemed to come from within, and the air around him
wavered and danced as if afire. It *was* really happening.

Yan wasn't about to leave and miss it.

"Your fate is upon your own head, magician."
Zephem fell to his knees and began to pray.

"Behold the cleansing fires of Horesh!" Kerandiri's
voice was a shout from the center of the earth, and the
tops of the hut's walls burst into fire.

The wizard did not appear intimidated. He matched
Kerandiri's chant with one of his own; his voice was deep
and low. Yan did not understand the words, nor most of
the postures; they went by too fast. Yan did recognize
many imploring poses scattered through the wizard's
monologue.

The wizard's scales took on color in a bedazzling
array. His torso lengthened and sprouted another pair of
limbs, though whether arms or legs, Yan could not be
sure. A third eye opened on the wizard's forehead and
turned its baleful, amber glare on Kerandiri. Baansuus, it
seemed, was also listening, and was just as willing to
endow an avatar.

Kerandiri was a warrior of fire and the drakkenree
wizard had become a jeweled dragon. They lunged for

each other and fought, clashing soundlessly. Each time one of the combatants struck the other, a wave of power rippled out from them to splash against the walls of the hut. The energy was contained by some unseen barrier that had nothing to do with the logs of the walls. Yan felt himself tossed by the backwash of that power, a flailing seabird caught in the eddies and currents of a stormy sea raging around a rocky shore.

The manifest supranatural power frightened Yan. He backed away from the unearthly battle. As he neared the wall, a skull in a niche snapped at him. He jumped away from the clashing teeth. The skull pivoted to keep its empty eye sockets on him. Yan found a section of wall with no niches and put his back against it.

The supranatural battle raging at the center of the hut was intense, the light of the struggle too bright to look at. Yan huddled at the wall, keeping low and hoping to survive. The combat lasted an eternity—a handful of heartbeats—before the glare diminished. The dragon that was the wizard seemed larger than its opponent, looming over the crouching warrior. It spoke.

"You have bared your teeth with lowered head and challenged B'han'ssu'uss. There is no challenging God. You know this now."

"The world is wide. Horesh sees it all," Kerandiri sounded strong, but the light suffusing the löm was weaker, and fading.

"Horesh is a strong spirit," the wizard conceded. "Today He is not strongest. Today He must bow. Today B'han'ssu'uss is stronger."

"Today," Kerandiri croaked. He crumpled, no more the avatar. The löm lay on the floor of the hut, just a broken, beaten man. He coughed blood, befouling his yellow robes. Kerandiri still had defiance in him. "Beware tomorrow."

"Today is today," the wizard said. Returned fully to his drakkenree form, the wizard's tail shrug seemed oddly ordinary. "For you, priest of Horesh, there is no tomorrow. Death comes."

Between the spasms that racked him, Kerandiri managed to say, "I—do—*not*—raise my head."

"It matters not."

The wizard flicked his head in a motion Yan had seen drakkenree use to break the neck of a small animal held in their jaws. Kerandiri sprawled. His head tilted loosely on a broken neck.

Yan didn't need to examine the priest to know that he was dead.

With a scream, Zephem threw himself at the wizard. The invisible barrier stopped him. Howling, Zephem battered at the unseen wall with all the effect of a moth hurling itself at a lantern pane. The wizard turned his sightless eyes to the Baaliffite.

"Be still, Frazephem," he commanded.

The sword fell to the floor. Zephem slumped, standing like a beaten man. Two drakkenree warriors entered the hut and led Zephem away as darkness gathered again under the roof that rewove itself above Yan's head. It was a magical effect—but not magic as Yan understood the Art. The black-scaled drakkenree came and removed Kerandiri's goods and clothes and made a pile of them near the wizard's slab before dragging the löm's corpse away. Quiet settled on the hut. Yan found the wizard staring at him.

"You stood aside," the wizard said.

"The gods were acting. It was not my place to interfere."

"You think that the gods are separate from the world?"

Caution still seemed the order of the day. "They are Powers I do not comprehend."

"So you stand apart." The wizard inclined his head in the way his kind did to convey the same thing a merin would with a sad shake of a head. "Only a whole egg gives birth to a whole person. The gods are as much a part of us as we are of Them; as everything, seen and unseen, is part of the All."

"Tobiesel refuted that argument more than a century ago."

"I do not know Tobiesel."

Yan did not know him either, but he'd read his book. Not that he remembered more than the gist of the argument. But this didn't appear to be the time to make such an admission. "Tobiesel was a philosopher-wizard of the court of first Emperor Dacel."

"*First* Emperor Dacel? Time passes." The wizard was silent for a moment as if thinking. "You will tell me about Tobiesel. Yes, yes. I want to know his arguments. It seems to me he might have much in common with K'khanx. Clever one was K'khanx."

It seemed that Yan's life was going to be spared. Was he to be the slave of another drakkenree wizard? Not a pleasant future to contemplate. He hoped he wouldn't have to kill his way out of the situation as he had before.

"You look disturbed," the wizard said. "Tell me, Yan Tanafres. Do you think me given to darkness?"

"I don't know." It was an honest answer.

"But you want to know."

"Yes." Another honest answer.

The wizard laughed. "We *are* brothers in the Art."

27

TELETHA FOLLOWED THE TRAIL of the three men to a logging burn, where they had met with a drakkenree. She recognized the three-toed prints. The meeting had taken place some time ago. She was losing ground on the men she trailed, owing to Sir Kopell's inability to keep up a good pace. There was nothing for it; she couldn't abandon the knight.

It was near dark, and they were moving downhill when Sir Kopell tripped on a root and fell with what Teletha thought a terribly loud crash. She crouched, awaiting attack. None came, but she heard the distant, contented lowing of *vekkanconday* from the direction in which the trail led.

Drakkenree used the *vekkanconday* as pack beasts.

They moved with greater caution. The trail left the jungle at the edge of the river floodplain. Staying in cover, they crouched and took in the panorama of the winding river and the great flat stretches of waving vegetation. A walled village squatted hard by a tight bend in the river. The obvious destination.

Between their vantage point and the village, a herd of *vekkanconday* grazed. Not wild ones; there were a pair of keepers watching them. Teletha could see more drakkenree—a lot of drakkenree—moving about on the walls of the village's stockade and within the log palisade. She even saw a black one, the kind Yan said could do magic. That one was smaller than most of the others; maybe it wasn't mature and couldn't do much magic.

Any magic was more than she wanted to deal with, especially without Yan around to do something about it.

The situation didn't look promising.

There seemed to be a single opening in the palisade, and that had a well-spiked gate. The walls looked climbable, if one chose an unguarded spot. Sir Kopell was in no shape to climb. She could, though, assuming she could reach the walls unnoticed. Teletha looked to the sky. V'Delma was already showing in the deepening blue; the moons would provide plenty of light tonight. More than enough light for a sentry to spot a woman crossing the stretches of open ground between the jungle and the village, even if the damned *vekkanconday* didn't bray out a warning.

Getting into the village might be possible—not smart, just possible. But what then? Teletha saw no merin, nor even any bregil. If Yan and the others were in the village, they had to be inside one of the huts. As she looked for some sign, her gaze settled on the hut at the center of the village. It was more stoutly built than the others. A ring of poles implanted in the ground surrounded it, and bone gleamed from the top of each pole.

"Do you see those skulls?" Sir Kopell asked.

Teletha nodded. "Want to bet against that being where the Wizard of Bones lives?"

"I'd sooner gamble with the Great One."

That was Teletha's sentiment, too, and the ruler of the Under Court was not known for losing.

If that was the wizard's hut, that was where Yan would be.

What was she thinking of? She'd be throwing her life away to try to get into the drakkenree village. Yan had

gotten out of worse situations without her help. He didn't
need her help.

But even his luck would run out one day.

Then again, so would hers.

Maybe Yan would just have a nice talk with the
Wizard of Bones and come strolling out without her having to do anything. Maybe the Great One would dissolve
the Under Court.

Any action before full dark would be too foolish even
for a fool like her. She sat down and began checking the
load on her pistol.

Night in the jungle was more frightening than day. All
the strange noises sounded ominous and threatening. Jerr
knew that the haunting cries and raucous screams
couldn't all belong to hungry beasts eager to eat her and
Galon, but the darkness made jokes of the arguments she
used on herself. She was glad Galon was with her; had
she been by herself, she would surely have run through
the woods like a frightened ninny and been eaten by
something. Without Galon's determination and quiet
strength, Jerr would never have made it this far.

Just as without her woodcraft and knowledge of
wildlife, he would not have made it. She shuddered,
remembering how he had nearly kicked the mason wasp
nest and roused the ire of those nasty insects. The nest
had been large and surely held enough warriors to have
easily stung Galon to death.

In reaction to her shiver, his arm, curled protectively
around her, drew her in closer. She was cold and he was
warm, a fire to chase away the chill. She snuggled, bur-
rowing toward his warmth. Up close she could smell the
man-scent of him. She liked it. His hand slipped down
from her shoulder and cupped her breast. She liked that,
too.

Jerr and Galon were all alone in the jungle, all alone in

the night, with only each other to rely on. They might have been Old Grandfather Rock and Old Grandmother Water, not as they were in most of the stories, but as they had been at the birth of time: young and newly woken to the land by the gods. The Old Grandparents had been all alone in a hostile land, too. Like the Old Grandparents, Jerr and Galon had each other.

She sighed as his hand slid across her chest and fumbled with the lacings of her kirtle. It would be good to forget about the dangers around them. She lifted her head to see his face. His mouth was waiting to fall upon hers.

They had each other, if only for the moment. She wasn't willing to let that moment pass. Her hand slipped down to his trousers and found his manhood hot and hard beneath the cloth. He understood the moment as well as she did. Her touch quickened him, and soon there was no turning back. Not that she would have wanted to; his touch told her that she was alive, his desire that there was hope that she would stay alive.

It hurt the first time he entered her, but she didn't let him know. What point? The pain had been brief, washed away in other sensations. It was better the second time they made love, much better.

As long as they were together, everything would be all right.

28

THE WIZARD RETURNED to his slab and lay chuckling to himself. The hut had returned to its original state as if nothing had happened. Bizarre and unnatural, but not so unnerving as the supranatural battle that had concluded only minutes ago. For all the weirdness of the Baansuus's power, Yan hadn't sensed the overt evil that he would have expected had the deity channeling its power through the wizard been steeped in darkness. He'd sensed strangeness, yes; inhuman strangeness. Yan was very aware of how close he stood to the edge of reality as he understood it.

What happened next surprised him, because it was so ordinary. A half-grown drakkenree, black-scaled, appeared at the door of the hut and made a servant's bow. There had been no summons that Yan detected, but good servants often operated in such a fashion, knowing when they were wanted.

"Bring meat for two," the wizard told the newcomer, then held up a hand to halt the small one's departure. To Yan he said, "Your kind cooks meat, yes?"

"We prefer it that way."

Nodding, the wizard told the servant, "Cook one portion."

The servant started to object. "L'grr'w will—"

"L'grr'w will do as you tell him. Say that I require it," the wizard said. "Yes, and see that the meat is not from the *maah'nn'kun'yee*."

The black drakkenree bared his throat, then left without further objection.

"Cooked," the wizard said with a saddened head slant. "Weak teeth. Comes of bad blood."

"I don't want to cause problems."

"Worry not, your meat shall be cooked. Let L'grr'w— he's the provider—complain. Not often a brother in the Art visits. There are courtesies to be observed, yes?"

Yan wasn't going to object to being treated courteously, even if he didn't understand the reason for it. Could the fact that the wizard had called Yan a brother in the Art have something to do with this friendly familiarity? Drakkenree seemed to have high esteem for magicians. Yellow Eye had taken Yan for a personal slave upon realizing that he was a magician. This wizard's regard had a different feel to it, for which Yan was grateful; he'd seen how drakkenree worked their ordinary slaves. At the moment Yan was being treated more as a guest than as a slave. He could accept that. But how long would it remain that way? He decided to use the opportunity to seek understanding; you must work while there's light, his father used to say.

He cleared his throat nervously before addressing the wizard.

"Honored one, the warrior who brought me here called you *kekess* Kedjaka'rak chay Foss Kaynee. It is a name I do not completely understand. I recognize the honorific, and I know that you are a wizard. But I don't understand the rest. My knowledge of your language is not as great as I would like."

"As it should be," the wizard said.

"All right. My command of the language is not as great as it should be." The gray rings appeared around the wizard's eyes. Yan found being the source of the wizard's amusement uncomfortable. His voice leaked some of his irritation when he asked, "Will you not explain your title to me?"

The wizard twitched his tail. "What is there to explain? I do the bone magic. It is my center, my heart of magic."

The bone magic. Had Zephem been right? Yan remembered how the skull had snapped at him. Animating the remains of the dead was the province of the dark masters of necromancy. "I do not know what you call the bone magic. Is it necromancy?"

The wizard did not answer at once, but seemed to ponder Yan's question. Did shame keep the wizard from admitting to the art he practiced?

"Necromancy?" The wizard imitated Yan's voice and intonation, suggesting that the word was new to him. "What means this word?"

"It is a magic that draws on the dead and the spirits of the dead."

"Your kind sets great store by this term, yes?"

"Some do."

"Terms are only words; they are unimportant. Importance lies in the nature of the heart, not the words used to describe it. The ancestors speak to me through the bones. I listen."

"Do you constrain them to speak?"

"It is wrong to put constraints on unwilling spirits."

That was an encouraging answer; necromancy was built on constraints placed upon the spirits of the dead, and such constraints were the foundation of the Church's objections to the art. "One of the skulls snapped at me. How could it do that without compulsion?"

The wizard was amused by Yan's question. "Who can compel the ancestors to do other than they will? I am honored to be thought worth protecting."

If the wizard could be believed, "Then your magic is

not real necromancy; it only appears so because of the forms of your foci."

"If you say so."

If only Kerandiri had been willing to wait and get an explanation from the wizard instead of acting on suspicions and assumptions. Of course, at the moment Yan only had the wizard's word concerning how his magic worked; but he felt confident that exploration and experimentation would confirm those words.

"You are not satisfied with my answers, yes?" the wizard asked.

The wizard had rewarded honesty before. "Well, I do have more questions."

"Kmm had more answers than questions." The wizard's pose suggested that he intended a shift in the topic of conversation. "You knew Kmm, whom you called Yellow Eye."

Was the talk going to turn to the matter that Yan feared? Wary, Yan answered as simply as he could. "Yes."

"You knew Yellow Eye's heart of the magic, yes?"

Yan had worked with Yellow Eye, but Yan had never understood the basis of Yellow Eye's magic. If he had, he thought that he'd understand much more of the writings Yellow Eye had left behind. By learning of this concept of a "heart of magic," he'd just learned more about drakkenree magic in general. But know Yellow Eye's heart of magic? "No."

"You lie," the wizard said without hint of rancor.

"I do not lie," Yan protested.

"You lie to yourself." Yan continued to protest, but the wizard silenced him with a peremptory gesture. "It is time to eat."

The black-scaled servant appeared at the door of the hut with the meat that the wizard had ordered. The servant presented the wizard with a slab of flesh that still dripped juices and blood; Yan's portion was cooked.

Badly: half charred and half almost raw. Yan smiled as he accepted the offering. Not wishing to offend his host, he tried the meat; it tasted gamy, as if it had come from some waterfowl. He ate it anyway. The wizard wolfed his meal, finishing well before Yan managed to chew his way through his chunk. The drakkenree laid his head down on the slab and waited. Yan thought the wizard fell asleep, but the wizard's head rose as soon as Yan finished his last bite.

The drakkenree poked among the pile of the things that had been taken from Kerandiri's body before the corpse was removed from the hut. He picked up the carved bone dome that had convinced Yan to become involved in this ill-fated adventure. "You recognize this, yes? Do you know what it is?"

"A talisman." Deciding to attempt to confirm a theory, he added, "It was made by you."

"It was, yes. And difficult it was. I sorrowed when it disappeared. A great loss it was, for I did not think that I would live long enough to replace it. I worked on," the wizard said, displaying the claws of his right hand. The talons had been shaped and sharpened into carving instruments. "I trusted God. Knowing that I was doing His work, I knew that She would not abandon me. Now, my work is returned to me, and under circumstances that can only be by the directing claw of God."

The wizard's talk of godly direction discomforted Yan. He didn't like thinking that his decisions had been motivated by supranatural influence. That was not the way the world was supposed to work.

"Do you understand the talisman's purpose?" asked the wizard.

Yan had not been able to fathom the artifact; there seemed no point in denying it. On the contrary, there might be an advantage; the garrulous wizard seemed more than ready to reveal secrets. "I was unable to achieve any real understanding of the artifact. Its magic seems incomplete."

"As it is," the wizard said, nodding. He produced another carved hemisphere from behind his slab. Bringing the two together, he joined them into a sphere. There was a flare of power visible even to the mundane eye. The wizard held the sphere out to Yan. "Look upon this now, as only a mage may see it."

Cautiously, Yan entered the *præha* state. There seemed little likelihood that the wizard would take advantage of his body's defenselessness, but he worried nonetheless. His first sight of the sphere's mystical shadow chased such worries from his mind. It was beautiful. Where carved surface had been, a solid silvery surface appeared. Beneath the glistening quicksilver surface, Yan could sense a void; the sphere, in its occult existence, was hollow. This artifact could contain and amplify whatever it held. Somehow the glyphs and images informed the arcane nature of the sphere, rendering it a near perfect resonator of arcane energies. Yan did not question how he knew the nature of the magic of which the sphere was capable; it seemed too obvious to him. He did wonder briefly how one could put something in the center of a solid object; in the physical world the artifact would have no hollow center. His thoughts were pulled round and round about the sphere as he pondered the familiarity he felt. There was a nagging similarity between the sphere and something Yan had once or twice encountered. As he studied the shape, he recognized an echo of the chamber in Scothandir where he had discovered the ancient drakkenree mages.

He understood then that this artifact was an application of an ancient form of magic. Primitive mages often used miniature representations of objects to focus their magics. More advanced mages just as frequently used symbolic models as ritual components to refine and distill their magics. This carved sphere was an elegant and sophisticated distillation of the principles of magic behind such usages.

"You have brought the key," the wizard told him.

"I have done no such thing."

"Another lie. I smell it upon you."

Yan knew then what could be put in the heart of a solid sphere. In his satchel, heavy upon his hip, lay the Serpent's Eye. The Eye was barely corporeal, woven of spells, moonbeams, starshine, and unknown magics. Yan's hand drifted down to the satchel. The wizard did not follow the motion; his sightless gaze was already riveted on the bag. The wizard knew what was in there. But how?

Did it matter?

Yan reached into his satchel and removed the Eye's box. The container felt warm. Maybe he shouldn't be doing this. But how else would he learn the Eye's secrets? He opened the box, revealing the pale ocher sphere that was the Eye of the Serpent.

The wizard rose from his slab and came toward Yan. He crouched, hands outstretched, fingers crooked to encompass the Eye, but he did not touch it. His attitude was one of extreme reverence.

"It is an Eye of God," the wizard said.

Yellow Eye and Yan had found it in a statue of Baansuus, but Yan knew that there was nothing of the supernatural about the Eye. It was magic, pure and simple. No, not simple, anything but simple. Still, purer magic Yan had never encountered.

"Tell me how it was made," he said. "Tell me its purpose."

"To understand, you must experience."

Yan wasn't surprised by the wizard's answer. He had heard the same phrase throughout his apprenticeship. To hear or read about magic wasn't enough. A magician had to experience magic to master it; he had to know it.

Know it in his heart.

With the cold amber light of the Eye shining on him, Yan recognized Yellow Eye's heart of magic. Recognizing it, he knew that he had known all along and just had not understood. Yellow Eye had been a finder; he'd found the Eye. This was the foundation of Yellow Eye's magic expressing itself. But Yellow Eye was a powerful mage and had possessed a twinned heart. Yellow Eye had also been a dominator; Yan had experienced that magic in his work with the drakkenree mage. Yellow Eye had tried to use the Eye to enhance his spells on the field at Rastionne, but Yellow Eye hadn't understood the truth at the heart of the Serpent's Eye. The Eye was wrapped in magics of seeing, bound by magics of knowing; it was not for domination. The Eye was for the curious, to know and to communicate. It sang of the power to improve and amplify.

It sang to Yan.

"You have seen with the Serpent's Eye," the wizard said.

Enwrapped in the mysteries of the Eye, all Yan said was, "Yes."

"God is mysterious. He makes plans, but She does not tell even His closest followers. We all stride forth at Her call. He orders the hunt, and She commands the strike." The wizard backed away, returned to his slab, and took up the sphere. Once again he crouched before Yan. "This is where the Eye must be. You feel it, yes? You cannot open the Eye, I cannot place it within. Together we can unlock the magic. You want to know the secrets of the Eye, yes? This is how you will know."

Yan looked at the sphere. He no longer had any doubt that the artifact had been prepared to house the energies of the Eye of the Serpent. The sphere would not house the Eye perfectly, but well enough. Clearly the wizard thought it to his benefit to have the Eye activated. Was there any reason not to? The Serpent's Eye was not a weapon, only a tool to increase knowledge. What was wrong with increased knowledge?

There might be other uses, uses that the wizard knew. Working with the wizard to activate the Eye was a risk, but Yan had used the magic of the Eye before; the wizard had not. Not only had Yan used such magic, he had wrested it away from a drakkenree mage. What he had done before, he could do again.

After all, the greatest mages were those who knew the most. Who could compare to one who knew the secrets that the Eye held? Yan's long-sought dream of being a great magician lay before him. With the Eye activated, he would see what had been hidden from him. He would have the knowledge he had sought for so long. All he need do was to act.

"Show me how," he told the wizard.

Snapping his jaws in satisfaction, the wizard settled to the floor. For a moment he concentrated, holding the sphere to the tip of his snout. A dark line appeared at the equator and then the sphere was no more. The wizard held a hemisphere of carved bone in each hand.

"This is the receptacle," he said. "To fill it, we must work together. To work together, we must be attuned."

Yan understood that. "I worked with Yellow Eye. I know the paths."

"Each is different."

"I know that, too."

"Let us swim in *ssess'trak'ka*."

"In *præha* we will meet."

And in *præha* they met. The wizard looked younger and healthier to Yan's arcane sight. Together they explored how their spirits meshed and learned how to work simple manipulations of the mana together. They were craftsmen trying each other's tools, finding those that best fit the hand. The wizard was more experienced than Yellow Eye had been; the task of learning to work together went smoothly.

"Ready, yes?"

"Ready."

The wizard showed Yan how to waken the Eye of the Serpent. Yan said the words and imposed his will on the mana. The sphere's ocher color lightened as the fires of energy within it kindled. The Eye blazed with a golden light as the sphere rose from the box, drifting like a soap bubble.

It floated toward Yan's face. He felt no concern, no fear. This was as it should be. The magic at the heart of the Eye was, in much of its nature, like the heart of his own magic. He had the gift to enhance the nature of things and processes, amplifying and intensifying their energies, making things more of what they were. This was the core of his magic, and the more he knew of a process or a thing, the more that he could do with it. Why he had failed to understand this clearly until now, he didn't comprehend. It didn't matter; he understood now.

He welcomed the Eye and the knowledge it brought.

"*Skendni*," the wizard shouted.

The drakkenree slapped the two halves of the bone sphere together around the floating Eye, but not before a spark escaped and dashed itself against Yan's forehead.

There was no physical sensation, yet Yan felt as if he had been struck a solid blow. For a moment his mind unfocused, and his vision dimmed. When he recovered, the first thing he knew was that the wizard had firm control of the magic they were working; Yellow Eye had gotten his talent for domination from his parent.

Outraged, Yan reached for the sphere. The wizard kept it from his grasp. Yan attempted to break their joining, but the wizard wouldn't let him go.

Yan retreated, considering his options. He looked about for something to turn to his favor and found that he had a sharper sense of the physical world than was usual when he was using his arcane senses. He could see the hut's physical existence as well as its occult energies. There were powerful spells reinforcing the log walls. Spirits coiled around each of the skulls. This was the wizard's lair; all here served him. There was nothing Yan could do for the moment.

Yan's eyes returned to his partner in magic. When he gazed into the pale, opaque orbs of the wizard's eyes, he saw himself reflected there, but the reflected image was not the one with which Yan was familiar from mirrors. Like many magicians, Yan's eyes were a mismatched set, each a different color. The reflection in the wizard's eyes showed a strange set of eyes, for Yan's reflection showed a third eye—a slit-pupiled, saurian eye—in the middle of his forehead. Yan put a hand to his brow; his physical fingers felt no change, but his head throbbed with power.

The wizard did not give Yan long to contemplate his condition. The drakkenree lifted their linked spirits through the roof of the hut and into the sky. They rose above the trees, higher and higher, until clouds rolled between them and the earth below.

"The Eye of God sees all," the wizard said.

Indeed, it did seem as if they could see everything that happened on the land below. Yan needed only to concentrate to bring his vision into closer and sharper focus. Beneath them a group of giant, long-necked saurians— t'hn'pah—smashed a path through the jungle in their search for more food to fill their rumbling bellies. To the west a young merin girl and lad struggled through brush; Yan wished them strength, pleased that Jerr and Galon were yet alive. The wizard wrenched Yan's attention to other things. Out to sea, there were storm clouds on the distant western horizon, a wall of them. The Wall, Yan realized.

Yan sensed that the wizard's attention was focused on those storms. The drakkenree was doing something to manipulate the winds and rains and lightning.

This might be the chance Yan had wanted. If the wizard

wished to play with the storms, Yan would let him. Yan drew upon his core and fed the wizard's spells.

The wizard laughed a coughing drakkenree laugh. "Not this time, Yan Tanafres. Kmm was my child and my student. Not a very good student, was Kmm."

The wizard's blithe dismissal of Yan's magic enraged him. He refused to believe that he could not overpower this old mage. The strength of the Eye gave Yan a power greater than he'd had when he had struggled with Yellow Eye. He drew upon it.

The wizard fought back. He did not bother with a physical distraction, as Yellow Eye had done. They struggled directly, grappling will against will.

The storm clouds were closer, roiling the air around them. Lightning flashed searingly close.

Yan pushed against the wizard's mastery, feeding the energy and opening the magical channels, pushing the wizard as he had pushed Yellow Eye. There was magic in the storms; Yan linked it to the spells and expanded them. The wizard laughed, daring Yan to do his best. Yan shouted his defiance.

For an instant all hung in the balance.

Then everything seemed to freeze. A bolt of lightning stood etched in its forked glory on the sky. The clouds no longer moved. Yan's heart stopped beating in midbreath.

Yan knew fear, deep fear.

"The directing claw of God," the wizard shouted exultantly.

The moment shattered.

Yan's vision splintered and the shards went wheeling away in a shower of fiery sparks. Nothing was as it was; all was as it might be. Perspective was gone, the storm was gone. The world was gone.

No longer were Yan and the wizard in a space Yan understood. There was no landscape and no horizon, just a formlessness that was not a void, but neither was it anything Yan knew. There were presences in that place that was no place, presences without form, but not without substance.

"Who?" one asked in a sepulchral tone.

Was it the voice of the dead? Had the wizard dragged Yan into necromancy after all? Yan dismissed those thoughts as he realized that the presences were alive. Elsewhere, but alive.

"I am D'jahnss'kk'lan," called the Wizard-Master of Ancient Bones.

"D'jahnss'kk'lan? You are old," said a second voice.

"And the other?" asked a third.

"Unimportant," the wizard replied.

"No," said First. "He has borne the Eye."

"Who are you, brother?" asked Second. "We know your taste."

"Yan Tanafres, a magician," Yan told them.

Confusion and concern roiled through the gray space.

"This cannot be!" said several voices at once.

"But it is," said Third.

"It must not be," said a fourth voice.

"It *is*," Third said, solemn as a judge pronouncing sentence.

"Maah'nn'kun'yee?" This fifth voice quavered.

Yan felt something touch him. He remembered an encounter with a band of ragged beggars in a backwater town of the coastal kingdoms; the beggars had run their hands along his clothing and poked their fingers into him and his goods. They had been curious to see a man dressed in islander style. They had been more than curious; there had been fear and greed in their probing. He had scattered those beggars by announcing his name and profession. Here that announcement started the disquieting probe. He endured. The touches departed.

"Maah'nn'kun'yee!" bleated Fifth.

"It cannot be!" protested Fourth and Second.

"But it is," said Third.

"It *must* not be!" said a sixth voice.

"It *is*," said Third.

"It is," echoed the others.

"It is," Sixth said forlornly. "Though it should not be, it is."

"B'han'ssu'uss stirs. It is time!" said D'jahnss'kk'lan, the Wizard-Master of Ancient Bones. "God shows us that it is time."

"Time!" cried Second. "Our time!"

"So soon, D'jahnss'kk'lan?" asked Third.

"Soon for you. Too long for me," said the wizard.

"D'jahnss'kk'lan, you are old," said Second. "You have grown old without us."

"I knew the cost," said the wizard.

"*Maah'nn'kun'yee.*" Sixth sounded distressed. "You come with *maah'nn'kun'yee*. This is not meet. It cannot be our time. It must be past our time. We are lost."

"Too late!" cried Fifth. "We have lost our place in time. We are lost!"

Great confusion and turmoil swept through the space.

"We are not lost!" D'jahnss'kk'lan thundered. "It is time to leave the egg. Time to walk past the walls. God has shown me that which we feared, that which we fled, is gone. I tell you that it is time. God's eye is open upon the world. The world is kind again. Look! See for yourselves!"

Yan's head felt as if it were swelling. He seemed to be seeing multiple views of the world all at once. Too much to comprehend. The images overwhelmed him, and he cried from the pain. He closed his eyes, trying to shut out the visions, but one eye remained open—the saurian eye. Images whirled past the eye at stunning speed; Yan could make no sense of them. The pain continued.

Then it was gone.

"The walls *must* fall," said First.

"The walls *will* fall," said Second.

Thunder crashed around them. Flash after flash of

lightning burned in the sky. The winds howled and raged
with the fury of the Under Court unleashed upon the
world. Yan was in the middle of the greatest storm since
Vehr contested with Baaliff to win the land free of the
sea.

"They fall! The walls fall!" the voices exulted.

Yan trembled in the sudden light that flared and beat
down on him with the heat of the hottest summer day.
He might have been looking into Horesh's eye, for the
way the burning glare blinded him when he sought its
source.

Was this the gaze of a god? Horesh? Or Baansuus? Or
something else?

"The greatest magic ever made," D'jahnss'kk'lan told
him.

Magic? Not any magic Yan knew. Yet he did not feel
the terror he'd felt when Kerandiri and the wizard had
called the godly power into themselves. This *was* different. He understood then that it *was* magic. Magic, pure
and bright, and more powerful than any he had ever
known, a magic to dwarf the creation of the Serpent's
Eye. His forehead throbbed, and a spike of pain stabbed
into it. He saw forms of magic undreamed of: strange,
antique magics, saurian magics. He screamed, frightened
by the glory of it.

What frightened him most was that he understood that
he had already been touched by this magic, touched and
marked, changed forever. In Scothandir, under the castle,
in the chamber of the ancient drakkenree wizards. So
long ago, yet only a moment ago. The time-warping spell
had placed its mark on him, set him apart. Now he saw
what lay behind that spell.

The drakkenree wizards had bent time to their will.
Now they were undoing their magic.

The force of the energies that roared around him was
awe-inspiring. Terrifying. This was magic beyond one
man's ability. How had the drakkenree mages done what

they had done? How could he consider asking now? He did not belong here.

Yan could not run in that place, but he ran anyway. The mana flow swirled and churned. Turning his back on the glare of the magic, he fled the raging maelstrom.

He felt the sky rip. Time was unraveling around him. He feared to slip into nothingness, as a black pit of timelessness opened beneath his feet.

Denying the pit, he hurtled above it as if he were winged. He refused to be dragged down into the dark. His place was elsewhere. Clinging to that thought, he sought that place. Returning to that place was what he wanted most. He bent his will to being there.

Howls followed him as he fled—anguished howls, joyous howls. Not merin shouts, but saurian screams, noise beyond hearing. Claws caught at him, demanding that he stay. He tore himself away. He would not be held. He wanted no part of the magic howling around him. The magic was strong. Too strong. He was lifted up and tossed by the mana storm and whirled screaming into darkness.

29

THE STORM CLOUDS CAME UP with unnatural speed. It might have been the gods answering Teletha's prayers, but she didn't think so. It was more likely sorcery. When the rain started falling, she reconsidered her guess as to the storm's source. Water fell in sheets, and within seconds she was soaked to the skin. Her pistol and the arquebuses would be useless. The storm was the sort of answer she was used to getting from the gods.

Still, it could be worse. The heavy downpour would make the *vekkanconday* hunker down and mind their own business, and it would drown any sounds made by a prowler in the drakkenree village. Was that a fair trade for losing use of the guns? What if you add the lack of visibility?

Lords above! She was debating like Peyto. If she was going to go, she should go. Things couldn't get worse.

She checked on Sir Kopell, trying to make him as comfortable—and as hidden—as possible. The knight's wounds were getting the better of him; he was barely conscious. She cautioned him about crying out, and he seemed to understand the danger. Vehr knew that Sir Kopell was a good soldier. The knight would do his best, but he might not be able to control himself if the pain grew too great. Teletha prayed that Vehr would honor

Sir Kopell's courage and give him the strength to master the pain. She asked for Mannar's mercy as well. It was all she could do; Yan was the doctor.

Time to go find him.

She started down the slope, going cautiously, for the earth was slick and becoming slicker. She discovered that she had miscalculated her path when she found herself sheltering for a rest at a rock that turned out to be one of the *vekkanconday*. The beast paid her no heed. And why should it? She was no threat to it. She looked about as best she could in the driving rain. She had passed several of the animals already, more lay ahead. The one nearest her shifted. She leapt back, but it was not rising to attack her; it was just getting more comfortable. Stomach rumbling, the *vekkanconday* settled back down, once more becoming little more than a big lump. She let herself breathe again. If they were all so docile . . .

The herd had been between her and the village. It would be shorter by a good bit to pass through the herd than to go around the beasts. If she went around, she might run into their keepers. The brutes were quiet and offering no threat, and there was more than enough space to pass between the lumpy shapes of hunkered *vekkanconday*. It seemed safe enough. The greatest danger looked to be avoiding the steaming piles of excrement.

Through the herd, then.

She was well into their midst when the lightning began. There was a lot of it. Bolt after bolt streaked down from the sky until the air hung heavy with the scent of the thunderbolts.

She'd been wrong about the greatest danger. The *vekkanconday* didn't like the lightning. All around her the stupid beasts were stirring. They bellowed and honked as they rose to their feet and started to jostle against each other. One lurched to its feet directly in her path. Teletha struck it with her fist, as she would have struck a horse, trying to get it to move away. She might as well have done nothing; the animal did not acknowledge her blow, lumbering on oblivious to her. More of the beasts were rising. She was in serious danger of being trampled by the clumsy brutes as they milled about.

Vehr, save a soldier, she prayed.

Someone had better look out for her, she wasn't being bright enough to look after herself. She had to get out from among the beasts. She ran, heedless of stealth, heedless of direction. She hoped she was still headed for the village, but she didn't really care. The *vekkanconday* were becoming more agitated. It was vitally important to get free of the herd before the stampede got truly started. She leapt tails and even scrambled over one or two of the slower beasts who had not yet gotten to their feet.

And made it—barely.

Bellowing with terror, the mass of pack beasts rumbled forward. Teletha heard someone shouting. One of the keepers? The sound was smothered by the herd's thunder, a sound that bid fair to rival the angry sky.

A deeper darkness loomed before Teletha: the village wall. She hit it at a run and went up it faster than a bregil seaman climbing a mast. She had a better motivation than any bregil seaman.

She rested on the parapet, as much to catch her breath as to ensure she had not been spotted. The weather had driven the sentries to cover. If they were good sentries, they would not have gone far. She could not afford to assume that they were not good sentries.

She found a ramp to the ground and headed straight for the center of the village. From the wall, she'd seen how the lightning concentrated around the hut with the skulls. That was the focus of the ruckus; that was where Yan would be.

Not only the sentries had been driven to cover. The village might have been deserted. She encountered no one and soon stood before the entrance to the skull-ringed hut. Light, pulsing and lambent, spilled from the doorway. Teletha didn't hesitate; she knew that if she did, she might never have the nerve to go into the wizard's lair.

She drew her sword and kissed it. *Vehr, save this soldier.*

She stepped through the doorway.

The roar of the rain suddenly seemed far away. It was hot and dry in the hut, like a furnace, but there was no fire. Nothing she could see accounted for the bright light filling the hut. The illumination revealed niches hewn into the walls, from which toothy drakkenree skulls leered at her.

The light also revealed a sight that made Teletha's breath catch: Yan sprawled upon the floor. It took her a moment to be sure that his chest moved; her breathing resumed when she was sure that he was alive. Clearly all was not well. A tiny flame like a candle's flickered on his forehead. The fire didn't seem to be burning him, but it could not be good. She needed to get him out of here.

But could she?

A small white drakkenree crouched beside a carved marble slab that might have been a sacrificial altar. She only needed to glance at the drakkenree to know that this saurian was the Wizard of Bones. Everything the drakkenree wore was made of bone or ornamented with bone. The white drakkenree looked as if he were made of bones himself. Tiny lightnings crackled around the wizard, their play intensifying as he lifted his eyes from the silver globe that he held and turned them on her. Those eyes looked blind, but Teletha did not doubt that the drakkenree saw her.

Was her sword faster than his spells?

"After so long, my brothers speak to me," the drakkenree said.

For a wonder, the wizard spoke Nitallan. The words were oddly accented, but Teletha understood them well enough. Given the power crackling around the wizard, she thought it better to talk than fight.

"I have no quarrel with you," she said.

"They are coming," the wizard said, as if she had never spoken. "The time has come to let loose time."

Whatever that meant. Had the magic rampaging here unhinged the drakkenree's mind?

"All will be as it was," the wizard said. He continued to speak, but it was in the growling, hissing language of his kind.

Teletha swallowed, her mouth and throat very dry. She wanted nothing to do with the wizard. She grabbed the shoulders of Yan's robe and started dragging him toward the doorway. The skulls in their niches hissed and gnashed their teeth, but the wizard did nothing more than stare into his silver globe, hissing and growling to it lovingly.

Teletha got Yan outside without interference. Promising all of her favorite gods sacrifices of thanks, she tried to get Yan on his feet. She surely couldn't carry him far. He might have been a dead man for all he responded. She managed to get him sprawled on her back and abandoned the lee of the hut. She hadn't gotten far before the wash of the rain roused him from his stupor. Gratefully she plopped him into the mud. He whuffed out a breath, but did no more.

"Come on, Yan. You have to walk for yourself. I can't carry you."

"Zephem," he said, slurring the name.

"What about him?" Teletha hadn't seen the Baaliffite in the hut. Nor Löm Kerandiri, for that matter, and the löm was more important. Why wasn't Yan worried about him? "What happened to Löm Kerandiri?"

Yan shook his head sadly. "Dead. He opposed the wizard."

Teletha was very glad she hadn't attempted the same course; she was no löm, with the power of the Celestial Court behind her.

"We'll be dead if we don't get going," she told Yan.

"They took Zephem away," he mumbled, resisting her tug on his robe. "We must get him."

"To hell with him." The Baaliffite had done nothing but preach against Yan. Let him rot. She was going to have enough trouble getting Yan out of the village.

"We can't leave him here," Yan insisted.

Teletha didn't see why not. Maybe the drakkenree would eat him; he'd probably give them indigestion. Rescuing Löm Kerandiri she would have attempted willingly. But the Baaliffite—

In the end they rescued him from the hut in which he'd been penned. Agreeing to do it had been the only way to shut Yan up. She wasn't surprised that Zephem wasn't grateful; the first words out of his mouth asked for more trouble.

"We must kill it."

"Kill it?" she asked, feeling that she knew whom Zephem meant.

"The Wizard of Bones. It is possessed of evil."

She had been right. The man was an idiot! "It's possessed all right. It's *possessed* of enough power to fry you."

"It must be killed. My Lord calls for its blood."

"You'll be spilling your own if you try to go after the wizard."

"We must leave this place," Yan said. He still seemed a little muddled. "Word must go out of what happened here."

Teletha didn't know what Yan was talking about—she wasn't sure she wanted to know—but she did know what would happen if they didn't leave. They would be killed.

"Do what you want," she told the priest. "We're leaving."

Zephem found it more expedient to stick with his merin comrades than attempt to take on the wizard alone. The storm continued to shield them. They headed for the gate; in his current condition, Yan couldn't manage the climb over the stockade. Unfortunately, the gate sentry was too diligent; he remained at his post.

Zephem stole a log from a woodpile and crept toward him. He rose up like a vengeance spirit and clubbed the drakkenree down from behind. Teletha didn't complain; the Baaliffite's actions made it possible for them to leave by the gate. Zephem appropriated the guard's weapon, a long-handled sword that looked to have a terrible balance. They left the village.

The warrior priest held his weapon ready, but they had no need for it; the worst opponent they faced during the rest of their escape was the clinging, mucky ground churned up by the stampeding *vekkanconday*. It was trial enough; Yan continued to stumble and require support. Teletha led them to the place where Sir Kopell lay.

The storm hadn't done the knight any good. His bandages were soaked and seeping blood again. "He's in bad shape," Teletha observed, feeling a little foolish at stating the obvious. Yan was the one with doctoring skills; he'd know better than her.

"He may die," Yan said. "I don't have any real healing magic, but I can help a little, I think." Yan knelt beside the wounded knight, bowing his head and closing his eyes. After a moment his hand reached out and touched Sir Kopell's forehead. Several long minutes later, Yan sighed and came out of his trance. He sounded shaky when he spoke. "He needs a true healer."

Yan looked up at Zephem.

"I am no healer," Zephem said. "My Lord has no need for healers."

"We will need a litter to get him back to the ships," Yan said.

"You care for Sir Kopell," Teletha told him. "Fra Zephem and I will make the litter."

The Baaliffite glowered at her, but he did follow her when she set out to gather materials. The continuing rain made the job harder, but it shielded them from prying eyes as well. Teletha didn't see a reason to complain. Zephem felt differently.

"This is a waste of effort," he whined.

"Shall I tell King Shain you think his knight not worth the saving? Sir Kopell is his picked man."

"That king has poor taste in companions." The bitterness in the priest's voice was deeper than a Baaliffite's distaste for helping the wounded could account for.

Teletha hadn't noticed the priest showing any particular dislike for Sir Kopell in the past; in fact, the two had seemed to get along rather well. What underlay Zephem's comment? "You were against this mission from the start, weren't you?"

"That is true," Zephem said. "Had I been successful, your Sir Kopell would never have come here to die."

Had I been successful?

The meaning seemed clear to Teletha. "You bloody Baaliffite, you're the one who tried to kill Yan!"

Teletha reached for her sword, but stopped when she saw that the priest made no move toward his own. He was no coward to stand meekly against her accusation. Why wasn't he ready to fight? He smiled grimly at her hesitation.

"A priest of Baaliff does no murder," he said, straightening up and standing tall.

"Your Master is the Lord of Blood. Tell me you don't know the ways of murder."

"The followers of Lord Baaliff are warriors, not the bloody-handed, mindless killers of Vehrite tales. We do no murder."

Could he be telling the truth? "If you didn't try to kill Yan, who did? Who else had reason and chance?"

"One whose scruples are different from mine."

"So you know who the villain is."

"Aye."

The Baaliffite's smugness offended Teletha. She drew her sword and put the point on his chest. "By Vehr's sword of justice, you will tell me the villain's name."

"Swear whatever oath you care to, you will not move me or cause me to speak. Your violence will not bring the name to my lips. I owe a higher loyalty."

"What higher loyalty is there than justice and honor?"

"Loyalty to the Celestial Lords and to Their laws."

"The Celestial Lords uphold justice."

"That They do, but They have passed down laws as well, and by Their laws I am bound to say nothing. Do not look at me like that! I do not condone stealthy murder, but I am bound. I learned what I know when I served as the ear of the gods. By the vows of my priesthood and the laws of the gods I may not reveal what I learned acting in Their stead. To no man, or woman, may I reveal what I heard."

Zephem put his hand on her blade and moved the point away from his chest. She let him. A priest acting as the ear of the gods *was* sworn never to repeat what he heard. Others had been placed in similar dilemmas ere now. They had found solutions, reasonable ones by Teletha's lights.

"Will you be justice yourself?" she asked.

"I am no Vehrite."

She had half expected such an answer, but there was something more in the Baaliffite's tone than the rivalry between the martial orders. There was clear hatred behind the contempt, and she didn't think it was directed at the Vehrite order. "You're hoping the villain will still succeed."

Zephem shrugged. "I will not mourn if the magician dies. He is corrupted and serves evil. He deserves to die."

"You're making me think that your friend with the different scruples does not exist."

"The villain, as you call him, exists. And I will tell you that he thinks to honor his god." Maliciously, Zephem added, "Perhaps he is misguided, but his end is laudable."

"You seem to be protesting too much."

"Much as I want to see the magician dead, I know it

must be done according to law, justice, and honor. He
deserves Great Horesh's cleansing fire. Every soul
deserves a chance to be purified, even that of a black
magician who sides with the ancient enemy."

Zephem delivered his speech with such venom and
sincerity that Teletha had to believe that he wasn't the
villain. When she thought about it, she saw that Zephem
wouldn't have been so open in his efforts to blacken
Yan's reputation if the priest was intending to murder
him. Why work to send Yan to the stake, when a knife in
the back would do the job? Zephem was a good enough
warrior to manage that.

So the villain wasn't Zephem. Who, then? Who would
attempt murder, then be concerned enough about his
actions to confess his attempts to the Baaliffite? Someone
who was still alive, or the priest wouldn't be holding out
hope that the villain might still succeed.

First things first, though. First they had to leave the
vicinity of the drakkenree village before the storm broke
and they were discovered. That meant finishing Sir
Kopell's litter. They had just about used up the saplings
and vines that they had gathered. They needed a few
more poles to make a good bed. Teletha sent Zephem to
gather them while she finished lashing what they had;
she didn't trust his knots. It was a foolish fear, she supposed, but she felt it all the same.

She was finished with her task and debating going to
find out what was taking Zephem so long, when she
heard a rustling in the brush. Someone dragging a load
of saplings shouldn't make so much noise as to be heard
over the rain.

She took up her sword.

No sooner had she done so than a naked drakkenree
emerged into the little clearing. Naked? The drakkenree
from the village had all worn harness. Sir Kopell's slave had
been naked, but that drakkenree hadn't been armed with a
sword.

A bloody sword.

"Ah, the magician's warrior," the drakkenree said. "I must be getting closer."

He charged.

30

JERR GAVE A PRAYER OF THANKS to Mannar when she got her first look at the river. As they moved along near the riverbank, she caught glimpses of the ships through openings in the trees. They'd done it! The nightmare of the trip through the jungle was over. The gods had smiled, offering them a respite from the rain that had dogged the last part of their journey. They were nearly safe now. It was only a little farther to the landing site, where the boats were waiting to take them back to the ships.

When they reached the break in the riverbank vegetation where the boats had been drawn up, Jerr saw that the boats were gone. How could that be? The ships were still anchored in the middle of the river. The boats were supposed to wait. Why wouldn't the boats be waiting? She started to ask, but Galon shushed her.

"Stay quiet," he said in a brusque whisper.

His tone was annoying. She turned to question his manner and saw the first of the bodies. Now that her eyes were no longer locked on the river's edge, she saw that corpses littered the landing site. The boat guards were dead. For how long? Long enough for the forest scavengers to have gotten to the bodies; but as she and Galon had learned, here in the jungle the scavengers were never far away. The massacre could have occurred as long ago as yesterday—possibly at the same time as the *sharkkain* were devastating the party that had gone inland—or it might have happened only minutes ago. The attackers might still be nearby.

She held her tongue, watching Galon survey the area. Finally he relaxed, apparently satisfied that there was no immediate danger. She still wasn't sure that they were safe. Still scanning the forest for signs of the killers, she asked, *"Sharkkain?"*

"Not unless the beasts have taken up gun and sword."

"Then who?"

"Soldiers from Jor Valadrem would be my guess. There are bregil footprints about." He walked to the water's edge and stared out over the river. "They didn't get everyone, though."

Jerr hadn't counted bodies. "How do you know?"

"The bregil didn't capture the boats. They're gone."

"Maybe the bregil sailed away with them."

"Not past the ships. Master Threok's gunners wouldn't miss."

"Maybe the bregil did take the boats, and maybe Master Threok did sink the boats."

"We would have heard the cannon."

They would have, wouldn't they? "Well that's good. The islanders can come pick us up."

Galon's response disappointed her. "They won't risk a landing to pick us up. The bregil will be watching the ships. Master Threok won't risk his sailors just for us. We'll have to get to the ships on our own."

Jerr wanted to ask why, but Galon's grim expression suggested that questioning his assessment wouldn't be a good idea. Besides, he seemed to think that they could get to the ships themselves. She didn't like his idea of making a raft, but it was better than swimming. They set to making Galon's plan a reality.

Jerr didn't have Galon's strength to heave the logs

about, but her fingers were as nimble as his with the knots. They soon divided their labor, working as quietly as they could and stopping often to listen. Galon feared that the bregil would be lurking about, and he worried that noise of the work might mask the approach of the soldiers.

She worried about that, too, but she was more worried about what would happen once they'd finished. She had to agree that making a raft was better than swimming, but by how much? She'd seen the crocodiles in the river. The raft they were building did not have the safe, high sides of the ship's boats in which they'd come ashore. A crocodile could crawl aboard as easily as it could haul itself onto the riverbank. Galon assured her that the reptiles wouldn't do that, but she wasn't sure she believed him. What did *he* know about crocodiles? Even Master Tanafres didn't know much.

She was still worried about the threat of crocodiles when they launched their makeshift craft. There were none of the reptiles in sight, but you never knew; the monsters could be lurking just beneath the surface of the water, ready to snatch away a person, the way she'd seen one take a cappylagom that had come to the river to drink. People were a lot bigger than cappylagoms, but she'd seen crocodiles much, much bigger than the one that had taken the cappylagom. She was careful to keep her hands and feet away from the edge of the raft.

Galon pushed them away from shore with a springy pole. There were rough but serviceable paddles—flat sheets of tough bark ripped from a type of tree she'd never seen before—for when the water got too deep for the pole. Galon said that they'd only use the paddles if they had to; the river current should do most of the work of getting them to the ships. Jerr was glad of that. She wasn't looking forward to using the paddles; using them meant being near the edge of the raft. The river water was too murky; she couldn't see into it at all.

"One more good push," Galon said, leaning into the pole.

The wood bent under his weight as he put his strength into it. He was leaning dangerously out over the water. Jerr grabbed for his shirttail to keep him on board. The linen strained, but it didn't part; Galon stayed aboard. There was a loud bang from the shore and a hole appeared in the cloth. Jerr didn't understand, but Galon did.

"Get down!" he shouted, diving onto her and making her do as he said. "We're being fired upon."

She stopped struggling to squirm from underneath him and hugged herself to the logs. Ugly, dark water washed up through the cracks between the logs and lapped against her face. There were more bangs, and something thunked into one of the logs.

How could the gods have let them come so far only to let them be killed so close to safety? It wasn't fair! They were so near to the ships. Near enough to see activity on the decks.

Two knots of sailors wrestled something to the quarterdeck rail. A ladder maybe? Galon was using one of the paddles to guide the raft away from that side of the ship. What good would a ladder do? They wouldn't come near the ladder.

But the sailors weren't readying a ladder. As the clumps of men separated, she saw that they were carrying small cannon. The sailors set the guns into fittings at the rail. The weapons must have already been loaded, for gunners set them off nearly at once. The two little cannon roared in unison, sending smoke rolling out over the water. Splintering crashes sounded from the riverbank. When Jerr's ears could hear again, she heard someone weeping on the shore.

There was no more arquebus fire from the riverbank.

Galon's guidance brought the raft to *Mannar's Handmaiden* so that the ship's bulk was between them and the hostile shore. There were sailors at the rail along the main deck, and this time they really did have a ladder. The wooden rungs clattered against the hull as the ladder uncoiled. Galon caught the ropes and held the ladder taut for her to climb. As she climbed she felt the relief of knowing that this time they *had* reached safety.

Captain Namsorn and Master Threok were waiting on the deck.

"You'd best have a good answer to why you're here and Löm Kerandiri is not, or you'll be facing the headsman and taking your excuses to the God's tribunal," said Captain Namsorn.

31

YAN LOOKED UP from the semiconscious Sir Kopell when he heard Khankemeh's voice. For a moment he was glad, then he heard the drakkenree's challenging roar and Teletha's answering shout.

What was he to do? He wasn't a fighter; he couldn't wield a sword against Khankemeh. Remembering his earlier encounters with Khankemeh, he knew that he would be killed almost at once. What help was a dead magician to Teletha?

For that matter, what help was a live one? Yan had no magic to blast the drakkenree. Since his experience with the Eye, he had a clearer understanding of magic, including destructive sorcery. But he did not have the symbolic tools or the finesse. He could not command the arcane energies with sufficient control to strike Khankemeh and leave Teletha safe. Such magic was not part of his heart.

"What passes?" Sir Kopell asked weakly.

"Khankemeh is attacking Teletha."

"No."

Denying it would change nothing.

"She must be helped," said the knight.

Too true. But how?

Sir Kopell struggled to rise. "No one can stand against a drakkenree unaided."

The knight's heart was in the right place, but his body was in no shape to help. Much like Yan. And yet . . . what about Yan's heart? What about his heart of magic? He had learned, and there *was* something he could do. His magic—*his* magic—might have a use.

He slipped into *præha*.

Teletha met the charging drakkenree with the point of her sword. The drakkenree was too canny to impale himself on the sword. He shifted to the left. She went right, ducking low to avoid his cut. Her slash sliced nothing but air.

They separated and circled, experienced sword fighters studying each other's form. Teletha didn't care to think how often this lizard had watched her practice at Sir Kopell's steading. She had never seen him use a sword.

She'd fought drakkenree before, but never alone, and then the lizards had always been less cautious than this one. Was this one showing respect, having seen her skill in practice? Or was he toying with her?

Teletha relied on speed and skill. The drakkenree was fast, too, though maybe not so fast as she. Certainly he was stronger; she couldn't allow a weapon bind or get close enough for him to grab her. His skill remained to be tested, although it was clear that he was no novice swordsman. She could only hope that he put most of his reliance on his strength and size. If so, she might have a chance; she'd used her advantages to beat that combination before.

But never against a drakkenree.

She feinted. He shifted, showing that he understood the danger of her point. It had been too much to hope that he wouldn't. They circled. The soaked ground didn't make for the best of footing.

"I am Khan'kmm'eh," the drakkenree said.

As if she cared.

"I am your death," he added.

Not if she had anything to say about it.

Her best chance was to keep the drakkenree busy until Zephem returned. Together they could beat it; she felt sure of that. All she had to do was stay alive until the Baaliffite showed up. Until then, she had only herself to rely on.

Or did she?

Strangely enough she felt as if she was not facing the drakkenree alone. She sensed a presence real enough to be spoken to.

Yan?

She was sure that it was Yan. Somehow—it had to be through his magic—he was with her. There were no words, but she felt as if he were reassuring her, offering her strength. She was thankful for the encouragement, and glad that someone thought she might survive this fight.

Maybe things weren't as hopeless as they seemed.

She launched a spoiling attack against the drakkenree. Her first thrust was supposed to be a feint, a potential threat to set the drakkenree up for her next maneuver. She placed her point so well and executed the move so smoothly that she nearly scored. Khankemeh seemed surprised. That was fair—so was she.

The drakkenree recovered first, launching a pounding series of cuts that beat against her guard and threatened to overwhelm her by sheer strength. Her arm strained against the brute power of Khankemeh's blows. And failed her. The drakkenree's sword slammed down, forcing her own blade down. Khankemeh's edge came down on her left arm, hacking open the sleeve of her sodden buff coat, cutting through her shirt, and slicing her flesh.

It wasn't a bad wound, but the pain was a white-hot reminder that she needed to make the fight go her way, or lose it. She threw herself back, out of the reach of the drakkenree's sword.

Fight your own fight, Yan seemed to whisper to her.

Good advice, she told herself.

She took that advice. Making the best of the sloppy ground, she adopted a hit-and-run strategy. She made much use of her point, employing techniques with which the drakkenree ought not be familiar. Her strategy worked, somewhat; the damned lizard was quick and kept himself from any wound deeper than a scratch. On the other hand, he failed to cut her again. The fight was turning into a stalemate in which stamina would tell. She was good for a long battle, but the endurance of drakkenree was legendary. In the end, Khankemeh could wear her down.

Unless she did something to shift the odds.

She didn't like to gamble, but she was running out of options.

A few more passes showed her an opportunity. Khankemeh was weak in his low guards and slower to his right than his left. She ran another exchange, pushing—just a little—along that line. The opening was low, very low. Going for it would be a risk requiring an unorthodox ploy. She could get herself dead quickly.

Or she could wait, until Khankemeh wore her down. Either course promised death, and Vehr hated a coward.

She went in low, sword first, and kept going, diving to the ground. She half slid, half rolled through the mud. Form wasn't important here, only speed. Khankemeh's sword cut air and rain in the space where he'd been expecting her to stop. She'd made it! Teletha scrambled to her feet, taking up her guard. Khankemeh was slow in turning; blood flowed from a deep furrow in his haunch.

She'd scored!

They fell to circling again. The drakkenree was showing new respect for her as an opponent. And well he should. She'd lasted longer than she'd thought she

would, and she wasn't as tired as she should be. She'd
demonstrated that she was a threat. Maybe she wouldn't
need help against the drakkenree after all.

Then again . . .

Teletha caught a hint of movement behind
Khankemeh. Yan? Zephem? Vehr would be taking her
to His standard, if it was another drakkenree.

A figure emerged from the brush: Sir Kopell.

The man was wobbling, barely able to stand, but he
had an arquebus in his hands. In the rain, it would never
fire. The knight knew that. He raised the gun over his
head like a club as he stumbled forward.

How could she take advantage of the new situation?

The drakkenree caught the change in Teletha's focus.
Damn, he was canny! Instead of taking advantage and
attacking, Khankemeh backed away. Did he think she
was trying to draw him into a trap?

The drakkenree opened the range between them. The
lunge she'd just decided upon would be difficult now.
Khankemeh maneuvered to his left, past the litter,
putting the rickety frame of saplings between them. No
hope for the lunge now; if she tried, she'd likely end up
on her face, and it would be all over. Still, she had to do
something, or Sir Kopell was a dead man.

The knight was moving faster than she had thought
him able. He was almost upon the drakkenree. Too late
for plans now.

Somehow, the drakkenree sensed the threat to his
rear. He turned as Sir Kopell closed the last of the distance between them.

"Treachery!" the knight shouted as he swung his
makeshift club.

Incredibly, the drakkenree did no more than raise his
arm to ward his head against the blow. The arquebus butt
struck the arm. Teletha heard bone snap. Hissing,
Khankemeh backed away from the angry knight.

Sir Kopell swung the arquebus wildly before him as he

advanced. Khankemeh backed away faster, opening distance between them. The drakkenree made no move to attack the knight. Had the saurian been so surprised by the flank attack? Teletha thought that unlikely. Khankemeh's retreat wouldn't last long; he would soon realize how feeble Sir Kopell's threat was. Teletha hurried to the knight's side. Before she reached him, Khankemeh turned tail and dashed into the jungle.

Teletha halted her rush. The mighty drakkenree warrior running away from a wounded man with a club? It didn't make sense to her. Even with his arm broken, Khankemeh could have overwhelmed Sir Kopell. The lizard hadn't even defended himself. It just didn't make sense.

"Stinking treacherous lizard," Sir Kopell huffed. "Coward, too."

The knight was wobbling. Teletha caught him before he collapsed. The knight leaned gratefully on her, his body shaking with tremors. The arquebus clumped to the ground. He didn't seem to have any strength left.

"I don't feel well," he said, and fainted.

Teletha struggled with the knight's weight. Then Yan was there, helping her.

"Let's get him on the litter," he said.

"But it's not finished. Zephem went for more saplings."

"Zephem won't be coming back," Yan said.

He sounded awfully sure. "How do you know that?" she asked, suspecting that she already knew the answer. Magic.

"The only living humans nearby are Khankemeh, who is heading away at speed, and a party of drakkenree warriors, who are coming this way, though not so quickly."

Much as she hated magic, she knew its efficacy when practiced by true magicians. Yan was a true magician. If he said there were enemy on the way, they were in trouble.

"We won't be able to outrun them."

Yan nodded. "I know."

Together they managed to get Sir Kopell to the litter. The frame was complete; it could be hauled. The bed was still barely formed, but it would have to do. She did what she could to tighten the lashings.

"Is there something you can do?" She didn't want to rely on magic, but it seemed their only chance.

Yan never stopped work on settling the knight on the litter. "If we can get away from this immediate vicinity, there might be."

She hoped so. For all their sakes, she hoped so. Einthof wasn't one of the gods to whom Teletha prayed regularly—not in His role as patron to magicians anyway—but she asked Him to help Yan in whatever way He could.

It took both of them to haul the litter out of the clearing. They left a trail that a blind beggar could follow. Teletha didn't see how the drakkenree could fail to track them, and said so.

"I'm working on it," Yan said. He was breathless already. He wasn't the strongest man, but they had not been hauling the litter long enough to have winded him. Something else was sapping his strength.

Magic, she realized. It really was the only way they were going to get out of this trap.

Yan sat down suddenly. "Guess I'll have to try here."

You'll have to succeed. Teletha heard a drakkenree shout in the distance; they'd discovered the trail. "You'll succeed. I have faith in you," she told Yan, but he was already deep in trance.

Just as well. Her words didn't sound very confident to her. She would rather have put her trust in a dozen arquebuses wielded by stout soldiers.

Lord Einthof, are you listening? Will a mass be enough, or is Your price higher? I'll pay it. Is my oath as a solider surety enough?

"Yes." Yan sounded a little surprised. "It's working."

He'd always been better with magic than he thought he was. If he felt confident of the success of his spells, they must be achieving fabulous results. She heard the still-unseen drakkenree. They were moving away.

"Have you sent them on a false trail?"

"They have seen all the evidence they need to know that we made a meal for a drakkenkain. They are returning to the village."

"An illusion?"

"It looked and smelled real enough to them."

The best thing about magic was having it on your side and not arrayed against you. Even then, she didn't like it. Today, however, she wasn't going to complain.

32

JERR AND GALON FOUND A PLACE for themselves near the prow of *Mannar's Handmaiden*. It didn't have a lot of privacy, but at least it was away from Master Threok and Captain Namsorn. She didn't want to see either of them after the awful way they had treated her and Galon. The two men seemed to think that she and Galon were responsible for the *sharkkain* attack and the deaths of everyone else who had gone inland. Jerr supposed that the only reason that Master Threok and Captain Namsorn hadn't ordered some awful punishment was that they couldn't agree on a single course of action. They were still arguing about whether to attack Jor Valadrem or to try to escape downriver.

Jerr liked the idea of escaping, but it worried her, too. She and Galon had survived the *sharkkain* attack. Others might have as well. If the ships left, they would leave any survivors behind.

"I think the rain may be easing," Galon said.

Jerr didn't think so. The gap in the storm that had let them reach the ships was long gone. While the storm was weakening, it was a long way from finished.

"We'll sail when it stops," he said.

She wasn't so sure. "Master Threok still wants to attack the city."

"Captain Namsorn will have his way. He has charge of this expedition now."

"He hasn't convinced Master Threok of that. He doesn't argue well."

"But Master Lennuick does, and he agrees with Captain Namsorn that we need to tell the emperor what has happened."

"Tell the emperor! Tell the emperor! What about King Shain?"

"The king, too," Galon said so mildly that Jerr was embarrassed by her outburst.

To hide her chagrin, she turned away to stare between the supports of the rail. She was out from under their protective blanket, getting wet. Galon—bless him—said nothing. He just moved closer and tugged the blanket around her shoulders again.

Jerr stared at the rain. Her eyes traveled along the dimly seen bank. What was she looking for? She didn't know; it was better than arguing with Galon.

Through the shifting curtains of rain, Jerr glimpsed two figures struggling out of the jungle into the clearing where the boats had landed so long ago. One wore tattered black robes and the other, a woman, wore the bedraggled garb of an islander soldier. Jerr couldn't believe what she was seeing. She knew those two silhouettes. Those weary travelers were Master Tanafres and Mistress Schonnegon. They were alive!

"Look!" she shouted, pointing toward the shore. "Look! There at the landing place. It's Master Tanafres and Mistress Schonnegon."

Men came running to the foredeck, Captain Namsorn and Master Lennuick among them. Jerr and Galon's private place became crowded with anxious sailors and soldiers ready for war. They demanded to know the cause for alarm. Jerr kept pointing and shouting, "Look!"

"They're dragging someone with them on a litter," Galon said excitedly. "A man."

"I cannot see," Captain Namsorn said. "Is it Löm Kerandiri?"

"I don't think so," Galon said.

He would be hoping that it was Captain Schell. Everyone would hope it was the person he most wanted to see. Except Jerr; she was already seeing whom she wanted to see. That relief let her observe more honestly.

"I think it's Sir Kopell," she said. Though it would disappoint Galon, she hoped that she was right; she liked the knight. "See the colors on the man's chest? Those are Sir Kopell's colors."

"Kopell." Captain Namsorn didn't sound pleased. "Foolish to expect otherwise. It has come to pass."

The Solonite captain wasn't making any sense, so Jerr asked, "What are you talking about?"

"The betrayer betrays again," he said, as if it explained everything.

Galon looked troubled. "You can't mean Master Tanafres."

"The Great God knows His enemies and sets His soldiers upon them. Rastionne was a lesson."

"With respect, Captain Namsorn," Master Lennuick said. "You don't know what you are talking about. You weren't at Rastionne."

"I know about the betrayal at Rastionne. Who are you to deny it?"

"I will tell you about the real betrayal," Galon said boldly. "I heard about Rastionne from General Iaf Smyth, and I—"

"Another dupe of the corrupted one. Keep such drivel to yourself, boy." Namsorn glared at him. "And take your hand off your sword. Men lose their heads for attacking their superiors. A boy's neck is no different to the headsman's ax."

Galon did remove his hand from his sword, but she didn't think that he was afraid of Captain Namsorn. Captain Namsorn held the emperor's commission, and

Galon had too much respect for his emperor. Galon's expression promised that the matter was not settled, even if he no longer challenged Captain Namsorn.

"Someone has to help them," Jerr said; she wasn't sure to whom. "Master Threok says that there are still bregil soldiers in the jungle. They could be attacked. They could be captured." Or killed, but she didn't want to say that; it might make the possibility real.

"The monkeys may have the magician," said Captain Namsorn. "Let him reap the rewards of treachery."

"Without accusations, I suggest that the treachery is on the water, not the land," Master Lennuick said. "Sir Kopell is the representative of King Shain of Kolvin. Surely, Captain Namsorn, you cannot be considering abandoning him?"

"Spare me, clerk. Like you, Kopell is corrupted. King Shain is better off without such knights."

"It is not your decision—"

"I am the ranking representative of the emperor here!" Captain Namsorn roared. "I will not be defied! If the God finds them worth saving, the God will save them. I will not. None of my soldiers will go ashore. We are short-handed as it is, and I won't risk them unnecessarily. I will not waste good men to give that one another chance to spread his corruption. It is too dangerous. Do you understand the danger, clerk?"

Master Lennuick didn't answer, but he stopped arguing.

"Someone has got to do something," Jerr whispered to Galon. She hoped he would have an idea.

Galon nodded. Apparently he had an idea. He left her side and headed aft. Jerr lost sight of him as he descended the companionway to the main deck, and saw him again as he climbed to the quarterdeck. Galon went straight to Master Threok. Jerr watched him argue with the bregil sailing master. She saw Master Threok gaze in her direction. The argument didn't last long after that.

Master Threok and Galon left the quarterdeck. Activity stirred aboard *Mannar's Handmaiden* in their wake. Master Threok mounted the companionway to the foredeck. Men made room for him at the rail. Setting his spyglass to his eye, he gazed toward the landing place.

Lowering the glass, he said, "I had not thought to see it, but I can't say I'm surprised."

Jerr couldn't tell if Master Threok was pleased or angry. "Will you send a boat for Master Tanafres?" she asked.

The sailing master looked at Captain Namsorn rather than Jerr when he answered, "I will."

"You will not," Captain Namsorn said.

"The ship is my command, and that makes the boat my command as well. Deny *that* in your emperor's name and see how far it gets you."

"He's got you there," Master Lennuick said to Captain Namsorn.

The Solonite captain glowered at both of them.

Master Threok turned to Jerr. "Girl, you're apprenticed to Master Tanafres. Have you any magics to ward the boat?"

"I don't have any, uh, appropriate magics."

"You're *his* apprentice, all right." He chuckled. "Well, you're coming along anyway. Maybe your presence will motivate *him* to ward the boat." He turned away and started for the main deck, shouting orders for the boat to be readied.

Jerr scurried after him. She didn't know what she could do, but she wanted to help Master Tanafres.

It didn't take long to ready the boat. Captain Namsorn refused to allow any of his soldiers to go, but Master Threok had more than enough willing sailors. And one other.

"My commission is not in *your* regiment, Captain Namsorn," Galon said as he stepped to the rail. He snatched an arquebus from one of the soldiers and started down the ladder, adding, "*I* was taught to honor pledges of protection."

Jerr wanted to cheer when she saw the scowl that the remark brought to the Solonite's face. She was glad she hadn't when Captain Namsorn started down the ladder. He couldn't be thinking of taking up his quarrel with Galon now, could he?

The boat rocked as Captain Namsorn dropped into it. "Don't think to shame me, boy. I know whom I'm pledged to protect."

"Shove us clear," Master Threok ordered from his place in the stern. Sailors butted the oars against the *Handmaiden*'s hull and shoved. As soon as there was clear water, they dropped the oars into the locks and began to pull.

"Better hurry," Master Lennuick called down to the boat as it came around the *Handmaiden*'s prow. He was pointing to the shore. Jerr looked and wished she hadn't. A mob of bregil was flowing out of the jungle toward Master Tanafres and Mistress Schonnegon. Master Threok saw them, too.

"Pull, you rat-gnawed scum, pull! Bend those oars; they won't break!" he shouted at the rowers. Under his breath Jerr heard him say, "Going to be a close run."

Jerr looked worriedly toward their destination. She couldn't see Master Tanafres, but she could see Mistress Schonnegon; she had her sword out and was fighting off the bregil. Already two lay on the ground.

"Vehr, what swordsmanship!" Galon exclaimed.

Jerr couldn't tell good swordsmanship from bad. All she could tell was that the poor woman was outnumbered. She did seem to be holding the bregil at bay; fortunately there were not as many as Jerr had first thought. But, Jerr saw with horror, maybe one too many. In the brush at the edge of the clearing one bregil was loading an arquebus. Jerr pointed him out to Galon.

"Coward," was his remark.

Galon began to blow up the match to his arquebus. In his haste to fit the cord to the lock he nearly dropped it. Ashore, the bregil arquebusier had finished loading. Galon managed to get his matchcord into the lock. He opened the pan cover and dumped in some priming powder. Putting the stock to his shoulder, he took aim. The bregil was taking aim as well. With a deafening bang, Galon's arquebus belched smelly smoke over the boat.

The bregil with the gun went down, his weapon unfired.

"You've only prolonged the inevitable. We'll not get to them in time," Captain Namsorn said, pointing at another, larger group of bregil soldiers moving through the trees toward the landing site.

Master Threok urged his sailors to greater efforts with a string of oaths and insults. Strong backs bent to the oars, but it seemed to Jerr that they were in a race that the soldiers of Jor Valadrem were winning.

On the shore, Mistress Schonnegon had dispatched all but the last of the soldiers. Soon even her skill would not be enough. The new soldiers had nearly reached the clearing.

A roar echoed through the trees and across the water. The drakkenree Khankemeh strode out of the jungle, stalking toward Mistress Schonnegon.

The boat was too far away. They could not possibly get there in time.

33

YAN WAS SURPRISED by Khankemeh's appearance. He'd known that the drakkenree warrior was lurking nearby, but he had expected that Khankemeh, being wounded, would let the bregil do his work for him. This attack caught Yan unprepared and broke the spell he'd been weaving around Teletha.

What the drakkenree did surprised Yan even more.

Khankemeh's charge took him not at Teletha but into the midst of the newly arrived squad of bregil soldiers. Khankemeh tore into them. His snapping jaws, slashing claws, and bludgeoning tail scattered the soldiers. They fought back after the initial shock, their swords hacking into the drakkenree. He fought, he killed, but there were many of the bregil and Khankemeh was unarmed, save for what his god Baansuus had provided him. He went down, but he had given Teletha the chance she needed to take the last member of the first squad.

The boat from *Mannar's Handmaiden* slammed its prow into the shore. A terrified Jerr sat wide-eyed in the stern as shouting sailors piled out and raced to engage the bregil soldiers. The combat broke into a swirling melee. Yan saw Galon plunge into the fray just before the fighting shifted from the clearing into the jungle.

For the moment, nothing threatened them. Yan looked to Teletha.

"I'm fine," she said. "Just tired."

She collapsed in a panting heap. Yan didn't think that she had taken any serious wounds. He trusted that she would have told him. Khankemeh, their savior, was not so well off. Yan could see at once that the saurian was mortally wounded. He knelt by Khankemeh's side, hoping to do something to ease the drakkenree's pain.

Khankemeh raised his head weakly. "Have I atoned?"

Atoned? "For what?"

"My *hrr'g'nk*." It was not a word Yan had heard before. Khankemeh didn't hear his request for an explanation. "I am property for as long as the *kedj'k'krr* lives. Sir Kopell Mastillan lives; I am his. My *hrr'g'nk* was wrong. Unjustified."

"Then you can die happy, lizard," Teletha said. "Sir Kopell is dead. Chasing you away killed him. He's been dead since shortly after you fled."

"No!" Khankemeh hiss-growled something in his language. He was outraged, everything about him said so. Heaving, Khankemeh tried to get to his feet. His good arm reached for Yan, taloned fingers extended. Yan sprawled, trying to get away from those reaching claws. Fortunately for him, Khankemeh didn't have the strength to complete his attack. Falling back, the saurian curled into a ball, writhing and coughing up blood. Yan got to his feet, still careful to stay out of Khankemeh's reach. Khankemeh was dying, but every time the spasms left him, he tried to crawl toward Yan.

The drakkenree died cursing Yan's name.

Yan stared at the corpse. He was supposed to be the expert on drakkenree. He didn't understand this.

"Behind you," Jerr shouted.

Yan spun in place, expecting to see a bregil soldier creeping up on him. Instead, he saw Captain Namsorn standing not three yards away, a pistol in his hand.

Threok stood behind the Solonite's shoulder, a harsh grin on his face.

"I know not the Great God's plan in this matter," Namsorn confessed. "I thought it better that you had died in Kolvin, before you brought a good and holy man to corruption and death. Yet the God saved you again and again. I never fathomed the reason, but I know that His ways are not those of men. I pray that someday I may be granted some small measure of understanding. Perhaps you can ask Him to send enlightenment my way, when you stand before His judgmental eye."

"I thought murder was abhorrent to the followers of Solon."

"It is not murder to kill a rabid dog that has turned on its own kind."

"Whom am I supposed to have betrayed?"

"Do not pretend innocence. Your soul knew its first corruption when you took up magic; but that, by the laws of the Church, is insufficient to cast you out from the company of wholesome men. Had that been your only failing, you might still have been saved. But Lord Renumas knew of your deeper corruption. He knew that you had delved into forbidden things. You did, didn't you? Do not deny it! I have seen with my own eyes how you called the ancient enemy out of the forest to defend you. Your pact with them is revealed!" Namsorn cocked his pistol. "I will pray for your soul, though I know there is no salvation for it."

As he raised the pistol, Namsorn's eyes widened. Teletha surged to her feet, ready to take advantage of the lapse in Namsorn's concentration, ready to fight despite her exhaustion. But her defense was not needed.

Namsorn's knees buckled. He fell, kneeling, as his arm slowly drooped. The pistol fell from his limp hand. Namsorn pitched forward, smashing face first into the ground.

The dripping blade gripped in Threok's tail was thus revealed.

"If you can't watch your own back, you need someone to do it for you," Threok said. "He should have thought about that."

"He trusted his back to you," Yan said.

"Me? I just happened to be standing here. Namsorn seemed awfully intent on you, magician. I don't think he knew I was here."

"What you did could be considered murder," Teletha observed.

"Really? Some places I've been would call what I did good sense. Looked to me like Namsorn was about to kill a helpless man, and that's murder everywhere. Stopping him makes me a hero, by some lights. How would the gods take it, do you think?" Threok shrugged. He pulled a rag from his pouch and began to clean his tail blade. "Paid and paid I thought we were, Yan Tanafres. And now perhaps the balance has shifted. He would have taken your life, had I not taken his. Should I have let him?"

"No." How could Yan answer any other way? Who wanted to die? "You might have tried something less lethal than a knife in the back."

"It was expedient. You know me. I'm an expedient man."

Know Threok? Hardly. "Just who are you, Threok? What is your real interest in these matters?"

"My interests? I'm just looking out for myself. Like I said, you know me, magician. I'm a merchant, a trader in goods and services."

"Services such as killings."

"A good merchant diversifies his goods and services," Threok said, with a flick of his tail. "A fair price is all I ask."

"It is difficult to barter after the sale."

Threok smiled. "I'm a fair man. You're an honest one. I'm sure we can work out a reasonable deal."

"Honest, are you? Did you know Namsorn was the one trying to kill me?"

"I knew nothing of what happened in Kolvin. I did see him near the lines to the spar that nearly got you. I suspected."

"You didn't share your suspicion with me."

"Could have been anybody aboard rigged those lines."

"You don't believe that."

Threok shrugged and looked away. That would be the end of that line of questioning. That dismissive attitude *was* something Yan knew about Threok.

"I have some vague understanding of Namsorn's motives in trying to kill me, misguided though they were," Yan said. "But I don't understand why he destroyed the balloon. I never understood how that would have harmed me. The damage would have been discovered before the first flight."

"He didn't."

"Do you know who did?"

Threok nodded, but gave no other answer.

Yan saw an answer, but not a reason. "You? Why?"

"Doesn't much matter now. You went upriver anyway."

"You always argued against that, didn't you?"

"Doesn't much matter now."

"Surely it does. Why didn't you want us to go upriver?"

"I will concede that I have interests of my own."

"I want to know."

"Always inquisitive, even when it gets you in trouble. You want to know? Try reading my mind, magician," Threok said with a wicked grin.

He knew magicians couldn't read minds.

The seamen and Galon were returning, victorious in their skirmish with the soldiers of Jor Valadrem.

"So much for a quiet, private conversation," Threok said.

"This isn't over, merchant."

"You're right, magician. We haven't settled on what you owe me. But right now, we'd best be getting back to the *Handmaiden*."

34

FOR TWO DAYS THEY REMAINED ABOARD the ships, awaiting a turn in the weather and hoping for the arrival of other stragglers. The steady succession of storms slowed, though the river grew swollen with the unseasonable rains. The only member of the ill-fated exhibition to be seen again was one of the soldiers. The man's bloated, half-eaten body floated by amid less noisome debris borne by the flood.

"There is no more reason to wait," Peyto said, watching the corpse pass. "Anyone who survived would have returned by now."

Yan wasn't so sure. In the past two days his heightened awareness of the world had encouraged him to scout the land surrounding them with his arcane senses. He'd sent his spirit form back along their trail, looking for survivors. He hadn't found any, but he hadn't satisfied himself that all who had gone inland were accounted for. Now, with the weather easing, he had to look to the future; word of the end of the Wall needed to be carried back to the empire and to Kolvin, lest they be caught unawares by the drakkenree who would be emerging from the egg of their spells.

But to warn the world they must first escape Factor Choshok's trap. Through conferences with Threok and the other captains, Yan had developed a plan to do just that. The plan was chancy and depended heavily on Yan's ability to achieve magical effects beyond any he had yet successfully achieved.

Yet he felt confident. Though he had not yet had time to appreciate the implications, he was different now. At the very least, through enlightenment, his understanding of the world had changed. Since escaping the hut of the Wizard of Bones, Yan's perceptions had grown deeper and expanded more broadly. He had made a breakthrough in his journey to mastery of the Great Art.

The world around him looked different, though he knew that it was much as it always had been. He was just viewing it differently. He seemed to be nearly always in a state close to *præha*, a constant condition of heightened arcane awareness. His perception of the mana flow and his sensitivity to its nuances were greater now, and his new sophistication gave him a better understanding of how a magician touched the mana and used it according to his will. He saw more clearly how he could control the magic, and how the magic could control him; and that discovery offered him new insights into his place and role in the constantly changing system that was the world. It was a leap of comprehension as great as the one he'd made the first time Gan Tidoni had opened him to the *præha* state.

He would need time to come fully to grips with it.

Time that was not yet allowed him.

"I'm ready to begin turning the ships," Threok announced.

Turning the ships around within the channel would take time, time enough for Yan to finish his final preparations. His satchel, along with all his ritual tools and aids, had been left behind in the wizard's hut. He'd worked out substitutes for what he needed and with the help of Peyto, Jerr, and Galon had nearly readied them all. There was little left to do. A week ago he would not have trusted such makeshift tools to let him accomplish magic, but now. . .

"Ready enough," Yan said.

Threok looked worried. "You sure you can do what you said?"

"I don't see an alternative."

"You don't *want* to see an alternative," Threok said.

"*Your* alternative is unacceptable."

"If you can do these magics—"

Yan cut him off. "What can be done under some circumstances cannot be done under all. Magic in battle is too chancy to rely upon. Much too chancy to trust when it is paramount that we leave this place. What we've planned is risky enough."

"It had better work, mage. Don't make me regret saving your life any more than I already do."

Yan had no desire to do so. "Do what you need to do, Threok. I'll do my part."

Threok said nothing more, but went off to give orders.

The turnabout was a complex process in the narrow confines of the channel. It involved considerable bustling on all ships, boats passing back and forth, and an almost continual cacophony of shouted orders, curses, and work chants. Once the ships were pointed downstream, there were other last-minute preparations before they sailed. Such things were done.

A party of soldiers and seamen had been set ashore to act as pickets, to watch the city from the spit between the two channels and to guard against further attacks from the city's soldiers. As the last thing to be done, a boat went ashore to recover them. The pickets reported Jor Valadrem quiet.

Yan and his friends were aboard *Mannar's Grace*. She was the best of the three ships for what Yan intended. Threok's *Handmaiden* was larger, but she was also older, and her stem post had a flaw. The crack in the timber was not enough to endanger her for years to come, but it was enough that she would not serve Yan's need.

Yan made his way to the topcastle, Teletha climbing behind him. Where once he had feared to scale the lines so high above the deck, he now did it without concern. He understood that the wood beneath his hands and feet was strong, a part of the ship. The lines were well tied; if not, he avoided them and trusted his weight to other lines as he climbed upward. The rocking of the ship on the river no longer upset him, for he found himself anticipating the slight shifts and compensating for them in advance of their effects. His magical confidence was making him physically surer as well.

Teletha had carried the materials that he could not, and she helped Yan array them within the cramped space of the topcastle. She worked quietly and did all he asked, but she wouldn't stay.

"Too near the magic to be comfortable," she said. She didn't go far, though, finding a place lower on the mast, where she could wrap her limbs in the lines for a stable perch. "I'll get a good enough view from here."

He understood. She was supporting him as best she could. Magic was something she wished did not exist, and something he could not live without. It would forever stand between them.

Threok gave the order to get underway.

The ships began to move. The *Handmaiden* led as she always did, and the little *Breath* took up her station in the rear of the line, as she always did. From his perch in the topcastle, Yan watched the trees thin until he could catch glimpses of the stony cliff and the towers of Jor Valadrem hunched upon its crest. There was no turning back now. The city's sentries would be spotting the mastheads and giving warning. Factor Choshok would have Captain-general Lorm's soldiers ready for them when the ship's hulls came into sight.

There was a trick, simple enough when one knew the

secret, that entertainers used to project their voices across the width of a room and pretend to have conversations with dolls or give tongue to inarticulate objects. Many magicians used the trick in one way or another to enhance their mystique. The trick took constant practice to perfect; Yan had never managed the knack of not moving his lips as he spoke. That didn't matter here; here he would be using the trick to another end. Envisioning himself standing upon the parapets, he cast his words into the mana stream and let the flow carry them across the water. His voice went where he could not.

"Factor Choshok, I call upon you to let these ships pass in peace. Send the word to your minions at the lower tower. Bid them remove the chain barrier. In the name of the Emperor Dacel and of all men of goodwill, do not oppose our leaving. Do not turn to violence, lest your violence turn upon you."

His reply came from a cannon. The ball whistled past the ships edging into the main channel and crashed into the far shore.

Not an unexpected response.

The other guns would fire momentarily. The choice of violence was Choshok's. With regret, Yan reached down and took up the linstock with its trailing tail of matchcord. He blew up the slow match, then touched it with his magic.

Here and there, it is; similarity makes this be that.

Holding the image firm in his mind, Yan made it so. He felt the existence of other linstocks, other matchcords. Some were on the ships, some in Jor Valadrem. He concentrated on those in the city, superimposing the image of the linstock and cord he held over those others.

What is here, is there. Sputter. Burn. Flare and spark.

His match flared, burning with extraordinary speed. Sputtering and throwing sparks, the match looked like a festive holiday sparkle cord.

As here, so there.

He touched his linstock's cord to the keg of dark powder at his feet, encouraging the sparks to find their way to similar kegs. The powder in his keg was false, a look-alike compound with just enough of the real stuff to establish the occult correspondence. Those other kegs would be full of real firepowder, powder that sparks could cause to—

Explosions blasted smoke and rock from the walls and gun positions of Jor Valadrem in a thunderous string of detonations. Men died in those explosions, their souls torn screaming from their bodies. The mana roiled, tainted by the anguish of the dead and dying.

Yan cringed, knowing what he had done to keep the ships and their crews safe. But he had more yet to do. He set about it, trying to think only about what must be done.

Air was not an element that bent easily to Yan's will, but smoke was a phenomenon of more than air. Its heart was made of solid things—tiny things that partook more of earth than air. Reaching to touch those particles was difficult so near the spreading occult turmoil centered on Jor Valadrem, but Yan managed. He bade those tiny pieces of earth to stand firm, to resist the tug of the air.

The smoke hung in thick roiling clouds that masked the walls of Jor Valadrem.

Yan's arcane assault was not a complete success. Some of Jor Valadrem's guns still spoke. Though the gunners were firing blindly, there was still a chance that they would cause damage.

The mana around the city was too disturbed to manipulate safely, but more needed to be done to silence the guns. From the quarterdeck of the *Handmaiden*, Threok looked up at Yan. He was ready; Yan could hear him calling for permission to open fire. The city was a large target, and it didn't move, making it an easy mark for the shipboard gunners. Still, the ship's cannon were mostly too light to do significant damage. That, too, Yan had taken into account.

As they had agreed, the sailing master was waiting to give the order to fire. Yan was to strengthen Threok's voice that all gunners aboard the three ships would hear him at once, the better to ensure that the ship's guns would speak as one. A single volley was better for the magic Yan intended. He had been hoping that this step would not be necessary; the first had cost too many lives. Vainly he called upon Choshok to silence his guns. Cannon fire replied to his plea. Clearly the masters of Jor Valadrem were not ready to cooperate. The surviving guns still threatened the ships. The next step had to be taken.

At Yan's instruction, the cannon of the three ships had been loaded with stone balls instead of the usual iron shot. Stone was not as strong, but it was far more subject to his influence. Yan had done the final shaping for each of the projectiles, putting his touch and certain symbols upon each of them, creating a link for the sorcery he intended. He used that link to call upon the stones, reawakening their bond with the greater mass of rock from which they had been carved. He reminded the stones of their place within the earth and of the fires in which they had once swum.

The fire will touch you again, he told them. *When it does, remember. Remember your strength, remember how great the whole of you once was. Carry that memory with you and bring it to the walls of Jor Valadrem. Be, each of you, what you were.*

The stones heard his words. With the stately slowness of the earth and in accord with Yan's will, the stone cannonballs gathered their memories. There was no time for Yan to admire the interplay of mana and matter; no time to delay. Yan prepared his next spell and signaled Threok.

Threok's amplified command to fire boomed across the water. Seconds later the cannon of all three ships

boomed, scarcely louder. The volley stuck Jor Valadrem
with the force of a mountain crashing down. Stones tumbled into the river as the walls of the town shook. No
cannon replied to the ships' volley.

Yan found the effect oddly gratifying; the magic he'd
wrought had been effective beyond his expectations. The
crafting of the Art had been successful, wildly so. Yet he
was terrified, too. He had not studied the Great Art with
the intent of causing such devastation. The Great Art was
not supposed to be about destruction.

Yan bade the smoke from the ships' cannon to hang
about them, hiding the ships from the city. The smoke
would do nothing to hide Yan's shame; he would have to
live with it. He had done what needed to be done.

Hadn't he?

Now was not the time to consider such matters.

The *Grace* cut inside *Mannar's Handmaiden* at the bend
in the river, taking the lead position for the little flotilla as
planned. *Handmaiden*'s sharp falling off was not as
planned. Had she taken damage? Another matter that
there was no time to consider—for the barrier chain, still
stretched across the river, loomed in the path of the
ships.

Mannar's Grace moved toward the barrier, gathering
speed. The stem post of the *Grace* was as strong as Yan
could make it. The effort tired him, but wood, however
strong, did not master iron. There was still work to be done.

Most of the chain was encrusted with muck from the
river bottom. Beneath the muck was rust, and rust was
what Yan intended to use. Yan felt along the chain,
searching for a point at which the rust dominated the
iron. He found such a section near the tower, where the
legacy of rising and falling water levels marked several
links. This was where the air fought its battle most
fiercely with the fruit of the earth's womb. Upon that part
of the battlefield, air was winning; the red rot of air's
meddling cut deep into those links.

Yan selected the weakest link.

And found that there was little he could do to that link. Iron was the bane of magicians and was not his to command. He had known that. But he had thought that he could subvert the iron, using the rust, iron's own bane, to eat away at the link and cause it to fail as he had once used rot to eat away at leather and cause a girth strap to fail. Yet as he tried to heighten the rust's control of the link, he found that, in a way he did not understand, the rust was still too much like the iron itself. The rust resisted his efforts.

The *Grace* moved inexorably closer to the barrier. She would wreck herself on the chain unless Yan succeeded. To the air he offered his strength, urging it on in its slow assault on the chain.

Take the iron. Chew at it.

The ship nosed against the barrier. Creaking, the iron stretched taut. *Mannar's Grace* groaned with her effort. Yan willed strength into her wood; the strain stretched him until the blood began to pound behind his eyes.

Make the iron yours, Yan urged the air. He was desperate. There was little time. *Faster, faster!*

Mannar's Grace slowed, losing headway. *Theris's Breath* crowded close upon her. The chain gave against the pressure, but only its slack. Its strength remained sufficient to stop the ship. Disaster was imminent.

Yan refused to let dumb iron win. Once he'd beaten iron, but that had been a wild magic, the mana effect warped and twisted by the unpredictable presence of a battle; the success of that folly, along with his newfound awareness, had led him to believe he could make the chain part under his will. He had been overconfident. He had chosen the wrong course, and doomed them.

No! It couldn't end this way! There had to be something else he could do! Wildly he looked about, searching for something to tip the struggle in their favor. He saw nothing. The chain's guardian tower seemed a finger lifted in insulting mockery.

The tower.

Sitting on its base of crumbling rock.

"Teletha," Yan shouted, "fire your pistol at the cliff."

"What?"

"Don't argue. Just do it."

Trusting, she did. The lead ball struck the rock. It was too small to do much. A few rock chips flew and tumbled downward, touching the surface of the rock.

Down! Yan commanded the rock. *Part of you is falling, all of you is falling. The part is the whole, the whole is the part. Let it be. Let it be!*

Pebbles clattered down. Not enough.

The lesser unto the greater. Fall, fall!

He abandoned his efforts to bolster the *Grace* in her struggle; either the ship would stand the strain or she would not. He bent his will to the rock; it was of the earth, and earth he knew.

Pebbles gathered cobbles in their downward slide.

Faster! More! Greater!

The rock obliged. The shower of stone became an avalanche of boulders crashing down to the river. Most crashed clear of the chain, but one stone struck the growing talus slope and rebounded, arcing out into the river.

Yes!

By Yan's will or by luck, the boulder came down upon the chain, striking the weakest of the links. The link snapped, iron shrieking as it snapped.

Released from the strain, the *Grace* surged forward. Huzzahs rose from the deck. The barrier had broken! They were through!

The *Breath* sailed over the sinking corpse of the barrier. The small ship seemed eager to run for the sea. They were free!

But where was *Mannar's Handmaiden?*

"They're striking the Imperial pennon," Teletha cried, pointing back at the lagging ship.

Yan looked. It was true. Another flag was going up on the line to the top mast of *Mannar's Handmaiden*. This was not in the plan. What had gone wrong?

Exhausted, Yan struggled to focus his senses on the captain of *Mannar's Handmaiden*. Though the projection was easier than when he had last attempted it, he still took some minutes to achieve success. The slow build of rapport allowed Yan to perceive eddies in the mana stream. He listened to the echoes in the stream, hearing the sounds of Threok's quarterdeck. He knew Threok would hear him when he spoke.

"What do you, Threok?"

The sailing master started, surprised to hear Yan's voice. He looked about, trying to see where Yan stood. Fruitlessly. Threok recovered quickly; he turned toward *Mannar's Grace*. "Mage?"

"It is I. What are you doing?"

Threok grinned. "You need the *Handmaiden* to cover your retreat, mage. Choshok may organize a pursuit."

They both knew that there were no ships at Jor Valadrem.

"You do not do this for the emperor," Yan said.

"Who says I don't? And what does it matter why I do it?" Threok asked. "You are past the chain; take your chance and go. Nensk is more than enough captain to get you back to the empire."

"And leave you here?"

"I'm not asking you to stay." Threok interrupted their conversation to bark orders to his crew. *Mannar's Handmaiden* started to tack upriver; Threok was taking his ship back to the city. "I'm telling you to go."

"One ship against Jor Valadrem? That seems a little mad."

Threok gave a bregil shrug that ended in a nervous

flip of his tail. "They've been softened up, and *Handmaiden* has a picked crew of good men, mage."

For the first time Yan noticed that all the bregil from the fleet had somehow now managed to end up aboard Threok's ship. Had Threok intended this adventure all along? Though Threok's motives remained unknown, many of his actions and much of his counsel began to make sense.

"This is what you wanted, isn't it?" Yan asked. "The cannon turned against the river are silenced. There are none to fire upon you should you make for the dock."

"Your magic sight tell you that, or are you guessing?"

Yan didn't need to use his arcane vision; he felt the destruction of the guns. "My magic silenced the guns. Had I not done what I did, your plans would have foundered on the rocks of Jor Valadrem's walls and cannon. You yourself would most likely have been killed."

Threok scoffed. "You did what you did for your own ends. That it aided my ends is pure happenstance."

"Happenstance, Merchant Threok? I think you bargained for it when you killed Namsorn. You've gotten your worth of my life. We are paid and paid, merchant."

For a moment Threok said nothing, frowning across the growing distance between the ships. Then he roared out a laugh.

"Paid and paid it is, mage. A fair wind and good seas to you; I'll make a better bargain next time." He laughed again. "Now take your immaterial self off my quarterdeck. I've got work to do."

"Fare you well, merchant," Yan said, but only with his physical voice; and only the wind heard.

There were storms on the horizon to the west when they emerged from the river mouth and turned to the north, but the wind was rising behind them, freshening into a fair breeze. The sails filled. *Grace* and *Breath* leapt forward as if eager to return to their home ports in the islands.

Home?

Yan had once sworn never to return home until he had proven himself a magician of note. What had he done this day, if not that? Yes, Yan could go home now.

But first they sailed to Sharhumrin. He had a tale to tell to the emperor.

ROBERT N. CHARRETTE was born, raised, and educated in Rhode Island. Upon graduating from Brown University with a cross-departmental degree in biology and geology, he promptly moved to the Washington, D.C. area and entered a career as a graphic artist. He worked as a game designer, art director, and commercial sculptor before taking up the word processor to write novels. He has contributed three novels to the BattleTech™ universe and five to the Shadowrun™ universe, the latter of which he had a hand in creating, and is now developing other settings for fictional exploration.

He currently resides in Herndon, Virginia with his wife, Elizabeth.